The First Time

"I can't make love to you," he said. "It wouldn't be right. It'd be taking advantage."

"I think we should stop talking right now," she said, losing her patience. "We seem to do nothing but argue when we try to talk." She held out her arms to him. "Give me your hand!" she insisted, taking hold of it.

Unbuttoning her blouse, she placed his hand on her breast, feeling an immense delight in having solved the problem so simply. He came forward and kissed her, then lowered his mouth to the base of her throat.

"That's lovely," she whispered, falling back, her fingers in his hair. "That feels so nice."

"I can't stop," he said, all caution gone as he pulled at her blouse. "I can't!"

"I don't want you to stop," she said, helping him...

Love Life
by Charlotte Vale Allen

LOVE LIFE

CHARLOTTE VALE ALLEN

BERKLEY BOOKS, NEW YORK

This Berkley book contains the complete
text of the original hardcover edition.

LOVE LIFE

A Berkley Book / published by arrangement with
the author

PRINTING HISTORY
First published in the USA by Delacorte Press
Delacorte Press edition published 1976.
NEL edition / June 1981
Berkley edition / July 1987

ISBN: 0-425-10012-X

A BERKLEY BOOK ® TM 757,375
Berkley Books are published by The Berkley Publishing Group,
200 Madison Avenue, New York, NY 10016.
The name "BERKLEY" and the "B" logo
are trademarks belonging to Berkley Publishing Corporation.

PRINTED IN THE UNITED STATES OF AMERICA

10   9   8   7   6   5   4   3   2   1

To Walter, Norman, and Lola
and to Helen, because . . .

LOVE LIFE

PART ONE

TEDDY

1

She grew up in an extraordinarily happy atmosphere. So happy, in fact, that she took pleasure as much for granted as other children did hand-me-down clothes or battered toys that had been played with by many more than one other pair of hands.

The ripest visual memories of her childhood always centered on an image of sunshine flooding through the windows of her mother's studio, catching and illuminating dust motes that seemed drawn to the sunlight; the sounds of Vivaldi or Beethoven pushed, somewhat tinnily, from the small black Victrola it was sometimes her privilege to crank. And Amanda, her mother, caught in the sunlight as she stood before her easel, her brush poised midair, her head turned slightly, as if listening to something only she could hear.

If she concentrated on remembering those years of childhood, the effect was one of overlapping films of her mother: Amanda in the studio; Amanda in the kitchen, absent-mindedly adding herbs to a simmering pot of stew as she talked knowledgeably about something or other; Amanda patiently answering one after another of Helen's questions.

It was a time so completely satisfying in her mind that

she was never totally willing to relinquish the idea that it was gone, irretrievable. Those sunshine days cushioned every other day of her life, affected every action she undertook. She was able, for the most part, to approach every tomorrow with the attitude that whatever happened, nothing could interfere with that insulated corner of her brain that sheltered the remembrances of those childhood days.

She was born in Port Zebulon—never actually a port—but remembered nothing of it, because Amanda sold the house there and moved to the city when Helen was almost two. Helen's father died five weeks before she was born in an influenza epidemic at the close of 1920. Helen was born in January, 1921, when Amanda was thirty-eight years old.

Almost from the moment Helen was born, Amanda viewed her with her artist's eye, rather than her maternal one. She couldn't help herself. Helen was so unlike anything she'd expected, small and exquisitely pretty in a way she herself hadn't ever been (and doubted Lawrence had been either). Helen wafted joyfully through babyhood and into childhood. She toddled through the large, dusty rooms on uncertain legs, smiling and confident of an enthusiastic reception at her destination.

Initially the house seemed far too large for just herself and Helen, but Amanda was determined not to allow her loneliness for Lawrence to destroy the satisfaction she derived from the big, rambling house and from Helen. She hired a housekeeper to help with the cooking and cleaning, and immersed herself in her work with renewed concentration.

Her painting and pottery were as important to her life as her daughter, as living itself. The ordinary things—tending to the house, enduring dreary social functions, watching and enjoying Helen grow—were in some ways nothing more than diversions, necessary interludes between work sessions. She recognized her compulsiveness; her total need for self-expression hinged on her ability to give herself over to her work, capturing with paint or clay a mood or an emotion that was not satisfied

4

simply by being voiced aloud. She gave in to these needs totally, not even minding the backaches and stiffness that followed her bouts of intense effort.

She felt contented, at peace with herself. Her work sold so well that she couldn't keep up with the demand, and early on she gave up trying to perform to order. She simply followed her inner commands, throwing fresh clay on the wheel when the need to feel growth beneath her fingertips overtook her, ordering new supplies of paint, canvas, and brushes when she felt she had to paint.

From time to time her preoccupation transferred itself from her work to Helen and, scooping the child up into her arms, she spent long hours with her in the garden studying the flowers and insects or simply lying on the grass watching Helen explore the fringes of the flower beds.

Helen didn't seem to mind being alone, appeared quite happy to play on her own for hours, running along the upstairs hallway or piling her blocks into elaborate structures, laughing when they collapsed. She loved the zoo in the park across the way, and in particular the aviary with its high vaulted ceilings, which echoed with the exotic cries of the birds.

Fearing, though, that too much isolation might harm her, Amanda sent her off at almost three to a nearby nursery school. On the first morning she waited outside the door, prepared to see Helen reappear within moments. But the child stayed inside, and, peeking through the door, Amanda was both pleased and oddly disappointed to see that Helen had forgotten all about her and was merrily engaged in playing the triangle in the nursery-school band.

The house seemed empty with Helen away every morning. But, afraid she might do damage by removing Helen from the school strictly for the sake of her own comfort, Amanda made the decision to take on several students. She didn't really want to teach, but she was wary of making any mistakes with Helen by making her the human center of her existence.

So, three mornings a week, half a dozen youngsters arrived at the studio door, eager and impatient to learn.

And she soon discovered she enjoyed this new aspect of her capabilities: the capacity to convey to others the basis of her own distraction. She was able to teach about color and sensation and form. Soon the teaching became an addition to instead of a detraction from her own hypnotic attachment to her work.

There were occasional men who came to dinner bringing wine and flowers and personal needs they hoped she might fulfill, but she found, with some sadness, that she was no longer interested. She didn't feel forty-two, scarcely gave any notice to the passage of time or the small physical changes taking place in her. It was just that, with Lawrence's death, that part of her that had needed a man had also died. He'd been so much one of a kind that it didn't seem probable she'd find his qualities in another man.

The sexual loss didn't bother her at all. She'd always had a certain take-it-or-leave-it attitude about the physical aspects of love, a detachment, as if it were something to be involved in only to more fully cement her emotional relationship with her husband. In many ways she'd found lovemaking exceedingly pleasurable. It was more that she hadn't ever had the preoccupation with sex that so many of her contemporaries had. What she'd never especially savored, she didn't particularly miss. What she did mourn was the loss of wonder that went along with being young, and the sharing of marriage. She frequently found herself turning to include Lawrence in some thought or concept, to hear his reaction to one thing or another, only to find a shadowy, imagined outline where his real person should have been. She missed him.

At five Helen, still tiny but even lovelier than she'd been as a baby, was a semi-serious child with a rapidly developing fondness for words and books. She spent hours curled up in an armchair in the corner of the studio, studying picture books while Amanda gave classes or worked on her own. At times Amanda would turn to see Helen smiling out at her from the depths of the chair, several books tucked between the cushion and side of the chair, another open in her lap. At those moments Amanda wondered about Helen's future—what she'd do, what she'd become.

She had a certain way of smiling that was startlingly mature. It seemed as if she had an understanding of the goings-on around her and found them neither displeasing nor curious, but, rather, just the way things were. It was a somehow perceptive smile of recognition, as if she had already achieved a knowledge of her own identity within the proscribed boundaries of her world and saw no reason to question either her own personal definition or her mother's.

Following nursery school, Amanda enrolled Helen as a day student at a girls' prep school. And within a few months little girls began appearing at the front door asking for Helen and the noise of children at play upstairs filtered down to Amanda in the studio. Helen was very sociable and very popular. Children as well as adults were drawn to her enthusiasm and prettiness and openhearted interest.

The next summer, after a most successful exhibition that made her a good deal of money, Amanda purchased a small cottage up north. It was situated in a cove with its own private beach, approachable from either side of the beach but, as it was between other privately owned summer homes, entirely protected from the possibility of strangers happening accidentally onto their stretch of beach. With Jessie, the housekeeper, along, she began the first of their summer expeditions north.

On those mornings when Amanda painted close to home, Helen tagged along, sitting some distance away, watching. During the intervals when Amanda rested, enjoying a cigarette, they talked. It was while observing her mother roughing-in in charcoal a gnarled old tree slightly up from the water's edge that Helen asked, "How did you get me?"

"What, dear?" Amanda asked distantly, glancing over.

"Where did I come from?" Helen repeated, curling her toes in the sand.

"Oh," Amanda said, setting down her brush. "You came from your father and from me," she said.

7

Carefully, aware that this moment signified the ending of one era and the beginning of another, Amanda selected her words with caution, for fear of implanting misconceptions in her daughter's mind. She explained the anatomical differences between the sexes (the teaching side of her warming at once to the aesthetics) and then proceeded to the more difficult literal description of the physical process wherefrom children are conceived.

"Is it something people like to do?" Helen asked thoughtfully.

"Yes," she said simply, preferring a shaded lie to her personal truth. Perhaps it would be very different for Helen.

"Good," Helen said enigmatically, getting up and wandering off down the beach.

Amanda watched the small figure move away down the beach and wondered if she'd said and explained it all in the best of possible ways. She thought of Lawrence. He'd been a man who hadn't ever been vocally overt about sex. Lovemaking had been an activity he'd relished but wouldn't readily discuss. But still . . . She stood a moment longer, her eyes caught by the sensual memory of his fine, long body lying warmly over her own. And she felt again his loss.

Helen's first views on sex, then, were closely tied to her mother's paintings, to the nude studies of men and women she was allowed to examine, to the art books in the studio and at the cottage. Her conception of sex, of making babies, was one of fluidity and beauty filled with splashes of explosive color. She thought often of making babies, of someday having one grow right inside her. And every time she thought about it, a little shiver of excitement ran through her, making her smile.

2

People came to the cottage. People who knew of Amanda's work, seeking to offer praise and be accepted as students. After a moment's reluctance, she set up two afternoon classes a week. And then there came a tide of people dropping their cigarette stubs in the sand and carelessly splattering both their canvases and themselves with paint.

Helen stayed away from the beach on those afternoons, preferring to rest indoors with her books, occasionally looking out the window to see her mother in the center of a circle of students, using her hands and shoulders to add emphasis to something she was saying.

She loved her mother fiercely, intensely, thought of her as someone special, someone very much her own. Times when people came to their beach, her mother seemed to become someone else: someone whose words held unquestioned authority and whose laughter was invariably echoed by those around her. It was evident these people knew too how special she was and did not dare violate the sanction of being invited into her presence.

And yet Amanda expressed a certain small displeasure at being catered to in this fashion.

"They don't offer argument," she said, seeming saddened. "They won't challenge what they see as an accomplished route to success. There's not one of them with any real fire, with the exception of Jennie Gilroy. It's a pity that child's father won't allow her to come to the city to study." Jennie was the daughter of the local postmaster, and paid for her lessons by posing at alternate classes. "She's a bit tentative but has a good eye for line. A pity."

She dropped these comments before Helen with a tired air, as if teaching the classes was something she'd have preferred not to do.

"Don't you like teaching?"

"Sometimes." Amanda peered over the top of the outsized newsprint pad she was holding on her lap. "There's always the chance that one will display genuine ability. It's worthwhile looking for." She returned to the one-minute sketches she was doing of Helen.

"What would you do if there was one with real talent?"

"That would depend." Amanda's hand flew over the page, scattering dusty bits of charcoal.

"On what?"

"On all kinds of things. Do sit still, darling. It would depend on who it was and the circumstances. I've offered to send Jennie to school, but her father won't hear of it. But, in general, I can't say what I'd do until the time came."

"You mean if someone else came along who was very, very good, you might offer to send them to art school too?"

"Something like that. Talent deserves its chance. No more talking now."

Helen accepted the presence of those others on the beach and in the cottage as part of their summer lifestyle, but she still missed those afternoons when her mother was entirely her own. During the classes she followed Amanda's eyes, watching, waiting to see if she would suddenly proclaim she'd found one more with talent. She learned, in studying her mother, to recognize which work held promise and which merely showed unrelated lines on paper. It was a slow process of understanding that seeped into her consciousness by constant closeness to someone who knew precisely how to go about looking.

The year Helen was eleven, Amanda decided to make one final appeal to Mr. Gilroy to allow her to subsidize Jennie's art studies. He came to the cottage and sat in a straight-back chair, erect and stiffly correct in his postman's uniform. He listened to Amanda's proposal, then coughed, pulling himself even taller in the chair as he said, "Jennie will stay here and help out, as she's always done. You've got no right to put wild ideas in that girl's head. It's bad enough she comes out here and . . . She's shameless."

"I see," Amanda said. "You don't plan to allow her to decide her own future?"

"Well . . ." He shrugged, shifting uncomfortably. "I'd best be getting along now."

"What exactly is so shameful about having talent, Mr. Gilroy?" Her neck and cheeks had turned very pink.

"You summer people. I think—"

"I'll tell you what *I* think," she said, leaning toward him, "I think you're an arrogant, stupid old horse's ass, Gilroy. It actually makes me rather sick at the stomach to think you could've fathered someone as fine and sensitive as Jennie. You haven't the right to stunt that child's growth with your rural ideas on sin." She got up, glaring at him. "My 'bohemian' life, as you call it, has been one of utter satisfaction and reward. I doubt you have the intelligence to fully appreciate that, but it can't be helped. You really are a sickeningly ignorant man. Your condemnation of me and my lifestyle makes me tired, just tired. Go collect your mailbag and truck and deliver your letters! God willing, we'll neither of us have to suffer each other's company again. I just want you to understand that I condemn your ignorance and narrow-mindedness as much as, more than you condemn my lifestyle. You don't have the comprehension of a five-year-old when it comes to talent or other people's right to freedom. Go on," she said, crossing the room, keeping her back to him. "I've seen and heard quite enough. I hope you'll be very happy knowing you've harmed Jennie's future."

"You can't justify yourself to me!" he said, red-faced

and insistent, "And you're going to infect this child with your foolishness about talent and art!"

He glanced nervously at Helen, who looked at him with round, startled eyes. He knew instantly he'd made a mistake. Amanda whirled around, her eyes flashing.

"I'd rather have her infected with a joy for living than an obsession with sinfulness and joylessness. Get out, Mr. Gilroy! Get out before I say a number of things I'd prefer not to say, because you are Jennie's father after all, and I'm trying to keep that dismal fact centered in my mind."

"I'll go now," he said, backing away several steps.

"Do, for God's sake!" she said, her fists clenched at her sides.

After the door had closed and the sound of his truck's engine was no more than a faint buzzing in the distance, Amanda walked over to the sofa and sat down beside Helen, looking very worn all at once.

"He's not very nice, is he?" Helen said sympathetically, not sure she'd understood all that had been said.

"He hasn't the right to obstruct her future," she said wearily. It's her God-given privilege to make her own decisions. I'll try never to interfere with yours. I just hope you don't choose to become a civil servant." She laughed halfheartedly. "God! To think of spending one's life fighting with rigid people who refuse to give any credence whatsoever to the possibility that their life mightn't be the only good way to live. And then to have that rural bumpkin come at you with more of the same! It's too much!"

Helen stared at her mother, mystified.

"I didn't know you were fighting."

"Not in the way you understand it, darling."

"Did you really mean it about doing whatever I decide to do?"

"Yes."

Helen thought about that for a while. "It seems like a very grown-up thing, to make my own decisions."

"You'll learn how. Let's go for a walk. It's too gloomy in here. I just hope to heaven that fool doesn't fly back to town and take it all out on poor Jennie."

Glad of the opportunity to put the whole unpleasant incident behind them, Helen reached for Amanda's hand as they went down to the beach. Amanda seemed to relax after a while, her shoulders easing down.

"Doesn't Mr. Gilroy like your paintings?" Helen asked, still going over the argument in her mind.

"He can't help it," she said, draping her arm around Helen's shoulders. "He thinks, for some reason, that being an artist is just one step removed from being on the stage or taking up life as a whore. I'll never know where he got that idea. It's such rubbish! We won't talk about it any more now."

The next afternoon Amanda asked Helen if she'd like to pose. Delighted, she stripped and sat as her mother instructed. While she posed, gazing down at the sand, she felt something very strange happening: a tightening of her muscles, then the relief of sudden release.

"Something's happening to me," she said softly.

"What, dear?" Amanda asked, looking up.

"I'm not sure. I feel funny."

"Are you ill?"

"I don't know. It feels funny here, at the bottom of my tummy."

"I think I know," Amanda said, putting down her brush. "Come, get dressed. We won't work any more today."

"Why not?"

"I think it would be a good idea for you to stay warm and relaxed for the rest of the afternoon. Come along. Jessie's made some soup. That'll make you feel better."

Helen dressed as Amanda collected her things from the beach. They sat together at the table in the kitchen, each with a mug of soup. It had clouded over outside, and Amanda said, "It's going to rain. It's good we came in when we did."

"I'm so sleepy," Helen said, suddenly chilled. "I'm going to lie down for a while."

Amanda reached across to put her hand on Helen's forehead.

"Go take a little nap, darling. I'll come see you in a bit."

In her room, Helen sat on the bed looking out at the gray sky for a few minutes, knowing her mother had meant they would talk when she came in. Helen sensed that what they talked about was going to be important, but she felt too drowsy to think about it. She settled down and pulled the comforter over her. She slept and dreamed she was swimming. It was good, restful. But then she came out of the water and she felt wet and cold. Very cold. She shook with it. She awakened to find Amanda sitting beside her on the bed.

"I feel wet. I hurt."

"I brought you some things," Amanda said softly, smiling.

After she'd changed her clothes and come to an understanding, through Amanda's quietly voiced explanations, of the process that was taking place, Helen stood with her arms around her mother, wanting to cry but not aware why.

"Does this mean I'm all grown up, a woman?"

"Oh, not quite yet." Amanda laughed. "It means you've started readying yourself. You'll know when you're a woman. This is just one part of it."

"How will I know?"

"You'll know. You'll feel it."

"But I'm not a little girl any more either," she said, the tears coming at last.

"It's not something to cry about, darling. Everything changes, grows. It's the way of life, the way things are meant to be."

"But I don't want anything to change. I want it all to stay exactly the way it is."

"Most of it will. It's you who'll change. Your whole life is in front of you. It's very exciting."

"Could we make popcorn in the fireplace tonight?"

"Why not?" Amanda laughed. "Let's light a fire."

3

During the next two years Amanda observed, with mingled fascination and pride, the formative changes in Helen.

Although she remained petite—Amanda assumed she'd take after herself in stature—Helen was unexpectedly long-bodied. Her legs were slender and beautifully shaped, her hips narrow, and her waist sharply in-curving. There was an interesting breadth to her shoulders that offset and balanced the rounded prominence of her full breasts.

Her hair was a rich brown, thick, curling at the ends. She seemed foreign somehow, with her straight-on manner of looking at people, things. Her demeanor was disarming and unassuming. Totally unselfconscious, she had no false modesty. She accepted the fact of her physicality much as she accepted the routines of their life. If one of the local models failed to show up for a class, Helen obliged without hesitation, quickly discarding her clothes to stand as directed.

And while she posed, turning this way and that as requested, she studied the people who carefully studied her. She examined the way their eyes traveled the length of her body, having learned with time which of the students saw with a genuine artist's eye and which merely skimmed her surface in a dutiful attempt to render an image on their paper.

She'd walk past the easels while the group stood together smoking and drinking coffee at the midway point of the session, nodding to herself at the success of her judgments. She was rarely wrong about the ones with talent.

"It doesn't make me feel one way or another," she told her mother, "being right or wrong doesn't seem to matter. It's just something I think I understand. At least"—she laughed—"if I can't paint or draw, I can recognize talent when I see it."

"Recognition of other people's ability is a talent in itself," Amanda said. "Is it that you're disappointed at not being able to paint, Helen?"

"Oh, I'll be good at something," she said. "Making babies, probably."

"Perhaps you will."

Time passed quickly. Amanda painted. Helen watched or read or daydreamed. She went to school, came home, enjoyed her active social life. She and Amanda discussed F.D.R., or the girls who'd had to leave school because the family money had run out. Amanda made faintly disinterested responses and comments to Helen's social and political remarks, coming to full attention only when Helen said, "We really should be doing something. It doesn't seem fair to have as much as we do and not share a little of it."

"There's not *that* much, Helen," Amanda corrected, "and you can remember me as being selfish, if you like. My efforts are to make life pleasant for both of us. It's the only tangible gift I have to give you."

"You give me everything," she protested.

"Of course I try to, within reason. I don't believe in making children wait for the death of a parent to benefit from the hoardings of a lifetime. I'd rather be here right now seeing you grow, knowing life is presenting you with as many opportunities as possible, not seeing you kept in suspended animation, hoping you'll suddenly come to life at my death because of money. It's really a savage tradition. I don't believe in it. I wanted you, Helen. You're not something that involuntarily happened to me. It was a choice I made. Understand that! It's something of a miracle," she said, looking at her, "making a baby." She shook her head slowly. "The ultimate creative act, if one cares to see it that way. I love you deeply. Part of the pleasure of creativity is in knowing that what you've created gives other people as much or more pleasure than it gives you. Don't you think that, having derived my own selfish compensation from having had you, I should contribute to your well-being?"

"I don't know. When we talk, everything you say makes perfect sense. But then I go to school or out with my friends, and I listen to all the things they say and what their parents say, and I'm not sure what to believe, or who."

"Go on."

"I mean, you say so many things about children, babies, and creativity, and the way things are *supposed* to be. But nobody else's parents do the things you do."

"Don't you like your life?"

"Oh, I do! I love it. I love you and all the things we do, the places we go, and the people. It's just that . . . I don't know."

"Perhaps I can say it for you. You don't have a father, to begin with. And your mother often sleeps in the morning and stays up late at night working. And the parents of your friends get up early and go to bed early and have jobs and tell their children what to do every step of the way, every day of their lives, and chastise them if they happen to step out of line. Is that something like it?"

"You're angry."

"I'm not. I had a family exactly like that myself, Helen. I didn't hatch out of an egg with a paintbrush in my hand, you know. My life—our life—is the way it is because that's the way I've chosen and worked very hard to make it. If you elect to disagree with my choice, that's your prerogative. I'd no more think of insisting you adhere to my principles than I'd consider turning you out on the street in the event you might disagree. However you live, it'll be your option, not mine. I can only hope that you'll live in a fashion that allows you to grow to your full potential, whatever direction you take."

"Maybe I'll just spend my whole life with you. We'll stay together forever."

"Nothing stays the same, darling. Don't wish for it! I, most likely, will remain fairly much as I am. At my age one doesn't have the tendency to rush headlong into ill-suited ventures. I've arrived at a place where I want to be. Now it's a matter of learning, improving. But you're still a child. You have everything to experience before you accept or reject any one mode of living for any other."

"You mean falling in love and getting married."

"Possibly. Some women never do. It's not necessarily how your life will go, although I suspect it will. But, Helen, because your talent doesn't fall into line with mine doesn't rule out the chance you have something else. Talent is like truth. Its perspective differs depending on the viewer. Do you see? I think what you're experiencing is the beginning of the world for you, darling. You're finding out that other people don't live or even think the way we do, and you've begun asking yourself if there isn't a very real chance that I'm wrong and all the others are right. It's a question of numbers, I know. When one sees that the larger percentage of numbers fall heavily to one side of the scale, one tends to doubt the other side."

"I don't know what I want. I think so much about falling in love, having babies. I can't seem to think about anything else. I keep thinking, if I can do those things, it doesn't matter that I can't do what you do. I love you because you can do the things you do, but I'd love you even if you were different."

"It's sometimes very difficult for me to reconcile my perspectives about you, Helen. It's true. I can see all sorts of potential in you. Men will find you tremendously attractive—it's something you should be prepared for. I can see it, but I can't truthfully say—when I remind myself I'm your mother and not just a member of the audience—that it vicariously excites me. Living through one's children rarely gratifies people, I've found. But right now, this minute, I want to keep you with me just as much as you want to stay. It can't last, though. It won't. Something, someone, will come along and everything will be different. Because *you'll* have changed. It's inevitable."

"I do wonder about talent, though," Helen confessed. "I don't seem to have any at all."

"It's such a nebulous thing. To me, talent is ability. Not just being able to paint or pot. Cooking well is a talent. Speaking beautifully is a talent. I think perhaps you'll have talent with people. I have little gift, if any, with people. I simply cannot tolerate stupid people, slow people. It's something I work to overcome, but I'm impatient, anxious to get on with things.

"You're not like that. I've watched you with your friends, seen the instinctive patience and kindness you show them. You're a giving person, Helen. Without any compunction whatsoever, you give of yourself. Sometimes I envy you many things: the life you've still to live, your beauty."

"I don't see that the outside of me matters. I mean, the person I am is inside, isn't it?"

"A great number of people would prefer not to think that. It's very easy to be drawn by superficial 'skin' qualities. What you have to offer is important not only because you're going to be a beautiful woman, Helen, but mainly because most beautiful people succumb to the trap of their own beauty and live strictly for the sake of it, not *because* of it or to its benefit. You must grow to be your own person, not a carbon copy of me or anyone else. Because what you are, what you'll be, will be the original.

"Maybe I'm not a very good mother. I don't know. Motherhood for me is, often, an unnatural condition. Just, please, don't fly at your life believing it's all urgent. Everything will come to you. In time."

There were fewer students the summer of '36. The houses on either side of the cottage remained closed. Helen roamed the beach with a quiet sense of isolation, feeling, in spite of her mother's assurances that the

Depression would pass, the desperation of the times creeping closer to their front door.

Much as she loved Amanda, she found it difficult to understand her ability to ignore what was happening around them. When Amanda explained, with more patience than she felt, that she was an artist and was unable to surrender that in order to develop a social conscience, Helen was bewildered.

"I had to make a choice long ago," Amanda said, hoping to settle the question of her selection of lifestyle once and for all. "It was a matter of living a fragmented life—breaking up parts of myself to apply them here and there like so many bits of colored paper in a collage—or of concentrating on what I do best, what I know best, what I'm driven toward. I may be a social ignoramus"— she laughed—"but at least I know what I know."

"But if you live in the world, you're supposed to care what happens," Helen argued lamely.

"Of course I care what happens. But what I care most about is my own continuing growth and awareness as an artist, as a person, and, naturally, your growth. It's not that I don't *care,* darling. I'm not an earth-mover or a political activist. I care in my own way. We each have our own methods of achieving goals. You have to learn to accept other people as being what they are. You can't inflict your conscience on others. It doesn't work. One must be very careful to see all the viewpoints, not just one's own."

"I know you're right," Helen said. "And I know you get tired of explaining it all to me over and over again. But if I accept that you are right, then I have to know why."

"Of course. So don't stop demanding explanations. You're starting to find out."

Throughout July and half of August, she steered clear of the classes, avoiding the group on the beach. She posed once, when Jennie sent a note at the last moment saying she was ill. Otherwise, Helen spent most of her time sitting in the sun, thinking, reading, attempting to come to terms with her growing awareness of herself and of the differences between herself and her mother.

Coupled with these philosophical self-examinations was a new interest in her own physical structure. She was having a hard time trying to equate what she suspected were childish emotional reactions to people to the fact of her own body and its well-developed state—its completion of growth something almost separate from the person she felt she was inside.

She investigated herself critically, looking at her body as if it might have been something her mother had painted, trying to find some way to relate her blossoming physical cravings to her lagging emotional and intellectual comprehension. Her body confused her. She accepted that it was hers, that she had to care for it, keep it clean, and provide it with food. But at times when, with astounding importunity, it demanded a different kind of attention, she was perplexed as to how she might appease its appetites.

Amanda was aware of this conflict, and had moments of fear about it. She was worried that Helen could, from mistaken motives, be drawn to those dangerous superficial realms where her sexuality might inevitably be satisfied but little else. She kept her fingers crossed and said nothing, hoping that all their previous and continuing communication would serve to direct her.

A new student came, midway through the summer, arriving at the front door of the cottage late on a Thursday afternoon.

"I'm Theodore Jennings." He smiled down at Amanda. "My dad's Raleigh Jennings. I believe you know him."

"I do indeed," she said, opening the door to invite him in. "I've known your father since Port Zebulon days. How is Raleigh?"

"He's just fine," he said, moving into the armchair by the window. "Asked to be remembered to you."

"Are you staying close by?"

"We've taken the Gooding House round the way. Dad ran into Mr. Gooding in town and they struck up a conversation and one thing led to another, the upshot being they made a deal on the house. Then, when Dad heard you were here, he insisted I come see you to ask if you'd take me on while we're here."

"You plan to be an artist, Theodore?"

"Teddy. No, ma'am, an architect. But I've been taking art and anatomy classes at college, and I'd like to keep my hand in, you know."

Helen arrived at the back door, dipping her sandy feet in the basin of water kept on the porch. She came in, saw Teddy, and stopped.

"This is my daughter, Helen," Amanda said, watching him rise politely, his eyes suddenly filled with Helen.

"Helen, I'd like you to meet Teddy Jennings, the son of a very old friend from Port Zebulon."

Helen stood very still, staring at him. She hadn't ever seen anyone who looked cleaner, more sharply defined, than this tall young man with bright blue eyes, a happy sunburned face, and carroty red hair.

"Hello," she said. "I'll just get dressed and be right back."

Amanda knew instantly they'd be seeing a great deal of Teddy Jennings. She identified the look in Helen's eyes, and as she indicated to Teddy that he should resume his seat, she felt a small uneasiness.

When Helen returned, wearing a new blouse she hadn't worn because she'd insisted she had no need for new clothes, Amanda half nodded to herself. She was right.

Helen tucked her legs under her on the sofa and sat listening to her mother and Teddy talk about the classes, all the while studying this unusual person. He wasn't at all like the other students, didn't even look as if he could hold a brush in his large, awkward-looking hands. But she liked him. She felt drawn to his relaxed manner and frequent laughter. He smiled often, showing his teeth, and she watched, brimming with curiosity.

"Where do you go to school?" she asked finally.

"Yale. I'm going to be an architect."

"Oh." That explained why he didn't look like the others. "Are you going to come to Mother's classes?"

"I hope so. Well, I'd better get back," he said, wondering as he got up how old Helen was. "We're still unpacking. Dad wanted me to come by and say hello and invite you to cocktails this evening if you're free."

"That would be very nice."

"And you too." He smiled at Helen. "If you'd like to."

"Thank you," she said, guessing his father wasn't expecting anyone but Amanda but thinking she'd go anyway and perhaps wear her navy dress with the white piping.

After he'd gone, she said, "He's got a sweet face, don't you think?"

Amanda stubbed out her cigarette carefully. "He's handsome, Helen," she said. "Sweet is for girls."

"I know that," she said impatiently. "I mean, he seems like a sweet person."

Mildly surprised, Amanda said, "I'm quite sure he's all of that, darling. I can't say I much care for your tone of voice."

"I'm sorry," she said, her face falling. "I didn't mean . . ."

"I know what you meant. Why don't you wear your white dress? It looks wonderful with your tan."

"All right," Helen agreed, sensing her mother knew something she didn't.

She spent a considerable amount of time in her bedroom, brushing her hair and staring at herself in the mirror, leaning close to the glass trying to see, really see, how she looked. She couldn't locate the beauty her mother claimed was there. It didn't matter. She felt excited, a low stirring in her stomach, as if something big and important was about to happen. It made her restless and fidgety, eager to be moving.

Unable to remain still within the confines of the house, she walked through, paused at the door to her mother's room, listened but heard nothing, and continued on out the back door.

She walked for several minutes at the water's edge, unable to shake off the sensation of impending change. She needed something to do that would assuage her tremendous pent-up energies. Throwing off her clothes, she began to run along the sand as fast as she could, hearing her feet pounding down on the firm-packed sand, the reverberations of her movement filling her skull. When she arrived at the bend of their cove, she whirled and ran back. Directly in front of the house, she hurled herself into the water, swimming with every ounce of her strength toward the raft. She climbed up and lay on her back, catching her breath. She felt wild, like an animal, wanting something ferocious, nameless. She lay with her arms outflung until her breathing subsided to a more normal rate, then sat with her arms around her knees, gazing at the horizon.

She perceived, feeling the air turn cooler as the sun moved down, that she wanted something totally her own, something that didn't come to her reflected from her mother, something that she didn't think had anything to do with talent or gifts of giving. She wanted a feeling. She could almost reach out and grasp it, but there was no name she knew to apply to it. It had to do with the panic inside her body, the inner demands wanting to be made on someone, something. She wished she knew what.

The sun was dropping fast, but she was reluctant to leave the raft. If she stayed only a while longer, it might become clear to her. She might obtain some clue to her need. But then she remembered they were going to see the Jenningses, and her attention shifted to Teddy Jennings and his large hands and sunburned cheeks, and the panic quickened in her stomach. She held her hands over her breasts, imagining how his hands might feel on her. It was ridiculous! Jerking her hands away, she dived back into the water and swam to shore, gathering up her clothes as she ran to the house.

She was ready long before Amanda, and sat in the living room leafing through the new issue of the *Post*, unable to concentrate. She smoothed down her dress, thinking it made her look awfully young. Amanda appeared, cutting off her thought of changing dresses.

As they walked along the road, Amanda showing the way with her flashlight, Helen kept pace, thinking anyone would know her mother was exceptional. Everything she did, even walking along a dark road carrying a flashlight, had such decisiveness, as if she knew exactly what she was doing at all times and, not only that, also why she was doing it. And, knowing all these things, she hadn't any time to waste giving it consideration. Her mind, apparently freed of the requisites of attending to routine details, was able to move in other directions. It was amazing, Helen thought, that she could be so utterly sure of who she was that she hadn't any need at all to pay attention to how she came across to others. How one looked to other people didn't count nearly so much as how one appeared to oneself and how true one was to one's own personal and artistic integrity. Helen understood that, logically, this included how she treated others and her behavior in her own eyes. It all had to do, Amanda said so often, with exercising a positive awareness of other peoples' feelings. One had to be concerned with the why's of others, not what they did or didn't think of you. Honesty was bound to transcend artifice.

Nearing the Gooding House, Helen wished, for one fervent moment, that she could already be at the point of self-understanding her mother was. But that took so long. And they were already on the porch.

Teddy came to the door, and Helen felt her panic rising again. She followed Amanda and Teddy inside and acknowledged the introductions gracefully, all the while letting her eyes follow Teddy. He came over at last, and stood beside her.

"Would you like something to drink?" he smiled.

"Oh, I'll have a Coke or something," she said, sounding childish to her own ears.

"One Coke coming up."

He headed for the makeshift bar, and she watched, liking the way he looked in his white shirt and sweater vest, his navy bow tie. She imagined all the boys at Yale must look that way.

"How old are you?" she asked as he handed her a glass.

"Twenty-two next month. You?"

"What do you think? Guess!"

He turned to look at her with an expression she knew

25

well. It was one her mother had upon occasion when her eyes were caught by some subject that intrigued her. He was an artist.

"Seventeen?" he guessed.

"I'll be sixteen in January."

"So, you're fifteen and a half." He sounded very self-congratulatory.

She was suddenly angry, but even more excited.

"I am not a child!"

"No, I wouldn't have said so. You don't look like a child."

"Well, I'm not!"

"No," he agreed, attempting to demonstrate patience, "you're not. Would you like to go for a walk?"

"Why?"

"Because"—he glanced around the room—"I'm not wildly interested in the good old days, and I don't think anyone will mind if we do."

"All right."

Amanda watched them go. Their departure created a number of conflicting reactions in her, but she set them on a mental upper shelf for later review, returning to her conversation with Raleigh and Lilah.

Helen bent to take off her shoes, and Teddy said, "Here, let me!" and took them, jamming one in each of his pockets.

"You look very funny," she laughed, the anger gone now and only the marvelous excitement remaining. "I'll race you to the end of the beach." She ran, knowing he'd follow. Animated images flicked off and on on an interior screen, and she viewed these scenes with a mounting sense of anticipation. So many things could happen! She stopped at the turn of the beach and waited for him to catch up.

He bounded over and dropped onto the sand, catching his breath. She sat looking at his profile in the moonlight, liking his face more each minute. She especially liked the shape of his mouth, the pointed bow of his upper lip. Like a child's mouth somehow, relaxed yet ready at any moment to display petulance.

"You don't get much exercise at school, do you?" She watched him take a pipe out of his pocket and start filling it from a leather tobacco pouch.

"I usually skip workouts, gym, that stuff. They're a waste of time."

"How long have you been smoking a pipe?" she asked as he held a match over the bowl and puffed rapidly.

" 'Bout a year," he said out of the side of his mouth. "It gives me something to do with my hands while I'm thinking."

"I see," she lied.

"Fifteen and a half, almost sixteen," he said, leaning back against a rock. "You're almost six and a half years younger than me."

"What does that prove?" she asked, looking up at the moon, wondering what was going to happen.

"That depends on what you're talking about."

"I don't know what I'm talking about." She laughed.

"Good! Neither do I!"

"How many more years of school do you have?"

"A few. You're beautiful. I guess you know that, don't you?"

She looked over at him, trying to see his face, but he was in shadow now.

"People say so. I don't understand it, though. I mean, I can't see it. I just feel like me. Whatever that is."

"What do you want to do?"

"When?"

"When you're older."

"Oh! I don't know. I'll probably go to college and study languages. I'm not talented like my mother."

"And what'll you do after you've finished studying your languages?"

"Teach, perhaps. I haven't thought that far. It seems like such a long way away."

"It comes fast enough. The older you get, the faster time seems to pass."

"You talk as if you're so old. You're not!"

"I'm at college. It's an older type of life."

"Maybe. But you're still only twenty-one. It's not that old."

"True. But sometimes I feel more like forty-five or fifty," he said tiredly, puffing on his pipe.

"Why?"

"Oh, loads of reasons. It's hard playing the game with my folks, pretending we're making out when we're just barely squeaking through. There's only just enough. Just enough for two drinks for everyone, measured carefully. Just enough for my tuition. Just enough to rent a summer house for a month at the end of the season. Just enough for almost everything. But not really."

"I think you're lucky. Most people don't have enough for anything at all. Do you think this Depression will ever end?"

"Probably. I hope we keep on having enough until it does. It's damned hard sometimes to know when Dad's telling the truth."

"Why? Does he lie?"

"I don't think so. It's more having to preserve appearances. For himself as much as for me and my mother."

"But that's very kind of him. He's a nice man, and he's trying to give you a good life."

"Oh, I know. That's what makes everything so difficult. I'm afraid to do the things I want for fear of letting him down."

"What things?"

"Just things," he said, knocking his pipe against the rock so that the tobacco fell, a dark, still-burning lump on the sand. "Tell me," he said, leaning close to her, "have you been kissed by a lot of boys?"

Her heart pounded. "No. Not by any."

"That's impossible," he said, laughter lurking at the edges of his words as he took her hand and held it in his large palms.

"I never lie," she said, finding it a strain to talk, to concentrate on words.

"Maybe you do and maybe you don't," he said, running his fingers over the back of her hand. "You're so small.

28

Look at this hand!" He laughed, holding it up between them. "It's not possible to have a hand that small!"

"Of course it is!" she said, trying to draw her hand away. "You're making fun of me."

"I wouldn't ever do that," he said, keeping hold of her. "You're much too beautiful to make fun of."

"Oh, stop! I hate hearing about beautiful."

"All right. We won't discuss it. Come on," he said, pulling her up, his attitude formal all at once. "We'd better head back."

She was terribly disappointed. He wasn't going to kiss her after all. She stood, shaking the sand off her dress, trying to gather herself together. These few minutes talking that way had unsettled her, so that she now felt somehow separated from herself.

"Here," he said, "turn around. Let me."

He held her arm and turned her, slapping at the back of her skirt to loosen the sand. She stood, aware of his hand on her arm, her shoes stuck in his pockets, and thought how crazy they both were.

"You're not going to kiss me."

"I thought you didn't want me to," he said, letting her go, his face puzzled.

"I don't remember saying that."

His mouth was very soft as he touched his lips to hers for a brief moment.

"Is that all?" she asked.

"No," he said, putting his arms around her so that he could feel her breasts against him.

She felt so many things all at once when he kissed her the second time, covering her mouth with his soft, smooth lips. She felt small and fragile, yet enormously powerful. And also she felt a resurgence of that wildness she'd experienced on the raft, and pressed closer to him, touching his lips with her tongue.

He broke away abruptly. "Who taught you to do that?"

"Do what?"

"Kiss that way?"

"No one taught me. I wanted to know what you taste like."

"My God!" he said, holding her arms at her sides.

"Shouldn't I have done that?"

"You're only fifteen." He released her. "You make it hard for a fellow to remember that."

"What does my age have to do with anything?"

"It has everything to do with everything. Come on. Let's go back."

He started off along the beach and she ran after him, exasperated and humiliated.

"Why are you running away from me?" she demanded, tugging at his sleeve, forcing him to stop.

"Don't you know the facts of life?" he asked sharply.

"Of course I do!"

"Then you should know better!" he accused.

"Better than what? I don't understand you."

He turned, opening his mouth to tell her precisely what he thought of teases, then stopped, looking at her expectant face.

"I'm sorry," he said, wondering what it was about her that had him standing there apologizing for what *she'd* done. "I'm behaving like the fifteen-year-old. I'm very attracted to you."

"And I to you."

"We're talking about two different things," he said disconcertedly.

"I don't think so," she said, sliding her foot into the water. "I know about lovemaking. Because I haven't done any doesn't mean I'm ignorant."

"If you do know, then you must also know that at fifteen you're too young to be playing games."

"You talk such nonsense! I don't know a thing about playing games. I wanted to kiss you, to know how you tasted. It gave me a good feeling. Is it that you didn't like it?"

He turned away. "People don't talk about those things."

"Well, maybe people ought to. Didn't you like it?"

"Yes," he admitted, facing her again. "Yes, I did."

"Then why on earth are you so annoyed with me for liking what we both wanted to do?"

"I'm not annoyed with you."

"You're certainly annoyed with something. If not me, what?"

"Look, this is turning into an inquisition, for Pete's sake! Let's drop it now. They're going to be wondering where we are."

"Will you kiss me again?"

"I thought I just explained myself to you."

"Oh, to hell with you!" she exploded. "You're a fool!"

Avoiding the hand he put out to restrain her, she ran away down the beach toward home.

"Hey, wait!" he called.

"To hell with you!" she shouted, racing away.

He stood there for several minutes until he was sure she wasn't going to come back, thinking she was the most outrageous and beautiful girl he'd ever seen. But there was something about her that had him stumped. He started back to the Gooding House. Leaving her shoes beside the veranda, he went inside to explain to Amanda that Helen hadn't felt well and had gone home. And as he offered his feeble lie, he encountered that same puzzling aura in the mother that he'd seen in the daughter. The way they looked at him—as if they were capable of exercising extraordinary powers of knowledge and vision.

"I'd better run along," Amanda said. "It's good to see all of you." At the door she paused. "We'll expect you Saturday, Teddy."

"I'll be there," he said, questioning the good sense of attending the classes.

Helen was in the kitchen, having changed out of the white dress and into a pair of shorts and a shirt, drinking coffee, and trying, again, to read the *Post*.

"What happened?" Amanda asked lightly, pouring some sherry.

"He kissed me, then got mad."

"I see."

"Well, I don't. That boy's crazy!"

"Not at all, darling. I think most likely he's confused by you."

"I thought he was so nice, and then there he was acting so annoyed, accusing me of playing games. I don't know anything about games."

"As I said, he's confused by you. What were you hoping for from him, Helen?"

She looked up. "I wasn't hoping for anything."

"Think about it. Perhaps you were."

During dinner Helen attempted to determine what she'd been hoping for and why she felt so let down at the way things had concluded on the beach. It was best to put the whole matter out of her mind, she decided. She wasn't getting anywhere at all in her examination of the episode.

They were on the beach the next afternoon. Helen was resting between poses, engrossed in a discussion with her mother on the merits of Vassar versus Radcliffe.

Teddy came down the beach and stopped in a quandary, aware that it was too late to turn back without being seen. Trying to appear nonchalant, he continued ahead, realizing with a shock that there was that damned girl posing nude for her mother.

It seemed impossible to avoid confronting some naked aspect of this incredible, impulsive girl. He felt suspicious of the casual attitudes of this pair. People he knew didn't act the way this mother and daughter did. Their relationship defied anything he knew or understood—they seemed like friends, and that didn't make sense. He was accustomed to girls who were always on the edge of disagreement with their mothers. Girls who laughed but merely used their laughter as an enticement, girls who said dozens of things they didn't mean simply to appear bright and engaging. And now here was this girl, claiming she was everything she said, claiming she didn't lie, acting spontaneously because her mother obviously encouraged her to do so. It wasn't right.

"Oh, here's Teddy!" Amanda said with a wave of her hand, making it impossible for him to retreat.

He plowed ahead, carrying Helen's shoes, trying to avoid looking directly at her, although she didn't seem bothered either by his presence or by the fact that he was seeing her nude.

"I brought back your shoes," he said, wondering where he could drop them before making a fast escape.

"Thank you," Helen said, holding out her hand for them.

He was forced to look at her then, to give her the shoes, which she accepted—her breasts lifting as she raised her arm. She set the shoes on the sand beside her, glancing questioningly over at her mother.

Teddy stood mesmerized by the sight of her high, full breasts, the nipples darkly pink; the length of her thighs; the concave lure of her pelvic structure. As an artist he wanted to examine every nuance of her construction, the magnificent application of flesh to bone. As a man he was profoundly embarrassed, and backed away, coughing to cover his discomfort.

"May I?" he asked, indicating the canvas as he approached Amanda.

"Do!" she said, moving to one side to allow him to view the painting. She was aware of his embarrassment, and questioned the training that wouldn't allow him to react openly and honestly to the situation. His performance of gentlemanly discretion made her angry, since he was destroying the pleasant mood that had existed before his arrival by refusing to admit to his confusion. Only Helen, it seemed, was unaware of the negative contagion of his reactions.

"It's beautiful," he said, grateful he'd worn his baggy trousers.

"Will you have some iced tea?" she offered, looking at Helen, who hadn't budged.

"Oh, no." He forgot himself and looked at Helen again. "I've got to get back. I just came about the shoes, you see."

"Of course. Perhaps you'd like to have dinner with us this evening," she said, surprising herself. What did she hope to achieve by that?

"Well . . ." he said, unsure.

"No one will bite you." Helen laughed. "Or kiss you, for that matter."

That did it. "Okay," he said defiantly. "What time?"

"Seven." Amanda looked at her wristwatch. "That'll give us another hour here, and time for a swim."

"Fine!" he said firmly, casting a challenging look at Helen. "I'll see you later, then."

"Don't be late!" Helen called to his retreating back.

"That wasn't needed," Amanda said when he was well down the beach.

"What?"

"You didn't have to be cruel. He was very embarrassed."

"Why, for goodness sake?"

"A dozen reasons. Primarily, I'd say, because in his world women don't show themselves. Not their bodies, certainly. And their brains only rarely. You've an exquisite body, and you've never been told it's something to be ashamed of or self-conscious about. He most likely hasn't ever come face to face with anyone as uninhibited as you are."

"That's unbelievable!" she exclaimed.

"No. A little sad, perhaps. Try to be understanding, darling. You're going to find the world chock-full of young men and women like Teddy. They're merely acting out the roles they've been given to play."

Dinner went easily enough. Teddy's defiance melted away as he saw that Helen wasn't going to be difficult. Involuntarily his eyes returned again and again to appreciate the seductive swell of her breasts, the vulnerable flawlessness of her throat. He sure wouldn't fluff a second chance with her, he promised himself, tease or not. He'd show her a thing or two. He could barely keep his attention on the conversation, he was so involved in his yearning for another viewing of her delectable body.

Amanda excused herself after coffee, saying, "I have some letters to write. Good to see you, Teddy."

She retired to her room and pulled out a sheaf of stationery, but couldn't begin. The temptation to hurry back out and issue warnings to Helen was almost insurmountable. But what good would it do? She'd known from the moment he'd appeared at the front door that

Teddy would alter their lives. If it wasn't Teddy, it was bound to be someone else, because there was no legitimate way to shield Helen from exposure to the ways of society. *If only he wasn't so damnably receptive to Helen's physical appeal!* she thought. But perhaps she was being hasty. She picked up the pen and forced herself to start the letter.

Helen and Teddy got up from the table as Jessie came out to clear up, and they sat on the sofa, silent. Without Amanda, conversation had dwindled away. Helen turned on the radio, rolling the dial until she tuned in some music, then sat down once more, feeling stifled by the stuffiness of the cottage.

"Let's go for a walk," she suggested.

"Okay. The beach or the road?"

"It's up to you."

"The beach, then," he said.

They left their shoes on the back porch and started along the sand.

"I'm sorry about last night," he said, reaching for his pipe.

"That's all right. I don't suppose Mother and I are much like other people you know."

"You sure aren't. I won't forget in a hurry."

"It's so warm. Let's wade in the water."

"Why not?" he said, jamming the pipe back into his pocket and reaching for her hand. "Come on!"

They ran splashing through the shallows, overtaken by laughter. Teddy kept thinking, not without guilt, that he was defying some code—something vague he knew he ought not do—in allowing her freedom to spread over him like a light, flexible net. But he was caught up in it, temporarily unheeding of important admonitions because of the delight of such spontaneity.

Helen felt giddily happy, totally expectant. And Teddy watched her run, her hair streaming out behind her, her shoulders and throat pushing out the music of her laughter. When they fell on the sand, still laughing, Helen lay back looking up at the sky, thinking how good it felt being with him.

As he bent over her, it was without the premeditation and thoughts of vengeance he'd earlier entertained. He was too trapped in the enchantment of freedom to act other than instinctively. He kissed her for a long time, opening his mouth over hers, touching her tongue, her teeth, her lips until she was weak with desire. When he drew away she sat up, saying, "Have I done something wrong again?"

"No." He shook his head, resting his elbows on his knees, his senses threatening to return. "It's just that I want so much to touch you."

He spoke so softly that the rushing water almost drowned out his words. But she heard him.

"Why don't you? I'd like that."

"Helen," he groaned, "I can't. It's not right!"

"Why not?"

"I don't know. I don't make the rules. It's just the way things are. You don't make love to young girls from good families."

"Bad families, then?"

"No."

"Have you ever made love?"

"Oh yes," he said, gazing out at the water. "I have."

"And she was from a bad family, whatever that is?"

"No. It was different."

"Why?"

"Because she was older. It was all right."

"I don't see why you keep dragging up age."

"I can't with you. I don't feel that way about you."

"Oh? What way do you feel about me?"

"I care for you," he conceded hoarsely. It was like being tickled to death: painful pleasure.

"I see. You only make love with women you don't care for."

"God, that's not how it is at all! It's just that I *care* for you. I didn't plan it that way."

"Well, I care for you too. But I certainly don't understand you. I can't make sense out of you."

"For one thing," he said, attempting to induce a reasonable note into the situation, "we've only known each other for a few days."

"It still doesn't make sense. Do you have some kind of waiting period? I can't see why, if you care for me and want to kiss and touch me, you shouldn't do it."

"I can't make love to you. It wouldn't be right. It'd be taking advantage."

"Okay," she said, losing her patience, "when *will* it be right?"

"I don't know. How can I answer that?"

"Well, how can I?"

"Oh, I don't know."

"I think we should stop talking right now. We seem to do nothing but argue when we try to talk." She held out her arms to him. He made a strangled noise and looked away.

"Give me your hand!" She was determined to put an end to all this foolish talking.

He didn't answer.

"Give me your hand!" she insisted, taking hold of it.

Unbuttoning her blouse, she placed his hand on her breast, feeling an immense delight in having solved the problem so simply. He came forward and kissed her, then lowered his mouth to the base of her throat.

"That's lovely," she whispered, falling back, her fingers in his hair. "That feels so nice."

"I can't stop," he said, all caution gone as he pulled at her blouse. "I can't!"

"I don't want you to stop," she said, helping him.

"Don't let me do this!" he said, sounding as if he'd cry as he clasped her to his chest, his hands flat on her back, his mouth reveling in the scented curve of her neck.

"But I want you to," she urged, touching the whorl of his ear, curious, avid.

"Don't do this, Helen," he said.

"Teddy, I'm not a child. Let's stop all of this!"

She stood up and pulled off the remainder of her clothes. "I'm fully grown," she said, turning in a circle as if to illustrate this fact. "And you've been with women before. Now you'll be with me."

"I have to," he said, frantically undoing his clothes, his eyes sweeping over her lush body. "I have to."

He took charge then, spreading her skirt on the sand, lowering her down onto it, finding her yielding, unresistant. He traced patterns over her arms and legs with his fingertips, turning her this way and that as if she were a doll, examining her scrupulously with a sense of holding a miracle in his arms. His joy was so consuming he wanted to cry, to spend an eternity lost in the perfection of her flesh.

Entranced by his involvement with her body, she reached to touch him, familiarizing herself with him. It was as if she left the thinking part of her being off to one side while turning a new switch in her brain, one that involved her wholly in the uniqueness of what was taking place.

When he kissed her breasts she felt the pull deep inside like something stretching—some invisible, previously unknown chain linking the outside of her to the inside. She wished it were possible to be kissed everywhere at once, thinking of many mouths clamped to her body, tightening that chain that was growing more taut as his caresses became more explicit. She was turning to water, her bones dissolving as he continued touching her.

He was moving down, and when he eased her thighs apart and put his head between them, she smiled, thinking what a strange thing that was for him to do. But her amusement ceased as his mouth opened against her, and she relaxed for a moment, enjoying the feathery sensations. He reached to touch a part of her she'd previously ignored. And as he kept on, her concentration began to intensify until she was begging him not to stop. Every particle of her being was closing in, focusing on a point on the horizon she was striving to get to, a point his mouth was driving her toward, until she was clutching his head to her blindly, imploring him to help her to her destination, pressing herself closer, harder against this source of transport, opening herself to it until nothing else mattered. And all at once, lost in writhing frenzy, she threw herself forward into it, shuddering, a low sobbing moan escaping from her mouth as she was convulsed.

She collapsed on the sand, her eyes wide and slightly vacant as she fought to get her breath.

"That was fantastic!" she sighed when he lay down beside her. "Whoever taught you to do that?"

"A woman I once knew," he said, looking at her face, in love with her delicate profile, her heaving breasts.

"She must have been a genius!"

"Oh, no." He laughed, amused by her innocence.

"That was the most amazing feeling of my entire life," she said, shaking her head in wonder. "I'd like to make you feel that way too."

"It makes me feel good that I can do that for you."

"But I could do the same for you?"

"Perhaps," he said, running his fingers lightly over her breasts and down across her stomach. "God, you're wonderful!" He let his hand rest on her thigh.

"We have to do it all properly," she said. "You must come into me."

"I've never been with a virgin," he said, frightened. "I'm not sure I could. I'd be afraid of hurting you."

"But you must. You've been with other women. I can't see that there's any difference. I want to give myself to you."

She drew him over her, reaching to touch him. He trembled.

"It feels good, doesn't it?"

"Yes, yes," he whispered, urgently kissing her mouth and neck.

"You want me," she said, moving her legs. "It isn't fair for you to give me so much and you to have nothing. Let's do it. I want you to."

There was a moment—not more than a split second—when he believed that what he was doing was completely right. But no sooner had this insight come to him than the conviction that he was committing a moral wrong erased that belief. But he'd trespassed too far to go back. He wanted somehow to hurt her, and didn't know why. The wanting blinded him to a great number of things, made him suddenly forgetful of her age and inexperience. He was aware only of the need to ease his overwhelming desire.

"It's all right," she whispered, holding him. She stroked his arms, sliding her hands down the length of his back, thinking it would be good and beautiful.

In one powerful thrust, he came fully inside her. She cried out, hanging suspended, impaled on pain, incapable of movement.

"You hurt me," she said, her voice shaking, a coldness between her breasts, along her spine. "I . . . I think we'd better stop."

"No, no," he said, thinking she was deranged, crazy to say one thing one minute and tell him to stop in the next, "it'll be all right."

"But—" She fell silent, swallowed by the monstrous rending pain of his performance.

"Do you like it now?" he asked, determined that she would.

"Yes," she lied, coming slowly away from the pain, not wanting to spoil his pleasure, and a little frightened by his refusal to stop. For a moment she almost hated him for what he'd done. But her hands continued to encourage him, and her mouth opened to his kisses.

Despite her small dishonesty, she found herself responding, aiming at that once more accessible point on the horizon.

He waited, held back as she struggled to separate the parts of herself once again in order to fully participate in this act of giving. He stopped waiting as she moved beneath him, her eyes looking surprised as her breathing quickened. She felt him drawing up inside of himself, tapping some remote source in his body, and she retained her awareness long enough to feel him filling her with springing warmth. She was deeply moved and flooded with caring for him as she took flight in a soaring spasm of completion.

"I love you," she said, holding him, "I really do."

He listened in disbelief, unable to form thoughts.

The pain returned as he withdrew, and a sob escaped

her involuntarily. "I'm going to cry," she said, freeing her arms from him as tears rolled from her eyes.

"I didn't want to hurt you." He watched her cover her eyes with her arm, thinking she was undergoing an inevitable guilt. "Please don't cry like that. It's terrible to see. We shouldn't have done it."

"I'm not crying because I'm sorry," she said, confounding him. "But it did hurt. I never imagined anything could feel that way."

"It only happens once," he said, wondering why he felt so stinking guilty when she obviously didn't.

"Well." She wiped her nose and eyes on the sleeve of her blouse. "That's a very good thing, don't you think?"

"God, I love you!" he said, astounded at himself. "I did the very first minute I saw you dipping your feet in the pan of water at your back door. You looked so beautiful."

"I wonder what will happen," she mused, attempting to project her thoughts into the future.

"We'll probably get married and have seven or eight kids."

"I hope not," she said remotely. "I plan all kinds of exciting things for my life before I get married." She looked down, frowning. "I think I'm bleeding."

He felt faintly sickened and looked away.

"Let's go for a swim." He took her hand, his head buzzing with contradictions. "It'll wash away. We'll talk about the future later."

She floated on her back, locating stars and naming them aloud, her voice sounding inconsequential in the nighttime silence. *It's curious,* she thought, *that one minute you're one thing and the next minute something else.* She wasn't the same now as she'd been two hours ago. It was quite something, that changing of self. She was anxious to know how her mother would explain how one's self could be altered that way.

"What are you saying?" Teddy asked, sliding his arms under her so that she was resting against him, her hair drifting like brown seaweed over his arms.

"I was naming the constellations. Just a game. I'm very

41

happy," she said, putting her arms around his neck. "Is this the way it's going to be?"

"Oh, I don't know. I wish we could just stay this way forever. But we can't, and I'm scared."

"Of what?"

"Your mother's bound to find out. What'll she think of me?"

"I'll tell her. We don't keep secrets. We aren't like that. Mother's always told me I'm responsible for myself, to do what I believe is right. I haven't done anything wrong."

"Maybe not in your eyes, but I feel rotten. I can't help it. I'll have to marry you. It's the only decent thing to do."

"Put me down!" She pushed at him. "Let go of me!"

He followed her out of the water, watching as she sat on her skirt, reaching for her blouse to wipe her face and hair.

"Why do you have to be so concerned with 'the decent thing to do'?" she asked hotly. "Haven't you any instincts of your own? Can't you follow your own feelings? Do you do everything because somebody tells you to? What makes you think I want to be married? You keep insisting on telling me how young I am. Well, I am. And it's certainly not time yet for me to even think about getting married. I don't see why I should have to think about it at all. It's not in my plans at this moment. And I'm definitely not going to do anything just because other people think it's the thing to be done."

"I wasn't talking about tomorrow," he argued, shaking the water out of his hair. "I meant eventually."

"I don't see how you can be thinking about eventually when we're here right now. Why do you bother yourself about the future? What difference does it make? It seems to me as if all that 'eventually' thinking could only ruin what's happening right now."

"It makes a whole lot of difference," he said. "I care about you. I have a responsibility for you now. And I want you with me. For more than just a night on the beach. There'll never be anyone like you."

"What about your other woman? The one who taught

you so well? What about her? She must have been someone special."

"Not like you. She was married with children, not a young virgin."

"You don't talk about her very nicely. She must have cared for you to make love with you."

"Oh, she liked me well enough, I suppose. I never really understood it. She made herself available, and I wanted her. Who wouldn't? I mean, a pretty woman offers herself to you. I'm a normal man with normal impulses. Why would I pass that up? But it was all over almost as soon as it started."

"Have you had other girls?"

"A couple. But I've never felt this way before, the way I feel for you."

"Do you mean it?"

"Yes, I mean it! I never wanted anyone the way I did you."

"But that's just physical. How do you *feel* about me?"

"I can't be sure yet. We hardly know each other. I need more time. I think I'm in love with you. I don't know."

"I love you."

"You're too young to say things like that."

"I wish you could get past this age business."

"It just scares me the way you make the kind of committing moves and remarks you do. Aren't you ever afraid of being wrong?"

"If I'm wrong, I'm wrong. What's the good of worrying in advance?"

"You're shivering. I'd better get you home."

They dressed and walked back to the cottage. He sat down on the steps to put on his shoes. Putting her fingers lightly on the nape of his neck, she asked, "Will we see each other every day?"

He sat up and took her hand. "I'm going to see you every chance I get. At least until I figure you out and why I'm going into some kind of tailspin over you."

Well, that must mean something! she thought, watching him walk away. She went inside to the bathroom and started the water running in the tub. She felt sleepy, satiated, and smiled at the thought that a great number of things had happened that fell into adult categories. Changes. So many of them. She'd tell Amanda in the morning.

Amanda guessed. Helen was so incandescent; her skin seemed to radiate sexual satisfaction. While Jessie prepared their breakfast, Amanda suggested, "Let's swim before breakfast. Have we got time, Jessie?"

"Plenty," the housekeeper said, preparing a tray of muffins. "Go on."

In the water Amanda said, "Come out to the raft," and Helen followed, admiring her mother's strong, smooth stroke. It was a hazy morning, but from experience they knew the haze would burn off before midday, leaving the afternoon clear and hot.

"Do you want to tell me about it?" Amanda asked, pulling off her bathing cap.

"You know!" Helen examined her mother's impassive face. "Do I look different? Does it show?"

"Not particularly. It's more a sensation I have than anything else. Did you choose this for yourself, Helen?"

"What do you mean?"

"I mean, was it something *you* wanted?"

"Yes, I did. He didn't want to." She let her feet dangle in the water.

"I see," Amanda said soberly. "I'm not honestly sure how I feel about this."

"I know how I feel. I love him."

"Darling, don't delude yourself! It's all too easy to convince oneself it's love when it's physical attraction."

"You've told me about that, Mother. I know the difference."

"You think you do. At fifteen it's hard to be sure. And, whatever happens—whether you do or don't love him—you can't ever go back to what you were. You've entered into a situation with serious considerations involved. I hate to think you might be hurt and wind up losing in the end, not knowing or understanding why. There are certain things, kinds of knowledge, that really only do come with time and experience. You're very young yet.

"Don't misunderstand, Helen. I'm not condemning or criticizing. I'm simply attempting to point out various truths you'll have to come to grips with. What about Teddy? How does he feel?"

"He's not sure yet."

"Well, at least he's honest."

"Don't you like him? I thought you did."

"Whether I like him or not isn't the issue. I like him well enough. I expect I'll know a good deal more about him once I've seen his work."

"Are you angry with me?"

"No. A little sad, possibly. I don't know. In its own way, it's such a final gesture, Helen. You haven't known enough boys to be absolutely certain this is one you love. But if you're happy, I'll try to be happy with you. Did he take any precautions?"

"How?"

"To protect you from getting pregnant."

"No. I don't think so."

"Ask him to use something. Talk to him about it. He'll want to do what's right. When we get back to the city you can go and see Leon."

Helen nodded, brought down by her mother's matter-of-factness about having her see their doctor.

"Don't look that way," Amanda said, putting her arm around her. "It's a little difficult for me too just now. I've been going along thinking of you as a child. I have to make adjustments in my way of thinking. I want whatever makes you happy. It's only that I'm not altogether convinced this is it. I've always tried to be totally honest with you, Helen. I don't intend to change that now. I don't advocate sexual license in an indiscriminate sense. I've tried to make you see that making love should be a natural outcome of a deep, abiding affection—love—you share with someone. Sex for its own sake—unless you're entirely brainless—can't ever mean as much as lovemaking with someone you deeply care for. I'm not so old I've forgotten how it feels to want to *know*. But I'm not so

45

young either that I don't see the pitfalls you might encounter because of your drive and beauty. Please, all I ask is that you try to be honest with yourself. If you are, everything else will sort itself out. And we'll have to stop the portrait."

"Oh, why?"

"I'm not sure. As your mother . . . I don't really know. I just know I've lost the feeling for it, the mood. You're not the same girl who began the sittings. Your aura would be . . . is . . . different. It would come out as two portraits, I think."

"Do you still love me?"

"Of course I still love you. Do you think people just suddenly stop loving each other? That's not life, Helen. You have your own directions to follow. Just because you're not going along in my footsteps doesn't mean I withdraw my love. We each have to find our own dimensions. Take your time, darling, and be very sure what you're doing is really what you want. The portrait doesn't matter. I'll do another one some other time."

Teddy came to the class that afternoon, setting up his easel with care, arranging his paints, brushes, and palette with methodical precision. He greeted Helen genially, whispering they'd talk after class, then turned his attention to the model.

Helen hung around in the background, observing him work, guessing he was going to be good. Amanda stood behind him for a long time as he roughed-in. There was an affirmative strength to his lines that was powerful. She stepped close to Helen for a moment. "That lad's no architect," she said, sotto voce, "he's a painter." She patted Helen's hand, then returned to the group, moving from student to student, making comments. As she went, it was becoming clear to her that Teddy was engaged in an interior battle—one she was all too familiar with. It was the war between one's sense of loyalty to family traditions and directions and the yearning to give vent to the drive in one's soul for creative expression. She empathized, but somehow doubted that he had sufficient courage to win the battle.

Afterward Teddy seemed drained as he carried his equipment along the beach.

"Let me take something," Helen offered, reaching for his paintbox.

"Thanks."

"Is this the way you always are after working?"

"I guess so. Let's sit down here for a minute."

He sat on a rock by the shore and stared at the water.

"You don't really want to be an architect, do you?"

"No," he said, folding his hands over each other. "It's what Dad's always wanted for me."

"But you should do what *you* want."

"I can't, Helen! I owe it to him."

"He's your father. Doesn't he want what will make you happy?"

"That's not the way it works." There were tears building in the corners of his eyes.

"But, Teddy, you're so unhappy. Surely he must see that."

"I've tried to tell you. He sees what he wants to see. He's just ordinary, like other men."

"But you're not. You're very talented. Mother knows it, too. You could be a fine painter."

"It's out of the question." He blew his nose loudly. "Let's not go on about it. How do you feel today?"

"Perfectly wonderful. How about you?"

"Mixed up. But knowing I was going to see you today made me happier than anything has in ages. I don't know what the hell to do."

"Mother says I must tell you to take precautions."

He looked at her, his face a mask of incredulity. "You *told* her?"

"She knew. I didn't have to tell her."

"And she didn't raise holy hell?"

"Of course not."

"Jesus Christ! She even talked to me as if everything was perfectly normal!"

"She just wants us to be discreet and careful. Careful about babies."

"God above! No one has a mother like that! She's not real!"

"Certainly she's real. What a thing to say!"

"Don't get mad. That's not what I meant. This whole thing is . . . I don't know. What I wouldn't give for just one parent like that!"

"Your parents seem like very good people, Teddy. You make them sound like monsters."

"They're not bad or anything. They're just so god-damned typical! Their whole life is a pretense. Nothing's real except what other people will think. Who cares anyway what other people think? I wish to God I didn't."

"Then don't! Be what you want."

"I don't have your kind of training. It's too late for me."

"It's never too late."

"Look, let's take this stuff back and then walk into town for a soda or something. I don't feel like sticking around here this afternoon." He also didn't feel like arguing or going into a lengthy discussion about Amanda Kimbrough. He couldn't get over the idea—the woman had simply accepted the fact that her fifteen-year-old daughter had given her virginity to someone she'd known only a few days. There was something going on here that scared the hell out of him, and he felt as if he was being decoyed into some trap that would spring closed and kill him.

"Okay," she agreed, lifting the paintbox. "I wish you could feel happier, Teddy. Couldn't you try not thinking about all that while you're here?"

"I'll give it the old college try." He laughed, kissing her, thinking maybe he was mistaken; maybe he'd landed feet-first in a gold mine. "Maybe my luck has changed." He smiled, sliding his hands across her breasts before jumping to his feet.

The days burned off like the early-morning mist. They spent all their free time together. In the evenings they wandered the beach, making love on the sand or in the

Gooding boathouse, or on the pier at the empty Hewlett house. They never spoke of it again or remembered Amanda's advice about precautions, and went ahead with their lovemaking with abandon, experimenting. Teddy had the rare, luxurious sensation that he'd been fortuitously provided with the ultimate erotic fantasy: a beautiful girl to whom he could do practically anything, one who was willing to take instruction without hesitation, who found no part of him displeasing or untouchable. Just thinking of her, visualizing her naked form, he wanted her. He couldn't leave her alone, couldn't resist the temptation of her face and body.

Helen felt she was living in a state of perpetual arousal. She wondered what was happening to her, if this was what it meant to be in love. Alone in the early morning on the raft, she lay staring up at the sky, trying to put her feelings about Teddy into logical order. But she couldn't. There was something that nagged at her, gathering momentum until it actually came poking at her brain while she was in the midst of making love to Teddy. It wouldn't leave her alone, and she couldn't stop returning again and again to question her own feelings, to try to be very sure that what she felt was love.

Every night she'd run to him, filled with anticipation for talk, communication. And for ten or fifteen minutes, distractedly, he'd play at conversation. It was obvious he didn't really listen. It bothered her, especially when he repeatedly, fervently swore he loved her. She wanted to believe the things he said to her. It was very important to make it all turn out right. But she didn't think he really heard what she said. When he wasn't touching her, his eyes seemed to be, and that caused her to lose track of what she'd been attempting to say. She had to place her unfinished sentences to one side, because his touching made her lose control of her thoughts.

She wanted to believe that eventually they'd arrive at a point where he'd pay attention. So she went along, convinced that that point was coming closer. Once they became accustomed to each other, she reasoned, they'd be able to talk openly, honestly, the only way she felt genuinely comfortable. Until that time arrived, it seemed she and Teddy were playing a game, a practiced pretense that was routine in a love affair. They made promises about the future, planning a life together, how they'd raise their children, how they'd live and where.

"I'll be going to Vassar," she said. "It's not so far from New Haven. You'll be able to come see me. And I to see you. Then, if we still feel the same, we can think about getting married."

She threw herself into the spirit of the affair with the belief that making these vague promises was all part of what was done when people were in love. It was all fun, all delight, and the future was a million years away. And how important was it really if he didn't listen properly? He'd learn how.

"Won't the fellows just die of envy when I show up with you?" He laughed. "You'll be far and away the most beautiful thing any of them've ever seen. I want to show you off to the whole world. I'll never let you go. Never!"

Most evenings he dined at the cottage. Amanda listened to their weaving of plans in silence, refraining from contributing in any way, preferring to let events run a natural course, determined not to be responsible for influencing the final outcome.

The night before the Jenningses were to leave, he came to the cottage early to talk to Amanda. They went out on the porch and settled themselves in the creaky wicker chairs.

"I feel I should explain. I mean, I know it must seem like just another summer romance," he began, finding it hard to meet her eyes. "But really, that's not how it is. I really want to marry Helen, Mrs. Kimbrough." He clutched his kneecaps with tense fingers. "I love her. I want to look after her. You have to know that I'm sincere." He stopped, waiting to see if she'd respond, but she said nothing. "It's not that I've taken advantage of her," he continued, convinced despite Helen's claims to the contrary that this woman had to consider him pretty low, doing what he had done to her daughter. "I know it looks obvious from the outside. But it's real. We're in love.

"I wish I didn't have to go back to school at all. I'd give anything to be in the city near her. But I have to go back. My dad expects me to finish up at Yale and go on to my postgraduate studies. I owe it to him to do it. And that's another three years before I can even start thinking about having a wife. It's so damned long!"

For several moments she studied his hands. *Remarkable, the construction of those hands,* she thought, noticing the prominence of the knuckles, the breadth of the palms. Atavistic appendages. Primitive. She visualized those hands on Helen's body, and for an instant was gripped by a revulsion that threatened to make her physically ill. She quickly looked away.

"I don't doubt your sincerity." She weighed her words. "Nor do I doubt the feelings you claim to have for Helen. But three years, as you say, is a long time. And Helen isn't yet sixteen. Wouldn't it be wise to let things happen in their own time?"

"But my feelings won't change!" he insisted. "They'll never change!"

"Perhaps," she said. "One can never be certain of emotions." Seeing him about to protest, she hurried on, anxious to conclude this confrontation. "In any event, it isn't for me to make her decisions. Whatever she chooses to do, she'll do. If marriage is what you both want, then that's how it'll be. It isn't necessary to convince *me,* Teddy. I'm not directly involved. I do not believe in making my daughter's decisions. Now come along inside. Helen's jumpy as a cat wondering what we're going on about."

"I guess I couldn't ask for more," he said, baffled by her attitude. "I'll always do my best for her."

"Do what's best for yourself. Follow your own instincts, Teddy. Don't attempt to do things because you think they're expected of you. I haven't any expectations of you." She met his eyes, finding them a somehow dissatisfyingly uncertain shade of blue. "How could I possibly? After all, you're a grown man with definite opinions and leanings. I am not your mother or anyone whose influence should affect you unduly. I can, naturally, affect Helen. But only, hopefully, with common sense. I won't stand in your way. But I won't go to bat for you either. This is between the two of you."

Helen toyed with her food, eyeing Teddy and her mother, conjecturing what had been said. Outwardly they seemed as always. She looked at Teddy's jaws working as he chewed, following his hands as they moved back and forth between the plate and his mouth. She was fascinated by everything about him: the almond shape of his eyes, the length of his blond-red lashes, their downward sweep, the straight line of his nose, the outflaring of his nostrils, the square angle of his jaw. She studied the scattering of freckles on the backs of his hands, the breadth of his shoulders. She was seized with wanting him. Waiting for the meal to end was a lengthy agony, to be endured strictly for her mother's sake, because there were proprieties she did observe. Dining properly—relaxing, conversing between courses—was a household rule. It was, Amanda claimed, unhealthy and neurotic to gobble up one's food without thought or appreciation for the qualities of taste and presentation, or consideration of the opportunity to exchange thoughts in a comfortable atmosphere. "If there is tension around the table," she'd once said, "there's utterly no sense in sitting down to a meal. It'll be a wasted effort for all concerned."

Helen sipped her wine, acutely aware of tension at the table. Teddy ate, rarely looking up, pausing only to offer compliments on the food—as he usually did. Amanda drank several glasses of wine with an expression of slight distaste, as if she'd found a hair in her wineglass. But all Helen could think about was that tomorrow morning the Jenningses would be getting into their car to drive Teddy to New Haven. She pictured him carrying his bags to the dorm he'd told her about; unpacking his shirts and sweater vests and bow ties; placing his easel and paintbox at the back of some closet, where they'd stay, probably unused, throughout the semester.

Amanda lit a cigarette, signifying the end of the meal. Teddy lit his pipe.

"I sure will miss Jessie's cooking," he said, holding his fingers over the pipe bowl as he puffed to get the tobacco burning evenly. "I'll bet I've gained ten pounds this past month."

"Quite," Amanda said obscurely, glancing over at Helen, who was peering into the depths of her glass. She had a sudden—thankfully fleeting—impulse to tell these two children a number of truths about the so-called state of love they thought themselves in. It seemed so clear that Helen was infatuated with Teddy's image, what she *thought* he was. And Teddy—of course he wanted to marry Helen. It was probably the only time in his life he'd meet someone who gave of herself, in every way, so unstintingly.

"Why don't you two run along," she said. "I'm sure you have last-minute things to say to each other."

Helen got up from the table, impatient for Teddy to come. But he took his time, thanking Amanda for her kindness and understanding, shaking her hand with solemn formality.

"I thought it would never be over," Helen said as they stepped outside. "If you'd gone on for one more minute being polite, I'd have started screaming."

"You're too impatient, Helen. You really have to learn to slow down."

Words of rebuttal rose to her lips, but she swallowed them as he took her hand and they headed in the direction of the Hewlett pier. They walked along silently, following the dim beam of Helen's flashlight. They stood at the edge of the pier, looking down at the inky water lapping against the pilings.

"I can't stand saying good-bye," she said, bursting into tears, although she'd vowed to herself she wouldn't.

"Gosh, don't!" he said, taking her in his arms. "It makes me want to cry too. I feel as bad as you do. We've got to decide this very minute where and when we'll meet. Once we've got that settled, we'll both feel better."

They agreed he'd come collect her on the night before Thanksgiving.

"We'll go somewhere for dinner," he said, thinking he'd borrow on his allowance.

"It's such a long time," she said, "three months."

"Not so long."

"Oh, it is!" she said fiercely. "It's forever! What'll I do for three whole months alone?"

"Probably forget me," he said, more than a little convinced of it.

"I wouldn't ever! Let's hurry. I've been aching for you for hours."

"So have I."

"Do you hurt wanting me? It's like a pain to me. I want to touch you, hold you. Hurry!" she said, taking off her clothes, which he spread hastily on the damp wood of the pier.

She found the initial meeting of their bodies reassuring. She lay very still, clinging to him, basking in his warmth. His body always felt very warm. Eyes closed, she waited for his mouth. And when he came over her, she felt a kind of confirmation, something in her mind that said, *I can give this. This is something I can do.*

She broke away and looked at him, studying his heavy-lidded eyes. For an instant she found him ugly. His open mouth and eager breathing seemed almost bestial. But then she looked down the length of his body and he was beautiful again as she kneeled to put her mouth on him. After several minutes she got up and turned. She looked at him again, then straddled him, lowering herself slowly, taking him fully inside her. It was momentarily painful, but a pain she craved because it erased everything else, and she forced herself to relax around him.

"Hold me," she whispered, placing her hands on his chest.

She rode, driven into motion by his hands, the pressure of his hands on her thighs. She was lost, dancing crazily, and sank her fingers into his shoulders, kissing him hungrily until he sat up and threw his arms around her, lifting her up and down as though she were weightless, driving into her, hurling her backward on the pier. He cried out, locking his hands in her hair, searching for her mouth.

He continued thrusting into her, going on and on until he'd lost track of the number of times she'd gone into quivering contractions. With a raging half shout he let go, falling onto her, his breath coming in huge, racking sobs.

She waited, crushed by his full weight.

"I can't breathe," she said, pushing at his chest.

"I'm sorry," he said, kissing her, shifting. "Did I hurt you? I'm sorry if I hurt you."

"You frighten me a little," she said, shivering as the cool air wrapped itself around her.

"Why?"

"I don't know why. It's as if . . . It doesn't matter." For some reason she didn't know, she couldn't tell him just how much and why he frightened her. She had an idea that voicing her fears would cause him to hurt her more.

"I love you," he whispered. "I want you again."

"Give me a minute," she said softly, watching him swell against her hip.

"I can't wait!" he said, covering her breasts with wet feverish kisses. His need was so enormous, so violent, it frightened him too. Feeling her come again and again around him gave him a sense of something—*Power,* he thought—something that made him want to keep on and on until they were both dead from it. He wanted to engulf her in his love, swallow her with it, imprint himself physically on her body so that no one else could ever have her.

"Please wait!" she said, sucking in her breath as his fingers swooped down, pressing hard. "I'm sore, Teddy. You're hurting me. Please!"

"No, no, no." He kept on, ignoring her arguments.

Her eyes were round and fixed as he came down on her, her body taut under his, their arms and legs starfished together.

"Please," she cried as he held her pinned. "Teddy!"

He watched her face as, with short, sharp thrusts, he hammered at her, feeling as if he could drive her down through the splintery wood of the dock, down through the layer of air and water, down right into bedrock. He saw her eyes roll back as she stopped fighting him.

"You're mine," he whispered, moving harder, faster, slamming into her, keeping her nailed in place. "I love you. God, God! I love you."

She wept, tears trickling down the sides of her face, her body contorting insanely, trying to escape him yet to contain him too, driven beyond thought, beyond reason, by this possessive torture. He was kissing her, caressing her, sliding smoothly in and out slowly, for such a long time, then suddenly bearing down, lifting her from underneath, making her come again when she thought there wasn't anything left inside to give. And when he fell finally, biting at her mouth, his hands still locked under her buttocks, she closed her eyes, trying to suppress the hysteria that seemed about to overtake her.

He tried to hold her, to explain.

"I wouldn't purposely hurt you," he said, trying to make her look at him. "It's just that I love you so."

"It doesn't matter," she said coldly, unable to move, terribly hurt.

"Tonight will have to last us three months," he said, folding his sweater and putting it under her head. "That's a hell of a long time to be without you."

"Yes, I know," she said, feeling the fluids slowly seeping out of her, picturing a tubful of soothing hot water.

"My little lover." He laughed, completely unaware of her feelings, kissing her hands. "Look at your hands! It's impossible. How can anyone be this small? Even your feet! Like a kid's, so tiny and narrow. It doesn't make sense you could be so small and yet have the body you do."

"It makes perfectly good sense to me," she said coolly. "It's my body, after all."

"I love it." He rubbed his face against her belly. "I love you. Promise me you'll never give yourself to anyone but me!"

"Teddy! I don't know that."

"Better not," he said, only half smiling. "I plan to keep you all to myself."

"Don't!" she said, sitting up, reaching for her clothes.

"Hey!" he said softly, watching her fumbling to fasten her brassiere. "You're my girl."

"It's not something we have to say all the time, Teddy."

"I like to hear it."

"I'm your girl," she parroted. "And I suppose you rape all your girls."

"What?" His happy expression crumpled. "No! I didn't."

"I asked you to wait and you wouldn't listen. How could you do that, Teddy? I don't understand you. How can you swear you love me and then . . . hurt me that way?"

"Oh my God!" he said softly, paling visibly even in the darkness. "I'm sorry," he whispered, at once in tears. "I didn't mean . . . I'm sorry. I *do* love you. You can't think I meant to do anything like that."

His tears had the effect of erasing her fear, so that instinctively she sought to comfort him, letting him seek shelter in the circle of her arms.

If he could be so abjectly contrite, so obviously distraught over his own actions, the least she could do was forgive him and try to understand his repeated apologies and I-love-you's. By the time they were walking back along the beach, he'd become familiar to her again. The glow of his pipe was something she recognized. His voice making plans was low and assured. *It was a mistake*, she thought, putting the idea of fearing him out of her mind. How could she dislike someone she loved? Someone who wept so brokenheartedly over causing her pain? A mistake.

4

Amanda kept hoping Helen would come to her to talk about Teddy, but she didn't, and Amanda didn't want to press the issue. They closed up the cottage and returned to the city. The house seemed far larger than when they'd left. She and Jessie set about restoring things to order and unpacking while Helen walked up and down in her room, missing Teddy for the first time. She hadn't thought she'd miss him to the extent she did. It disturbed her that nothing else could hold her attention for more than minutes. Her mind withdrew into safe dark corners to examine Teddy—his fervent words, demanding embraces—replaying their month together day by day, until that entire time was endowed with a romantic cast she hadn't been aware of when she was actually with him.

He telephoned the night after they arrived home, and she reached for the telephone as if for a lifeline, starved for the sound of his voice, for the words of love and desire he was bound to utter.

"I miss you," he said. "It's lonely here. A damned good thing my schedule's so heavy, or I'd drop everything and roar down there like a shot. How are you? Do you still love me?"

"Of course I do." She was caught up in his eagerness.

"I'm trying to get ready for school, but it doesn't seem possible I've got to put on my uniform and go back to Miss Evans's School. It's been so long since you left. Do you think about me all the time?"

"Constantly."

They talked for twenty minutes, renewing their promise to be together the night before Thanksgiving.

Later she complained to Amanda that three months was too long, that she'd never make it.

"Once you're back at school, the days'll fly. It'll seem like no time at all."

"I don't think so."

"Would you like to talk it out, Helen?" she asked gently.

"I can't." She shook her head slowly. "I don't know yet. I'm not sure what I think."

"I see. Well, you know I'm always here."

"I know."

In the weeks after Helen returned to school, Amanda found herself stopping from time to time—her brush or fingers held a fraction of an inch from the canvas or clay —to stare inward, her eyes trapped by an inexplicable image of herself, Helen, and Teddy caught in a frozen gray landscape where there was no movement or sound. The image was so real that it seemed to superimpose itself over everything, forcing her to stop working and go seek Helen out, hoping somehow to be heartened just by the sight of her. But there was no relief in seeing Helen's head bent over her books or her rapt profile staring off into space.

There were other times when Helen's eyes met hers and stayed, connected, and searched for long moments before breaking away to silently resume their inspection of books or empty space.

"Are you all right, darling?" Amanda would ask, knowing in advance the answer as her fingers stroked the thick, glossy luxury of Helen's hair.

"I'm fine, Mother," she'd say absently, her eyes preoccupied. "Really."

"All right," Amanda would reply, drifting away to try again to direct her concentration toward her work.

She managed for long hours to lose herself in what was evolving on the canvas or wheel, but her work showed the strain of everything unsaid between them.

The days dragged for Helen. She studied, doing her utmost to keep her grades at top level so there'd be no chance of being refused by Vassar. In the evenings, after dinner, she sat in her room looking out the front windows, wondering what she'd think and how she'd feel if Teddy suddenly appeared. A month passed. He wrote at least once a week, saying that the pressure of his studies left him little free time. And invariably he made references to her body or to her lovemaking that she read with a feeling of vexation. He never replied to the questions she asked, and rarely gave news of his activities. His letters were all about her body, her beautiful body. And nothing about *her*, about her hopes or plans or the person she was. Just her long, smooth thighs and beautiful breasts. She tore up his letters after reading them a second time, appalled at the idea that her mother might inadvertently find and read them and sense that Teddy seemed to be in love with her lovemaking and not with her. But at least he wrote. And perhaps in time he'd learn to say the things she wanted to know.

She replied, describing her feelings of being outside the mainstream of things at school. She could not reciprocate in writing the loving claims he made with such facility. She was sure she loved him, but somehow putting it all down on paper didn't seem the right thing to do.

In the middle of October she came home from school feeling ill. There were stabbing pains low in her belly, and she wondered if she might be pregnant, but couldn't imagine how that could be possible. She hadn't missed a period. On the contrary, she'd been bleeding slowly, steadily, for almost a week. And these pains, she was sure, weren't a typical part of pregnancy. She waited out the evening, unable to eat. Finally Amanda said, "What's wrong, darling? Your face is all twisted."

"I don't know. I think I'll go up and lie down."

As she got to her feet, the pain expanded to such

intolerable proportions that her mouth opened with the shock of it as she put her hand out toward her mother, took a step, and screamed, seeing the floor rushing up to smash her in the face.

"Helen!" Amanda knocked over her chair in her haste. Jessie came flying in from the kitchen.

"Call an ambulance!" Amanda cried, bending over Helen, whose face was completely drained of color. "Dear God," she whispered, noticing a spreading stain of blood on the floor, "what is it?"

She rode along in the back of the ambulance, watching in horror as the two attendants performed a cursory examination and packed thick wads of absorbent cotton between Helen's legs. She wanted to look away but couldn't, and sat the whole way to the hospital riveted to the sight of brilliant red blood inching its way over the wads of cotton. Helen was wheeled off to an examination area while Amanda waited for their physician, Leon Schindler, to arrive. He came rushing in, peeling off his hat and coat as he hurried over to her.

"Sit over here, Amanda." He touched her hand. "I'll let you know the instant I have something to tell you."

She sat, oblivious to her surroundings, chain-smoking, praying Helen wasn't going to die. The thought of it terrified her. An hour went by, then another. An aide stopped to ask if she'd like coffee, and she looked up blankly.

"Please, leave me be," she said, lighting a fresh cigarette.

The waiting, just sitting doing nothing, was torture. Not knowing, having only conjecture for company. She kept seeing Helen as a small tot, peering into the flower beds, turning to smile before pulling the heads of half a dozen chrysanthemums, then crying brokenheartedly when Amanda admonished her. What was it all for, if what you loved and valued most was lost to you?

Finally, after three hours, Leon emerged from the operating room. The front of his white coat was spattered with blood.

"We had to wait to get the bleeding under control." He sat down beside her, lighting a cigarette. "We're getting her ready now for surgery."

"What is it, Leon?" she asked, holding her hands down in her lap, grappling with her fear.

"It looks like a Fallopian pregnancy. I can't be positive until we have her in surgery and can take a look. It's not good, Amanda. I won't hedge with you. She's lost a hell of a lot of blood. Her pressure's dangerously low. I truthfully can't tell you anything now."

"Is she going to be all right?"

"I hope so. Look," he said appeasingly, "we're taking her up. There's a waiting room. Go to the third floor. I'll let you know the minute we're through."

Woodenly she walked to the elevators and rode up. For three more hours she sat, smoking, thinking, reviewing her life and Helen's, hoping it wasn't all going to come to an end in this place. She glanced every few seconds at the operating room doors.

That damned boy! she thought, wanting desperately to take her anxiety and fear out on someone. *This is all his doing.* But it wasn't. It was impossible to ignore Helen's role in the affair. Amanda knew how it felt to be pursued by an attractive young man, knew that first leaping of physical curiosity. She couldn't place blame. What good would blaming someone do if Helen were dead? *God, she can't die!* She stubbed out her cigarette and started another. Dying, death, Helen's ashen face, a pool of blood. The tears offered no respite. They came, continual streams of them, painting her face with water. Two hours more. She mopped her face and drew a deep breath as, soaked with perspiration, Leon came out, pulling off his surgical headdress. He slumped down beside her, saying, "She'll make it."

She let out her breath slowly, handing the cigarettes to him. "Thank God!" she said.

"I was right," he said, smoke curling from his nostrils. "A pregnancy of that nature is a serious enough matter. But there were a number of complications. The worst of it, I'm afraid, is one of her ovaries was badly diseased. The other was on its way. We had to remove them."

"Oh, Leon, no! No!"

"There was no choice, Amanda. Another few months or so and it could have been a damned sight more serious. She won't have children, but at least she'll be a healthy functioning woman. I'm terribly sorry." He looked down at his hands.

She'd been kicked in the stomach. It hurt miserably. In a paroxysm of total outrage, she cried out. "Leon, it's so unfair! I want to—God, *break* things! It'll destroy her!"

"It won't," he said reasonably. "I assure you, it won't."

"You don't know! It isn't fair! Not at fifteen. Her whole future . . ." She looked at him, her throat constricted. "When can I see her?"

"She's in the recovery room. About an hour or so. Listen to me, Amanda. I'm not much of a philosopher, and I detest people who offer nice little homilies in situations like these, but listen. This has to seem a monstrous slap in the face to both of you. But she's young, and youth is in her favor. She'll be up and around in a matter of weeks. She's *alive,* Amanda, and that's the important thing here. Knowing you, knowing Helen, I have no doubt you can both cope with this. Sometimes, you know, one's life can be shaped according to circumstance. Her life needn't be damaged in any way by the loss. It is possible to use an experience like this to good advantage. I know it's all so much gibberish to you now. But hear me out, please!

"It could be a turning point in her life. I think you're getting the drift of what I'm trying to say. If everything one wants is not handed out on a platter, as you know, it makes what we do obtain infinitely more valuable. Because it's been won through sincere effort. Keep it in mind! She'll be coming in for a series of X-ray treatments over the next few months to make sure we've got it all. I'll tell the nurse to let you know when she's conscious." He got up, pressed her shoulder wordlessly, and left her.

Helen was not yet fully conscious when she went in. The faint hovering smell of anesthetic nauseated her. All those hours of waiting, her relief, and now this smell made her hurry out of the room and into the corridor, where she gulped down mouthfuls of air, trying to calm her stomach.

I need some fresh air, she thought, heading toward the elevator. Once outside, the cold air revived her, swept away part of that cloud that had been looming over her for the past eight hours. Pulling her coat closed, she started walking. Just a lap or two around the block would get her blood circulating again, get her mind working.

She was thankful Helen was alive. But the rest . . . Having to tell her. There was no gentle way to impart this, no sense to playing games with the truth.

She ducked into a doorway to light a cigarette and continued along the street, smoking, ignoring the lifted eyebrows of passers-by, trying to sort out her thoughts. What did her smoking in the street matter at this time? She couldn't be concerned with social niceties now. The drugstore at the corner was open. She went inside, sat down at the counter and ordered a cup of coffee.

Adding cream, watching the cream swirl through the dark liquid, blending, gradually becoming absorbed until its color and the coffee's had merged to yet another color altogether, it occurred to her that by telling Helen the truth, by pouring it in slowly, Helen would be altered— the very tone and hues of her life transmuted.

God! she thought, pushing away the cup. She closed her eyes for a moment, praying everything she'd tried to teach her was sufficiently ingrained to help Helen withstand this blow.

Amanda sat on a small wooden chair beside the bed, staring at the waxen face on the pillow. Blood dripped into Helen's right arm, drop after drop, while a clear liquid fed into the other. All the equipment was further testimony to the seriousness of Helen's condition.

She opened her eyes and looked at Amanda.

"Helen." Amanda touched her icy hand. "You're going to be all right."

"What happened?" Helen asked faintly, trying to

moisten her lips, her eyes fearfully taking in her surroundings.

"You'll be all right, darling," Amanda repeated, stroking her hand.

"I can't move. Why can't I move?" Her eyes were
terror-filled now as she tried to raise herself.

"You've had surgery. You're strapped down."

"I hate it! I want to move! Make them take it off!" she
cried. "Please!"

"In a while. Rest now, darling. Don't fight against it,
you'll hurt yourself."

A nurse came in, her uniform rustling like newspapers.
"You're awake!" She smiled. "Good, good!"

"Could I have some water?" Helen asked. "I'm so dry."
She looked at her mother appealingly.

"I'm afraid you can't have anything for several hours."

"Can't you do something for her?" Amanda asked,
keeping her voice controlled.

"Well," she said, looking at Amanda's drawn face,
"perhaps a wet washcloth to suck on."

"Anything, please!"

She went into the bathroom and returned with a wrung-
out cloth, which she handed to Amanda, saying, "Don't
let her have too much. It'll only cause her pain, and no
one wants her to suffer."

"Thank you."

"I'll bring you some coffee," the nurse volunteered.
"You look all in."

She brought a carafe and a cup, warned Amanda not
to stay too long, then tiptoed out. Amanda held the cloth
to Helen's lips, watching her labor to swallow.

"That's better," Helen said, her voice stronger. "I was
so dry." She looked at her mother. Amanda looked so
tired, her hair disheveled, dark shadows under her eyes.
Her appearance triggered a warning in Helen's brain. If
her mother looked so haggard and worn-out, something
very serious was going on.

"How do you feel, darling?" Amanda asked, touching
Helen's face, glad to see some color returning.

"Sore all over. What's happened to me?"

"You've had surgery," she began.

"Why? What was wrong?"

Here goes, she thought, taking a firm hold on Helen's hand. "You had a Fallopian pregnancy," she said.

"What? I don't understand."

"Lie back now and listen. I'll explain everything. Do you want the cloth again?"

"No, no. Just tell me."

"You were pregnant," she began again, keeping her eyes fastened on Helen's, warming her hand in her own. "It was growing in the Fallopian tube instead of the uterus. Leon had to operate to save your life, remove it."

"Oh." Tears welled in her eyes; her mouth began to tremble.

"There's more, Helen."

"More?" She didn't understand. All she could think of was some unseen pair of hands opening her up, taking away her baby. "What more?"

Helen's eyes looked vacant. Amanda continued chafing her hand, waiting for her attention to return.

"Was it a boy or a girl?" Helen asked, coming back, searching her mother's face. "Did they tell you?"

She hadn't been prepared for that. "No way of knowing," she said, fighting down the tears.

"Tell me the rest," Helen said, gathering the bedclothes under her fingers, her knuckles white.

"In the course of the surgery," Amanda continued, "Leon discovered that your ovaries were . . . damaged. They had to be removed. A biopsy was done this morning. There was malignant growth."

"You mean cancer?" Her face was that of a disbelieving stranger's.

"He wasn't specific," she lied. "He assured me everything is fine now."

"Everything is fine," Helen repeated, closing her eyes, assembling these facts. She couldn't contain it all, didn't want to. She opened her eyes again to look at Amanda, and knew from her face that this wasn't a dream. She started to speak, but a stricken cry was rising from

66

deep inside. She wanted to put her hand over her mouth to hold down the sound, but her arms were strapped down, so the sound came out, filling the room, hurtling against the windows, piercing her skull, shattering everything.

"Don't, darling! Don't!" Amanda begged, coming to the bed, trying to take her in her arms but frustrated by the tubes and straps, holding Helen's head against her instead, trying to cushion the pain, whispering shushing sounds, calming sounds, stopping that agonized lament.

"Tell me it's a dream," Helen sobbed. "It's a bad dream, isn't it? I'm dreaming."

"No, no. I wish to God it was. It's not a dream, Helen."

"Mama, hold me. I hurt so badly. I can't bear it."

"I know, darling," she said, caressing her face, her hair, urging her to accept the truth. "I know how it hurts. I know how you feel, darling. I know. It seems like the end of the world, but it isn't. It isn't."

"I'll never have any more babies," she cried, thrashing under Amanda's hands. "Never! How could they do that? How could you let them do that?"

"There was no choice involved, Helen. No one is responsible. It's just the way things happened. Do you think I'd allow anyone to harm you? Do you think I'd give my consent to have you hurt? I love you, Helen. Your life is important. I couldn't let you die. You have your life."

"How long do I have to stay here?" she asked, her voice and expression going cold.

Amanda sat down exhaustedly in the chair.

"Three or four weeks."

"Why?" Helen wailed, the coldness instantly gone. "Everything's done. Why do I have to stay? I hate this place."

"You have to stay until you're well. You are going to get better and come home. This will all be over very soon."

"Is this real?" she asked, looking beseechingly at Amanda. "I'm lying here, we're talking, we sound the same as we always do, but it's still a dream. Oh, Mama! What's left of me?"

"Your whole life, darling, everything."

"People my age don't get cancer." She pictured the interior of her body as being like an infected, berserk colony of ants running every which way.

"They do, Helen," she said, with more composure than she'd known she had left. "It's very fortunate it was discovered and caught in good time. Think of it as lucky."

"I can't think at all! I can't!"

"You'll be well and home very soon. Right now you must sleep, rest. We'll talk more later. Please, don't make yourself miserable going over and over it. That can't help or do you any good. Try to sleep. I'll be back this afternoon and we'll talk again. No more now."

She bent to kiss her. Helen was already falling back on the pillows with a look of embittered resignation, whimpering.

"Don't be afraid, darling. Try not to think. Just sleep," Amanda said softly, blotting the tears from Helen's face with agitated fingers. "I love you very much." She kissed her again, renewed her promise to return later, and left.

Helen stared at the green ceiling, feeling the pinch of stitches running down her abdomen. If only she could turn, move, relax herself somehow. Being strapped down was a nightmare. She looked at the tubes in her arms, the blood on one side, the liquid on the other. Turning her head until she thought her neck might snap from the impossible angle she was forcing herself to, she read the label. Glucose. Nothing made sense. She flexed her knees experimentally. Something between her legs. Another tube. Too many tubes. Spreading her fingers, she touched a metal object with her right hand. She lifted her head, to see it was a buzzer. Depleted from these small explorative efforts, she dropped her head back onto the pillow and pressed the buzzer. The nurse came immediately.

"What is it?"

"Please, untie me. It's awful being strapped down this way."

"It's for your own protection, dear, so you don't harm yourself."

"Please." She was in tears again. "Please take it off!

I promise not to move. I'll lie perfectly still! Please!" She felt like a helpless baby.

The woman stood for a moment looking at her, then turned decisively toward the foot of the bed.

"What is the tube between my legs?"

"A catheter, until you're able to evacuate by yourself. Would you like me to sponge your face?" she asked, attempting to read Helen's eyes. "It'll refresh you."

She nodded, feeling the straps come away. The relief was colossal, a return to sanity. Her body seemed to sink down several inches as her muscles untensed. The nurse went into the bathroom and returned with a cloth and an enamel basin of water. Pulling down the top of Helen's gown, she gently rubbed the cloth over her neck and shoulders, then squeezed the excess water into the bowl and bathed Helen's face lovingly. "That's much better, isn't it?" she crooned, smiling. "You're such a beautiful girl. I have a little girl," she said, her smile changing, becoming commiserating. "I think I know how you must be feeling. But honestly, before you know it you'll be home and all this will be forgotten. This is such a wonderful time of your life. You'll forget in time. It's amazing how you forget all the things you swear you never ever will when they happen. But somehow time passes and we forget. Try to rest now." She readjusted the gown.

"How old is your little girl?"

"Nine."

"What's her name?"

"Bonnie."

"Bonnie. That's pretty. Thank you for taking those awful things off."

"Close your ears and your eyes, and don't think of anything but getting better, sleeping. If you need anything, just use the buzzer. And remember, don't move about."

"I won't."

She slept fitfully, waking to see the tubes still in her arms, the needles taped to her veins. She thought about water, the sound of it, the clear, even flow of it, and slept again. She had no idea of time. The curtains were drawn over the window, carefully overlaid so that no light could enter. She coughed, and scalding pain shot through her. Her fingers groped over the bedclothes, clutched the buzzer, and, sweating, she pressed down as hard as she could. The nurse came at once.

"Did you sleep well?" she asked, setting a thermometer under Helen's tongue so she was unable to answer. "I'll just take your pulse." She slid her fingers onto Helen's wrist. "Good," she said, "I'll be back in a bit for the thermometer."

She was going to cough again and held it down, dreading a return of the searing pain. But it wouldn't stay down, and the thermometer fell from her mouth as her body rose rigidly from the bed. She screamed, swallowed alive by white-hot fire. The nurse came flying back.

"What is it? What's wrong?"

"Help me!" she cried. "Please! It's so bad. Give me something, help me, please!"

"Now, now, don't cry!" The nurse retrieved the thermometer and read it before shaking it down. "I'll check the doctor's orders and see if you can have something."

"I want to die! I want it ended. They should've let me die! I don't *care* any more!"

"Oh, now," the nurse said, looking very perturbed, "you mustn't think such things. You're far from dying, dear. Every hour you're that much closer to being well again. This evening you'll be sitting up, and tomorrow you'll dangle. By tomorrow afternoon you'll be able to sit in the chair there for fifteen minutes."

Helen stared at her dumbfounded, her tears subsiding.

"Oh yes," she went on, encouraged, "Dr. Schindler believes it's imperative to have our surgery patients up and about as quickly as possible. It promotes rapid healing, revitalizes the incised muscles. It's quite revolutionary, but it really does work. You'll see! Now just rest your head on the pillow, and I'll see what can be done about medication."

"Why are you trying so hard with me?" Helen asked suspiciously.

"Why?" She looked for a moment like an instructor with endless patience confronted by a disputing student.

"Because it's my job to help you get better. I wouldn't be a nurse if I didn't think I was serving some purpose, helping. What an odd question!"

"I didn't mean to be rude. It just seems you're so . . . involved."

"Look, my dear." She smiled, letting her hand lie on Helen's shoulder. "Just because I don't know you doesn't mean I don't care. You're young and you've been through a frightening ordeal and now you tell me you'd prefer to be dead. I would prefer you not to be dead. If you were my daughter, I'd feel no differently. No one likes to see other people suffer. Not unless they're sick themselves, or evil or something. Accept it. Humor me." She laughed softly. "Get better and go home with your mother. She certainly doesn't want you to die. She spent eight hours while you were in surgery hoping you weren't going to die."

"*Eight* hours?"

"That's right. You came close, dear. How do you think it would make her feel now, after all that, to hear you talk about dying? Now, enough. I'll get your medication."

In the interim before the medication took hold, she tried to think, to align her thoughts. All she could see was an image of Amanda waiting eight hours to find out if she was going to keep on living. Eight hours. No wonder she'd looked the way she had. *Poor Mother,* she thought, crying again for her mother's sake.

Teddy. She saw him and was instantly stiff with fear. Why? She couldn't remember why. She closed her eyes and saw herself and Teddy making love, taking him inside her body again and again. So many, many times they'd been together. And they'd made a dead baby. It was very real. She could see it: blue, unaspirated, its tiny arms and legs curled into a self-protecting ball. Dead. And inside her there was nothing. She saw a narrow glass door running the length of her abdomen and looked inside, sharply drawing in her breath as she saw the clean, pink emptiness. Just curving bones and desolate space. Nothing. And all the lovemaking in the world could never fill that void. A lifetime of opening herself to Teddy would only throw endless fountains of seed into the hollows; then it would all just flow away again, out of her, leaving her eternally empty.

She was swept away then, riding lightly like discarded wrapping tissue caught up by the wind, wafting away from herself, from her life, from her barren frame. She slept.

5

She changed. Some major part of her optimism, her belief in the unending possibilities of life, was left in the hospital. She felt prematurely forced into adulthood, knowing that nothing was ever going to be as uncomplicated as before.

She practiced walking in the hospital corridors, clutching her stomach, afraid it might come open at any moment. As her muscles regained their elasticity and she stood straighter with each day's passing, she attempted to come to terms with her future as a woman—what her life might be without the chance ever of there being children.

What was the point of thinking of marriage if one of the primary reasons for entering into a married relationship was to have children? None that she could see. And what was the point of keeping on with Teddy, being abused and then apologized to, prior to further abuse? If that was love, she didn't want it. There had to be something more to loving than physical exchanges. So slowly, sadly, she came to the realization that perhaps she hadn't ever actually loved him as she thought she had.

She looked at his continuing letters, reading his proclamations of love with aversion. All that business about her body, her beautiful body. It was boring, disagreeable. She stopped replying to his letters, stopped reading them, began crossing out the address and penning in "Return to Sender" in the corners. And finally they stopped coming.

At home she climbed the stairs slowly the first two weeks, still afraid for her body. But after the third week, when the bandages came off, she examined the incision, marveling that cutting just half a dozen inches along her flesh could have been responsible for such consuming pain, for such momentous alterations in her outlook and philosophies.

For many weeks, when she closed her eyes at night she was back in the hospital, strapped into the physical torment and madness she'd experienced. She stayed awake, picturing her mother pacing the corridors, smoking, thinking God knows what. She was alive, and that mattered to both of them. So she made plans, mapping out her future: the courses she'd take at Vassar, the years at teachers' college, her career. She diligently charted a life course, steering clear of thoughts of men, love, marriage. She wasn't ready yet to think of those things.

Teddy began telephoning. She refused to talk to him. At the outset Amanda gave alibis. But Helen's rejection of the boy was unfeeling, and Amanda couldn't continue lying for her.

"He has no idea what's happened," she said. "You should at least talk to him, tell him that you don't care to see him again. This isn't right, Helen. Whatever your reasons, however you feel, he does love you. It's cruel to treat love with such disregard, even if it is something you don't want. At least respect his feelings."

"I haven't anything to say to him. I don't want to talk to him."

"You cared enough a few months ago to think about marrying him. Don't you think you could handle a small explanation?"

"I guess you're right. Next time he calls, I'll talk to him."

"Do, please, darling! If the positions were reversed, think how you'd feel in his place."

But he didn't call again. At first she was relieved. Then, as the days went by and the telephone didn't ring, she began to think, feeling guilty, that the affair had ended as badly as it had begun.

Back at school, the girls greeted her enthusiastically, asking about her operation (Amanda had told Miss Evans she'd had a ruptured appendix), wanting to know all about being in the hospital and what it was like getting cut open. Their naive curiosity was very touching, and, with new depths of patience, she created acceptable lies. Feeling far older than her friends, she strove to be ever more tolerant and kinder to them, regarding them with a sort of maternal affection. She believed she knew, in part at least, some of the things the future held in store for them.

Tactfully she discouraged new friendships, sidestepping social obligations and attending those few activities that were unavoidable. The letter of acceptance came from Vassar, and she turned her thoughts in that direction.

It struck her, during those last months at Miss Evans's School, that she'd become two people. One was a schoolgirl who put on her uniform, knee socks, and oxfords and went off each day to play it out. The other was a woman who'd had a lover, lost his child, and had a hysterectomy. She hoped that once she was out of this prep-school environment she'd feel more unified, more her own self.

She passed up attending the graduation ceremonies, and they went up to the cottage two weeks earlier than usual. Jessie had retired, and there was a new housekeeper, Mary O'Riley, who was thirty, widowed, and "off men forever," she swore, although Amanda confided privately to Helen that she had her doubts. Mary rarely returned from her days off without a sanded-down, complacent look that bespoke more than merely friendly all-female outings. But she cooked very well, cleaned up a storm, and doted on Helen, claiming, "The poor wee thing needs a good bit of fattenin' up, what with bein' in hospital 'n' all."

Helen traveled back to the city for her final checkup

with Leon, closing her mind to the indignity of lying on the examining table, her intimate emptiness nakedly exposed to his probing fingers.

"Good as new," he announced with a grin, patting her on the knee as she sat up. "The X-ray treatments were a good idea. We'll have you in again in six months for a routine look. Otherwise, have yourself a good summer. Give my love to your mother."

"Good as new" was a defective record that played incessantly in her mind all the way back to the cottage. She wouldn't think about it any more, she told herself, stepping down from the train and into Amanda's welcoming embrace. She'd erase all of it, everything.

She ate as much as she could of Mary's bland, heavy stews and lopsided chocolate cakes, working off her dietary excesses by swimming for hours between the shore and the raft until she wanted nothing more than a good book and then sleep. When Amanda asked if she'd pose for the class one afternoon, she breathlessly refused, backing away. Her expression couldn't have been more incredulous if Amanda had asked her to step in front of a firing squad.

"All right, darling," Amanda said softly. "I understand."

"Do you?" She looked at her mother's hands, noticing her knuckles were swollen. "Do they hurt?" she asked, nodding at them.

"Sometimes. Let's not change the subject just yet," Amanda said. "You're going to have to stop pretending nothing's happened, Helen. I'm beginning to get very worried about you. You can't spend the rest of your life in the water avoiding everyone."

"I'm not avoiding anyone. I just want to be by myself."

"You have a scar. Are you afraid of having it seen?"

"No. I don't care about that."

"What *do* you care about?"

"I don't know. I just know I don't want to take my clothes off and have everybody look at me. I couldn't stand that."

"Do something for me," Amanda said, gathering her into her arms.

"What?"

"Go to your room and have a good, long look at your-self, Helen. And while you're there, I want you to be sure to notice what's happening to your face. If you see what I see, try to do something about it. At the rate you're going, in another five years you'll have become what you merely *think* you are now. You're young, darling, and capable of having much much more in life than a batch of bad memories and locked doors in your head you're afraid to open. Do it now. Then let it all go, please. You're making me as unhappy as you with this grieving."

Helen broke away and stood open-mouthed, her eyes boring into her mother's. Then she whirled and ran into the cottage. Furiously she tore off her bathing suit and flung it against the wall. She sat on the edge of her bed, her chest heaving with anger, her fists clenched with it.

Why am I so angry? she asked herself. After all, what had her mother said that was so unreasonable? She got up and walked over to the mirror.

At first she could see only the view that met her every day of her life: the same face and body, with the seam from her navel down to her pubic hair, neatly bisecting her stomach. She stepped closer, narrowing down the range of her inspection. And as she stared, she began to see it: a slight furrowing of the forehead, a crease at the bridge of her nose, a faint pursing of her mouth. She looked indignant, unhappy. She moved back somewhat and turned to study her side view.

"My God!" she said aloud, seeing the beachball look of her stomach, her shoulders hunched forward so that her breasts drooped. She jerked her shoulders back, tightening her stomach muscles so that her breasts lifted and the wings of her diaphragm had their usual definition.

Why haven't I seen it before? she asked herself, facing forward as she relaxed her facial muscles. How long had she been going around looking that way? She tried a test smile at the mirror, and suddenly she—herself, the person she knew—had returned. Grabbing up her robe, she threw it on and ran out. Amanda was having a cigarette on the porch, and Helen watched for several moments through the screen door.

"I'm sorry," Helen said through the door.

"Come talk to me," Amanda said, not turning. "Come out."

Helen pushed open the door and sat in the old rocker.

"I didn't know," Helen said. "You should have told me."

"As long as you know now," Amanda said, smiling.

Helen got up and knelt on the porch, resting her head in Amanda's lap.

"Get on with your life," Amanda said, stroking her head, relishing the solid, physical reality of her. "Forget what's happened. Forgive him and forgive yourself. You haven't done anything that deserves the kind of punishment you've been giving yourself."

"I love you," Helen murmured, breathing in the scent that belonged only to her mother—the scent of sunshine trapped by the warm surface of her skin, the lemon-vanilla freshness of her cologne, hints of turpentine and solvent, and the thick, glutinous aroma of oil paint.

The following week she spent an entire afternoon trying to write to Teddy, to explain what had happened. But everything she wrote came across as so melodramatic that she finally abandoned the project, thinking she'd call him once she was back in town. It would be far easier to talk things through.

By the end of August she was actually looking forward to talking to Teddy. She considered last summer and how in love they'd been, and wished she hadn't been so cavalier in trashing his letters. At least they'd been tangible proof of his claims of love. All she had left now were ethereal memory images that failed to conjure up any convincing essence of someone she'd believed she loved.

As the day drew near for their return to the city, she became more and more stimulated by the thought of seeing him. The night before their departure she went to bed early and lay in the darkness recalling how they'd made love that very first time, the ways in which they'd touched each other. And, to her surprise, she found herself unable to sleep, agitated. She wanted him again, longed for the exchange of caresses. She closed her eyes and ran her hands over her body, imagining Teddy, seeing Teddy, wet with renewed desire for him. She touched herself as he had, sighing softly, shifting to accommodate him, lifting her hips to accept the penetrating thrust of his body. Her fingers were his mouth, and she opened to the pleasure he was bringing her, almost hearing the small, wondering sounds he made. And at the moment when her body was racing headlong to the brink of orgasm, she said his name, came all around his name, fell with it, and slept, finally, enveloped in the sound of it.

She tried to call several times, but no one answered on her first three attempts. The fourth was picked up by Mrs. Jennings, who said, "Teddy's spending the long weekend away before returning directly to New Haven." Her tone was cool, and Helen guessed he'd told his family about their breakup. She thanked Mrs. Jennings and hung up knowing it really was all over. Too late.

Amanda agreed to allow her to draw on her trust fund for a small secondhand car to take to school.

"Just make sure," she warned, watching Helen run her hand over the fender, "you pay close attention to what the other drivers are up to. I'm not so much worried about your abilities as I am about the rest of the people on the road."

Helen liked Vassar, threw herself zealously into her studies. Freed of the confining childish atmosphere of Miss Evans's School, she felt her life to be more honest, more in keeping with her altered interior status.

Her room in town was large and cheerily sunlit. And as she made friends she began to unbend into the routines of college and stopped thinking, as best she could, about Teddy. But every so often, when she least expected it, he'd come into her mind, forcing her to remember how happy they'd been at times and how badly she'd treated him. But it was over now, and nothing good could be accomplished by rehashing something that hadn't worked out.

She hadn't planned to attend the last big dance of the school year, but Betsy Bigelow, a fluttery blonde with enormous, myopic blue eyes, who was also a compulsive but charming talker with a capacity to captivate anyone willing to listen came rushing into Helen's room two days before the dance.

"You've got to save my life!" she announced, flopping onto Helen's bed, holding her hand over her chest.

"Who's after you?" Helen laughed.

"Dear girl, this is catastrophic!" Betsy said, her eyes on Helen's breasts. "Lord, I do envy you," she sighed, momentarily sidetracked. "I'd give just about anything in the world to have a figure like yours."

"We were going to talk about saving your life," Helen prompted.

"Oh, yes," she said, raising her eyes to Helen's face. "I've done the stupidest thing! They'll probably cut me up in little pieces and bury me all over the campus."

"Who will?"

"If you don't do it, I don't know *what* I'll do. They'll *murder* me!"

"Who, for heaven's sake?" It always amazed Helen that Betsy, who eternally seemed up in the air and scatter-brained, was a mathematical wizard, studying advanced calculus as well as several other courses in physics and science.

"I'd already asked Jimmy. But then I didn't hear from him, so I naturally assumed he wasn't going to come after all, and I went ahead and asked Stu Brainard, too. I don't dare cancel either of them out. They're both excited and filled with seductive plans. Which one will you take? You can have your choice, since the mistake was mine in the first place."

"I don't want either of them."

"You have to! You wouldn't want to see a potential contributor to world welfare hacked up into stewing meat, would you?"

"Perish the thought!"

"Then which one will you take off my hands?"

"Oh, I don't care," Helen acquiesced. "Just send one

of them along to pick me up at eight. And don't ever do this to me again! I'll have to borrow a dress. I didn't bring anything with me. I hadn't planned on going."

"I love you!" Betsy sang, throwing her arms around her. "And you're coming along this very instant to pick out something of mine. I'm sure we'll be lifelong friends," she said. "But I must be honest. I really could hate you for your bust. Why does nature make these hideous mistakes?" she asked, glaring down at her narrow chest. "Oh, well," she hurried on, "I do have hidden assets. If all goes well, I'll have an absolutely back-breaking weekend."

"You're mad!" Helen declared, allowing Betsy to tow her away.

The only dress of Betsy's that came even remotely close to fitting was one of white satin that only just fit, and Helen modeled it doubtfully, saying, "I don't know. It's awfully big on the bottom and small on top."

"A tuck or two at the hips and you'll be sensational. I have to wear hunks of cotton with it, you rat. My luck to have a body like a carrot. Go on, take it! I'd never wear it again, having seen it on you. I won't tell you which of the boys I'm sending, just to get even with you for looking so damned sex-u-al in that dress."

She was having fun, she realized, brushing her hair the night of the dance. Her mysterious date had sent a camellia corsage with an unsigned card promising to pick her up at eight. She was actually grateful to Betsy when Stu Brainard arrived. He was dark, older than she'd anticipated—a senior at Cornell—and smiled when he shook her hand, displaying a mouthful of perfect, even white teeth.

"I was going to be mad as hell at old Bets," he said, in a deep, resonant voice, "but now I'm not sure I won't just send her some flowers or a cake. I'm awfully happy you could make it."

They went in her car and Stu drove, looking over every few seconds to smile, showing those luminous teeth.

"Did she mind when you borrowed the dress?" he asked, tapping his fingers on the steering wheel.

"Who? Bets?"

"No, Jean Harlow. She's the only other woman I've ever seen who could wear something like that and look right in it."

"Thank you, I think." She smiled.

"You're too good to be true!" he stated, pulling into the parking lot. "Thank you for going along with this whole farce. You're a good sport."

"You're a better one. You offered to take Betsy." She laughed, adding, "I didn't mean that quite the way it came out."

"I know *exactly* what you meant."

He danced beautifully, guiding her around the floor with relaxed confidence.

"What are you studying?" she asked, glad he wasn't sweaty-handed and clinch-oriented like some of the others she'd dated during the year.

"Medicine."

"Oh?"

"Believe it or not, I'm going to do psychiatry."

"Really? Why?"

"Because I want to know."

"Know what?"

"Why people do the things they do. Why you're the way you are, why I'm the way I am. Why Betsy would look like anyone's best bet for the fruitcake of the century and really has a mind like a whiz. Why people so often seem like one thing and turn out to be something else entirely. I want to understand what makes some women beat their children and other people jump out of windows. I want to know it all."

"What happened to you?" she asked, sensing something about him.

He stopped dancing and stood, his arm still around her, their hands held in midair.

"I'll tell you what," he said quietly, searching her eyes. "I'll tell you my secrets if you tell me yours."

"Oh, I don't think so."

"And why not?"

"Because my secrets aren't worth talking about. But I think yours are."

"Aha! Let's have something to drink, and we'll see if we can't tempt you to reveal all those secrets."

"I'll have a drink, but I'm not promising I'll do any talking."

"I like you," he said, leading her off the floor. "You're another one of these people who look like one thing but are really something else entirely."

"You think so?"

"I know it. I'll give you several examples." He handed her a cup of punch, pausing to light a cigarette. "Example one: Almost every really good-looking girl I've ever been out with has spent the major part of her time looking around here and there, checking out the competition, making sure she was being seen, paying little if any attention to conversation beyond the usual niceties about the weather and how wonderful she looks, thank you very much. You laugh," he said, "but you don't know, because you haven't done any of that. Example two: Said good-looking females often titter at inappropriate moments or look serious when somebody says something funny. Zero score on brains. Mostly they quit college midway through their sophomore year to get pregnant or married or both. You're laughing again." He smiled. "But that's because you're smart enough to recognize that type. And you're not one of them. I've got lots more examples, if you're interested."

"And what about you?" she asked, taking a fancy to his easy manner. "You're not any more typical than you claim I am."

"Why don't we step outside?" he suggested. "It's awfully close in here. We can continue this cross-examination outdoors."

There were crowds of people pressing together, and they made their way through, heading for the doors. Stu collided with someone and apologized. Helen looked up to see Teddy staring at her, red-faced. Stu noticed, and turned from her to Teddy and back again with a puzzled expression.

"Hello," Teddy said, unsmiling.

"Hello. I'd like you to meet Stu Brainard. Teddy Jennings, an old friend."

She watched the two men shake hands, sizing each other up, and wanted to leave them both there and go home. She'd gone cold at the first sight of Teddy.

"How's school?" Teddy asked, ignoring Stu, who crossed his arms with an air of bemused patience and stood beside her, waiting.

"Fine. Good. We were just going out for some fresh air."

"Sure. Stu wouldn't mind if I steal you for one dance, would you?"

"Not at all," he said good-naturedly. "Carry on."

Before she could say or do anything, Teddy had taken her arm and was leading her back on the floor. They danced in silence, and she found it hard to follow him. She was too nervous. When the number ended he took her hand and led her off the floor in the opposite direction, away from where Stu was waiting, and outside to the parking lot. She went along, fearing a scene.

"Where are we going?" she asked, disengaging her arm.

"Somewhere we can talk privately for a few minutes."

"This isn't the time, Teddy. It isn't fair to leave Stu just standing there—"

"I think you owe me a few minutes," he said evenly, taking her arm again, opening the door to a Packard sedan, ushering her into the back seat.

She sat against the far door, smoothing the dress down over her knees as he climbed in and closed the door.

"I tried to telephone you a few times," she said, watching him light a cigarette. "When did you start smoking cigarettes?"

"A while ago," he answered, rolling down the window and flicking out the burned match. "I didn't get any messages that you'd called."

"Well I did. Several times no one answered. And then, the last time, your mother said you were away and going straight to school from wherever you were."

"What happened, Helen?"

"Oh, I . . . I was ill."

"That sounds like a lie."

"It's true. I was in the hospital for over a month, and then I had to recuperate at home for six weeks after that."

"Sure. And that's why you sent back my letters and didn't even have the decency to talk to me on the phone when I called."

"That is why."

"And what mythical ailment were you afflicted with?"

"I think I'd better be getting back now."

"No, stay and talk a bit longer."

"Why? So you can accuse me of all kinds of nasty things? I don't think so, Teddy."

He threw his cigarette out the window and reached for her, pulling her hard against his chest.

"I loved you," he said acidly. "I loved you so much. And without a word, not one lousy word, you ended everything. I want to know why. You owe me an explanation."

"I've told you why. It's the truth."

"So you got sick and that was the end. I'm sick, so to hell with Teddy."

"You're not going to believe anything I say. Please, let me go back to my date."

"You're even more beautiful," he said, thawing, running his hands down her arms. "How the hell is that possible? I wasn't good enough for you, was I?"

"That's not it at all. I missed you," she said, shivering as he continued to stroke her arms. "I thought about you a lot. I tried to write to you dozens of times, but I just couldn't."

"Because you were ill." His voice was quiet now. "Would you care to know how I felt, what you did to me?"

"I'm sorry. I know it was cruel. It wasn't what I intended. It just couldn't be helped . . ."

"You've changed." He smiled, placing his hands on her neck, his thumbs on her throat. "Grown up, haven't you?"

"I suppose so." She was finding it increasingly difficult to talk. His hands were distracting.

"Did you ever love me, Helen?"

"Of course I did. I believed I did."

"You loved making love. I used to go to bed at night wanting you. I couldn't think of anything else, the way I wanted you."

He brought her head forward and kissed her, his hand reaching inside the gown, drawing in his breath as he touched her bare skin.

"God!" he said, breaking away to look at her. "I still want you."

"Stu's waiting for me. I really have to—"

"Only a minute," he said, kissing her again, robbing her of her willpower, so that she didn't know what she was doing. She thought about Stu standing by the door, probably wondering where she'd gone, what she was doing. But this. All those nights of saying his name and recreating their affair. And now he was here, sliding the gown off her shoulders, down around her waist, lowering his head to kiss her breasts, taking her nipples into his mouth, making her boneless, utterly pliable with wanting him all over again.

"We shouldn't," she reasoned as he lowered her to the seat, pulling the gown up around her hips, deftly sliding her step-ins down.

"Sssh, no," he said, kissing her mouth, easing his hand between her thighs.

"Teddy, please, not here! Anyone might come by. See us."

"You want me, I can tell. And I want you. God! You're wet," he said, burying his face against her breasts as he slid his fingers inside her, making her wetter.

"Please, please! We can't do this here."

"It's all right, all right," he said, unbuttoning his trousers, parting her legs. "I want to come in you again," he whispered, kneeling on the seat, his fingers moving. "Come in you," he repeated, his face swooping down on hers as he lunged forward, making her cry out with the suddenness of it. "Come on, baby, come on," his hands under her, gripping hard as he bore down, filling her.

"Oh, God, Teddy," she sighed, lost, lifting herself, wrapping herself around him, "I wanted you so much. I never wanted to hurt you. It's so . . . so . . . good, Teddy. Oh, God!"

He let his weight down, kissing her wildly as she clung to him, moving madly against him, then arching, quivering, her legs locked like steel around his hips. He pounded into her, crying, "Oh, Jesus, Jesus! Oh, *Jesus!*" as he came spilling forward.

There was complete silence in the car. She lay with her eyes closed, holding him, her body still happily filled with him.

"It was so good," she whispered, touching his face. "I'd forgotten how good it is."

Without a word, he pulled away, reaching into his pocket for his handkerchief as he withdrew from her abruptly, wiping himself, then straightening his clothes, closing his trousers. She watched, seeing a hardness overtaking his eyes, a tightening of his mouth, and for a moment she thought he might strike her. But he patted down his clothes, fixed his bow tie, then opened the car door. He got out, closed the door, and leaned in through the window.

"Quite a little picture," he laughed, waggling his finger at her. "You look like what I should've always known you were. Just a slut."

"What are you doing?" She sat up, trying to pull her dress around her.

"Going back to my fiancée." He laughed, lighting a cigarette. "You owed me one," he said. "I figure that about evens the score. I'll hand you one thing, sweetheart," he said, tossing away the match, the smoke from his cigarette rising around his head, "you're one hell of a fabulous fuck. See you around."

He banged his hand hard against the car door and strode away.

Shaking violently, she got her dress back on. She looked around for something to clean herself with. Sobbing, she picked her step-ins off the floor of the car and used them. Then she got out of the car and stood on the gravel of the parking lot with the soiled underwear in her hand, feeling violently ill. She hurried toward the shrubbery, where she discarded the step-ins and threw up. When she'd finished, she moved away, turning slowly, looking at the rows of gleaming cars. She was standing in the same spot when Stu found her.

"I knew something was wrong," he said, coming over to her. "Come on." He put his arm around her. "We'll go to your car."

Halfway there, she stopped and looked at him.

"You know what happened," she said. "You can see exactly what happened. There's no need to be a gentleman. Do you want to have me too? I don't see why you shouldn't. I've ruined your evening. We can go somewhere. It doesn't matter. Nothing matters." She couldn't stop crying.

"Hey!" he said, touching her wet face. "Whatever's going on between you two, that's your business. But you're a sweet girl, and I don't think you really mean any of that. I saw him come whistling in, and there was something about the look on his face that made my hackles rise. Forgive my saying so, but I think your friend Teddy's a son of a bitch. You're not the type who gets her kicks in the back seats of cars in parking lots. If you want to talk about it, I'd like to listen, to help if I can. If he hurt you and you want me to risk getting pulverized, I'll go back in there and defend the hell out of your honor." He smiled gently, coaxingly.

"Why?" she asked as he lifted the strap of her gown back onto her shoulder.

"Why not? I like you. A lot. Come on, get in the car."

He brought out a flask and induced her to take a drink. "Drink some. It'll make you feel better."

She did, then handed the flask back.

"Now, mop up." He laughed, handing her his handkerchief. "I'll buy you a coffee," he said, throwing the car into gear. "It goes well with brandy."

"I don't understand you," she said, dabbing at her face. "What does this get you?"

"Why does it have to get me anything?" he countered, looking over at her. "Sit back and enjoy the ride. I know a nice, quiet little restaurant a bit farther along here."

"Are you hungry?" he asked as they were settling into a booth at the rear of a small Italian restaurant. "I'm famished."

"I guess so."

"Okay, let's eat up a storm. I have it on good authority that there's nothing like a hearty weeping session to work up a woman's appetite."

"I think your good authority has something there." She smiled.

"I love it when you smile," he said, patting her hand. "See! Nothing you can't solve with a plate of pasta and some cheap red wine."

He added brandy to their coffee later and turned sideways in the booth, lighting a cigarette.

"Let's talk now," he opened, dropping his match into the ashtray.

"No, Stu, really. You've cheered me up, and I feel much better now. I went to pieces back there. I'm sorry. About everything."

"All right. Perhaps you'd like to hear the story of my life?"

"I would."

"I'll just bet. I wouldn't dream of boring you. There are so many things that seem world-shattering when they happen and look so inconsequential in retrospect."

"There was something that *wasn't* inconsequential, wasn't there?"

"Oh, sure! Ask any ten people and you'll always find that certain something there somewhere. We've all had our crises, our traumas. What was yours?"

"Teddy," she said, tired of fencing. "We met almost two years ago. He . . . we . . . were in love, I guess. I'm not sure. I got pregnant. A Fallopian pregnancy. When they were operating, they discovered I had cancer, so they took everything out. That's all."

"Christ! That's not *all*. What about him? Did you tell him? What happened?"

"I handled it badly," she admitted. "I stopped answering his letters. Tonight was the first time I've seen him since it all happened. But I'd been thinking about him,

89

going over it all in my mind, thinking I really had been cruel just leaving him to think whatever he wanted. He used to write me the most embarrassing letters, though. He claimed to be so much in love with me, but all he ever referred to was the way I looked, my body, lovemaking. He never asked about my life or my plans or what I thought or felt. He seemed to take it for granted that being in love was entirely making love. All his references to it made the whole affair seem squalid somehow. I kept throwing the letters away, and he finally stopped writing and calling.

"I should have known better tonight. But he came at me so quickly, I forgot all the things about him I really didn't like. Can you understand that? I was so involved in wanting him, I didn't think. He said some ugly things and then walked away and left me in the back of somebody's car. I kept thinking of you standing by the door, waiting for me, and I felt so terrible about everything. God, the whole thing was so *sordid!* I behaved like a complete fool."

"Why didn't you tell him what had happened?"

"I tried to. I planned to. But he wasn't prepared to believe anything I said. He was too bent on . . . avenging himself, I suppose. So what was the point? Could I have some more of that brandy?"

"Are you going to get plastered on me, Helen?"

"I don't think so. I've never had it before. I like it."

"Okay. Why not?" he said, adding some to her cup.

"I'm sure none of this was what you had in mind for this evening," she apologized, thinking he had nice eyes, gentle eyes.

"I don't know what I expected. But I'm certainly not disappointed." He laughed softly, clinking his cup against hers. "Cheers!"

They drank, then sat staring at each other.

"Tell me about you," she said. "I'd like to know."

"My father lost all his money in the crash," he said, gazing at her over the top of his cup. "He'd made a fortune buying on margin, and when the walls started caving in he couldn't raise enough to cover himself. The only assets left were a couple of insurance policies he'd had the foresight to sign over to my mother. It's not an uncommon story. He stuck a gun in his mouth and blew the top of his head off. The insurance came through, and there was a good amount of it. She—my mother—seemed all right at first. I don't think it really hit her for a long time. She just quietly sat down and wrote checks to cover what Father owed, then sold the house and moved Larry, my younger brother, and me and herself into an apartment. She pretended she was still living. But I went around all tensed up, waiting for the explosion, wondering how long it'd take for it to penetrate. Don't misunderstand," he added quickly, "I wasn't *hoping* something would happen. I just knew it would.

"Larry was coping. He's younger than me, and didn't have too good an idea what was going on. But they'd been so close, my parents. She couldn't seem to get going again after he died. When you talked to her she stared right past you as if she was seeing someone behind you. It gave me an eerie feeling. Sometimes I'd actually turn around, fully expecting to see someone—my father—standing there.

"She tried awfully hard. I admire the way she tried. She sent Larry off to St. Paul's as soon as he was ready, and made sure I was back at school before she did it.

"The cleaning lady found her. She'd written notes for both of us, me and Larry, then got herself ready. Our family doctor told me about it later. He thought I'd want to know, because I was going to be a doctor and I'd understand. He kept shaking his head, saying it was one of the most remarkable and tragic experiences of his medical life.

"You see, she'd been a nurse before she married my father. So she knew exactly what happens when someone . . . dies. She gave herself an enema then . . . plugged herself up, all neat and tidy. Because she didn't want to cause anyone any trouble. Then she sat down on the bathroom floor and cut her wrist and held it under the hot-water faucet in the tub. No mess anywhere." He lowered his head mournfully. "She was so pretty. Would you like to see her picture?"

"Very much."

He brought out his wallet and handed her a studio portrait of a young woman with a pale, wholesome face and slightly intimidated eyes.

"I think women have such a lousy deal in life, for the most part," he said, putting away the wallet. "We men do such . . . *things* to them, and then expect them to go on and on putting up with it all, making do, getting along. It isn't easy. Would you like some more coffee?"

"Please, I would."

He beckoned the waiter, then lit a fresh cigarette and smiled at her.

"I'm a sucker for women," he said, pushing a teaspoon across the table at her. "I don't like to see nice people, good people, getting pushed around for irrational reasons. I want to know the reasons why. I think old Teddy's an irrational bastard. I've got a good mind to go back there and sock him in the mouth. What he did to you was brutal. You're so young."

"So are you. I'm terribly sorry about your parents. You've gone through such a lot, losing them that way. It makes me ashamed—when I hear about your life—to think how I've coddled myself."

"We do not allow that sort of sorry talk at this table," he said as the waiter set down fresh cups of coffee. "There's no need. For either of us," he added, handing her the sugar.

"You're very nice," she said, noticing the clean parting of his hair. "Where are you going after Cornell?"

"Baltimore."

"We won't see each other again, then."

"One never knows."

"No," she said, looking at his mouth, then down at his long, slender hands, "I don't think so. I'm very glad I met you, Stu. I think you'll be a wonderful doctor, help a lot of people. I mean it."

"And what are you going to do?"

"Teach French. It's what I've always planned to do.

That's the only thing in my life that hasn't changed. That and my mother. She's an artist."

"I know."

"You do?"

"Oh, sure! Old Bets told me everything but your glove size."

"Stu?"

"What?"

"Come back to my room with me."

"I told you, Helen, you don't have to do that."

"I know that. It's not because of having to. I'd like you to stay the night with me, sleep beside me. I've never spent an entire night with anyone. I want to hold you, have you hold me. Will you come back with me?"

"You know I will. But why?"

"Because. A lot of reasons. You've been hurt and it makes me sad. I'd like to do something, give you something, make it better, if that's possible. And you're kind. I think you'd be gentle with me. I feel a little scared sometimes. Life is so big. There are so many nasty surprises. We've both had them. I think it would be nice to do something that turns out well. For both of us."

"You shouldn't ever be afraid," he said, taking her hand, holding it. "You're beautiful and sensitive and intelligent, and living well sometimes means an awful lot more than just being able to make babies. You'll get over it."

"I know. I'll remember you, Stu. Will you write to me if I give you my address?"

"Will you write back?"

"Yes."

"All right, then. Let's go. It's getting pretty late, and I want very much to hold you. As much as you like. More."

The next morning when she awakened, he was gone. On the pillow he'd left a note with his address saying he'd looked in her handbag and copied hers off her driver's license. There was a big heart and a row of x's, followed by a line she never forgot:

"When you've lost your life, you've lost everything. Keep yours. It will be all you wish it to be."

PART TWO
STU

6

She doubled up on classes the next two years, hoping to maintain the fatiguing pace of the workload in order to complete her degree a year early. It was harder than she'd anticipated when she'd conceived of the idea, and she wandered about the campus from one lecture to another in a state of dizzy abstraction, her mind reeling with declensions and multi-language verb tenses.

Betsy dropped by infrequently to divert her, endlessly prying, hoping to unearth some tidbit of what had happened the night of the dance with Stu.

"Nothing happened," Helen said repeatedly. "We're friends. We write. Here." She tossed over one of his letters. "Read it for yourself. Just news, that's all."

"What a disappointment you are!" Betsy complained. "All that beauty and body, and here you sit getting all skinny, wearing yourself down to the bone so you can graduate a year ahead of time. You should be out and about having a grand time with the rest of us."

"I haven't got time."

"Who'd ever have thought you'd be such a grind?" Betsy shrugged her shoulders. "Well"—she looked around the book-cluttered room—"I'll scram and let you get on with it."

Helen was afraid to slacken up for fear of losing the momentum, sucked into a paper hurricane of theses to be written, exams, standards to be upheld. And she didn't know why she'd climbed aboard in the first place. She'd just started toward a goal and couldn't stop.

Letters arrived from Stu about once a month, newsy pieces filled with amusing comments on his internship and hospital life, and reiterated pleas for more information on her activities and comings and goings. These letters were something she came to rely on, eagerly sitting down to read what he had to say, then settling back for a few minutes to think about him, about how kind and encouraging he'd been.

Amanda came from the city for the graduation ceremonies, observing the proceedings with interest, commenting on what she saw.

"I can't wait to get out of here," Helen said, handing her her diploma, then throwing aside her cap and gown. "I feel like a prehistoric bird in this outfit."

Amanda laughed, tucking the scroll into her voluminous carryall. "I must say, the purpose of all the solemn black escapes me. Wouldn't you think educated, intelligent people would know black is a negative noncolor? Yellow, now. That would be lovely. Row upon row of girls in a good cadmium yellow. Like daffodils in full bloom."

"I suppose so," Helen said, collecting her bags.

"Who was the fey little blonde sitting just across from me?"

"Why?"

"She seemed particularly interested in you, applauded deliriously when you received your honors."

"Oh, Betsy." She smiled, checking to see she had everything.

"A friend?"

"Of sorts. We can go now. I've got everything."

"You used to have so many friends. All those children coming to the door asking for you. Are you planning to do without people altogether?"

"Of course not. I've just been too busy."

"I see. Well, you certainly have left the place tidy."

"Let's go, Mother. I don't want to spend another minute here."

Several thoughts came to Amanda's mind, but she held back on voicing them, noting the almost manic air with which Helen hurried back and forth, taking her things to the car. She seemed so determined, completely dominated by a fixation Amanda couldn't find a name or reason for.

"Are you unhappy, darling?" she asked, lighting a cigarette.

"Unhappy?" She smiled suddenly, a brittle, glinting smile that reminded Amanda of a piece of broken glass on a beach. "I feel wonderful, just wonderful. I can't wait to get up to the cottage and get some sun, forget about books and exams for a while. Do I seem unhappy?"

"I'm not sure. You don't talk the way you used to. God!" She laughed. "The questions you used to ask me!"

Helen glanced over, her smile more natural now. "What questions?"

"Everything conceivable. Time's gotten a little away from me. I was just thinking how grown up you are. Just a few weeks ago you were a round, fluffy thing picking the heads off my flowers. You favored chrysanthemums especially."

"Did I?"

"Yes. Cried as if your heart was broken when I said you weren't to do that." She laughed softly. "I can see you so clearly."

"I'm going to be twenty."

"Right this minute, you seem older."

"Do I?"

"That pleases you!" Amanda's eyebrows rose. "Why, for heaven's sake?"

"Oh, I'm tired of school and girls and studying. I want to get on with . . . things."

"Nineteen is hardly the far side of life, darling. Slow down a bit, take some time out to enjoy yourself."

"I will once I've got teachers' college out of the way and I'm actually working. I want to get past all that."

"What's your hurry? I don't understand this new compulsion to race through life."

"I don't know," Helen said. "I've started, and now I can't stop. It *feels* like a race. If I don't do all the things I should today, every day, I know I'll never have the day again, and I feel somehow it's important to fill up every single day."

"Try to relax, Helen. You've got a few months to unwind. If you continue on at this pace, one day you'll wake up to find you've rushed right past all the lovely, valuable moments, the important introspective moments. You should take the time to be with yourself, darling. All this feverish haste. It's not good, not healthy. You'll burn yourself out."

"But you're just the same, staying up nights working, doing the things that are important to you."

"That's a little different, Helen. I *know* the length of each day and how much I can put into it. I don't think you do."

"Maybe later I'll take the time to be introspective. Right now, I want to do first things first—get home and get ready to go up to the cottage."

"Maybe later you'll have forgotten how to stop."

"Maybe later I'll be dead."

"Helen!"

"It's always a possibility."

"Not one you should be disturbed about now."

"I'm not disturbed, just aware of it."

"If I'm not dwelling on that awareness at my age, why should you?"

"Because you're going to live forever. I've always thought that."

"Let's change the subject," Amanda said, chilled. "I'm not enjoying this conversation."

In that same state of fixed determination, she hurried through the next two years at a frantic pace that kept her verging on breathlessness. There were dates she accepted, but many more she refused. And the men whose invitations she chose to accept all seemed so much alike that later, trying to remember where she'd gone with whom, she was unable to match occasions to faces. She wondered if she was equally faceless to her escorts. All that really mattered was getting through school.

If I can't have children, she decided, *at least I can spend every day of my life surrounded by them, giving them something.* The *something* she considered giving was nebulous and hadn't anything to do with teaching. It was a feeling she had of imparting more perhaps than just knowledge. When she visualized herself standing at the front of some imagined classroom, she felt lifted and warmed by the prospect of sharing in the lives of children.

There were other times when she became impatient with herself, demanding answers to her need for this mad dash through time. But she hadn't any kind of satisfactory responses to give to her own questions. So she closed her mind to as much as she could, fearful of losing her momentum. Speed was essential, and, caught up in it, she lost sight of how and why she'd embarked on the race in the first place. She only knew that if she stopped, she mightn't ever be able to get started again. So she kept on. And on. Going forward.

With teachers' college over finally and nothing more to anticipate but the actual commencement of her teaching contract in September, she carried her various books and papers up to the attic, then looked around the house, feeling vaguely adrift. She was no longer hurtling headlong through each day—she was moving with slow-motion unreality. She went shopping, sorted through her closets, discarding things, suddenly trapped into the need for killing time.

Amanda watched with a sense of apprehension, hoping something or someone—or, better, a renewed sense of self-awareness—would intercede and set Helen back on a more substantial footing. She sensed it best to say nothing.

Helen's correspondence with Stu had continued, subtly growing more intimate with time. In the midst of her sorting, shopping, discarding, she wondered if she'd ever see him again. When she closed her eyes and tried to remember him, all she was able to summon up was a recollection of slender hands and a brilliant smile. She was still in the process of trying to resurrect him mentally when he telephoned.

"Helen? It's Stu."

"Stu! Where are you? How are you?"

"I'm here in Baltimore. I'm just fine. How are you?"

"Fine. Good. I'm so surprised. I was just thinking about you."

"Well, that's nice. Hey! Guess what?"

"What?"

"I'm coming to town. My brother's getting married, and I was hoping, if you haven't got other plans, you'd be my date."

"When is it?"

"Next Saturday."

"Stu, I'd love it. When are you coming in?"

"Friday afternoon."

"I'll meet you. Would you like me to? Where are you staying?"

"I was just about to start making calls on it."

"Stay here!" she said impulsively. "We've got loads of room, and I'd love to have you meet Mother. There's so much to talk about. Could you do that?"

"You sound like you're in a terrific hurry." He laughed.

"No, no. I'm not."

"That's very generous of you, Helen. Are you sure it wouldn't be inconvenient?"

"Don't let's be polite and formal, Stu. I very much want you to stay here, if you'd like to. It's so good to hear your voice. I'd forgotten."

"Same for me."

"Tell me your arrival time and I'll meet you."

She was almost an hour early, and paced back and forth in the station, wondering if he'd be the same. At first she didn't recognize him, and stood staring along the platform, examining the faces of the disembarking passengers. He waved and called to her, and she ran to meet him, annoyed with herself for having forgotten how attractive he was. *How could I have forgotten that?* she wondered, running to join him.

"Hey!" He laughed, hugging her. "You forgot me! I saw you searching all over the place, trying to remember what I look like." He held her away, looking at her appreciatively. "You're even better," he said, hugging her again.

"So are you." She laughed, infected by his gaiety. "I didn't realize until this minute that I'd been missing you." Those same gentle eyes and that engaging smile.

"I sure missed you," he said, taking her arm. "Where are you parked?"

"Out this way." She handed him the keys. "You drive, I'll navigate. Did you really?"

"What? Miss you?"

"Yes."

"Even more now that I see you."

She looked at his fine, slender hands on the steering wheel, his straight, narrow nose and mobile mouth, and wondered if she'd ever really looked at him that night of the dance.

"I want to ask so many questions," she said. "Tell me everything. Have you found out yet where you'll be after Baltimore?"

"You're spoiling my big surprise." He smiled over at her. "I was going to announce it with a fanfare at some appropriate moment over the weekend. I'm coming back here. I've been accepted for my residency at The Pavilion."

"That's wonderful! You're going to be here. And I was so positive you'd be flying off to some romantic place like Duluth or Kokomo."

"Very romantic," he quipped.

"You're going to be here," she repeated, taking it in.

"And what about you?" he asked. "I want to hear about this school you're all worked up about. Everything. Don't we sound hilarious?" He laughed.

"There's not much to tell. It's just a high school downtown. I'm more interested in hearing about you."

They fell silent. Helen looked out the window, fiddling with the buttons on her coat.

"Have you . . . met anyone?" he asked, paying close attention to the traffic.

"No. Have you?"

"Not really, no." He reached across and plucked her fingers off the buttons. "That's great!" he said with obvious relief. "Really great!"

"It's so good to see you. I can't believe it's been three years. It seems like ten."

"Hey, it really does. I've been thinking a lot about you lately."

"We're here," she said, her pulse racing. "You can park in front."

From the first moment she saw him, Amanda felt a sense of rightness about Stu. She liked the way he treated Helen, the deferential and gentle but assertive manner in which he was able to slow her down. She also liked the way he came forward to take her hand, the warmhearted openness of his attitude.

"I've been reading about you in Helen's letters for so long, it seems I've known you for years," he said, kissing her cheek. "You're exactly as I imagined you."

"And you"—Amanda laughed—"are one of my daughter's well-kept secrets. Where have you been hiding this young man, Helen?"

Helen flushed happily. "You know perfectly well I've told you a dozen times about Stu in Baltimore."

"Show him up to his room. We'll talk over lunch."

On the way to the guest room he stopped at the door to her room and stepped inside.

"This is yours, isn't it?" he asked, looking around, taking in the chaise longue in front of the fireplace, the four-poster double bed set against the far wall, the polished antique desk in the bay of the front windows, the needlepoint rug on the floor.

"Yes."

"Couldn't belong to anyone else," he said, following her along the corridor.

She sat on the edge of the bed as he opened his bag and quickly distributed items in the chest of drawers, then carried his shaving gear and toothbrush into the bathroom.

"Come talk to me while I splash around," he called. "I like to see who I'm talking to."

She walked over and leaned against the door frame, feeling as if time had suddenly stopped—as if the ship she'd been sailing had finally landed, leaving her unable to walk on dry land, her sea legs still expecting the pitch and roll of the ocean.

"I thought we might go out tonight," he offered, "if you feel like it. Have dinner, take in a movie, go dancing—whatever you'd like."

"Don't you have to see your brother?"

"Just saw him," he said, lathering his hands in a way that looked as if he were scrubbing up prior to operating. "Larry came down to Baltimore on Monday to work out the details and talk money. Tonight," he said, reaching for the towel she held out, "I'm all yours."

"It's as if we've done all this before," she said. "Dozens of times. It's the oddest feeling."

He straightened his tie before turning to face her.

"I'm going to take up a lot of your time," he said, grasping her hands. "I made up my mind to that on the train. How could I possibly have let all this time go by?"

"You'll have to let me take my share of the blame. I don't know what I could've been thinking about."

"Just like me: busy being educated."

"God, how stupid! Wasting all that time."

"We'll simply have to make up for it now." He bent to kiss her.

Three years, she thought, putting her arms around him. *Three wasted years.*

"If we don't go down right now," he whispered in her ear, "I won't be able to stop."

"Just another minute," she said, holding on to him. "I can't believe you're here."

"I am, and I'm going to be around a long time, too."

Throughout the meal she sat, trying not to stare at him, listening to him and her mother chatting away like old friends.

"After my residency," he said between mouthfuls, "I'll be able to go ahead with my special."

"Your special?" Amanda asked.

"Specialize. Psychiatry," he explained.

"Now, that's fascinating," she said. "I've always thought I'd like to know someone who studied and understood human motivation."

"We'll have to have a talk about it. This is the best food. You would not believe a hospital—a place that's supposed to cure the ill—would do its damnedest to kill everyone, including the staff, with its food. The worst stuff imaginable! Most of us have been living on Hershey bars out of the vending machines. And terrible coffee!" He grimaced, then smiled at Helen. "If you're not going to eat that, I will."

"Do," she said, pushing her plate across to him. "I'm enjoying watching you eat. It's incredible."

"Perhaps," Amanda said, resting her chin on her laced fingers, "we should consider renting a room to a nice young doctor."

"Mother!"

"Depends on the rates," Stu interjected, starting on Helen's lunch. "The food's certainly a factor."

"You're so serious, darling," Amanda chided lightly. "I've got to run along. If I don't pick up those wallpaper samples today, we'll have to go to the cottage without them. And I will not spend one more summer in that place looking at those separated seams and water stains. You two take your time. I'll drop by the kitchen on my way out to tell Mary to give you all three desserts."

After she'd gone Stu said, "I think I'm in love with your mother. I might give some serious thought to renting a room in this establishment. It has a lot going for it."

"Don't let her twist your arm! She's liable to do it. You've certainly won her over."

"And how about you?" he asked, lighting a cigarette. "How much work will I have to put in?"

"Not a lot, I don't think."

Mary came bustling in with an oozing blueberry pie, which she set down in front of Stu. Helen laughed at the slow spread of color over his face as he thanked Mary, then looked over helplessly.

"I can't eat a whole pie," he protested.

"I bet you can."

He succeeded in eating half of it before easing himself away from the table with an exaggerated groan.

"I may die," he said, holding his hands over his stomach. "I just may die."

"Let's go for a walk in the park. You can work it off."

"I'm not sure I can get up, let alone walk."

"Come on." She laughed, going for her handbag.

At the bottom of the hill, he stopped and looked up at the house. A prepossessing, dormered house with an air of rightness to its situation, the lawns sloping gently down to the street. He wouldn't have been surprised to see a dainty lady in a bustle appear in one of the windows to lift a lace handkerchief in greeting.

"Have you always lived here?" he asked.

"Since I was two."

"Lucky girl. It's an impressive place. Not because it's big. Because it's lived in."

They crossed the street and went into the park, following the path until he steered her over to a bench.

"I've eaten much too much," he said. "Let's sit for a few minutes."

He lit a cigarette and sat looking at her. He smiled, remembering the night they'd spent together—how she'd trusted herself to him in sleep. Why hadn't he realized then that she was what he wanted? He shook his head at the idea of his lack of foresight.

"What?" she asked.

"Just thinking. Did you ever see that bastard again?"

"Teddy? No. Mother sees his parents from time to time. He got married."

"A girl with a lot of money, I'll bet, and no brains. What he did to you was vicious."

"I don't think about it."

"That's just as well."

"You were so kind. You must have thought I was insane, carrying on that way."

"Not insane. Human. I was just thinking about that night, asking myself why I didn't come for you a hell of a lot sooner."

"You're here now."

"I am. I want to marry you."

"What?" She looked at him with an expression of complete perplexity.

"You heard me. I want to marry you."

"Stu, we haven't seen each other in three years. And even then we were together only once. You can't be serious."

"I am. I want you to know that's what I have in mind."

"But why? I can't give you anything. You know that. I can't have children."

"So what? Do you think that's all there is to marriage?"

"I don't know what I think of marriage. I haven't given it any thought since Teddy. And that was when I was fifteen and thought the whole thing was a fantasy. I don't think we should talk about this now."

"Why not?"

"Because I can't even think straight, I'm so flabbergasted."

"Okay. We'll talk about it later. Hey! What's wrong?" Her face had lost its previous élan.

"I don't know," she hedged. "Could we walk some more?"

"No, tell me. There isn't anything that can't be talked out."

"Please," she said, feeling that her joy in the outing had been blighted.

"Okay. We'll walk."

They followed the path down to the zoo and on through to the aviary, avoiding each other's eyes. Helen gripped the guardrail and stood gazing at the birds, their incessant cries cutting through her head. Disturbed, Stu put his hands on her shoulders and made her look at him.

"Hey," he said. "What I said back there—that has to

do with how I feel about you, you know. It wasn't an attack. I'm in love with you, Helen. It hit me over the head like a sledgehammer when I saw you at the station. I don't know where my mind's been lately, but it sure hasn't been doing its job."

"How do you know, Stu? This has all happened to me before. Maybe I'm suspicious. I don't know. It scares me, having someone come at me with such conviction."

"Sometimes the spontaneous moments are the best ones. Couldn't you trust me? I won't let you down."

"I might let you down, though."

"I don't think so."

"Give me a chance to get to know you. I can't make up my mind to things the way I used to."

"There's all the time in the world," he said. "At least smile. And could we please talk somewhere else? All these beautiful, unhappy creatures—it's gruesome. I am morally outraged by confined beasts and birds."

"Are you serious?"

"Very," he said, taking her hand as they went out. "I believe in wildlife preserves, but cages, animals confined away from their natural habitats, I think that's wrong, cruel."

"You care about everything," she said wonderingly. "You'd have made quite a disciple a thousand years ago."

"Not me. I like having fun too much."

After a quiet dinner that night, they went dancing.

"You are the smallest, lightest girl," he said, enjoying the movements of her body under his hand. "When I danced with you that night at Vassar, I felt like Fred Astaire. Are you having a good time?"

"Wonderful. I love dancing."

"Then come a little closer," he said, reining her in. "You feel good."

"You seem different," she said, looking into his eyes. "So sure of yourself."

"I'm sure of one thing," he said, his arm tightening around her. "You're the softest, sweetest-smelling woman I've ever known. I love you." He nuzzled her ear. "When'd you cut your hair?"

"Years ago!" She laughed, tossing her head. "My last semester at Vassar."

"It suits you. You never bothered to tell me you'd cut it."

"It didn't strike me as something you'd care about."

"Wrong! See! I think if you'd just once written you were about to eat lunch or had just washed your hair or anything even remotely connected with the ordinary, routine things of your life, I'd have been back in a flash. I always got the impression you were holding back, keeping everything very cool."

"I honestly didn't think you'd want to read about all that."

"Wrong again! I really will have to straighten you out."

"When do you come up from Baltimore?"

"August."

"We'll be at the cottage then. Perhaps you could come up and spend a few days with us."

"We'll have to wait and see how it goes."

"Oh."

"Don't like it played your way, do you?"

"I don't follow."

"I was giving a demonstration of some typical Helenish reticence."

"Is that how I come across to you?"

"Only since we had our little stroll through the park."

"I don't mean to be that way. *Would* you like to come up in August?"

"I wouldn't miss it. You know what else?"

"What?"

"I'm going to kiss you right here in front of God, the orchestra, and all assembled."

She felt the heat rising from far below, spreading through her body into her face.

"You're blushing," he said softly, brushing his mouth against hers.

"I know it."

"I want you." He kissed her again.

"I know." She moved closer.

"Where?"

"We'll go home."

"What about your mother? I'd hate like hell to upset her."

"Her room's downstairs at the back."

"What about the housekeeper?"

"Next to Mother's."

"Okay, then, let's go."

"Yes."

They sneaked into the house like burglars, giggling at the creaky stair treads until Helen said, "This is ridiculous! Mother's out playing bridge and probaby won't be in for hours. And Mary's most likely in bed, snoring passionately, dreaming about her rugged Irish boyfriends. Go on. I'll be in in a few minutes."

She closed her door and sat down on the chaise. She'd wanted him since he'd taken her in his arms at the railway station. But the instant he'd uttered the word "marriage," something in her had closed down. She knew it was because of the way Teddy had frightened her. It was similar to an experience she'd had in her first year at Miss Evans's School when someone had thrown a firecracker in her direction on the Fourth of July weekend and it had exploded very near her ear. She'd gone running home, sobbing in terror. She could still remember the explosion and the way her head had snapped around as the sound tore through her ears.

I fear damage, she thought, undressing. She didn't believe Stu was capable of harming anyone, but then, she hadn't thought it of Teddy, either. She pulled on her dressing gown, trying to keep in mind that Stu had always been completely truthful and honest with her. He knew about himself, who he was, what he wanted. Teddy hadn't.

He'd turned off all but the far bedside light, and was sitting on the side of the bed, smoking a cigarette.

"That's very pretty," he said. "You wear lovely things."

"Thank you," she said, glancing around. "I don't know why I'm acting like a fool."

"Hey!" he said, stubbing out his cigarette. "You're acting perfectly beautifully."

She went into his arms and stood, his head against her middle, letting this moment of contact ease away her jittery feelings.

"Come here," he said, settling her on his lap. "You look like a vestal virgin about to be sacrificed."

"Stu, I haven't been with anyone since you."

"You'll think I'm smug, but I'm glad."

"So am I," she confessed.

"Lie down with me," he said. "Let me hold you."

She watched as he began unbuttoning her gown with his long, tapering fingers. But he stopped and reached for her hand.

"Would you rather not?" he asked.

"I didn't used to be this way," she said, trying to smile and failing.

"Out of practice." He smiled, keeping hold of her hand. "It doesn't matter, you know."

She looked at his wide shoulders and well-shaped legs.

"What's happened to me?" she asked, hoping he'd have answers. "I've been rushing, hurrying through the last three years, and I don't know why. And now you're here, and I'm being stupid."

"I don't know why you've been doing what you have but now you can stop. Should I put on some pyjamas?"

"No, I like looking at you."

"Oh, do you?" He laughed. "There's nothing wrong with you. You're just a voyeur. Ah! Watch it! You're smiling."

"Voyeuse," she corrected. "Did you mean it, Stu?"

"Now, of a variety of meaningful statements I've made today, which one is in doubt? You're smiling again."

"About getting married."

"Actually," he said, returning to the buttons, "I did. The Lord only knows what prompted me to do it, but I did mean it. And," he said, releasing her hand as he got to the last one, "I will say it any number of times until I convince you." He opened the gown and moved over her. "It's too late now," he sighed, as her arms came around him. "No going back from here."

7

She cried during his brother's wedding. When later, at the reception, Stu asked her why, she said, "They just seemed so—young. I don't know what's happening. Everything sets me off."

"They're both older than you are."

"I know that. Let's forget it."

"No, let's not. I think we should talk about why everything sets you off. What's bothering you?"

"Oh, I don't know."

"I think you do."

"Please let it drop, Stu."

"All right. Will you marry me?"

She stared at him, surprised.

"Will you?"

"No."

"Why?"

"This isn't the time or place to talk about it."

He looked around at the people nearby, who were engaged in conversation. "You don't think so?" He smiled at her. "People always talk about marriage at wedding receptions. It's the appropriate time and place."

"I don't think so."

"I see," he said, still smiling. "Your dinner's getting cold."

"I'm not hungry."

"So I've noticed."

She looked around, wondering why she felt so vigilant and watchful. As if she feared that at any moment he'd change before her eyes and become something directly opposed to what he was. She knew it wouldn't happen, but still she felt anxious.

"What?" he asked, following her eyes. "Are you all right?"

"I'm fine," she said softly, feeling very shaky. Her hands were cold.

"Let's get some fresh air," he said, getting up to hold her chair.

She dropped her napkin on the table, fearing they were about to have a confrontation.

"Will you stop looking that way?" he said quietly, smiling as he ushered her out through the hotel lobby and into the dimly lit bar.

"Why here?" she asked, taking in the deserted room.

"Why not?" he said, sitting down with her on a banquette in the darkest corner, his arm around her. "It's quiet and private. Now listen."

"I'm listening."

"I'm going to keep asking until I get the right answer from you. That's point number one. Unless, of course, there's something you really despise about me that you're just too polite to mention."

She smiled, and his arm tightened around her.

"That's what I thought," he continued. "So, point number two, I have something in my pocket I'm going to give you when you do change your mind. But you're going to have to do something about your nasty doubts about me, Helen. You keep looking at me as if any minute now my skin's going to unzip and some monster's going to pop out. It gives me an unpleasant feeling having you do that."

"I'm sorry."

"Point number three, we're going to go back now and enjoy ourselves. Okay? It's a celebration, after all, and you're obviously so involved with waiting for my inner monster to emerge that you've forgotten all about that. Now, no more."

He tilted her head back and, before she could speak, kissed her, unexpectedly hard. Automatically her arms went around him as she softened.

"I love you," he said. "Will you admit you love me?"

"Look, I—"

"That's good enough," he said, taking her hand and pulling her up. "Time to get back to the festivities."

As the waiter approached, he said, "Sorry, wrong bar," and led her out.

"You're hysterical!" She laughed. "You didn't used to be so funny."

"How would you know?" he retorted. "That was a very serious evening we spent, as I recall. I don't remember there being too much time for laughs."

"Touché. What's in your pocket?"

"I knew I'd get through to you!" He laughed. "Female curiosity. It never fails. You eat your dinner, and we'll see about what's in my pocket for dessert."

"And if I don't feel like eating?"

"Stringent rules. Serious trouble for not eating."

"Very well," she said, walking away from him.

Adroitly she pulled a baby mum out of the floral arrangement on one of the tables. "My mother says I favored these as a child." She smiled, feeling slightly crazy, out of step with what was happening.

"Helen!"

She popped the flower into her mouth, severing the stem between her front teeth. Dropping the stem casually on the floor, she chewed up the flower and swallowed it.

"You didn't!" he exclaimed. "I don't believe it!" He gaped at her for an instant before erupting into laughter. "Christ! You did it!"

"Of course I did. I'm like my mother. Neither of us says anything we don't mean." She turned away, heading back to the bridal-party table. He went after her, still laughing, thinking he'd never forget this scene as long as he lived.

"Eating flowers deserves to be rewarded," he said, mopping his eyes on his napkin. He passed her a tissue-wrapped package, which she turned over before opening. He lit a cigarette and leaned back.

"What's this?" she said in a surprised undertone.

"Best I could do in a hurry."

"Cracker Jack?"

"Hey! That happens to be one of the really good surprises, a genuine imitation gold-tin ring with red plastic ruby. Because I love you."

She held it in the palm of her hand and stared at him.

"I don't give them to just anybody, you know." He smiled.

"I'm sure you don't."

"So now, will you marry me?"

"Stu, this is getting unfunny," she began.

"The kids are making their break," he interrupted. "Come on. Maybe you'll catch the bouquet."

"Please, Stu." She was on the edge of tears.

"Come on."

Lucinda threw her bridal nosegay right at her, but Helen stepped aside, allowing the girl behind her to catch it. On the way out Stu held her back to ask why.

"I don't believe in superstition," she said. "And anyway, you planned it."

"I didn't."

"You did."

"No," he said soberly. "I honestly didn't."

"But I thought you did."

"Christ! You're unbelievable!"

"I'm sorry, Stu. I just didn't want to catch it."

"What would you like to do now? We could go out somewhere, have a drink."

"You decide. We'll do whatever you like."

Halfway to the car, she stopped and looked at him.

"What?" he asked, tossing away his cigarette, watching it fall in a small shower of sparks.

116

"You're hurt."

"Okay. Yes."

"Why?"

"Because you're treating this like a game. Oh, sure, there's some teasing and joking. But I'm very serious, Helen. Having fun is only part of it. I don't think you can tell the difference."

"Of course I can. I simply do not see how you can suddenly be so certain of how you feel."

"It's anything but sudden. It's always been there. I was too thickheaded to see it, that's all."

"And now that you've seen it, you're trying to pressure me into feeling the way you do. You can't force me to fall in love with you, Stu."

"Are you sure you're not?"

"I'm not sure of anything. I know I love being with you."

"I'm wrong, aren't I," he said, drawing her over to him. "You're being sensible and I'm pushing. We'll call a truce and let whatever's going to happen happen. Fair enough?"

"I think so."

"Could I have one small kiss as a show of good faith?" She smiled, and he kissed her softly.

"When I'm close to you, when we talk, when you touch me, I know I do care about you," she said, looking up at him.

"I know."

"You know," she repeated, studying his eyes. At that close range, all she could see were glimmerings of reflected light.

"I know."

"And because you know, you want me to admit how I feel. It does scare me," she said, breaking away. "I *hate* games!"

"Hey!" he said, grabbing for her hand. "What games? Where are the games? Show me!"

"You—I can't spar with you this way. I'm no good at it."

"Tell me about games!" he insisted. "Is it a game to spend three years writing to someone because you care—

117

however distantly? It's not, and you damned well know it. I think you'd like to reduce it all to something purely physical, make everything come down to pure sex. And you know that is *not* the way it is with us. It never has been. I'm not a goddamned Teddy, Helen! And no amount of trying on your part is going to reduce me to one, either. Is that one crummy experience going to turn you off forever? When are you going to get past all that ancient history and start dealing with this situation honestly? I'm me, not some sadistic son of a bitch who's going to fuck you, then try to make you spend the rest of your life feeling guilty for it. Dirty word, huh? Well, what was it he did to you? You want to call that loving, okay. Fine. I love you. I want to love you and marry you and take care of you. And not just because of your body or because you're wonderful in bed and I love making love to you. Not because of your breasts or vagina or any of your other physical attributes. I love you because you're smart enough to graduate from Vassar *magna cum laude,* and because you're a scrapper, and because you're generous and gentle and caring. A million reasons. I love the substance of you, the composite qualities that make you you. Call it soul or spirit. Call it anything you like, it doesn't matter. But it's all the things you are and the ways you can be. Do you think I couldn't find any number of girls to sleep with? There's never been a shortage. But someone to share with, someone whose depths and qualities make me think and feel and care—that's something else altogether. What do I have to do to get through to you? Tell me. I'll do it. Anything you want. You're everything to me."

"Words, Stu," she said, almost inaudibly, "just words."

"No, damn it! Not just words. I love you, you argumentative, hard-hearted, suspicious idiot. L.O.V.E. I want to spend my life with you, get you a gang of kids to look after, do anything that gives you pleasure and makes you happy. God! You are *really* making me mad! What the hell else do you think there is, Helen? It's just people caring about other people. My whole life is based on that. There happen to be certain people who come into your life that you want to care about more, differently. And that's what you are for me. I want to be with you in forty years, know you then, sit in our rockers and laugh, swapping the tag lines because we know each other so well we don't have to tell the jokes. If there's more, tell me. If you've got a better way or something I haven't found out about yet, for God's sake, tell me! I'll try it on for size. At least open your mind to the possibility that I mean what I say."

"You sell hard," she said, swayed.

"Damned right I do! You're what I want, and I know you care. I *know* you do. What do you think's going to happen to you if you admit it? Do you think God's going to come down and strike you dead? What's so awful about being happy? Every time I've seen you start enjoying yourself, you look around like a guilty kid, afraid somebody might've seen you. That's one hell of a lousy attitude to have at your age. You're all set, determined to live a tight little life. Maybe you'll hop into bed every now and then to relieve the itch. But don't give anything away. You tried it once and it blew up in your face. So you'll keep everybody at a safe distance. You might start feeling pretty deeply if you let someone get closer, and then the whole sky would fall in. Aw, Helen, it's crazy! Can't you see that? That's not living. It's skimming along on the surface without ever getting your feet wet."

"I don't want to get hurt again."

"Nobody *likes* it. Being alive is being open to all the pleasure and all the pain. But at least it's real. Isn't it better to have a little of both than nothing at all, life in a vacuum?"

"I don't know."

"Don't kid me! You sure do know. You've been taught all your life to face things, ask questions, believe in people. I know that from just two hours with your mother. What went wrong, Helen? Can't you loosen up and try to get past it? I'll do my share—more. Just try. I can't fight you every inch of the way. It all winds up as nothing that way."

"And what happens if I do all of it? Suppose something happens to you? I wind up with nothing."

"You dope! You wind up with everything. You wind up with your life. And you know you've loved, been loved, know how to spot the real McCoy when you see it."

"You're wearing me down, Stu," she said faintly. "I wish you wouldn't do this."

"Okay." He released her. "Okay. You know how I feel, what I think. It's your ballgame now. If you decide you want to play, let me know. Come on, we'll go home."

She sat staring out the window, listening to him light one cigarette after another. He pulled up in the driveway and switched off the ignition, then sat finishing his cigarette.

"My train leaves at four tomorrow," he said finally, breaking the long silence.

"I'll take you to the station," she offered, experiencing a miserable knotting in her stomach.

"You don't have to. It's all right. I'm not angry, Helen, just disappointed. But you can't teach anyone to swim in one brief lesson. I guess I'm a little brought down by the realization that I'm not as persuasive as I'd like to be."

He came around to open the door for her, holding out his hand.

"Hey!" he said, tossing his cigarette away. "Don't do that! Come on," he coaxed, "you know I'm a sucker. Don't cry."

"I can't help it. Everything you said is true."

"I said some nice things too, remember."

"I know," she said, clinging to him. "But all the rest made me sound so hopeless. It's not the way I want to be. I know you're not Teddy, nothing like the way he was. But I keep thinking of things we promised each other and the way it all turned out in the end."

"Listen to me," he said evenly, "I will share everything with you, even all your bad memories, if it'll help. Just let me in. We'll work it out together."

"I don't want to lose you, Stu. I don't. I know how good you are, how honest. Be patient with me, please. There's a lot to undo."

"Come on," he said gently. "Don't go overboard. I was only trying to get you to snap out of that trance you kept falling into. You're beautiful, Helen. You're generous with yourself in every way. All I'm after is a chance to give you something in return."

"I'll take it," she said, kissing him. "I will. I want to."

They went inside hand in hand.

"I love this room," he said, watching her hang up her dress. "It's so uncluttered and peaceful."

"It used to be Mother's," she said, pulling off the bed-spread. "But she prefers the big bedroom next to the studio. That way, if she feels like getting up at night to work, she's not disturbing anyone. What?" she asked, seeing an odd expression on his face.

"Just looking," he said, laying his hand across her breast.

She looked down at his hand and felt a kind of madness boiling up inside her. It seemed to center upon the sight of his hand molded over her breast, as if all her nerve endings had come together under his hand, as if, in making that gesture, he was illustrating love. And she was falling, could feel herself being caught in the eddying motion of the descent as he sat looking love at her.

His fingertips sensed the quickening of her heartbeat, the slow-rising heat of her body.

"It's very exciting," he said, caught up too.

"What is?"

"What's happening under here." He lifted his hand slightly. "It's hard to define. Something you do," he said. "You seem to settle into yourself for a moment or two and then everything starts happening."

"What do you mean?"

"I want to know," he said earnestly. "Tell me. Is it some kind of a switch you turn on inside when it's time to make love? Is there a signal? Is it because you want me?"

She considered it, gazing past him, her eyes on the far wall.

"Both," she said, looking into his eyes. "I want you, but I have to let myself know that I want you. Does that make sense? I have to have a second or two with myself to make the decision. Is that what you want to know?"

"Some of it."

"Then, tell me," she said, dropping her hand lightly at the juncture of his thighs, her eyes on his face. "What happens inside of you when I do that? Is what's happening now happening because I've touched you and you respond automatically, no matter what? Or is it me? I want you to tell me what makes my hand on you here different from any other girl's."

"I know who you are. And I'm not so very different from you, at least not inside my head. It's the same. There's the same switch that has to be turned when I tell myself this is a woman I love and want. I might be constructed more handily, so that it's a bit easier for me to respond. But it's the caring, the loving that makes everything matter. Is that what *you* want to know?"

"It's important, Stu."

"God, yes it is!"

For several seconds she sat gazing at him, her hand unmoving. Then she lay on top of him, her head on his shoulder.

He held her, thinking how small she was, how soft and utterly female. Her skin seemed to absorb his caresses, to swell under his fingertips. And for each caress he gave, she moved to offer more in return, instinctively reciprocating. He lifted her away, down beside him, looking at the spread of her body.

"This is like the first time ever," he said quietly. "Maybe it is."

"I want to tell you something." Her fingers wove themselves into his hair, bringing his head down to hers. "I love you," she said, closing her eyes. Her face was fiery red.

"That wasn't so hard to say, was it?"

"Yes it was."

"It'll get easier." He laughed. "With practice."

"Shut up, I want you," she whispered, opening her mouth on his shoulder. "I love you and I want you. I love you."

She held herself open, ready. And it seemed, in that moment it took to accept him, as if she had somehow actually managed to take all of him inside of her, into her soul, into her cells. And the idea of it, the magnitude of all her unleashed feeling for him, filled her eyes, brought tears spilling over.

"Darling." He paused. "Am I hurting you?"

"No." She held him fast. "No, I do love you. That's why."

"I know," he said. "I love you too."

He gathered her closer as she offered him her mouth, still crying, making words and sounds that shook him; made him despair of ever causing her pain; made their coming together a savagely gentle act of personal promise.

Some mornings, when he'd been on night duty, she waited outside in the car in order to have breakfast with him before going to school. When he was on days she went directly from school to his apartment to stay the night. And those times when he worked the middle four-to-twelve shift he called "no man's land," she went home for dinner with her mother, spent the evening with her before kissing her good night and driving downtown to prepare a late dinner for Stu. She was very happy.

Amanda saw her transformed.

"He's good for you, darling," she told Helen gladly. "Will you marry him?"

"Probably. I just want to be very, very sure."

The head of the French department eyed her for a long time, maintaining her distance. Helen was confused by her, unable to determine what it was about Fraser Hilton —aside from her name—that was so unusual. Just before school broke up for the Christmas holidays, Fraser ventured forward one morning to ask if Helen would like to have lunch.

Fraser was very tall, about thirty, with shoulder-length prematurely gray hair that fell softly about her slightly forbidding features. Despite a perpetual expression of wariness, she was a handsome woman with large gray eyes and a sensuously full mouth. She wore well-made clothes and moved with feline grace. A woman of contradictions.

Helen apologized for being several minutes late, explaining that one of her students had wanted to talk.

"I understand," Fraser said, in a rich, well-modulated voice. "There's a not-too-bad coffee shop nearby."

They found a booth and sat down, picking up the menus. They ordered and Helen sat back, trying not to feel uncomfortable under her superior's steady gaze.

"You're very beautiful," Fraser said at last, folding her long hands in front of her on the table.

"Thank you," Helen said, trying to guess where this was leading. She watched the woman's elegant hands wrap themselves around each other, thinking she ought to say something. "You're very attractive," she said, sounding shallow to her own ears.

Fraser didn't seem to notice. "I've been watching you," she said. "You've most likely gathered that. I'm not a subtle person."

"I'm used to people looking at me. My mother's an artist, you see, and I used to pose for her. One becomes accustomed to being stared at." *I'm sounding pompous,* she thought, finding the restaurant overheated.

"I see."

"Who's the tuna and who's the Swiss on rye?" the waitress asked, holding two plates in the air between them.

"Tuna here," Helen said, busying herself with the sandwich, anxious to get the meal out of the way so she could return to school.

Fraser ignored her food.

"I think you'll make a fine teacher," she persisted, as her eyes bore into Helen's. "The students like you."

"I hope so. I like them. I like teaching."

"*I* like you." She smiled. "I hope you'll come to feel the same about me."

"Oh, I'm sure I will."

"I find you very attractive, very desirable."

Helen put her sandwich down slowly and stared, thinking how naive she'd been.

"I see someone, Fraser," she said softly. "We're going to be married. I'm sorry if I gave the impression . . ."

"I had no idea," she said, her voice icing over. "Forgive me if I've offended you. You're very lovely. I had hoped—"

"I'm not offended," Helen cut in. "I'm flattered that you find me attractive. I take it as a compliment."

"I've embarrassed you," Fraser said. Her eyes looked glazed with shame. "You're very young. Please, do forgive me."

"I am *not* embarrassed," Helen said firmly, holding the other woman's gaze. "I know how it feels to be lonely, Fraser. I imagine I've felt much as you do. It's hard not having someone you love close at hand. The love isn't so very different, is it?"

Fraser stared at her in surprise.

"You're not disgusted—sickened?"

"Why would I be? I haven't ever been approached by a woman before. I don't think it's even entered my mind that it could happen. But I'm certainly not sickened. After all, love is love, isn't it? I can't see that it matters who one loves as long as it's loving."

"You've very secure in the love you have," Fraser observed sagaciously. "Could we be friends, do you think?"

Helen couldn't help but think how lonely Fraser must be to solicit friendship from someone she scarcely knew. *But then,* she wondered, *am I very different?*

"I think we could." Helen smiled. "Hadn't you better eat your sandwich?"

"I suppose so. I hope we will be friends. You intrigue me. Not just in that way. There's something about you, an aura. Would you allow me to give you a very valuable piece of advice?"

"Of course."

"If you plan on getting married, don't tell anyone."

"I don't understand."

"Are you serious about teaching? Do you plan to keep on with it?"

"I'm very serious about it."

"Then don't tell anyone, and I'll keep it a secret."

"I'm afraid I'm being dense, but I still don't see what you're getting at."

"They'll let you go once your contract expires. They won't keep you on if you're married."

"But why?" The last of the sandwich had lumped in her throat.

"God only knows why! It's a barbaric system the Board has always adhered to. Married women aren't allowed to continue on staff. Shocking, isn't it?"

"I'm stunned," Helen said. "I never dreamed that marrying Stu might mean having to give up my career."

"You could get away with it." Fraser smiled conspiratorially, looking all at once young and pretty. "I *am* the head of the department, after all, and nobody else has to know."

"Why would you want to do that?"

"Oh, a number of reasons." She smiled, picking up half her sandwich. "Every so often I like to beat the system. It's good for the soul. They only accepted me as a department head because Liz Conroy was too old and too ill after McGregor died, and I was the next in line. And then, I like you very much. I think you mean it when you say your career means something to you."

"You're right. It does. I'm very grateful you've told me all this. I'll have to do a lot of thinking about it."

She couldn't bring herself to mention it to Stu right away. It was vital now that she be completely certain of her feelings before committing herself one way or another.

Stu was working nights during the weeks before Christmas. Ever since those first calamitous reports about the Japanese bombing Pearl Harbor, Helen had felt uneasy— she had an ominous premonition that something was drastically going to disrupt the plans she and Stu were making for their life together.

Amanda said, when she told her about Fraser's warning, "If you think this woman is really to be trusted, I can't see a reason on earth why you and Stu shouldn't go ahead and be married. He doesn't object to your continuing to teach, does he?"

"Not at all."

"Then I don't see that you have a problem."

"Why can't I be sane and sensible like you?" Helen asked, putting her arms around her mother, kissing her.

"When you're sixty you'll find you secretly wish you were still young and giddy and bothered by unanswered questions. I find it hard sometimes to believe that I'm not as young outside as I feel inside." She smiled and placed the palm of her hand on the side of Helen's head. "Stop shrouding your life with anticipated problems, darling. Enjoy yourself. It all goes soon enough. You've got so much. You're young and lovely to look at. You've got a career you've worked hard for. And you've been fortunate enough to find a man who loves himself enough to love you well. Think about all that. Now run along and let me go to bed. This weather makes me stiffen up like wet wash in a cold wind."

When Stu came in from the hospital at midnight that night, she was sitting up in his bed, waiting for him. He knew from her expression that she'd made up her mind.

"I'm taking you out of limbo." She laughed, jumping up to embrace him. "If you still want to."

"If I still want to!" He laughed jubilantly, swinging her around. "I'd always want to."

"I'm not clean and tidy, Stu, and I loathe housekeeping."

"We'll get a cleaning lady."

"And we have to keep it a secret from anyone connected with the school."

"Explanation, please."

"They won't renew my contract if they know I'm married."

"What?"

"It's true. I've become friends with the head of the department, and she told me."

"But if she knows, won't she . . . ?"

"She's special, Stu. And she likes me. I trust her."

"If that isn't the damnedest thing I've ever heard. What do they think a married woman would do, anyway, corrupt the kids' morals or something? That's the biggest example of male dirty-dealing I've heard about in years."

"Well"—she shrugged—"it can't be helped. As long as you don't mind."

"I don't mind having our marriage a secret. But I sure mind about all the women whose lives they've screwed good and proper."

"I love the way you care about things—the birds in the aviary and all of us poor virginal teachers."

"How about the first of February?" he suggested.

"Fine. Good."

"Okay," he said, going over to the chest of drawers and rummaging around. "Now you get your lavish gifts." He returned and sat down on the bed with her. "We're going to talk about money for a few minutes, okay?"

"Okay."

"The bulk of my mother's estate went for putting Larry and me through school. Then, when Larry got married, we agreed he'd have Dad's things and Lucy would have Mother's jewelry. I want you to know where everything's been going. I don't believe in keeping financial matters out of a marriage. I've seen the disastrous results that can have."

"I have my trust fund, Stu. It's bringing in almost five thousand a year now. We don't need to worry about money."

"That's fine, Helen. But just hear me out. Mother left a will. She wanted to be sure that both of us would have something to start out on if we married. Larry got his when he married Lucy. When you and I are married, I'll receive the balance of my inheritance. It's not an awful lot, but more than enough to buy us a house and see us through until I finish my special. After that I'll be in practice and everything should be rosy. I love you for offering your money, but I want you to keep it, use it for all the things you'll want that I won't be able to afford to give you for a while. We can save your money for the years to come.

"There's one other thing," he said, lifting his hand. "This was Mother's." He put a small box in her palm.

"She would have loved you as much as I do, and I know it would have made her happy to know you'd wear it. Whenever you're not at school, that is."

"I wish I'd known her." She thought of that pale oval face and the large, apprehensive eyes.

"Open it."

Inside was a platinum engagement ring set with a round diamond.

"It's beautiful," she said, thinking it was like staring into the sun. "So beautiful."

"Now it's all on the up and up," he said, sliding the ring on her finger, "we're going to have the best life two people could have."

"The best," she echoed, bedazzled.

Christmas, the New Year, her birthday. A happy time sandwiched between hospital shifts. Stu walked around with a permanent grin.

"She's everything I ever wanted," he told Amanda on Christmas Eve. "I was positive once she got past comparing me to that louse and started trusting me, she'd be the way she is now—laughing, vivacious, happy. I know how she felt," he said, his eyes momentarily clouded with memories. "It's like waking up after being asleep for a long, long time, having had a lot of nightmares that are suddenly over. It's a matter of accepting that's what it all was: a nighttime horror."

"I know," she said. "When Lawrence and I met, our reactions were very much the same. I'd spent years, hundreds of them it seemed, arguing, bickering endlessly with everybody. And finding him was like finally being allowed to go to my corner, having the bell ring for the end of the round. He had your kind of caring, your zest for living things. You make me think of him." She smiled, knowing they understood each other. "You've done wonders, taken Helen back. These past months she's been the way she used to be—alive to everything. It's wonderful to see. I'm glad. For all our sakes."

With much laughter and sudden prolonged silences, Helen and Stu planned who'd attend the wedding, where they'd spend their honeymoon.

"It doesn't seem possible we're actually doing it," Helen said, curled up on the chaise longue in front of the fire.

"Hey," he said, dropping his cigarette into the grate. "Anything's possible. It's all happening."

"I know," she said, examining his hands, thinking how beautiful they were.

She was awakened at midnight the day before her birthday by the heavy, plodding sound of footsteps outside the apartment door. When the key turned in the lock and Stu came in, she knew at once something had gone wrong.

"What's happened?" she asked, pulling her cardigan around her shoulders as Stu slumped beside her on the sofa.

"You shouldn't be sleeping out here. Why didn't you go to bed?"

"I wanted to wait for you."

"I can't believe it," he said, reaching for cigarettes in his overcoat pocket. "I'm in a state of shock."

"God! What is it?"

"I've been drafted. I thought at first it had to be a mistake. I went over to the draft board yesterday afternoon on my way to the hospital. No mistake. They're sending me into the Army medical corps. Mine's got to be the first name they pulled! Jesus! I thought if it did happen it would take a while. A year maybe. Not a goddamned month. I can't believe it."

"It doesn't change anything," she said, her voice small and uncertain.

"It changes *everything,* Helen. We can't go ahead now. It'd be completely unfair to you. Who knows how long this idiotic war might go on? I'd hate to think of you stuck alone for months, years even, tied down to someone you couldn't be sure you'd ever see again."

"Don't say that! In the first place, I agreed to be tied, as you so ineptly put it. I want to be married to you. Nobody's forcing me. And in the second place, you don't even know yet where they'll send you."

"I've got a good idea. Right smack in the center of the action in a field hospital."

"You don't know that at all! This is the first time I've ever seen you behave like an adolescent," she said angrily, poking his arm. "If I'm willing, anxious, to marry you and wait for you, what difference does distance make? I'm surprised at you!"

"Nice try." He smiled grimly. "I know you too well to buy that, Helen. Your eyes look as if you'd been shot about an hour ago and the pain's only begun sending signals to your brain. Don't play it out for me. Just sit here and we'll be depressed together. What neither of us needs at this moment is a display of false heartiness and gung-ho optimism. Let's look at it as the worst that could happen and try to deal with it rationally, see what we can make of it."

Deflated, she sat back and watched him take off his coat.

"I'll make breakfast," she proposed. "You haven't eaten."

"No appetite," he said, looking at her. "Could you really take all this in your stride, knowing a couple of weeks might be all we'd have for years?"

"Yes."

"Why, for God's sake? After all the fighting and arguing and pressuring, I'd have thought you'd be grabbing at this opportunity to back out."

"Now you really are being an ass! I love you, Stu. L.O.V.E. You remember that little speech, don't you? How I felt and behaved before has nothing to do with the way I feel now. Do you really think that's all I am? I've got more staying power than you evidently give me credit for. If loving you, marrying you, means waiting, then I'll wait. That's all there is to it. Unless, of course, you have some other reason for wanting to call it all off."

"You know I don't."

"Then I'd say that ends this discussion. You relax, and I'll make breakfast."

"Helen, it really might be years."

"I know that."

"Do you have any idea of what you'd be letting yourself in for?"

"Do you?"

"Some."

"Look, Stu, I need you in my life. I love you. For the first time in years I can go to bed at night and sleep and feel secure, happy because I have you. Before you, I had a lot of fear and self-pity and not much of anything else, except a compulsion to be the world's fastest runner. You said yourself that people caring about people is all there is. I believe it. You've proven it to me. Are you going to do an about-face on me now and say it was all just a carnival pitch to get me to put down my dime and come into the tent?"

"No."

"Then take me at my word, as I have you. We're going to do it all as we planned. I've got my job, my mother, my friends. And you. That's everything I want, everything I need."

"I still feel like breaking windows or getting drunk."

"All right, I'll get the brandy."

It took little to get both of them high. They sat on the sofa for almost two hours, passing the bottle back and forth, until Helen said, "Time for breakfast."

They wove their way into the kitchen, where she poured more brandy into juice glasses, then set about attempting to make breakfast.

"You've only had three drinks," she accused, weaving toward the stove. "I don't believe you're drunk at all."

"I hate scrambled eggs." He screwed up his face. "How could you make scrambled eggs when you know I hate them."

"I don't understand it," she said, pushing the hair out of her eyes. "They weren't supposed to come out that way. Something happened."

"You haven't even finished your drink." He picked up her glass, the brandy sloshing down the side and over his hand.

"Don't wipe it off! That's a sinful waste, Stuart."

She sat down awkwardly on his lap, licking the brandy off his fingers.

"Hey!" he said, working his hand up under her sweater. "You've got nothing on."

"Nope."

"You had this whole thing planned."

"I did not! I was more comfortable without all that constricting underwear. Men have such advantages. No buckles, no straps, no garter belts, no seams in your stockings."

"There! You're doing it!"

"What?"

"Turned on that switch again. How the hell do you do that? We're going to do it this minute, right here."

He pulled off her sweater and threw it aside.

"Oh, Stu, I'm so drunk," she said, holding his head against her breasts. "On the floor?"

"Right on the floor."

As he came into her she said, "I wish we could make a baby. Oh, *God*, I wish we could!"

"We'll find you one the minute I come home," he promised, covering her face with kisses. "I'll get you the whole goddamned world."

She closed her eyes as the room tilted, glad of the plunging weight of his body. It was something real and substantial, something that kept her pinned safely to the earth, preventing her from being whirled away by the centrifugal force of the spinning room.

Afterward they were neither of them quite as drunk as they'd been before. Stu lay with his face against her stomach, and she stared at the ceiling, thinking she was very happy, regardless of the war and his leaving. But slowly, as she came back to herself, she sat up to look at him.

"Stu!" she whispered, stricken. "Darling, why are you doing that?"

He shook his head, and the gesture reminded her so much of something a small boy would do, she felt overpowered by love and a depth of caring for him. "Tell me," she urged. "Please."

"I'm scared. It's so goddamned stupid! I'm just scared." He sat up, dragging his handkerchief out from the tangle of clothes on the floor, and blew his nose. "I'm not some idealistic eighteen-year-old who thinks going off to fight for his country is what's owed in return for the privilege of being born here. I don't believe in killing people to prove how strong you are. It's wrong. And we don't even matter. We're nothing but tin toys they move around on their stinking maps, just ashes after the fire. They'll use up as many men as it takes to demonstrate who has the upper hand. A ludicrous, ugly game."

"Stu, get up!"

"What?"

"Get up. We're going to take a shower, get dressed and go see my mother."

"What for?"

"I'm not sure. I think she knows something about all this that I don't. I can't tell you what you need to hear, but I believe she can. Come on."

"Okay," he said, looking as if he'd never heard of her mother until that moment.

"Please don't take a cynical, show-me posture! I have something I think you need right now: a mother. I can be all kinds of things for you, but not that. My mother loves you. She'll know the right words. Okay?"

"Okay."

She left Stu in the living room while she went to find Amanda, who she knew would be up. She often spoke of finding it difficult to sleep later than four thirty or five, and had fallen into the habit of rising at that time to work for a few hours before breakfast.

"He's scared, Mother," Helen said. "I remember once when I was very young you said a number of things about how you felt about 'war games' and the military. Please talk to Stu. I don't know what to tell him, but I think you do."

"I don't have any special answers, darling."

"Not that. He needs a mother right now. Will you talk to him?"

Amanda got her coat and boots, and she and Stu went out for a walk. Helen never knew what they talked about, and never asked. But whatever was said seemed to do the trick. They returned to the house arm in arm, laughing, sharing a cigarette. And Helen felt lightened, able to breathe again.

When she invited her to act as witness, Fraser's eyes lit up with warmth and gratitude.

"I'd be honored," she said, attempting to smile. "More than that. It would be a privilege to attend your wedding."

From that moment on, Fraser yielded completely to her feelings for Helen, and during the week before the wedding they went out together every day for lunch to discuss the details. Their friendship was slowly but firmly cemented.

Fraser revealed her ardent interest in astrology and the supernatural, and Helen listened attentively as she described the effects of the planets on one's life.

"Perhaps you'll tell me sometime what the stars have lined up for me," Helen said as they were leaving school on the day before she was to be married. "I'd be most interested in seeing what you come up with."

"Give me the date and hour of your birth, and I'll make up a chart for you while you're away."

Helen agreed, writing the information on the back of an envelope she found in her handbag. "I'll be looking forward to seeing it."

"So will I," Fraser said ambiguously. "Most interested."

The ceremony was performed at City Hall. Then the small party returned to the house to celebrate. They'd limited the guests to Fraser, Larry and Lucy, and Charlie "Barnstorm" Barnes, an old friend of Amanda's who owned a gallery and waged a running battle with her about having her exhibitions there. He was a jolly, acutely intelligent bachelor with whom Amanda had been playing bridge and matching wits for almost twenty years.

Barnstorm took an instant liking to Fraser, and throughout lunch kept her amused and diverted with anecdotes about his arguments with Amanda over showing her work.

"You wouldn't think," he said, winking, "that a harmless-looking lady like that could be made of solid steel, would you? Don't be fooled, my dear! Tough as an old boot, that one. Absolutely incredible that she can paint those delicate little watercolors when she has a mind to. You'd think she'd turn out room-size canvases of battleships and artillery barrages."

Fraser looked over to see Amanda laughing into her hand.

"I'm sorry to say I haven't seen her work," she said, thinking this was one of the loveliest days of her life. "I'd certainly like to."

"After those two have gone," Amanda said, ignoring Barnstorm, "I'll take you out to the studio and give you a private showing. Hopefully," she added, "our senile guest will also have departed, taking with him his dubious wit and sarcastic stabs at intelligent conversation."

"Not a chance," Barnstorm said, putting his arm through Fraser's. "This statuesque charmer and I will take the tour together. After which," he said, looking at Fraser's mouth, "I plan to show this elegant creature some of the seamier aspects of our fair city."

Helen glanced over to see how Fraser was taking this attention, and was gratified to see she was reacting with pleasure. Her face was flushed with color, and she looked totally unselfconscious for once.

Stu was eating away, talking between mouthfuls to Larry and Lucy, who were to return to New York that evening.

To Helen, the day so far had had a dreamlike quality, an empyreal calm.

For one instant, after Mary had cleared the table and was bringing in the coffee, Helen looked down the table and suppressed a desire to burst into ecstatic tears. It was almost too much—sitting there, looking around at the faces of the people she loved, seeing their expressions of enjoyment and pleasure.

"Hey!" Stu said, squeezing her hand under the table. "Where are you?"

"Here." She turned to smile at him. "Just thinking."

He was about to say something when Barnstorm rattled his spoon against his cup and stood, lifting his wineglass.

"Ladies and gentlemen," he said. "Love flourishes. To the bride and groom. May they know peace and joy in their life together."

Fraser wept without making any effort to hide the fact as the party drank the toast. Amanda looked down the table at Helen and smiled, a smile that filled Helen with a flooding of love for all the goodness and sanity and understanding Amanda had always given her.

Stu tugged on her hand and said, "Now," and they excused themselves to change before leaving for the cottage.

After they'd gone, finally, ducking under the onslaught of rice and confetti, Larry and Lucy made their good-byes.

"Go give this woman her tour and then let us get on with our evening of festivities," Barnstorm told Amanda, pouring himself a generous measure of cognac.

"I believe you're declining into senility at a far faster rate than I'd imagined," she said, leading Fraser off to the rear of the house. "And don't drink it all!" she added.

Fraser was an ardently enthusiastic audience. Amanda enjoyed showing her her work.

"Beautiful," Fraser said again and again, drinking in the pieces Amanda set out. "I'm speechless."

Amanda, sensing something unusual in this woman, made a snap decision and said, "Come over here. There's something I think you'll like." She lifted the cloth off the easel and stood back to watch Fraser's face.

Fraser stood bolted to the spot, gazing at the new, nearly completed portrait of Helen.

"It's a wedding present for Stu," Amanda said. "Do you like it?"

"I . . . it's exquisite. God!" she said. "It's like pain. She is so beautiful, so utterly beautiful."

She loves her, Amanda realized, inexplicably touched.

"Perhaps you'd like to sit for me sometime," she said, scanning Fraser's face.

"Me?" she asked, breaking her hold on the portrait. "Why on earth would you want to paint me?"

"You've got a good face, unusual composition of features." She paused, considering. "Would you like me to do something about getting you out of this evening with Charlie?"

Fraser's eyes connected with hers.

"I understand now how Helen comes by her way with people," she remarked. "No. Thank you. I'm actually looking forward to it. He's being very . . . protective. I'm enjoying it. It's a welcome change."

"You live in both worlds, don't you?" Amanda asked, in a casual tone that failed to belie her curiosity.

"I have done," she said, turning to look again at the painting. "I do, yes."

"You're an uncommon woman," Amanda said, lighting a cigarette. "I hadn't expected, having heard Helen talk about you, that you'd be quite so honest. I hope you'll come and sit for me. I think we might both benefit from it."

"I think we might. I'd very much like to come again."

"Tell me something."

"Yes?"

"Why did you cry?"

"I'm not sure. I suppose because she's happy."

"And that makes you happy?" Amanda asked cautiously.

"Yes."

"Because you're living somewhat vicariously through Helen?"

"No. Because I love her."

She said it so simply, so truthfully, her eyes so candidly open, that Amanda was taken aback.

"You're quite something," Amanda said, stubbing out her cigarette. "I think we'd best get back to Charlie before he finishes off the cognac."

The snow was thick and deep, and they had to leave the car in the road while they cleared a space beside the house to park. While Stu went back for the car, Helen got a fire going in the living room and set a pot of coffee on the stove.

He came in, his cheeks red from his exertions, shaking the snow from his shoes.

"Why didn't we think about boots?" he said, tossing his coat over the back of a chair near the fire.

"There are tons of rubber boots under the cellar stairs. I'm sure there'll be something we can wear."

They ate bacon and eggs in front of the fire, huddled together for warmth.

"We'll never be able to sleep in any of the bedrooms," he said. "They'd find our frozen bodies six months from now. We'll have to drag a mattress in here and keep the fire going all night."

"Let's see what's down in the cellar. Mother usually keeps a little trove of goodies there." She went for the flashlight and came back waving to him. "Come on, let's go see."

They found two pairs of boots that would at least keep out the snow and several jars of peach preserves Mary had put up the summer before.

"What's over there?" he asked, directing the flashlight against the far wall.

"Probably one of Mother's canvases. They're everywhere."

"It's you," he said, shining the flashlight down.

"Yes." She remembered the day Teddy had come up the beach with her shoes.

"It's not finished."

"No. God!" She smiled wistfully. "I was so *young*. Look how young I was, Stu."

"You're not exactly elderly now."

"Come on. Let's go up. It's cold."

They undressed in front of the fire and crawled, shivering, under the blankets.

"Hey! Mrs. Brainard, are you happy?"

"I will be as soon as I thaw out. Your hands are like ice."

"Are you happy?" he repeated.

"Yes. Very, very. You?"

"Paralytically."

"That's descriptive."

"I'm too frozen to do better."

Every time the chill of the room woke them, Stu threw more logs on the fire, then dove back under the blankets to make love to her again.

"These four days may have to last quite a while," he said while she prepared steaks for breakfast.

"Maybe not."

"Do you realize we had breakfast for dinner and now you're making dinner for breakfast? You're creating seriously disorienting problems for my stomach. My body doesn't know if it's morning or night."

"This happens to be a genuine Texas breakfast—steak and eggs."

"Those Texans must have leather stomachs."

"Is that a comment on my cooking or a generalization?"

"Both. I didn't really believe you when you said you had no housewifely attributes. I believe it now, though."

"I want a divorce."

"No way. Anyway, at least the eggs are all right."

They bundled up and trudged down to the beach, surveying the frozen shoreline.

"Is there any chance I'll be able to come to see you?" she asked.

"I'll have to let you know once I get there."

"God, I'm afraid for you. Please, don't let anyone shoot you. Be a coward and hide in every corner."

"I'm no hero. You know how I feel about legalized murder."

"Come back a live coward, please. What will I do without you to talk to?"

"What will *I* do, stuck in some godforsaken place with a bunch of mangled kids to look after? It's not a cheery picture."

"Will you write to me?"

"Aw, come on, Helen. Who spent almost three years courting you via the postal service?"

"You said you weren't sure about anything until we met at the station."

"Not about everything. But I sure as hell knew something good when I saw you the first time. I never did thank old Bets. Three years."

"Don't say it. I can't stand to think of it."

"Are you really happy, Helen, really?"

"Deeply, blissfully. Words. There's no way to get past words. And none of them say enough."

"Nothing means more to me than you do," he said. "When this lunatic war is out of the way, we'll have all the time in the world to be together and collect up some kids to look after."

"I can't wait."

"I want you to listen to me for a minute. We'll get this out of the way and then we won't have to talk about it again. I want your promise that if anything does happen to me, you won't stop living—you won't go back into yourself the way you did after Jennings the Jerk."

"I refuse to even think about your not coming back."

"No, you've got to! It's something we both have to face. I'm not being philosophical now, Helen. It's not a polite attempt to put a good face on the most drastic possibilities. But if something does happen, go on with your life. Don't be driven backward into distrust and skepticism. People die in wars. They do. The thought of it scares me witless. But the thought of you giving up on life scares me even more. My mother did that, and it was a tragic waste of something good. I knew why she did it. She gave up her identity when she married my father. You've got to stay you, no matter what happens to me. If I die, you can't die too. It would make everything so damned pointless if both of us stopped living. I want your promise."

"I despise this conversation."

"No, think about it. Hopefully it'll never happen. Jesus! I don't want to die, Helen. But we have to live with the chance that I might. It would destroy all we've had

142

together if you let my death put an end to you. I'd know and come back to haunt you. You wouldn't want to have me spend eternity furious with you, would you?"

"That's a very unfunny joke."

"No joke, Helen. You've always smiled at my caring about the birds in their cages and all the living things that deserve their freedom, not peanuts from passers-by. I *believe* that!

"We all have to die one day. I'm not going off from here with the idea fixed in my mind that that's the inevitable outcome—that some crackpot with a grenade is going to be so stupid he can't figure out what a big red cross on a white background means. The odds are all in my favor. Doctors are valuable, regardless of which side they're on. I'm simply, sensibly accepting the remote possibility that something *could* happen. If I don't come back you have to go on. Promise me!"

"All right. I promise. But you're coming back. You *are!*"

"Let's get back to the cottage. I'm freezing."

They stood on the platform waiting for his train, both of them wanting to talk but neither of them able to start. Then they saw a train barreling down the line and flew into each other's arms, shouting above the noise. Their shouts subsided as they saw the train wasn't stopping.

"I thought that was it." He grinned. "I had a whole damned speech prepared."

"We're fools," she said, taking his hand. "We should be standing here saying all the meaningful things people say at times like this, and I can't think of a thing except that I wish to God you weren't going and what a long time it's going to be before we're together again."

"You don't know that. It'll probably all be over pretty fast, at the rate they're dragging any old resident into the service and turning them into majors."

"Put your arms around me and tell me how much you love me."

"I do, Helen. You're everything that's beautiful to me. You're waking up in the morning, and the best night's sleep, and laughter. Everything. I'll never forget that night I came to pick you up. I thought you were the most beautiful girl in the world and that I was the luckiest man. You're still the best. You always will be. If anything happens, don't stay alone. Don't."

"You promised you wouldn't bring that up again."

"I won't say any more. Just, please, don't stay by yourself."

"I'm going to go now," she said, holding him. "I'll never make it until the train comes. Take care of yourself, and call me the minute you're settled in. And write. Okay?"

"I will," he said, kissing her. "You go. It's a good idea. The train'll be along in a minute."

"I love you so much." She kissed him again.

"The major's wife." He laughed softly. "God, how I love you! Go now. Go on."

She tore herself away and ran. She got into the car, jammed the shift into first, and drove out of the station parking lot with her tires spinning wildly in the hard-packed snow.

She was halfway home to the city when the image of Stu standing alone on the platform sprang up before her. She pulled over and sat staring at the road. *I'll see him in a week or two*, she told herself. *He'll call me when he gets there and I'll go to him.*

What she needed was a drink. A good bracing drink to melt the clot of fear in her throat. She pulled back onto the road and drove until she saw a roadside inn.

Being that odd hour between late lunch and early cocktails, the place was uninhabited. She ordered a double brandy and sat, looking out at the passing cars. The brandy helped. Fortified, she paid, went out to the car, and drove home.

He telephoned two days later. The connection was poor and, in mutual frustration, they shouted to make themselves understood. They got cut off finally, and she was unable to reach him when she tried calling back.

The following week, she received a letter in which he

outlined the conditions at the base, warning that there was almost no housing or hotel space available and that she shouldn't get her hopes up about seeing him.

Amanda watched as every morning and afternoon Helen ran in to scan the day's mail, as every evening her eyes strayed to the silent telephone. And, nightly after dinner, she took a large brandy.

"To help me get to sleep," she said.

"Don't become dependent on that, darling," Amanda warned. "It won't solve anything."

"Perhaps not, but it helps."

"Concentrating on your job, on your friends and your life, would help a good deal more."

"I'm going up," she said, dizzy from the brandy. "I haven't finished storing his things."

"One way or another, you know, Helen, morning always rolls around."

"I know," she said, standing at the foot of the stairs. "That's what scares the hell out of me, Mother. All those mornings."

Stu wrote several times in the next weeks, saying how lonely he was for her, that everything was being stepped up even more—leaves had been canceled and all personnel restricted to base. It was impossible for them to meet.

Five weeks and three days after he'd left, he telephoned.

"They're shipping us out," he shouted over tremendous background noise. "I don't know where we're going. They haven't even told the officers."

"Are you all right?" she asked, unable to think of everything she wanted to say.

"Fine. Are you?"

"Fine. Good."

"Listen, darling, I've got to go. There's a line a block long for this telephone."

"I love you!" she cried, feeling him being ripped away from her. "Come home soon. I'll be waiting for you."

"I love you too!" he shouted and was gone.

She stood holding the telephone, wanting more, needing to hear his voice. After several seconds she put the phone down and stared at it, seeing it blur, wondering where he was being sent.

"He's going," she said hoarsely. "They're sending him away."

"Hold on, darling," Amanda said. "I know it's difficult."

"Come for a walk with me, would you?"

"I could do with some fresh air. Get your coat, and I'll join you in a minute. I have to do something I forgot to do earlier."

She hurried back to her bedroom and called Charlie.

"Barnstorm, I need a favor," she said when he came on the line. "Come meet us in the park and do some cheering up for Helen."

"They shipped him out, eh?"

"Exactly. Can I count on you?"

"Can't you always?"

"Don't let on that I called, will you?"

"I'll accidentally run into you down by the pond."

"Bless you, Charlie." She hung up and went to get her hat and coat.

Helen was subdued as they headed toward the park. When she first caught sight of Charlie and Fraser standing by the pond, she tugged at Amanda's sleeve, saying, "Isn't that Fraser with Uncle Charlie?"

"Where?"

"Over there, by the pond."

"Looks like them, doesn't it?"

"I didn't know they were seeing each other." She smiled. "Don't they look good together?"

"As a matter of fact," Amanda said, "they do."

"Let's go say hello. Is it possible they're having an affair?" she wondered aloud.

"Do them both a world of good if they are." Amanda laughed.

"Wouldn't it be lovely if they fell for each other?"

"I never guessed you had an inclination toward matchmaking, Helen."

"Oh, I haven't"—she smiled—"but they're both such lonely souls."

Fraser and Charlie played it well, jumping away from each other with a shade more realism than was absolutely necessary, greeting them effusively.

"Just out for a healthy constitutional." Charlie laughed, hugging Helen and nodding his head with feigned lordly dignity at Amanda. "And here we all are! The fortunes of fate!"

Fraser, looking girlish and rosy, actually giggled. "He's promised me dinner. Have you two eaten yet?"

Helen and Amanda looked at each other. "No," Amanda said. "Why not be a good scout and feed the women, Charlie?"

"Happily, madame, you do more smoking and talking than eating, else I might back off."

"Someday, Charlie, I'll deal you the ultimate blow and actually let you exhibit my work. After a couple of weeks you'll sit up and beg, I assure you."

"You two are crazy," Helen declared, amused as always at their never-ending volley of steaming insults.

"They've asked us to replace the Jack Benny show." He spread his arms in a herding gesture. "Come on, women! Uncle Charlie will buy you each a bowl of chili, or anything else under a dollar on the menu."

During the meal they observed the playful but delicate banter between Fraser and Barnstorm.

"I believe the old man's actually smitten," Amanda whispered.

"He's not that old, Mother."

"Actually, Charlie's about forty, give or take a year or two. Possibly even less. It's just that I've known him forever."

"Fraser's only twenty-eight."

"She looks older and younger. Hard to read."

"Stop that whispering!" Charlie said, summoning the waiter to order coffee and liqueurs. "This is no bloody hen-party at my expense. Pay proper respect to the host of this fiasco, or I'll run along home to my lonely trundle bed. Kindly remember, ladies, who is footing the bill for your unseemly demonstration of appetite," Charlie continued.

Fraser set down her cup and smiled across at Helen. "Come to the ladies' room with me," she said. "Keep me company."

Fraser sat down in front of the mirror and started powdering her nose. "You're curious, I can tell," she said.

"I admit it."

Fraser looked at Helen in the mirror as she applied her lipstick, then closed her bag with a loud snap and swiveled around.

"It's exactly what it looks like," she said. "Or what I imagine it looks like."

"Well," Helen said, nonplused, "that's wonderful."

"It won't last. It never does."

"Why do you say that?"

"Because it isn't anything really. Just two blind people staggering along the road together trying not to bump into the walls and telephone poles. We'll wind up friends, eventually. Neither of us has the right sort of glue, if you see what I mean."

"I'm not sure that I do."

"We don't stick, Helen. Our minds are elsewhere. It's merely a pleasant collision."

"My God, you have a low opinion of yourself, Fraser."

"Not at all. A highly realistic one, I'd say. I don't like men, or people for that matter, the way you do, for example. I'm too aware, I think, of my own separateness. I love well from a distance. Would you like to come have dinner with me one night next week, see my house?"

"Yes, all right," she said, her mind still working over Fraser's remarks. "Let me know when."

She went to dinner the next Thursday. The house was small and neat, filled with books on astrology. The garden Fraser spoke of so often was a tiny patch about ten feet square, situated tightly between her house and the adjoining one. Even though it was winter, Helen, looking at the carefully laid-out beds, could see that the garden was as precise and tidy as the little house, as Fraser herself.

She cooked passably well, offering Helen an overdone steak and underdressed salad, both of which she ate despite her lack of real appetite. Over coffee Helen asked why she'd never done the chart she'd promised.

"Good grief!" Fraser said, attempting to look forgetful. "I completely forgot. I promise, I'll get around to it one of these days."

"Why are you lying, Fraser?"

Knowing she was caught out, Fraser said, "I did do it, of course. But I made a mistake somewhere. I can't figure it out. It didn't come out right at all."

"Why didn't you simply tell me that? I'd have understood."

"I don't know. I suppose I didn't want to admit defeat. Nothing more, honestly."

If she hadn't added those last three words, Helen would have let the matter drop. But that extra bit of alibi persuaded her Fraser was still lying.

"You discovered something unpleasant, didn't you? That's it, isn't it?"

"No, no," she said. "People really don't believe in the stars, Helen."

"It was about Stu, wasn't it? He's not coming back."

"It was nothing like that. Nothing like that."

"I can't believe a thing you say now, Fraser. I can't tell when you're lying and when you're not."

She went over to her desk. "It's right here somewhere." She riffled through several sheets of paper. "Here it is."

"Let me see that!" Helen said, reaching for the page.

"No, I can't!" she said, knowing she'd made an error.

"Fraser, show it to me!"

She tore the page to shreds and then, before Helen could stop her, threw them into the fire.

"Why did you do that?" Helen asked, watching the paper catch and burn.

"I had to."

"Let's forget the whole thing. I can't imagine why I brought the subject up in the first place."

"Oh, the stars don't lie, Helen."

"Perhaps the stars don't. But you do, Fraser. I really had better go now. Thank you for dinner."

"You're not angry with me?"

"No, I'm not angry. Just tired. I'll see you Monday at school."

School was an oasis. She fled there each morning, armed
with enthusiasm and the beginnings of some new ideas
about teaching that served as a shield against the temptation to take to her bed and not get up again until the war
was over and Stu had come home. The responsibility she
felt she owed the children propelled her forward at the
start of each day, kept her moving until she was safely
behind the wheel of the car and on her way to the first
class of the morning.

The knowledge that the Board would let her go at the
end of her contract if they learned of her marriage outraged and infuriated her. She made up her mind to be the
best damned teacher that school would ever have, and
determined to arouse her classes' interest in the French
language. Believing the best way to accomplish that
would be to give them some feeling of the people, the
country, and its traditions, even its food, she began veer-
ing off from the established curriculum.

She brought in her own books, using time slots allo-
cated to grammar and vocabulary to read them the poetry
of Baudelaire, excerpts from novels by Colette (whose
writings she adored), Verlaine, Victor Hugo—all her
favorite French authors. She encouraged them to find writ-

ers they admired, to bring pieces to class to read aloud, and applauded their efforts when they did. She purchased a pot of herbs from Provence, which was passed around with her instruction to take in the aroma. She sat with her shoes off and one foot tucked under, enjoying the response to this experiment, then read them several appetizing recipes for Provençal dishes. The kids began trying to outdo each other in bringing articles of French origin to show to her and their classmates.

The principal, a man who prided himself on the quality of his staff as well as the broad scope of his personal views on progressive education, sat in on several of her unorthodox classes, impressed by the results she was getting. His interim report on her was filled with praise, and a recommendation that her contract be renewed.

Fraser complimented her on her success. "You're so inspired! I'd never have thought to do any of the things you've done."

"All part of beating the system." Helen laughed. "You're the one who gave me the idea in the first place."

Heartened by her success, she showed her students pieces of Alençon lace, gave them thimblesips of wine at Easter, telling them more and more about France, the people, their customs, and their legendary heroes. The children loved it all, loved her, showered her with gifts, and, best of all, walked off with the highest overall grade-nine class average in the school.

The school year ended. After mulling over the idea for months, Amanda decided to have the cottage winterized and add a small, new wing.

She found a local man to install the furnace, and she and Helen drove up the first Sunday in June to finalize plans for the new wing and see what else needed doing.

While Amanda was busy with Jake, the contractor—a jovial giant of a man with a rugged smiling face and a speaking voice that evoked distant thunder—Helen wandered through the cottage, stopping in the living room to notice the two pairs of boots standing beside the fireplace. Stu had been gone four months. It seemed forever.

His letters came, sometimes after a month of silence,

in twos and threes. Written days, weeks apart, they were consistently hopeful, amusing, and crammed with love. She wrote lengthy answers, then sat back to wait— always fearful the doorbell would ring and there'd be a telegram she was terrified of receiving—as more weeks went by. She read and reread the letters, trying to sustain herself on his outpourings of love and thoughts about their future. She tried to think of how surprised Stu would be when he saw the cottage with its new wing.

"We'll have the wall fronting the beach done entirely of glass," Amanda said, pacing out the dimensions while Jake took notes. "And the bathroom should have an outside door, so one can come directly in from the beach. No more pans of water, Helen."

"It sounds lovely," she said absently.

Amanda and Jake went off to talk money. Helen stepped out the back door, intending to go down to the beach, then changed her mind and went into the kitchen, watching her mother and Jake going over a list of figures. The deep drone of his voice was hypnotically soothing.

After he'd gone, Amanda sat smoking a cigarette.

"It won't be too expensive," she said, studying the totals. "This property's bound to increase in value after the war. It's a sensible investment."

She patted Helen's hand encouragingly. "I know, Helen," she said. "I do know."

"Mother, if I talk about how I feel, I'll go to pieces. I've never been a stoic. Are you ready to go back now?"

"I think so. You drive, dear. My hands are acting up today."

"I'll rub them for you," she said, taking her mother's hand. "They're so swollen. Do they hurt?"

"Oh, not badly." She smiled.

"It doesn't seem fair," Helen said, kneading the joints expertly, "getting arthritis in your hands."

"Better than in my feet." Amanda laughed and exhaled twin streams of smoke. "At least I can still stand up."

Helen looked up. "If you can laugh," she said, "I damned well can too!"

Amanda gave no classes that summer. Most mornings

Helen drove her to the marina or some picturesque spot in the vicinity, then picked her up again at midday. They'd have lunch; then Amanda would go to her room for a nap while Helen checked on the contractor's progress, interrupting him and his helper with cold beer and sandwiches. Jake was always laughing; the sound of his voice made Helen think of rich, dark chocolate. It was delicious, satisfying. She missed him when he and his helper finally loaded their equipment into the truck and said good-bye.

She wrote dozens of letters to Stu, racing to the post office in town every morning after dropping Amanda off, sliding her hand around inside the empty box, disappointment welling up inside her. Jennie Gilroy, having long ago given up hoping to have a career as a painter, had taken over as the town postmistress. She commiserated with Helen over the lack of letters. Her husband was also overseas.

Almost three months passed with no word from Stu. Then, their last week at the cottage, four letters came.

He'd had been gone for so long. She'd slept alone for almost a year, stayed alone, hadn't even considered going out for dinner with another man—although Jake had asked her, not realizing she was married. His profuse apologies and embarrassment had moved her, and she wondered if she shouldn't have accepted his invitation.

She was becoming inured to Stu's absence. Waiting was the major part of the routine which had evolved. The mixed-up groups of letters arriving in twos and threes were part too. Masturbating was routine. So were sleepless nights. And still, still, she believed he'd come back.

She moved into the new wing of the cottage the following summer, allowing her anticipation for the coming school year to carry her through as she planned new inroads to language for her prospective classes. It shocked her to realize she was projecting herself into a future alone. It was 1943, and there was no sign the war was anywhere near being over. She studied the newspapers, trying to determine how and when it would end.

She couldn't go on forever faking her way through

each day, telling herself he was coming back. His letters warmed her, enabling her to tolerate the sensation of emptiness inside. But they were only letters, and always months late. And she kept thinking, if only they'd been able to have a child—even an adopted one—that, at least, would have been something real to keep him alive for her. But there was nothing. Just letters and photographs and an ominous premonition never far from the edge of her consciousness. That unthinkable, intuitive premonition that laughed in the face of her dreams, cautioning her to beware of optimism. She had nightmares in which her fear took shape and silently strangled her at the edge of a precipice before dropping her over the side.

Fraser and Charlie came up to spend a weekend, bringing domestic champagne and a tide of caustic and clever dialogue. She and Fraser walked the beach, shielding their eyes from the sun.

"How are you two 'glueless' types getting along?" Helen asked.

"Amazingly enough," Fraser said, "we actually are getting along. I don't quite know how it happened. But we seem to be enjoying each other more and more. Maybe I'm getting too old to fight."

"You're only six years older than me," Helen argued.

"Inside," she said, gazing at Helen with a suddenly inscrutable expression. "Inside is old."

Days kept going by. *Maybe I'm deceiving people,* Helen thought, *and maybe I'm not.* But internally she felt dried up, dusty, decayed with disuse. She thought of Stu and found she couldn't remember what he looked like. It panicked her. She stared at his photographs, trying to find him in the black-and-white mirages.

For hours every afternoon she lay nude on the sand near the house, baking herself into a state of drowsy lassitude. Amanda kept people away from the cottage while she was on the beach, unwilling to disturb her. Helen was becoming increasingly uncommunicative and vague, and Amanda had a recurring vision of Helen going off to close herself into some private chamber where no one else had access. It was best to leave her alone. From her vantage point she watched over her daughter, wishing there were some way to spare her the self-inflicted agonies of her loneliness and fear.

Helen spent more and more time on the beach, lazily scooping up handfuls of sand, letting it slide through her fingers, gazing at the ashy residue left on her fingers and the millions of shimmering gold sun-dots she could see on her arms. She started sleeping on the beach during the hottest afternoon hours, letting the sun burn into her face, hoping it would burn right to her brain and destroy the seeds of her nightmares.

Somehow she managed to get through the summer.

Fraser greeted her heartily the first morning of school in the teachers' lounge, saying, "How tanned you are! You look lovelier than ever."

"I'm still waiting for my chart, Fraser. I thought you were going to do it over and prove to me you were telling the truth about Stu."

"Oh, yes. Well, I didn't do it after all," she said, that unreadable expression overtaking her features again. "So much to do, what with the garden and the cat having kittens and Charlie demanding home-cooked meals and other favors. I'll get around to it soon."

"You seemed so anxious to do it."

"Have you seen the classroom assignments yet?" Fraser asked, walking over to the bulletin board.

Helen passed it off as another of Fraser's eccentricities and started getting organized for her first class.

She assuaged her discontent by studying the faces of the children in her classes, loving the fresh-scrubbed look of them.

There had been no word from Stu since June. When school closed for Christmas, she began to fear the worst, her dreams assuming such bizarre proprotions that she usually slept only two or three hours a night.

Amanda tried to cheer her up. "You've gone months before. You're bound to hear any day now."

"Never this long."

"He might be somewhere it's impossible to mail a letter. Had you thought of that, darling? Try to be patient a bit longer."

"I'm slowly running out of patience. And everything else. This is never going to end."

"It will. You have my personal promise that it will."

"Your personal promise." Helen laughed sardonically. "I wish to God that were really so."

"You look so tired, Helen. Why don't you go up and try to take a nap?"

"I can't sleep. I'll be all right," she muttered, wandering away.

A letter came the next day, postmarked the second of December. She could hardly believe it. He missed her more than ever and was pining for Mary's cooking.

"He's fine," she cried, throwing her arms around Amanda.

"I told you you'd hear from him."

"Thank you for putting up with all my moans and groans, Mama. God, I love you."

"Go back to bed and try to get some more sleep, darling. I'll have Mary bring your breakfast up a little later."

"Yes, all right. Maybe I will. I'm so relieved, I think I might just sleep."

She unearthed one of Stu's old shirts and, along with a pair of tattered shorts she'd had for at least ten years, wore it daily that next summer at the cottage. She resumed her sunning sessions by the house, having found it the only successful means of keeping herself in one piece emotionally. She could sleep in the sun, although she rarely was able to sleep in bed.

The war ended. They heard the news, listening with held breath, each thinking Stu would finally be coming home. And yet to Helen it seemed as if nothing had changed. The endless waiting continued, as did the groping in the mailbox for letters, which had stopped coming altogether after that one in December.

June ended. July came and went. In the hot afternoons, while Mary and Amanda napped in their rooms, finding the sun too hot for them, Helen slept outside, giving up her mind and body to the numbing, anesthetic heat.

The second week in August Amanda, unable to settle in the sweltering airlessness of the cottage, couldn't sleep. Picking up her paper parasol, she went to sit on the steps at the front of the house, hoping to feel some slight breeze.

The heat was rising in curling waves from the tarred road, distorting what she thought she was seeing. But as the figure moved closer into her range, she was able to distinguish Jennie Gilroy on her bicycle, and she watched her gradually grow larger in the haze. It seemed she sat for hours watching the figure come closer and closer, until she was at last able to make out Jennie's features. She knew, from the downcast determination of her movements, the purpose of her pedaling all the way out from town in such sickening heat. Jennie laid her bicycle down in the shade of the big oak and came toward Amanda.

"Sit down, Jennie. You must be exhausted. It's a long ride from town."

Jennie nodded and sat on the steps, gasping for air, perspiration trickling down her temples.

"Would you like something to drink, something to cool you off?"

"No, thank you," she breathed, wafting her hand back and forth in front of her face in a futile effort to create a draft. "I wanted to come myself," she said, "instead of sending Junior. He usually delivers the telegrams. But when this one came through . . . Well, I wanted to bring it myself." She handed the War Department envelope to Amanda, meeting her eyes for the first time. "I know this probably doesn't mean much to you, but I'm truly sorry. I've always admired you and Helen so much." She got up and walked back to pick up her bicycle. "Mine came last week," she said, blinking into the sun. "It still hasn't hit me. I think this hit me harder, because it wasn't me. Does that sound right?"

"Yes, it does," Amanda said quietly.

"Tell her if she wants to talk it out, I'd like to help."

"That's very kind of you, Jennie. I'm sorry . . ."

"I know," she said, aligning the pedals, "we're all sorry."

She climbed onto the bike and pedaled away. Amanda

sat until Jennie was swallowed up by the distance. She looked at the envelope in her lap and had an impulse to tear it into a thousand pieces. *It wouldn't change anything,* she told herself, getting to her feet. An envelope containing a piece of paper. Some words. And a life was ended.

She walked through the house, feeling old and tired and sick at heart. She went into the new wing and opened the door, stepping out into the blinding sun. Helen was lying on her back, asleep. Amanda stood looking down at her for several minutes, wondering how fate could deliver yet another blow to someone who deserved it so little. She bent to put her hand lightly on Helen's cheek, whispering, "Helen," in a voice that didn't sound like her own.

She was dreaming, flying, and from a great distance she could hear her mother's voice. She soared down, her arms wonderfully effective in manipulating the weightless arrow of her body. She shivered, thinking a shadow must have gone over the sun. Then she heard it again, whispering her name. And she opened her eyes, sightless because of the sun's glare, trying to focus on the shadow leaning over her. *It's part of the dream,* she thought, confused by the darkness that moved closer.

"Helen," Amanda said again.

And then her eyes returned and she was able to see Amanda's face and the envelope in her hand.

"Jennie Gilroy just delivered this for you."

"I've been waiting for it."

"Would you like me to stay with you?"

"Please. I'll put on my shirt and we'll go inside and open it together." She picked up Stu's shirt and pulled it on, woodenly fastening the buttons. "Don't leave me," she said, her eyes huge. "You won't, will you?"

"No, darling, I won't."

They went into the kitchen and sat down at the table. Helen slit open the envelope with a bread knife and extracted the telegram. She read it slowly, then closed her eyes and pushed it across the table. To Amanda it seemed the cruelest way conceivable to announce that someone beloved, someone cherished, had been killed in a freak accident and was never coming back. She dropped the telegram on the table as if she'd touched something venomous.

"I'll be back in a minute or two," Helen said, getting up and walking out, down to the beach. There was a lot of debris on the sand, thrown up by the incoming tide after a storm at sea. *It will have to be cleared away*, she thought, kicking at a tangled clump of seaweed. She sat down on the damp sand, then got up again and walked along the water's edge, her feet gradually becoming accustomed to the cold water.

Being alive, being there on the beach, was part of the dream. She covered her eyes with her hands and peeked through her fingers at the seagulls wheeling overhead, screaming and swooping. They made a terrible sound—a sound like mourning—and she flew back to the cottage, unwilling to listen to their cries.

Amanda was sitting at the table, smoking a cigarette, waiting.

"Have you ever listened to those seagulls?" Helen said, sitting down to wipe the sand off her feet. "They sound like death."

"Oh?"

"They sound like widows wailing at a funeral, watching a coffin being lowered into the ground. I wish it was me," she said, letting her head loll back. "I wish somebody was putting me in the ground. I can almost hear the dirt falling over me." She closed her eyes, and Amanda thought her heart was literally breaking; she could feel the drag of it.

"There's a lot of garbage on the beach," Helen went on, her eyes still closed. "A ton of driftwood and broken glass. Bodies. The remains of people in love. Dead babies. It never ends," she said, her voice taking on a singsong quality. "It all goes on and on, and we knit scarves and roll bandages and say good-bye to dead men and smile and kiss them, let them touch us because they're dead after all and what does it matter. Children. Little boys with lingering hands going off with guns and grenades and bayonets to kill people. Not even old enough to vote, but they can kill. Dead babies walking around with a hundred pounds of equipment strapped to their backs, all trained and primed to kill. And an ambulance drives over a mine."

"Helen, stop!"

"Stu was no little boy," she said, oblivious to her mother. "He was a grown man. On his way home. Killed by a booby trap somebody forgot to dig up. We really must do something about the beach. It's a disgrace. People will think we're awful housekeepers if we don't clean it up. Why do those birds sound that way?" She opened her eyes.

"Helen, please, darling. Don't do this to yourself."

"Why? Why do they make that terrible sound? You know what I think, Mama? I think they're the souls of all those dead babies coming back to haunt us, screaming over our heads, darting down at us. They want our souls, you know," she said, her eyes glazed. "One ·afternoon we'll be out there and they'll dive down and lift the souls right out of our bodies, just rip them away, then go screaming off into the sky in search of others. What are we going to do about the beach?" Tears were pouring down her face. "We've got to do something about it."

She reached across the table, clutching Amanda's hands. "I'm falling to pieces, Mama. Everything's crumbling inside me. I can't think. I don't know what I'm doing. I want to die too."

"Don't, Helen! Please! Dying can't bring him back."

"I can't help it. My mind's crumbling. I *feel* as if I'm dying. Why can't it all be over? Why couldn't I go into the bedroom and lie down, close my eyes, and die? Why isn't it that simple? I don't want to go on without him. God, Stu!" She sobbed, choking. "*Stu!*" she called, standing up, knocking over her chair, "*Stu! It's over!*" she screamed. "*It's time to come home now, Stu!*" She heard the sound of her voice and stood, letting her arms drop, her eyes closed.

Amanda went to her, took her in her arms, and held her as Helen wept, asking "Why?" over and over, "Why?"

"I don't know, darling. I'll never know, any more than you will."

"I don't know why he died or where or what he did to deserve it."

"Perhaps it's best not to know."

"I can't even bury him!" she cried, breaking away, wiping her face on her shirt sleeve. "The goddamned Army gets to keep even his corpse. *God damn it!*"

Amanda was grateful to see the anger. She stood, hoping for more.

"I knew he'd die," Helen said bitterly, "I knew it. Why the hell did he have to die? God, I want to smash things!"

"Go ahead! Go on! Here!" Amanda said, reaching into the cupboard. "I've always hated these dishes. Do us both a favor and smash them to smithereens."

Helen looked at her for a moment, then picked up a plate and, receiving an approving nod from her mother, hurled it against the wall. Amanda handed her another, and with a shout of rage Helen sent it sailing through the top half of the kitchen window, shattering both the plate and the window. Amanda backed away and stood by the door until the last plate was broken and Helen was standing, sobbing, surrounded by bits of glass and china, her hands twitching at her sides.

"That helped," Helen said, looking the mess over. "That helped a lot. I'm going to get dressed now and go out for a drive."

"Do you think that's wise?"

Helen came across the room, picking her way over the broken dishes, to put her arms around Amanda.

"I love you, Mother. But I'm all right now. I'm not going to do anything foolish. I have to sort myself out. If I don't come back until late, don't worry. You have my word I won't harm myself. He made me promise before he left that I wouldn't do anything like that. If that promise doesn't mean anything, then all of it—the loving, the marriage—means nothing. And I have to believe in it. I want to go somewhere quiet and try to remember him for a while all by myself before everyone comes rushing to tell me how sorry they are."

"I understand."

"Don't wait up. I promise I'll come back."

She didn't drive far, just four miles down the highway to the roadhouse. She hadn't intended to stop, but the winking neon sign drew her eye and she pulled into the gravel lot and sat staring at the beer ads in the windows before climbing out and going inside. It was much cooler in the bar, where an overhead fan stirred the air. She sat in a booth near the window and ordered a double brandy, then drank it while she stared at her rings, twisting them around and around on her finger.

She was on her third double when a deep voice said, "Mind if I join you?" She looked up and saw Jake and said, "Help yourself."

"Nobody should drink alone," he said, beckoning to the barmaid. "Another drink for Miss Helen, and I'll have a double Scotch on the rocks."

The drinks came, and Helen looked at him.

"Tell me about you, Jake," she said, trying to smile. "Who the hell are you, anyway?"

He laughed and dipped his finger in the Scotch, submerging an ice cube. "News spreads fast in a town this size," he said, lifting his drink. "I had a feeling you might be out and about. It's no time to be alone. I know."

"Oh, do you?"

"Mmm, yes," he said, cradling the glass in his huge hands. "My wife died eight years ago. We'd been married eleven years. Happy. One night she complained she didn't feel well. Twenty minutes later she was dead. Heart attack. Thirty-six years old. I wanted to destroy the world, the universe. Kill everybody and everything, including myself. People, friends came around, wouldn't leave me on my own. And they were right, too. Got me over the worst of it, the rotten not-believing part of it.

"After a time, I sold out my business. Pretty good company I had. But I felt as if I was smothering in the city, couldn't get enough air into my lungs. So I scouted around and finally settled here. It's a good place."

"Do you have children?"

"One boy, married. I have a grandson. Gave me a funny kind of feeling, being a grandfather. I kept saying,

163

'I'm too young to be a grandfather.' But I guess age hasn't a thing to do with it."

"How old are you?"

"Old." He laughed. "Forty-seven."

"Not old." She shook her head. "Old is dead."

"You haven't eaten."

"No. And I don't plan to. I plan to sit here and get stinking and then quietly go to sleep somewhere."

"No, I think we'll have a little something to eat."

She shrugged her shoulders and started on the drink he'd bought her.

"You're a nice man," she said. "You really are. I like your voice. I feel a little dizzy."

"You'll feel a lot better when you've eaten. Trust me. I know about the grief."

"I'd like to sock you right on the jaw for saying you do."

"You can do that if it'll help."

"I smashed all my mother's dishes." She laughed, sliding into drunken hilarity. "She let me. Why the hell is everybody being so damned nice to me? I want to be mad."

"Get decently drunk for now," he said. "You'll have years and years to be angry."

"That's *exactly* why I'm so mad."

Things started getting very mixed up once the food arrived. Jake pushed food in front of her, and she ate a hamburger and some french fries. Then she started drinking again while she watched him eat.

"Take me home with you," she said, feeling the sorrow welling up again. "Would you? You're an awfully decent man. Would you be decent to me?"

His eyes were misted and sad and understanding, and she cried when he took her hand and said, "I'll take care of you, Miss Helen."

"Why do you call me that?"

"Because it's respectful and because you're young and grieving and I know that awful pain. We're old friends, the pain and me."

She drank a lot more, and at some point in the evening

he came around to her side of the booth and cradled her against his massive chest while she cried and drank and hit him with her fists and then drank and cried some more.

And then they were out on the road, walking.

"To my house," he explained, "just over there. See?"

She looked, but all she could see was an indistinct white shape across the road. He wasn't drunk, she realized in a moment of lucidity as she staggered along the road with him supporting her. He was taking care of her.

And then she was undressed and in his bed and he was kissing her, stroking her, easing the pain, murmuring sweet-sounding things against her throat and breasts, letting his giant body protect her from the grief for a short while, fitting himself tenderly inside her, telling her to let it all go away from her, telling her she was young and beautiful, with her whole life in front of her. But the words didn't prove it quite so much as his body did. His body brought her back, reminded her of her own self, and she held on hard to his smooth, muscular form, held on hard to the driving flesh that brought her peace and pleasure.

It was very late when she awakened. She stared at her watch, trying to see in the dark. After three. Knowing words weren't needed, she slipped into her clothes and left the house, making her way back across the road to her car. She was still a little drunk, and drove faster than she should have, missing the turnoff to the cottage. The car skidded and hit a tree at the left side of the road. She was thrown against the door, and sat for several minutes, her heart pounding, waiting for her panic to ebb. She rolled down the window, trying to determine the damage to the car. It was slight, just a bad dent in the door. As she straightened around she winced, feeling a spreading pain in her left hip. She ignored it, put the car in reverse, and easily pulled away.

Walking up the front steps made her hip ache badly, but she paid no attention to it, glad to be home, thinking only of sleep—craving sleep.

Amanda was sitting in the darkened living room, smoking.

"I'm glad you're home, darling," she said. "I'll go to bed now."

"Good night, Mother."

Every time she turned over, the pain in her hip awakened her. At six she got out of bed and limped over to look at herself in the bathroom mirror. Her mouth opened as she lifted her nightgown, seeing a huge, dark red bruise covering her hip from front to back. The sight of it scared her, since it didn't look like any bruise she'd ever seen. *If it doesn't go away in a day or two,* she promised herself, *I'll call Leon and let him have a look at it.*

It disappeared soon after, although the aching and stiffness hung on for weeks. But there was no time to think about it, because they were closing up the cottage then and returning to the city to pretend they were burying Stu.

PART THREE

GENA

10

During the next three years her moods alternated. She had bouts of depression, during the course of which she blamed Stu for everything from his death to her own inability to have children. There were nights when she abandoned all attempts at sleeping and wandered through the house searching for any improbable panacea that would eradicate the wound inside that refused to heal.

Then there were times when she found herself recalling every line of his face and body, every separate hair and pore, every word he'd ever written or spoken to her. And at those times she felt he'd given her so much that she wondered how she was able to summon up the anger she knew at those other times. He'd been so wise, she saw in retrospect. From almost the very first moment he'd known he'd be leaving, he'd taken pains to prepare her for the likelihood of his not returning. Had they both had those premonitions? She wondered. Their months together had been an intensive course in loving and letting go in order to continue on living, loving, letting go.

She came to discern a certain life pattern, a positive truth to life. That being, there was no permanence. She, like everyone else, was merely a transient—a vagrant soul gathering information and knowledge, learning lessons, before passing on to something grander, something perhaps more abiding and rewarding.

In this frame of mind, she started to gather up the ragged edges of her life, renewing her efforts at school, accepting dates, seeing friends again. But part of her knew that this era with its particular philosophy was also temporary and would pass. She knew it but still was able to comprehend the importance of going through this period, living it out until she was ready to move on to a new phase of her life that would be entirely unaffected by any residual, potentially harmful traces of her grief.

During these years she also came to understand what Fraser had meant when she talked of "collisions." Helen had many of them, accidents of need that threw her prone under the probing curiosity and desire of a number of men who offered, among other things, to love her or to marry her or to set her up in expensive surroundings that would give them continued access to her body.

She rejected them affably but cautiously. There were moments when, as she sat nursing her mind back to well-being, she tried to pinpoint what it was she'd thought she'd find in these encounters. For the most part the men were attractive and intelligent enough. But something was lacking. Some essential, significant essence was altogether absent from these attempts at communication.

She knew why Fraser called them collisions. What she hadn't yet been able to determine to her satisfaction was what exactly made them happen as they did, and what basic element was needed to elevate the incidents beyond collision status.

Amanda saw something in Helen's eyes that hadn't been there before: an expression that overtook her at rare moments, when she seemed almost melancholy, gazing off into space. An aura of distraction settled around her, encapsulating her in a transparent wrapper. It was almost possible to witness Helen's connection with this nameless thing—something she gave herself up to, although she was apparently not aware of it.

Helen went forward like someone with emotional cataracts, feeling her way along the passages and tunnels of time, sensing brighter light somewhere just beyond her present limited sight.

Each year, as another class went on, left her, and a new one came to take its place, she felt a small fear that time for her was destined to be permanently marked by the arrivals and departures of different groups of children and not by significant occasions or incidents within the framework of her own life.

Her loneliness, the longing for Stu, seemed eternal. Often she'd stare off into space, wondering how it was possible for someone to go away and simply never return. *Dead*. The reality of it was like a heavy brick she was unable to let go of. So she carried it with her, weighted down by her inability to absorb the horrifying finality of death.

Fraser had become her closest friend. She often came to visit at the house or asked Helen over for dinner. In the summers she came up to the cottage to spend a week or two or three, roaming the beach, her long, lean body like that of a sleek, prowling animal.

It was no surprise, but certainly a disappointment, when, as she'd predicted at the outset, she and Uncle Charlie broke apart and resumed their separate lives. What exhausted Helen's patience and caused her finally to blow up was Fraser's never-ending introspective attempts to analyze why the relationship had failed, especially because Helen thought her rationalizations were inaccurate.

"He refused to understand my needs," Fraser said, lying stomach-down on the sand, leaning on her elbows. "He wouldn't accept that there were people, women, I was drawn to. He talked about my selfishness, my refusal to admit to my own femaleness by trying to be both aggressive and passive at the same time. He said the ultimate goal for me would be to split myself and make love to myself. Those aren't his exact words, but you get an adequate idea. He wanted to have a child," she admitted, embarrassed. "Called me a cheat and a moral coward and said I didn't exist at all, that I was only a figment of his imagination that he'd thought he might transform into reality. The things he said and did sometimes terrified me."

"Why?" Helen asked, trying to hold down her temper.

"Because I think he wanted to trap me, make me surrender so that he could hold me down and write his name on me."

"Write his name on you?"

"You know what I mean . . ."

"He asked you to marry him?"

"Well, yes."

"And you refused."

"Yes, but—"

"And you can't see why he called you those things? Fraser, I'd like to hit you. God, you damned stupid fool! He's right. You are a cheat and a coward. He loved you. Love. The very thing you accuse him of denying you. He offered it all to you, you stupid, stupid woman! God, I want to hit you!" she said, jumping to her feet, her hands quivering with the desire to beat Fraser senseless. She couldn't ever remember having been so angry with someone, but she couldn't hold it back.

"How can you be so—so blind? Do you have any idea how lucky you are, Fraser? Do you? Once a month, regular as clockwork, you bleed. My God! Every single month of your damned, idiotic life, you have bright red confirmation of your life, absolute proof that you're all in one piece inside. I'm sure you think of it as just another tedious chore, one of the tiresome aspects of being a woman—something to contend with, just as you contended with Charlie and his weighty affections. And how do you think Charlie must feel, at his age, after living alone for so long, to care enough about you to want you to be a part of his life, even to give you a child if it's something you'd both be willing to do? And that doesn't matter, really, one way or another, having a child. But at least it's a decision you could make for yourself. You might feel quite differently if you knew there was nothing left inside, that the only decision you'd ever have to make was whether or not to give yourself—in whatever way—because the gift of caring, of loving, was *all* you had to give. It'd probably clarify all kinds of things for you! Your head's so full of wrong

172

answers to the wrong questions, I don't think you know any more why you do the things you do.

"You're spoiled, Fraser. You've taken so many things for granted for so long, you've forgotten—if you ever knew—what it means to love. You could so easily have said, Oh what the hell, what else is there anyway? and loved him back. You might just have found yourself in the process. But you're led around by the nose by your own stupid *lust*. For all the things you think other people might have and you'll never have a crack at. Envying me my face, my body. For what you *think* it is I have. And all the time, staring you right in the face, willing to give you everything, was the one person who was capable—eager, God help us!—to give you answers to all the questions you've ever asked about yourself. Fool! You're a fool! Has it ever occurred to you to pay attention to the things that are happening inside your own life and stop envying and cataloging the things you're afraid you're missing?

"Don't have babies! Nobody says you have to prove you're a woman. But stop using the fact that Charlie asked if you'd have his to hide the fact that you were just plain frightened of giving him more than your body and some superficial affection.

"You make me so tired, Fraser. If I believed the things you say, I'd lie down and die, because it would mean that everything I've lived for is just lust like yours, dozens of hopeless collisions for no worthwhile purpose. If I felt the way you do, if I even thought you believed most of the self-righteous garbage you spout, I'd prefer to die. But Stu was right. I know the difference. I can see between what's real and what isn't. I do care about people. I care about being a complete person. And I care about loving, and the willingness to enter into responsibility because of a shared loving. That's the important thing, the real thing. And I hope to have it again. I won't sit and listen to your trash, your egocentric maundering about your poor loveless, misunderstood self. You've had love in the palms of your hands and stared at it with fear, because you're right, you do love well from a distance. It's much much safer that way. At least from the distance you don't have to put any of your own self into the effort. You take no risks of being hurt or forced to grow. You can pretend you're participating when all the while what you're really doing is hiding out from the possibility that love might change you, and you don't want to be changed, Fraser. You enjoy your goddamned dual life too much to give it up to be either one thing or another! You're always waiting on the off chance that someone—male or female, it doesn't matter— might come along and be just a little more tempting, a little more appealing, than what you've already got. You *are* a coward!"

Fraser, whose face had completely drained of color, watched as Helen stormed away down the beach. She was tempted to give in to the luxury of self-pity and drown her fears in a torrent of gratifying tears. But she knew that much of what Helen had said about her was true. For several minutes she sat staring into her own soul, realizing slowly she was being given a second chance. Not with Charlie. It was too late for her with Charlie. But with Helen. And all it required was for her to get up and follow Helen, to reshape her ego in accord with the truth of her life. She didn't want to go after Helen. She wanted to dig a hole in the sand and bury herself in it. She'd just die and everyone would be very very sorry. But as she sat visualizing her own funeral, it occurred to her that the only person likely to attend the ceremony would be her own lost self. Because nobody else really cared that much. And that shocked her right out of her lethargy, set her on her feet running after Helen.

As she came to the turn of the beach, she stopped, seeing her friend sitting on the sand, staring out at the water. She gazed at Helen's profile, coming to an understanding of what it had cost her to state the reason for her childless condition. Helen was a totally private person in terms of her own self. She had never discussed herself on a physical level with Fraser, hadn't ever referred to the men Fraser knew she entertained. And now it was perfectly clear why. This understanding reduced her to tears. For Helen. Because, in telling her the condition of her very private body, she'd given Fraser an awesome gift of love: She'd given her back to herself. Not as someone divided in two directions, but as an entire person. She knew she couldn't change the habits and preferences of a lifetime. But what she could change was her own conception of herself, her understanding of why she did the things she did. And that made her weep, because she felt she had nothing to offer in return for this priceless mirroring of her soul.

She pulled herself together and went over to sit beside Helen on the sand.

"It's going to be a beautiful sunset," Helen said, her arms wrapped around her knees, her face an exquisite cameo against the sky.

"Thank you," Fraser said, directing her eyes to the horizon. "You're right, of course. I was being asinine."

"Sssh," Helen said, touching Fraser's hand. "We'll watch the sky now."

Time. Inching along, taking her past the grieving era and beyond, out the other side.

Amanda saw her correcting examination papers, writing comments on random batches.

"What are you doing, darling?"

"Some of these are so good, I just have to tell them so," she explained with glowing eyes, showing her a sample.

Amanda read it, then returned the exam, saying, "I'm not surprised these children love you. You're wonderfully considerate of their efforts."

"They're all new and untarnished, like shiny copper pennies. When they do well, I want them to know how much it pleases me."

Her eyes broke away, fastening themselves on some inner view. Her need—whatever it was—was almost palpable as it dropped invisibly into place over her.

"You'd be wretched without those children, wouldn't you? They're like flowers you have to water once a day or they'll wilt on you."

"I have no idea what you're talking about." Helen smiled.

"Nor have I, in any specific sense. It's just that there's something tied up in those children and that school and your motherly instincts. I'll know it when I see it."

"Sometimes I think you're too omniscient for my comfort. But I love you—for everything."

"And I you. For everything. Something's going to happen," Amanda said, her fingers light on Helen's hair. "It's coming. A time of change."

Before Helen could question this prophetic insight, Amanda bent and kissed her forehead and swept away, as buoyantly as a specter.

Fraser was more engrossed than ever in her astrological charts, and had been asked to give a guest lecture at the university. They went along, and were pleased to see that Fraser not only carried the whole thing off with impressive dignity, but was also a persuasive and literate speaker. They hurried to congratulate her afterward, and Fraser's only response was "I've learned it's not difficult to be convincing about something one believes in."

The first week of school in September of 1949, Helen's eyes were caught and snared by a pair of blue, almost violet eyes that searched her face. Helen glanced away, unable to meet that plaintive scrutiny. She proceeded with the roll call, aware she was reacting very peculiarly to this child's presence in the room. After all the years of looking without realizing she'd been actively searching for someone, seeing this child in the center of the class made her ponder what it was about this girl that was responsible for the giddy, stomach-tightening reaction she aroused.

Gena McLaren was delicately beautiful, with long, gleaming black hair, skin so pale it seemed transparent, and those haunting violet eyes. Helen found herself, in the following days, looking again and again at that face, at the tall, nervously thin body that seemed capable of swift flight at any moment.

It was a surprise, then, and a delight to discover that Gena had not only a quick and incisive intelligence, but also a gay, yet somehow frightening, sense of whimsy. This wasn't displayed in words so much as in actions. Helen's first introduction to the lighter side of the girl came near the end of September, when she found Gena closing the door of her car, looking guilty.

"Well, hello," Helen said, stopping short at the sight of Gena with her hand still on the door.

"Oh!" Gena's face broke into a bewildered half smile. "It was going to be a surprise."

"In that case, disappear and I'll be surprised."

Her eyes seemed to change color, become deeper, darker as she said, "I *knew* you'd be this way," and with her smile fully formed now, she ran off with her skirt rippling around her legs and her laughter trailing behind like the end of an interrupted dream.

Puzzled, Helen got into the car, to find a nosegay of violets tied to the steering wheel with a green ribbon. The sight of those flowers and the knowledge of who'd put them there gave her a thrill of pleasure the likes of which she'd never experienced. It was so fitting, such an exquisitely lovely gesture for the girl to have made, that she sat still for a long while, breathing in the scent of the flowers, before starting the car and heading home.

That was the beginning. After that, at the most unanticipated times, she'd find something or other that only Gena could have left for her. Never a note or an explanation. But then, none was needed, because the very absence of a signature to the gifts made them even more welcome.

There was the polished, perfect apple on the corner of her desk one Monday morning; then, just before Hallowe'en, a rough but cleverly drawn likeness of Helen riding sidesaddle on a broom. In November, a small box containing a polished pebble. And, following that, an envelope with a perfectly preserved pressed and dried rose. And, like a strange ghost from the past, a ring from a box of Cracker Jack attached to the car by a large pink satin bow.

Coupled with these gifts came a more complete viewing of that other, darker side of Gena. Helen became accustomed to seeing the girl simply tune out, staring unseeingly at her notebooks or doodling in the margins of her textbooks. At those times her face seemed on the verge of disintegration, transformed by grief.

They rarely spoke. Upon occasion, as she was returning from lunch alone, Fraser being on cafeteria duty or otherwise occupied, she'd turn to see Gena walking a short way behind her like a shadow, following her footsteps back to the school. Helen never stopped to wait for the girl to catch up. In her own time, Gena would impart her reasons for the game.

On a Saturday morning in early December Amanda said, "It's the oddest thing, Helen. A girl telephoned me yesterday afternoon and asked if she could model for me. She said she'd come around, and if I found her suitable she'd be contented to pose without payment in return for the opportunity of being part of my work."

"What did you say?"

"Naturally, I was intrigued, so I told her to come. She must have been very close by when she called, because she was here in minutes."

"And?"

"Come see for yourself," she said, leading Helen back to the studio. "She's like a summer-day apparition, something you see at the sun's peak when you can't be sure the light isn't playing tricks with your eyes. A rarely beautiful creature in an anguishing stage of transition."

"My God!" Helen said, studying the sketches her mother had made. "It's Gena!"

"You know her?"

"She's one of my students. Why on earth is she doing this?"

"Perhaps it's as she said. She seemed to understand just what was required, posed as if she'd never done anything else. I must confess, I found her tremendously charismatic. She offered—and looked terrified that I'd accept—to pose nude, and was so relieved when I said perhaps some other time that I actually began to wonder if someone wasn't hoaxing me. I even thought that fool Barnstorm might have sent her as some sort of practical joke. But he assured me he hadn't. And now we find she's one of your girls."

"Don't say it that way!" Helen said, studying the sketches. "You make it sound . . . I don't know. She's done a number of things . . . leaving flowers in my car, gifts. Do you remember, once upon a time, for a joke Stu gave me a ring from a Cracker Jack box?"

"Vaguely."

"She left a similar ring tied to the aerial of my car with a pink ribbon."

"Perhaps," Amanda said, stacking the drawings, "she's trying to tell you something about herself, darling."

"I know that. But what?"

"You'll just have to wait and see. I'm positive she'll be back. She scarcely said two words the whole time she was here. But her eyes seemed very pleased, very . . . elated? Yes, elated. She liked being here."

"Gena McLaren," Helen said with a toss of her head. "It's a mystery."

"I don't think for long. I'll tell you one thing, Helen. She's the loneliest child I've ever encountered. You could almost wrap her up in it, it's that real."

"Don't say that, Mother. It hurts."

"It does," she said, with a small, sympathetic smile, "doesn't it."

11

Helen too now felt the stirrings of imminent change. And she knew it would come borne by Gena's inevitable return to her home.

After Gena's brief appearance as a volunteer model, it seemed she no longer needed to leave little offerings. They stopped. Initially, Helen continued to expect them, believing that these gifts, which for the most part had been of earthly rather than financial value, indicated a wish to imply that Gena's desires had to do with intangibles such as only nature can provide. But with the cessation of the gift giving began two weeks of richly declarative visual communication. Gena's eyes were always on her. And the knowledge that she was being watched, researched in a way, failed to bother Helen. In fact, she was happy to fulfill her expected role in this eye-to-eye examination of her exterior self, in return for the pleasure it gave her to be able, just as freely, to contemplate Gena.

According to her severely abbreviated school history— Helen wondered at the terse nature of the information contained on the card—Gena's parent was one Norman McLaren. They lived in the fashionable older part of the city known as Remington Park, and Gena was almost fourteen. She had come to the school from an unnamed private school in California. Her grades at that school were not given. *And*—Helen read this several times, to be sure it wasn't a misprint—her IQ was listed as 184.

She returned the card to the office, trying to form a mental picture from the facts she'd gleaned, but she couldn't. All she could see, daily, first thing every morning, was that pale, comely face set like an exotic wildflower in the midst of a field of well-tended geraniums.

There were moments when, for no reason, she found herself smiling and receiving, in return, a beatifically radiant smile from Gena. *What we're saying to each other, God only knows*, Helen thought, deeply moved by that beaming face and its growing importance to her life.

"Are you aware," Fraser asked one lunch hour, "that we are being followed?"

"I am aware."

"Who is that child?"

"One of my grade nines."

"She's been doing it for days," Fraser said, surreptitiously glancing over her shoulder. "Have you any idea why?"

"Some."

"Oh?"

"Don't keep looking back, Fraser. It will upset her."

Fraser laughed nervously, peering at Helen's sunny smile. "You're enjoying it!" she declared. "Is it a game?"

"Of sorts. Just forget she's there. She'll vanish before we reach the door. She always does."

Taking a shortcut before her afternoon classes three days before the end of the fall term, Helen entered the mezzanine of the auditorium and stopped, hearing music. She looked down to the orchestra pit, to see Gena at the piano. Not sure if this was supposed to be a part of the game, Helen slid into a seat near the door to listen.

Gena played with facility and apparent unawareness of her audience. Her head bent to one side, the music flowed from under her hands with great control and poignancy. *One of the Chopin preludes*, Helen thought, trying to remember which one.

After the prelude, Gena continued on into a uniquely

individual interpretation of Vivaldi's lute concerto, and did it wonderfully well. Helen listened through to the end, then watched, her heart thudding like a trapped bird, as Gena drew her hands slowly from the keyboard and turned to look straight at her. Helen felt the penetration of those eyes all the way through her. She couldn't move. The noise of the piano bench being shoved back was jarring, and she thought she might cry. Gena stood looking up at her for another moment before fleeing. Helen related this incident to Amanda, who listened with an air of knowing.

"I think," she said, at the end of the narration, "you'd best prepare yourself. She'll come to you now."

"But why? What's going on that you can see and I can't?"

"Oh, I think you know, darling," she said. "It isn't all that complicated."

"Am I stupid? I just don't see."

"You will. Perhaps I'm able to see it because I'm your mother."

Helen laughed, reaching to massage her mother's taut, swollen hand. "You're not turning into one of those mystical batty old ladies on me, are you?"

"Never. I'm not in the least mystical or batty. One might say I have some well-earned eccentricities. But certainly not batty. What a thing to say!"

"You know what I meant."

"I most assuredly did. You're trying to fog the issue by turning me into a dim old dodo. You're far too perceptive to claim you don't know what's happening between you and that child. You're in love!"

"Mother!"

"Oh, not sexually. Sometimes you're so literal, Helen. She's a dream child, walking around, following you, giving you sweet gifts, demonstrating her talents for you. And you're enchanted. You've stopped flitting off into the hinterlands and come to earth at last, because you've found what you've been looking for since Stu died. Part of it, anyway. She wants you to love her. And you want it too. She'll be coming soon to stake her claim on your affections. And you are quite simply—quite wisely, I might add—waiting."

"Am I?" she said dreamily, caught up in the flow of her mother's words.

"Yes. This is a different brand of giving you've been yearning to do. If you want to know the truth, I think you're quite remarkable. I admire how you've handled yourself these past few years, how you've grown. I also admire your choice of children. That girl's face speaks to me. *She* speaks to me. You had such a dissimilar quality at her age. You were already off and running into your potential. This child is only beginning to make tentative approaches into hers. And she's hoping to include you. You need each other. It's no sin to care."

On Christmas Eve Amanda, with a counterfeit show of irritation, agreed to accompany Barnstorm to a concert.

"He's feeling sorry for himself," she said. "But I really would like to go. They're doing the *Eroica*, and I would enjoy hearing it. You don't mind being left on your own, do you?"

"Of course I don't. I'll do the tree."

Helen sent Mary off to her friends for the evening, refusing dinner. "I'll fix myself something later," she said, stacking boxes of ornaments inside the living-room door. "Enjoy yourself."

She listened to the radio, nibbling on some crackers as she circled the tree, thinking that, as ever, her mother had found one that had symmetry and definite character. Smiling, she picked up a box, and was about to start on the tree when the doorbell rang.

Gena was standing on the porch in a full-length mink coat several sizes too large.

"Gena! Come in."

"Is it all right?"

"Of course."

"I'll go pay the driver then," she said, skipping quickly down the steps to hand a bill through the window of the taxi that had brought her.

"It's wrong of me, I know," she said, returning to the porch, her hands jammed deep into the bulging pockets of her unlikely coat. "I wanted . . ." She looked around and shrugged.

"Come inside. You look as if you're freezing."

"Are you really sure? I hate doing this. I mean, this way."

"Come along inside," Helen said, extending her hand. "There's no point in both of us freezing out here."

Gena gave up her coat, saying, "It was my mother's. I wanted to wear it tonight. Sometimes I go for walks at night just to wear it."

"It's certainly heavy, isn't it?"

"Oh, I almost forgot," she said, shoving her hand into the pocket. "These are to put under your tree." She handed over two small, expensively wrapped packages.

"Thank you. That's very generous of you, Gena."

The girl looked away, letting her eyes sweep over every surface, her hands clasped behind her back.

"I like this house," she said, her eyes following Helen as she set the packages down on the hall table. "I wanted to be somewhere tonight. It was so empty at home."

"It's not much better here, I'm afraid."

"*You're* here."

"Have you had dinner, Gena?"

"No."

"I haven't either. Are you hungry?"

"I can cook." She smiled. "Would you let me cook for you?"

Helen laughed and took her hand. "I'd be delighted. The kitchen's through here."

"Do you trust me to cook for you?"

"I don't see any reason why you shouldn't, if it's what you'd like to do."

"All right. Then you sit down over here, and if I can't find what I need, you can tell me."

Helen sat and watched her tie on one of Amanda's aprons, then wash her hands at the sink.

"Do you like omelettes?" she asked, drying her hands.

Helen said she did.

"Good."

She found everything without having to ask. Helen relaxed, enjoying the sight of her efficiently cracking eggs into a bowl. The child's movements, Helen saw, had that same economy as Amanda's. She made no half gestures—everything she did was definite and precise and satisfying to see, like a ballet. Her face was flushed and furrowed with concentration. Her arms, where they emerged from her short-sleeved dress, were a little thin, and the sight of them filled Helen with longing to take this girl in her arms and hold her, rock her until she fell asleep. She herself felt pleasantly drowsy and contented in the heat of the kitchen, watching Gena move about.

Rousing herself, she went to the sideboard in the dining room to pour a brandy and a small sherry for Gena. Then she set the table.

They ate in a heavy silence, broken only by Helen's enthusiastic compliments on Gena's cooking. It really was very good. Gena pushed her food around, keeping her eyes lowered, then suddenly set down her knife and fork and looked across at Helen.

"My daddy was supposed to arrive back this afternoon from London. But he called to say he was fogged in and couldn't get another seat until tomorrow night. He was very upset, I could tell. He said so. I told him everything was fine, but then I put the telephone down and he wasn't there any more. It was as if he wasn't real if I couldn't hear his voice." She stopped and shook her head violently. "I wanted to *see* him!" she whispered, pushing her plate away. "I had to come." She covered her face with her hands, sobbing, "I had to see you if I couldn't see him."

Helen got up and walked around the table, standing uncertainly for a moment before placing her hand on Gena's head.

"I'm very happy you came," she said. Her hand stroked the gleaming hair, reveling in its unexpected softness.

"You think I'm crazy." She sobbed into her hands. "Everybody does!"

"I don't think that. Not at all."

"Oh, please," Gena cried, flinging her arms around Helen's waist, looking up at her imploringly, "please let me stay!"

"Of course you can stay," she said, holding Gena's head against her breasts, a deeply satisfied warmth spreading through her. "I want you to stay."

"You're so soft," Gena murmured, tightening her hold. "You always looked so soft to me. I wish I could stay this way forever. I hate growing up. I hate everything. If only I could stay this way."

"Growing up isn't so bad, Gena. It's nothing to be afraid of."

"It isn't that," she said, releasing her hold on Helen, laying her head down on her arm on the table. "That's not what I mean." The tears trickled from beneath her closed lids and dropped onto the table.

Helen brought her chair over close, then pressed her handkerchief into Gena's hand.

"Tell me about it," she said, watching Gena look at the handkerchief.

"This smells like you," she said, holding the crumpled square against her mouth. "I want to be you. You're so . . . I don't know."

"You don't want to be me, Gena. You just don't want to be you."

"I hate being me. I hate it."

"I don't hate you. I don't think your classmates hate you. It doesn't sound as if your father hates you. So why do you hate you?"

Gena laughed miserably, opening her eyes.

"You're funny," she said, studying Helen's smile. "I didn't expect you to be funny."

"One has to laugh, Gena. Really. It makes everything so much less painful."

"How do you know?"

"Because I do."

"I've done some terrible things," she said, her smile collapsing. "And I don't even know why I do them."

"Tell me about the terrible things you've done."

"I couldn't. You'd hate me!"

"I never would," she said, reaching for Gena's hand.

"No, I can't." She turned her head, refusing to meet Helen's eyes. "I'll clear away the dishes."

Before Helen could object, Gena had sprung up and begun clearing the table. Not wanting to pressure the girl, Helen got up, poured herself a refill of brandy, and wandered into the living room, settling on the sofa. She could still feel the impression of Gena's head against her breasts as she tried to imagine the very worst things Gena could tell her. She doubted Gena had committed any really reprehensible acts.

From the length of time she stayed out in the kitchen, Helen knew she was washing the dishes and replacing them in the cupboards. When she returned, Helen took advantage of the opportunity to study her. And she saw, in the few seconds it took Gena to come through the dining room, across the hall, and into the living room, that despite the too-short, childish dress, she had a very unchildish body. She wore no brassiere, and her breasts swayed slightly as she moved. There was something mature—a knowledge—in the way she walked. And Helen suddenly had a very clear idea of what "terrible things" Gena had done.

"Come sit with me," Helen said, folding her legs under her. "You needn't have cleaned up. We have a housekeeper."

"I like doing things I know I don't have to do," she said, dropping down beside Helen, searching her face. "It's because I don't *have* to do them."

"Who looks after you when your father's away?"

"I do."

"But you shouldn't be on your own . . ."

"Daddy keeps hiring housekeepers. I keep firing them again as soon as he leaves. I don't need looking after."

"Perhaps not," she said, caught by a sudden inspiration. "Would you like to tell me about your father?"

"Oh, you'd like him," she said, her features relaxing and a smile forming on her mouth. "Everybody does. We can't walk down the street without all kinds of people stopping to say hello, talk to him. He's very funny, sort of the way you are. And very intelligent—scary intelligent. As if he can look right into your mind and know exactly what you're thinking. I love him."

187

"He sounds very special. Tell me some more."

"Like what?"

"Anything you feel like telling."

"I know." She sat up on her knees. "I'll recite you his professional biography." She laughed, assembling her features into an expression of pretended seriousness. "A graduate of Choate and Yale, Mr. McLaren began his career as a stringer for *The New York Times* while attending Calhoun College at Yale. He majored in English literature and graduated with the Class of 'Thirty-two *summa cum laude*. He went on to receive his Master's and Ph.D., and is a member of the distinguished Phi Beta Kappa Society and all the rest of it. You don't want to hear this."

"But I do. I'm enjoying it."

"Really?"

"Go on."

"Okay. Where was I? Oh yes." She restructured her serious face and continued. "During the pre-war years, Mr. McLaren was a free-lance foreign correspondent whose work appeared in *The New York Times*, the Boston *Herald*, and the Washington *Post*, as well as other syndicated news publications.

"During the war he served as foreign correspondent for the Washington *Post*, covering the action in North Africa.

"He is the author of the much-acclaimed and best-selling novel *Legacies*."

"I'm very impressed," Helen said, smiling at Gena's pride in her father's accomplishments. "He sounds like quite a man."

"He is! He's coming home to stay now. He's going to do a book-review column and lecture at the university."

"I think that'll be very nice for you. It must be awfully lonely with him away so much."

"Would you like to hear about my mother?" Gena asked eagerly, ignoring Helen's last remark.

"If you like."

"I never knew her," she began, carefully noting Helen's reactions. "Daddy was living in Paris when they met. You'll never guess what she was!"

"I can't imagine."

"A chambermaid! Isn't that something? She was Irish. Her parents wouldn't pay for her to go abroad to study, so she took a job as a chambermaid at the Crillon to pay for herself while she studied. She was really determined!"

"It sounds so."

"Yes, well. Anyway, Daddy says she was a fierce, beautiful girl, and they fell in love and got married and had me. And then she died. I was only a baby, not even two. I don't know who she was. She was very young, only twenty-four. Would you like to know how she died?"

"I think you're upsetting yourself, Gena."

"Oh no," she said, her eyes contradicting her words. "I *want* to tell you. It's very *important* that you know. She had serious emotional problems, Daddy says. She left us. Daddy kept expecting her to come back, but she wouldn't. He hired a detective to try to find her. The detective came back to Daddy and said Madame McLaren was living in the Seventeenth Arondissement with a gentleman who was a known procurer and had a very, very bad reputation. A pimp," she said, her voice anguished. "She worked for him. Daddy paid the detective to keep an eye on her. It went on for a long time, almost a year. Then, one day, the detective came and asked Daddy to accompany him to the morgue, because there was a woman there he was positive was Madame McLaren. They had pulled her out of the Seine. She had a bicycle chain around her throat. Daddy didn't tell me that, of course. I read it later in the papers. She was murdered. They cut her. Cut off her breasts. Mutilated her. He . . . Daddy told me she drowned. But I always knew he was lying. And when we went to Paris two years ago so Daddy could do a piece on the Marshall Plan, I went to the newspaper offices and read about her. Daddy couldn't ever hurt anybody. It wasn't our fault. I don't understand how she could leave us that way. Do you understand it?"

"No," Helen said truthfully, "I don't."

"I look just like her. Isn't that something? I don't look the least bit like Daddy, not any part of me. I have her eyes and her hair and her skin. And her habits."

189

"What do you mean, Gena?" Helen felt silent alarms going off along the length of her nervous system.

"I have her body, too," Gena said. "Early maturation, they call it. I'm just like her. I couldn't help myself. When he said how lovely I was and started touching me, I didn't care about anything. Not anything at all. I thought how good it was to feel that way, how good it felt to be touched all over."

"Who?" Helen asked in a whisper.

"In California," she said, her eyes glassy. "The man at the school. I used to admire the flowers, and he seemed so kind. In the greenhouse. He put his hands on my body and kissed my mouth and said I was beautiful, let me do this, you're so sweet, I won't hurt you. It didn't hurt. I liked it very much. But after that I wanted to stop. But I couldn't. I had to go back because I wanted more. He was very pleased. I liked his face. It was so brown from the sun. And his arms, too. But under his clothes he was very white, and I thought, how beautiful. White skin. I couldn't think because he held me and I wasn't lonely and I wanted to show him I was glad not to be lonely so I let him put himself inside me and I felt happy and he cried against my neck and said he loved me. I believed that. But I didn't love him. I couldn't stay away. I went all the time. To the greenhouse. The flowers were in my ears and my eyes and in my throat, everywhere, drowning me. But then they found us. They came with a flashlight. Naked. I couldn't find my clothes and they said I was evil, wicked, a disgrace, put your clothes on at once, shameless animal. They sent the gardener away and told everyone what I had done and I begged them not to tell my daddy but they telephoned him in Africa and tried to make him listen to the terrible things I had done. But he wouldn't listen and made them put me on the telephone and he said, I'm coming to get you don't listen to what they say they don't know you I'll come right away. And he came and took me to my room and said don't be ashamed I love you and this doesn't change anything. But it did—I know it did. He said I would feel happier at a new school with girls *and* boys, that I would relate more successfully to my contemporaries in a less confining environment. But there was no one to relate to. Except you. Should I go home now?"

"No, no," Helen said, taking her in her arms. "You don't have to run away from me for that, Gena. It makes no difference."

"It has to," she said, crying softly against Helen's shoulder. "I have no morals. I'm just like her. It's what they said."

"I don't see that what happened in California has anything to do with your morals."

"You don't?" She sat back from Helen, confused.

"You were lonely. You took the only comfort that was offered to you. Sometimes, being lonely, we can't help ourselves. It doesn't mean we're immoral. It means we're human."

"But they said—"

"I don't care what they said. I'm saying you're not evil or wicked—just female, human. Everyone finds herself involved in situations that happen for the wrong reasons. It's not evil to make mistakes out of loneliness and need. You have to believe that, Gena."

"Why did they say those things, then?"

"Your father didn't, did he?"

"No. But that's because . . ."

"Because he loves you and understands how difficult your life is. He sounds very good, very sympathetic."

"Oh, he is! He's . . . beautiful."

"Those others were very cruel in their lack of understanding."

"Why do you see this when no one else does, except Daddy?"

"I don't know. Perhaps because I've done things other people might have found similarly evil. But I knew they weren't. And also, I was very fortunate. I have a mother who's wise. She's always told me to believe what I felt deeply inside myself to be the truth. I think what's needed here is someone who can explain that to you. I imagine it must be hard for your father. After all, it sounds as if he loves you very much. Surely he must be sorry he can't provide you with the type of attention he knows you need."

"He said almost those exact words. When he was bringing me back from California."

"So there you are, you see! He does know and understand. If your own father who loves you isn't willing to believe you're bad or evil, why should you?"

"But nobody likes me. They won't talk to me or pay any attention to me."

"I'm paying attention to you."

"But that's because . . ."

"Why, do you think?"

"I don't know why."

"Because I care," Helen said. "You know that. That's why you came here. Because you know I do."

"You're not old enough to be my mother, are you?"

"No, I'm not."

"I wish you were."

"Age hasn't anything to do with you and me, Gena. Not a thing."

"You don't think so?"

"No, I don't."

"Would you like me to get you another drink? Daddy lets me do his."

"That would be very nice."

"I know which bottle. I watched you do it."

She got up and went into the dining room. There were so many thoughts going through Helen's mind that she found it hard to hold down any one particular one. She knew only that she loved this girl, wanted to be close to her and respond to Gena's need.

Gena came back and gave her the glass.

"Will you tell me something about you?" she asked, resuming her place on the sofa.

"If I can."

"Why aren't you married?"

"I'm a widow." The word felt strange in her mouth. She used it so rarely.

"Oh, that's so sad!" She actually looked as if she might start crying again. "What happened to him?"

"He was killed in the war."

"Did you love him?"

"Yes, very much."

"*I* love you," Gena whispered, "I really do."

"And I you."

"You do?"

"Yes I do."

"Even with everything I've told you?"

"That doesn't matter. Would you like to stay here to-night? I know Mother would very much like to see you again. And if your father won't be arriving until tomorrow night, why don't you stay and have Christmas with us tomorrow? I'll get you home in time to see your father."

"I'd like to stay."

"Hadn't you better call home?"

"I told the housekeeper I was coming here. I'm very sleepy," she said. Her eyes looked it. There were darkening crescents beneath them.

"Come on, you can help me make up the bed in the guest room. Then we'll get you to sleep."

"I wish I lived here," Gena said as they were going up the stairs. "This is such a nice house."

Helen found a nightgown for her, then stood in the middle of her own bedroom sipping her brandy, waiting for Gena to get herself into bed. Helen heard her leave the bathroom, and she went back to the guest room. Gena looked so young, so fragile, Helen felt drunk with caring for her. She set her glass down on the night table and perched on the side of the bed.

"Can you sleep in a strange place?" she asked, touching Gena's cheek.

"This isn't a strange place," she said softly. "It's not strange at all."

"Is there anything you'd like before I go?"

"Would you let me kiss you good night?"

Helen leaned forward, and Gena's arms came around her.

"I love you so much," she whispered in Helen's ear. "You're so nice to me."

"I love you too. Go to sleep now." She kissed her, then gently disengaged herself, picked up her drink, and turned out the light. "Sleep well," she said, closing the door.

At some time in the night, long after she'd finished the tree and Amanda had come in and gone directly to bed complaining (as she rarely did) of pain in her hands, Helen was in bed, in the dark, thinking, when the door opened and Gena came in. Helen closed her eyes, keeping still. Gena stood beside the bed for a very long time, her fingertips barely grazing Helen's cheek. Then, as silently as she'd come, she went away.

12

"I don't know why," Helen was saying at breakfast the morning after Christmas, "but she lied. What I don't know is which part wasn't true."

"You've got ample material to choose from," Amanda said, thinking about the details of what Helen had told her. "That business about her mother is just ghastly enough to be true. I confess, I'm as confused as you."

"Something is strange. The worst of it is, I don't honestly think she knew she was lying. I think she believes every word of it. That's what makes it so impossible to put my finger on any one thing she said and say that that particular part wasn't true."

"What will you do?"

"What is there to do?"

"Nothing I can see. But be careful, darling. I think it would be a mistake to promise her anything. She's a desperately unhappy little girl. Desperate people are capable of doing damage."

"I'm not worried about myself. I'm frightened for her. She *hates* herself."

Back at school, Gena kept her distance. Helen was disappointed when, as the days passed, Gena failed to make any sign or acknowledgment that any communication had ever taken place between them. Helen saw her, at various times, standing on the fringes of some group or other outside the school and caught sight of her one evening in February standing by the fence gazing up at the windows of the house. By the time Helen got downstairs and opened the front door, she was gone.

In early March, as she was being driven downtown to dinner by a date, she spotted Gena in her shabby mink walking slowly down Old Street, passing through the Saturday-night crowds like a sleepwalker. On impulse, Helen asked her date to pull over. She slid out of the car and caught up with her.

"Where are you going?" Helen asked, smiling into the abstracted stare on Gena's face.

"Did you come for me?" she asked, examining Helen's face as if she were someone she'd never seen before.

"Let me take you home, Gena," she said quietly, taking the girl's hand. "Would you let me?"

"Nobody's there. I'm afraid of being alone at night."

"I'll take you home and stay with you." Helen looked around, glad to see her date had had the good sense to follow them. "I have a friend with me. We'll take you home."

"No! Please!" Gena pleaded, her face losing that unrecognizing mask of distrust. "Take me with you! I'll be good! I won't make any trouble. *Please*, take me with you."

Helen was torn between going back to explain the situation to her date and staying with Gena, but she feared that if she released her hand even for an instant, she'd lose her in the crowd. Well, she decided, Bob was just a casual date whose intentions for the evening he'd already made clear. And while she'd been anticipating a certain pleasure in being diverted for a few hours, it was much more important not to leave this child.

"What's wrong, Gena? Can you tell me? I'd like to help."

Gena shivered. "I'm cold. I'm always cold here. California was so warm."

"Where is your father? Is he away?"

Gena smiled. "He's in Berlin," she said, leaning closer. "You won't tell him about this, will you?"

Don't promise! she thought. *Don't say you won't when there's a chance you'll have to tell!*

"Come with me. My friend and I will take you to dinner."

"Oh, I *want* to be with you," she said, putting her arms around Helen, burying her cold face against Helen's neck. "I won't misbehave, I promise."

"The car's back here," she said, easing Gena away. "Come with me. Give me your hand."

Bob rose several notches in her estimation by his unquestioning acceptance and smiling agreement to take Gena along to dinner. "Couldn't do better than two beautiful girls," he said, steering the car back into the flow of traffic. Helen gave him a look that promised a later explanation, and they continued downtown with Gena holding tight to Helen's hand as she stared through the window at the passing stream of people.

She spoke only to express her preference for dinner, then lapsed into smiling, submissive silence, her eyes traveling back and forth from Helen to Bob and back again to Helen.

There was little doubt now in Helen's mind that Gena was very disturbed, and she wondered how best to handle the situation. Lost in thought, she scarcely noticed when Gena got up from the table mumbling something about going to the ladies' room. Bob leaped upon the moment to ask, "What's going on? Who's the girl?"

"One of my students," Helen said.

"Kind of remote, isn't she?" he observed. "What do we do with her now?"

"I'm trying to figure that out. Thank you for going along with all this. I really couldn't leave her roaming about on the streets."

"No problem," he said, reaching for her hand. "We can drop her off wherever she lives and go somewhere for a quiet drink."

The waiter began removing the dishes, whisking the crumbs off the table, and Bob turned to order coffee.

"She's taking her time," Helen said, sensing something was wrong.

"Girls her age like to take their time," he said, applying a meaningful pressure to her hand. "She's a great-looking kid, though."

"I think I'll just go see." She got up and walked out of the dining room, suddenly positive Gena had left. When she saw the deserted ladies' room, her heart sank. She stood, trying to think what Gena would be likely to do, but found she couldn't imagine it. Returning to the table, she sat down, saying, "Look, I know this is turning out to be a three-ring circus, but Gena's gone. I'm terribly worried about her. Would you indulge me and drive around a bit, see if we can't find her?"

He was annoyed, but he checked it and said, "Sure. I'll get the tab."

It was hopeless. They drove up and down the streets for forty minutes but couldn't spot her.

"Stop by that phone booth and let me see if she didn't go home."

She looked up the number in the directory and dialed. No one answered. She let it ring and ring, then tried dialing again on the off chance she'd misdialed the first time. Nothing. On a hunch she dialed home, knowing Amanda would be there.

"She's here," her mother said. "Arrived in a taxi a few minutes ago."

"Keep her there, whatever you do. Has she said anything?"

"Not a word. Not even hello. Just came along inside and sat down in the living room."

"I'm not sure what to do, but I'll be there in twenty minutes. Something's going on."

"I would say so. I'll sit on her if she tries to leave." Amanda laughed. "On second thought, I'll get Mary to sit on her. Don't panic, darling. I don't think she's planning to go anywhere. She seems quite contented where she is. I'm looking right at her."

Helen returned to the car.

"I'm sorry," she said. "Gena's gone to my house. I have to go back. Could I take a rain check on tonight?"

"Oh, what the hell, why not?" he said, slamming the car into gear. "This sure hasn't been dull. Weird, but definitely not dull."

"I know you're disappointed, and I am too. You've been very patient. I promise you, next time will be different."

"You bet it will. Next time, I'll take you out of town for dinner." He laughed, and the tension was eased.

She kissed him good night, pulling away with a smile when his hands reached inside her coat.

"A rain check," she said, opening the door. "Thank you for understanding."

"I don't understand. Don't give me any kudos for that. Call you during the week," he promised, and drove away.

"I haven't been able to induce her to take off that mildewed mink," Amanda said, meeting Helen at the door. "In fact, I cannot get a word out of her. What will you do?"

"I don't know. Do me a favor and try calling her home number again. It's in the book. Remington Park."

"All right. Then what?"

"Then I don't know."

Gena smiled when she saw her, moving over to make room for Helen.

"What are you doing, Gena? Why did you leave the restaurant?"

"I thought you wanted to be with him. I was interfering. So I came here to wait for you."

"You should have told me you wanted to leave. I was very worried about you."

"Oh, I'm sorry. I didn't think you'd mind." She sighed contentedly, looking around the room. "I love this house. This is probably my favorite place in the whole world."

"Take off your coat, why don't you?"

"This is my mother's coat, you know."

"Yes, I know. You've told me that. Here, let me help you."

Like a small child, she allowed Helen to unfasten and remove the coat.

"I'll get you some brandy," Gena offered. "Would you like me to?"

"No, Gena, thank you. I don't want anything. Do you know it's dangerous to be out walking alone at night downtown?"

"Nobody sees me," she said earnestly. "Nobody ever does."

"Of course people see you. I did, didn't I?"

"Yes, that's true. How did you know where to find me? I was so surprised to see you, I didn't even know who you were at first. You looked so beautiful. I couldn't understand why you were talking to me."

"Has something happened, Gena? Something to upset you?"

"I hurt myself," she said, her chin quivering as tears filled her eyes. "I hurt myself."

"How did you hurt yourself? Where?"

"I fell down. It hurt very badly."

"Where have you hurt yourself? Show me."

She stood up and pulled off her sweater, turning around. Helen gaped at an enormous discolored bruise across the center of Gena's back.

"How did you do that, Gena?"

"I fell. Off a chair."

"A chair?"

"I was standing on the chair to look at myself in the mirror and I fell down on my back."

"Put your sweater back on," Helen said, trying to visualize her standing on a chair to look in a mirror. It didn't make sense.

"I'd like to go to sleep now," she said, folding up on the floor, resting her head in Helen's lap. "I'm very tired."

"Yes, all right," she said, absently caressing the girl's hair. "Come along and we'll put you to bed."

Amanda came in shaking her head.

"Gena's going to go to sleep now," Helen said, out of resources, as she looked down at the suppliant figure at her knees. "Get up, Gena. We'll go upstairs now."

With an exhausted sound, Gena got to her feet and walked out of the room and up the stairs.

"What are we going to do with her?" Helen said, "I don't know how to reach her father. And no one answered, did they?"

"No. The only thing we *can* do is put her to bed."

Again, as before, Gena asked to be kissed good night. Helen held her, trying to transmit reassurance as she kissed the girl's cheek.

"I spoiled your evening," Gena said. "I didn't mean to. I'm sorry."

"Hush now. Nothing's been spoiled."

"Why are you so nice to me?"

"Because I love you. I want you to be happy."

"I'm happy when I'm with you. When I'm not with you, I forget your face. I don't understand that."

"It happens. Sleep now. I'll be here if you need me."

She started to turn onto her side, but her face contracted into a grimace.

"It hurts," she complained. "It didn't hurt before."

"When did you fall, exactly?"

"Sometime. This afternoon, I think."

"Don't you know?"

"It was this afternoon. I remember now. I had to lay on the floor for a long time because I couldn't catch my breath. I thought I was dying, I tried so hard to catch my breath. Make it better," she asked. "Make the hurt go away."

"I don't think I can, darling. You'll have to lie very still and try not to move. If it still hurts badly tomorrow, we'll take you to see a doctor."

"Yes, that's a good idea." She blinked, smiling. "Darling."

As Helen watched, her eyelids flickered closed and she was instantly asleep. Filled with a sense of futility, Helen got up, turned off the light, and went out.

She was asleep and came slowly away from it as she realized she was being touched. Someone was whispering to her. Her heart was pumping violently as she came awake, opening her eyes to see Gena's face very close to hers, her lips whispering, "Mama, Mama," as her hand opened and closed over Helen's breast. She lay still, waiting for her heart to resume its normal rhythm, as her sleep-clouded brain grasped what it was Gena was trying to do. Muddled, trying to throw off the claiming grip of sleep, she felt her nightgown being eased down as Gena lowered her head.

"Gena," she whispered, taking hold of her hands, "it's time to go back to sleep now."

"Mama?"

"Yes. Get up now, darling. I'll put you back to bed."

Gena submitted to being led back across the hall and tucked into bed. Helen, trembling as she visualized what the next step was to have been, returned to her bed, burrowing deep into the warmth as a sob escaped her. She put her hand over her mouth in an attempt to hold back the hysterical cries. She turned onto her stomach and hid her face in the pillow to muffle the sounds of her crying.

After a time, eased, she sat up, trying to think what could be done about Gena. Something had to be done. But what? There didn't seem to be any ready answer. If only her damned father was around. And why the hell wasn't someone looking after this child? Left to her own devices, anything might happen. Helen pounded the pillow into a comfortable shape and, determined to get to the bottom of it, went back to sleep.

Sometime in the very early morning, Gena dressed and left the house. Confounded beyond measure, Helen went straight to the telephone. Gena answered, sounding very much in control of herself as she said, "Thank you for letting me stay. I had a very nice evening last night," and hung up before Helen could say a word.

"She wanted to be nursed," Amanda said. "I'd say she's in some sort of regressive state."

"She's in a lot more than that," Helen said wryly. "I knew what she was doing. What I do not know and simply cannot for the life of me understand is why that child isn't being supervised. There's nothing I'd like more at this moment than a confrontation with her father. I don't care who he is or what he is, he can't be too busy to see that his only child is going off the deep end."

"That's conjecture, Helen. For all you know, the man is half out of his mind with concern for her. Just because you're upset, don't start placing blame. At least not until you have a clearer picture of the true situation."

"I'd still like to have a few words with him. Something's going to happen to her if someone doesn't do something. I can feel it."

"What else is it, Helen?"

"What do you mean, what else?"

"There's something more bothering you."

Helen looked at her for a long minute, thinking.

"It wasn't just Gena," she said finally, looking very frightened. "It was me. For one moment—less than a second—I wanted to let her go ahead. And then I thought, What the hell am I doing? It scared me. God! What am I turning into?" She held her hands over her face, closing her eyes. "What the hell is all this?" she asked, opening her eyes again, searching her mother's face.

"Motherhood," Amanda said quietly. "Instant motherhood."

Monday morning Gena was in class wearing that haunted look Helen was coming to know. She wanted to talk to her, but Gena fled from the room the minute the bell sounded, and, utterly frustrated, Helen watched her race down the corridor and into another classroom for her next lesson.

At lunchtime she tried again to reach someone at Gena's home. No one was there.

Just before the end of her last class of the day, she became aware of a great deal of activity in the corridors and heard raised voices in the stairwell, then the sounds of sirens and stepped-up traffic in the halls. She asked one of the girls to monitor the class and stepped outside just as Fraser came running down the hall, her face ashen.

"Come with me!" she ordered. "Get your bag! Dismiss the class!"

"What's going on?"

"Just get your things!" Fraser repeated, pushing Helen back through the door.

As they ran down the stairs to the teachers' lounge, Fraser said, "It's that girl. The one who follows you."

Helen's heart froze. "What is it?"

"Get your coat! I'll tell you on the way."

"*Fraser*! For God's sake!"

"She jumped from the guardrail of the third-floor landing into the stairwell."

"Oh my God!"

"They've taken her to the hospital. I'll drive you."

"Is she badly hurt?"

"I don't know, Helen. I really don't."

Fraser broke every speed limit getting Helen to the hospital. She went with her to the emergency room, then retired to the lounge to wait.

The doctor on duty took Helen to one side.

"Are you her mother? Are you assuming responsibility for her?" he asked.

"I don't understand. How badly is she hurt?"

"We're trying to determine that now. We need information in order to admit her. Can you do that?"

"I'm not her mother, but I can do it. I'll take the responsibility."

"Go with the nurse. I'll talk to you again as soon as I have something to tell you."

Helen turned to leave, then stopped.

"Call Leon Schindler," she said. "He's our family physician. He'll attend to her."

"Okay. I'll have him paged. The sooner you give the nurse the information, the sooner we can get her into surgery."

Surgery. The word ripped through her, demanding her attention while she was giving the nurse all the information she could. She went directly from the nurse to the public telephone to try calling the McLarens' number again. This time, a woman answered.

"Is Mr. McLaren available?" she asked.

"No. I'm sorry, he's away until the end of the month. Would you like to leave a message?"

"To whom am I speaking?"

"Who's calling, please?"

"This is Gena's teacher Helen Kimbrough. It's absolutely imperative I get in touch with Mr. McLaren. Can't you tell me where I might reach him?"

"Has something happened to Gena?" The voice had lost some of its starch.

"Who *are* you?" Helen asked again.

"I'm Mrs. Olsen, the housekeeper."

"Where in the *hell* have you been?" she demanded. "I've been calling this damned number for *days!*"

"I don't have to answer that!"

"I think you do. If not to me, to someone. Gena's had an accident. She's at The Pavilion. You find her father and tell him that! I'll stay with her until I hear from one of you!" She slammed down the telephone and stood shaking, trying to quell her fury.

"Can I do anything?" Fraser asked, touching Helen's shoulder.

"Yes!" she snapped. "Buy me a gun! I'm going to shoot someone!"

"Can't you get through to anyone?"

"I'm beginning to think she made up her father as well as everything else. What the hell should I do? Think of something!"

"I think we'd better sit down and wait."

"I want to know what's going on in that family."

"Come on, sit down," Fraser said sensibly. "You're not going to help matters by going berserk with a gun." She tried to laugh. "She may not be that badly hurt."

"Tell me exactly what happened," she said, calming down a little.

"I'm not sure. I had study hour, and was on my way out of the office when one of the boys came tearing in, white as chalk, shouting he'd just seen a girl jump. We all went running out, and there she was. It was awful. I'm sure it must have looked worse than it actually was. But

205

she . . ." She rubbed her arm, searching for words. "She looked like a smashed toy." She swallowed hard and shook her head. "She was so still, so quiet. And her face! Jesus!" She closed her eyes, blanching. "I thought she was dead. When I realized who it was, I came to get you."

"I knew something was going to happen. But not this. If she dies . . ." Her voice trailed off.

"I'm sorry, Helen. I know how fond you are of her."

"You have *no* idea! Forgive that," she said. "I didn't mean it."

"It's all right. I understand."

After an hour had gone by and no one had come out of the operating room, Helen's mind began conjuring up images of Gena lying in the stairwell. It was unbearable. "What's taking them so long?" she wondered aloud.

"I don't know."

"Fraser, you don't have to stay. Why don't you run along home? You look very tired."

"No, I don't mind. I'll stay."

"You're doing it for me, and I'm fine. I'd prefer you to go. You could do me a favor and call Mother, tell her what's happened."

"Are you sure?"

"I'm sure. Thank you for everything."

"I hate to leave you here . . ."

"Go on now, Fraser. Really! I'll talk to you later."

She sat a few minutes longer, then got up, saying, "You'll let me know, won't you?"

"Yes."

About forty minutes after Fraser left, Leon came out to talk to her.

"I understand you're footing the bill for this kid, Helen."

"I am, yes. How is she?"

"Messed up. From the injuries, I can only guess she must have changed her mind and tried to save herself. She succeeded, too. She tried to break her fall by throwing out her left arm. It's a bad break."

"What else? Tell me."

"You want it all?" he asked.

"Just tell me, Leon. Please."

"You don't happen to have a cigarette, do you, Helen? I always seem to be running out." She opened her bag and handed him one from her pack.

"Okay," he said. "She's got a fractured skull. It's not too bad, all things considered. A couple of swell black eyes. Broke her nose, which we've reset; a split upper lip, which took four sutures. The left ulna was completely shattered. She'll probably have to have additional surgery on that arm. Six broken ribs and a perforated left lung, fractured hip, and a clean break in the left tibia. Oh yes, and two broken fingers on the left hand. She took the worst of the fall on her left side. As I said, it looks as if she changed her mind and threw out her arm and leg to break the fall. Tell me something," he said. "You obviously know this kid and care a hell of a lot about her. Why in the name of God would she want to do something like that?"

"I don't know. I just do not know."

"Well, listen, they're taking her up to her room now. She's been asking for you. I want to warn you, Helen, she looks bad."

"Okay."

"I noticed on the admit you listed her father as the next of kin. Where is he?"

"That's a damned good question! One I intend to get an answer for."

"Take it easy," he said, putting his hand over hers. "Go on up. Just don't stay for more than a minute or two."

"Thank you, Leon. Really. I'm very grateful."

"Glad to be of service."

Gena started sobbing hysterically the minute Helen entered the room.

"Gena," Helen said, trying to locate some unbandaged spot where she might touch her. "Don't cry, darling. Everything's all right. I'll stay with you."

"I'm sorry," she cried, trying to pull herself up. "I'm sorry."

"Lay back," Helen urged, her hand on Gena's thin shoulder. "Sssh! No one's angry with you."

"But I thought I'd die. I thought I would. And then I didn't want to but it was too late and I couldn't stop falling. It *hurts!* I hurt everywhere. Don't tell Daddy! Please, don't tell him!"

"You mustn't worry now. Try to rest. Your father will come to you as soon as he can."

"I don't want him here! I don't want him to know. He mustn't come here! Don't tell him!"

"Of course he'll come, Gena. He loves you. He'll want to see you. You'll be better soon, and then you'll go home."

"I don't want to be better. I want to be dead."

"No, you don't. *I* don't want you to die. Nobody wants you to die. You're the only one, and I don't think even you do. Close your eyes, darling. Go on, close them."

She maintained a steady flow of quieting sounds until the convulsive heaving of Gena's chest subsided and her breathing evened out. Then she sat back and tried to concentrate on not being ill.

A nurse appeared a few minutes later, saying, "I'm afraid you'll have to go now. She's had a sedative. She'll sleep through the night."

"Yes," Helen said, reluctant to leave. "I'll come again in the morning."

She was able to hold down the sickness until she arrived home. She ran up the stairs to the bathroom, where she threw up, then stood sweating feverishly as she ran a glass of water and rinsed her mouth. She washed her face and neck and went downstairs.

"It looked as if someone had taken a hammer to her face," she told Amanda as they sat in the living room with their drinks. "I don't think I'll ever be able to forget how she looked. That poor little girl. God! She kept apologizing because she'd lived through it. It's a nightmare! An insane nightmare!"

That night she lay in bed seeing Gena's face—the black-red eyes swollen to slits, the blood-crusted nostrils and the distended, cotton-packed nose, the huge upper lip with its lacing of black thread. And the bandages covering her skull. The leg in traction, the plaster arm. She got up and took two sleeping pills and smoked a cigarette, waiting for the pills to take effect. Every surface of her room became a projection screen where that brief film of Gena's face and body played, until Helen was sick again from the sight of it. And, after that, she finally slept.

When she returned to the hospital the following morning, Gena's bed was empty, and when she opened the closet door she was confronted by a tangle of empty metal hangers. At the desk the duty nurse said, "She's been signed out."

"But that's impossible. By whom? Where has she been taken?"

"I'm not at liberty to give you that information."

"But I assumed responsibility for the payment of her bill. Surely—"

"It's all been taken care of."

"My God!" Helen said. "This is mad! Isn't there anyone who can tell me what's been done with the girl? How could she be moved in that condition?"

"Look," the nurse said softly, "I'm not supposed to do this. But I'll tell you she was taken by ambulance to a private hospital in Connecticut. I could get into all kinds of trouble for even telling you that much."

"I understand," Helen said. "Thank you. I don't suppose Dr. Schindler's on duty?"

"He's off today. I'm sorry."

For days she tried to reach someone at Gena's home. Finally she wrote a note to Gena's father, asking that he contact her as soon as possible. She waited three more days, hoping to hear something, but he never called.

"It's insane!" she told Amanda. "Taking a seriously ill child out of a hospital in the middle of the night, spiriting her away to some private place in Connecticut. What's going on?"

"There has to be a logical answer for what's happened. You still haven't heard from the father?"

"Not one stinking word! If I ever meet that man, I will murder him on sight."

"Poor unhappy girl," Amanda said. "What a thing to do! She's lucky she wasn't killed."

"I'm beginning to wonder," Helen said.

When weeks passed with no word whatsoever from Gena's father, Helen's anger and confusion slowly boiled down and became a need to know the truth. She thought of Gena constantly, wondering how and where she was, and who, if anyone, was looking after her.

She had recurring dreams in which Gena, her ruined face leering out from behind white bandages, stood on the front porch in her voluminous mink coat pleading with Helen to let her come inside. And, horror-stricken and ashamed at her own hesitation, Helen held out her hand, to find herself gripping the bones of a skeleton's hand. She screamed as the figure recoiled from her touch and ran, crying, down the front steps and disappeared into the night. For the first time in years, she was afraid to go to bed at night, knowing that as soon as she relaxed into sleep the dreams would return.

Amanda was busy cataloging paintings for her annual showing, which she had agreed, after all the years of refusing, to hold at Barnstorm's gallery.

"Help me with these," she said. "It'll help take your mind off that child."

"I won't be satisfied until I have some answers," Helen replied, taking the pen and paper from her mother. "It's been almost two months since her accident. I've written three times and telephoned at least a hundred times. And I can't even raise a busy signal."

"You may never get any answers, you know."

"I know. Christ! It'll haunt me."

"Charlie's very anxious to show that portrait, the one I did of you for Stu. Would you mind if it was included? Not for sale, of course."

"No, I don't mind. It's not as if it's really mine."

"Well, yes and no. But at the time I did it, I hadn't considered that a study of you might be included in one of my shows."

"I could care less. I don't mean that the way it sounded,

Mother. I honestly don't mind. It was Stu's painting, not mine. And I'm long since over not wanting to show my body. You do whatever you like. Anyway"—she laughed —"it's not as if you're showing me in the flesh."

"Only by reflection," Amanda said, setting the painting to one side.

It was a spectacularly successful exhibition. In less than two hours, every painting had been affixed with a small red dot in the lower right-hand corner, indicating it had been sold. Uncle Charlie, pleased and proud and looking very natty in a white tuxedo, did it up royally with champagne and caviar, gliding through the place with an air of regal happiness. Amanda was down near the front of the gallery, talking to a group of old friends and admirers. Helen took a glass of champagne from the waiter's tray as he was passing and leaned against the wall, observing the flow of people circulating noisily through the rooms.

She'd been standing there for about twenty minutes when there was an opening in the crowd and her attention was drawn to a man who was talking to her mother. He was a subtly elegant man, she thought, studying him. In fact, she'd never seen a man who looked so utterly unaffected. He wasn't good-looking in a traditional sense, but there was something about him. The longer she looked at him, the more she wondered what made him so attractive.

His clothes were the best, meticulously cut and tailored. Everything was just right, even his shoes. He was bald, except for a circular fringe of hair running the perimeter of his nicely shaped head. He did have an appealing head. It looked smooth, something that would be pleasant to touch. His forehead was high and broad, his nose long and straight with an agreeable width. His mouth was wide with a full, deeply bowed upper lip. A cleft chin. Because of the way he was standing, she couldn't see his eyes, but she wondered if they'd fit the picture.

She simply couldn't stop looking at him. Her eyes took in his height, guessing him to be about six feet tall. And he had the firm, solid-muscled trim build of an athlete. Like Amanda, he used his hands when he talked, and she noticed with interest that he wore no jewelry, not even a wristwatch.

He looked up just as the crowd moved in to close the gap, blocking him from view. But she'd seen his eyes in that moment before her inspection had been curtailed. And they were round and dark, liquid. *A beautiful man,* she thought, relinquishing her contemplation of him, focusing on other faces, other forms around her. She was startled then when, not more than five minutes later, he appeared in front of her.

"You're Helen," he said in a husky voice, his eyes even darker, more luminous at close range.

She nodded, smiling.

"I'm Norman McLaren," he said, extending his hand, taking hers, suffusing it with warmth.

Her heart gave a terrible leap, then settled suspiciously.

"I'll get my bag," she said, putting down her glass.

On the way to his car he apologized, saying, "I called your home. The housekeeper told me you'd be here. I know it's an imposition, but I had to see you."

"I've been wanting to see *you,*" she said, unable to summon up her anger. It refused to come.

"I'll fill you in over dinner. Do you like Chinese food?"

"I suppose so."

"All right. Chinatown."

Everything he did managed to come across as gentle but persuasive, even the way he drove. He seemed to know exactly where he was going and went at it without haste. At just the right speed—relaxed, confident—he maneuvered his way.

She watched the lights from passing cars throw themselves across his face, amazed at how totally desirable she found everything about him. Despite her apprehensions and anger, there was something about him that was so serene, so lacking in pretense, that she found it difficult to summon up the reservoir of outrage inside her.

"I just arrived back and I'm hungry," he said, glancing across at her. "You don't mind? You haven't already had dinner?"

"No. No, I haven't."

"Good."

In the restaurant, when the headwaiter started to direct them to a table in the center of the room, Norman put his hand on her arm and said, "No. The one there in the corner." And he was right. It was quieter there, out of the direct stream of scurrying waiters. He held her chair and she sat down, trying to keep the fact that this was Gena's negligent father fixed firmly in her mind.

"Is there anything you don't like?" he asked, picking up the menu.

"No. Order what you'd like. I'll have some brandy, please."

"Perfect."

He gave the waiter their order, then sat back and lit a cigarette, looking at her.

"Whatever it was I expected," he said, "you're not it."

"Oh?"

He smiled for the first time. "Schoolteachers have gray hair, glasses, and orthopedic shoes. They are not young and beautiful and daughters of fine painters."

"Thank you," she said quietly, waiting.

"Now," he said, pulling his chair closer, "I owe you explanations, apologies, tying up all the loose ends. It'll take a while. Have you made plans for this evening?"

"I'm at your disposal."

"Would that you were." He laughed softly, the sound of it making her realize that it was going to be very difficult to maintain her sense of proportion with him. He had great charm.

"All right," he went on. "We'll start at the back and work our way to the front. Gena's at The Clinic in Hartford. I didn't know they'd put her there until almost a week after it was a *fait accompli*. That damned-fool nurse, when she couldn't reach me, went into a tizzy and called up my lawyer. The two of them decided that that's where Gena belonged."

"What nurse?" Helen asked.

"Olsen." He spit the name out angrily. "Much as I deplore the cloak-and-dagger manner they used, I've just arrived back from another trip up there to see Gena, and she *is* in the right place. What makes me even sorrier is that I didn't get in touch with you sooner.

"There are things it's damned hard to explain to an outsider, someone who's never had to live day after day with an emotionally disturbed child. So many well-meaning people who don't know anything about the pressures and stresses want to offer advice, suggestions on better ways to handle your 'problem child.' After a while you just close the door in a lot of those faces and try to get on with it as best you can. I had no way of knowing you weren't simply another interested observer. So I've kept the phone switched off and ignored your letters, thinking you'd go away. I'm sorry. It was wrong of me, but none of this started just days or weeks ago, you know. It's been years, and I'm about at the end of my rope. Anyway, I want you to know I'm sorry. I can imagine how you must've felt."

"I doubt it. Go on. How is Gena?"

"Not good. Oh, she's pretty well recovered from the fall. Everything but her arm. She's going to have to have at least two more operations on that. But emotionally she's in very bad shape.

"I have to be honest," he said, pausing to light a cigarette. "I probably wouldn't have called you at all if she hadn't kept asking for you. I'm up to here with the whole thing. I suppose it sounds uncaring and callous to you, but let me tell you a few things. I've spent the last eight and a half years trying to do what I hoped and prayed was best for Gena. She didn't start life this way. I'll get to that later. At the beginning, I tried to cope alone. She's my child and I love her. But have you ever tried to merely *talk* to a child who screams and screams and won't stop? I started feeling as if I'd lose my own reason just trying to get through to her. Wetting her bed three and four times a night at age ten. Taking off her clothes in public places. Screaming. God, her screaming!

"The last thing in the world I thought I needed right now was for some involved schoolteacher to leap in with the best intentions and start trying to tell me where I'd gone wrong. I'm not going to do a whitewashing job and try to make myself out to be the injured party. I've made all kinds of mistakes with Gena. But please try to understand that I've got all the guilt I can handle right now. I've been back and forth between here and Hartford twice a week since I got back, a week after the fall. In between times, I've tried to get on with my work and not go under from the weight of my own omissions and guilt. No excuses," he said. "I simply didn't feel up to anything else. Now, please tell me what Gena told you and I'll try to fix the picture."

"How do you know she didn't tell me the truth?"

"Look," he said quietly, "I know you must think I'm the bottom. I don't feel far from it. But I do know Gena, and I also know she hasn't any real idea what the truth is any more. If we approach this one step at a time, hopefully we can get some of the misunderstandings ironed out."

While he ate, Helen repeated the stories Gena had told about her mother and the school in California.

"It's worse than I thought," he said, eating hungrily. "Please eat something! I feel bad enough as it is." He smiled engagingly, and she picked up her fork.

"First of all," he said, "Nancy, Gena's mother, was a lovely, quiet girl who was totally incapable ever of doing the things Gena accused her of. The part about her being a chambermaid at the Crillon is true. And she was Irish. But Gena was almost five when she died, not two. She's done a good job of bending the facts to fit her story.

"In truth, it began with Nancy's breast tumor and ensuing mastectomy. That's a part of the mutilation she described. After the operation we were led to believe that was the end of it, that she'd get better. But they'd 'spared' us the truth. The cancer spread like wildfire. There was no way we could keep Gena from seeing the effects. I tried endlessly to explain, in simple terms, what was happening to her mother, but she fantasized, even then, refusing to accept our explanations. She barged into the bedroom one morning as the nurse was changing the bed linen and I was helping Nancy into the bath. She looked very bad by then —she'd had surgery three times, and was down to about eighty pounds. Anyway, I think seeing her mother that way was the final straw. She refused to go anywhere near Nancy after that, it broke her heart. I was helpless. Nothing would induce Gena to go to her mother.

"I imagine the detective Gena created was Dr. Thibeault, who was treating Nancy when she died. The whole thing, from beginning to end, lasted about fourteen months. Gena never recovered from the shock of it."

"How sad for all of you," Helen said, setting down her fork, her appetite gone. "I'm terribly sorry. You must have felt so torn, not knowing what to do."

"It was bad. I brought Gena back to the States soon after Nancy died, thinking a change would do us both good. And at first things seemed to be going well. She was nine before the first signs of just how disturbed she was became evident. I started her seeing a psychiatrist, and that, again, seemed to help. For a while.

"Then, when she was eleven, she started menstruating. And that finished everything. For some reason, she associated her own bleeding with her mother's death, and was convinced she too had cancer. It was the only time she even openly referred to how her mother died. I tried every way conceivable to assure her that it was a perfectly healthy, normal function of her body, but it took months before she believed that she wasn't dying.

"When I thought we'd managed to get past that, she came home from school one afternoon, hysterical, claiming that her mother had been murdered, that I'd always lied to her. On and on, incoherent. Every time I tried to talk to her, she screamed. It was all catching up with her. And I no longer had any idea what to do with her. She'd back away from me if I went near her and start that hideous screaming.

"Finally, her psychiatrist and I agreed I'd go out and check on the hospital in California. And what the hell can you tell from the outside looking in? They show you this and that, their physical-therapy room, their occupational-therapy room, their cafeteria. And it all looks good enough, because everything is clean and the nurses and staff look fairly intelligent and none of the patients appear maltreated. So, I sent her there. Jesus!" He closed his eyes for a moment, pressing his fist against his mouth. "The next thing anyone knew, one of the attendants was dragging her off at all hours of the day and night, having her in the greenhouse. He wasn't any goddamned *gardener!* He was on their stinking staff, paid to look after—well, I had to go out there and bring her back. All they'd managed to do was terrify her into a state of submissiveness and leave her with screaming nightmares of electroshock therapy. But she actually seemed quite controlled, rational, even optimistic when we got back.

"So many false starts," he said miserably, "dozens of them. Every time is a new beginning, and you go ahead thinking, *This time! This time she'll come out of it.* But it never happens. And after a while, all you remember is that terrible sobbing in the night. You feel so helplessly empty-handed. And what else is there to do but hope like hell and go on trusting doctors, people who're supposed to be able to help?

"Because it's either go on trusting or put her away somewhere and pretend she never happened. I can't *do* that to Gena! I can't! I *won't* do it to her.

"We started her back with her psychiatrist here, and after six months of daily sessions he felt it might do her good to go to a regular school with regular kids. So here we are! She climbs up to the third-floor landing and takes a dive. And now it's back to the institutions and the therapy and the wishing that this time'll be *the* time. Except for you. You managed to accomplish something with her. She wants you. I believe it would help her enormously to see you."

"I'll go to see her."

"I was hoping you'd say that."

"Were you?"

"Don't misunderstand," he said. "I take nothing for granted. I merely hoped that for Gena's sake you'd bypass the way I've botched things and want to go to her."

"I will. But I want to say my piece."

"Please." He made an openhanded gesture.

"I love your daughter," she said. "I love her. And I've

217

gone through weeks and weeks of absolute torment not knowing where she was or what had happened to her. I can see you have enough guilt without my adding any more to it. I believe you when you say you're bothered by everything that's happened. But I want you to know I've been actively hating you all these weeks."

"Not without reason. Do you believe how sorry I am?"

"I don't know. That isn't the issue here. But can *you* believe that I'm now at a temporary loss because I wanted to despise you and I can't?"

"You do love her, don't you. Why?"

"Yes. I can't offer you a pat explanation. I think, to be completely truthful, I'd been looking a long time for something. When I saw Gena, I realized she was it. She did lovely things, left flowers and little gifts for me. She needed someone, and so did I. It simply happened."

"Not simply," he mused, reading her eyes. "You've expended quite a fair amount of understanding and affection on Gena. She's my child. I know her problems. It makes me stop, forces me to reevaluate when I consider that the others—all those eminently qualified others—couldn't reach her. But you did."

"They didn't love her."

"Do you realize what that implies?"

"Of course I do."

"And you'd keep on?"

She looked into his eyes, seeing there a mixture of hope and something else she couldn't—didn't dare—speculate on.

"I wouldn't stop caring for her because she's been removed from my reach. I have an obligation to keep on loving her, especially now, when she needs it. I know what you're thinking," she said. "But I couldn't have prevented what happened. There were too many unknowns to contend with. Not to mention wishing to do permanent damage to her eternally absent father because I wanted to blame someone for not being there to help her. Perhaps you're right. Perhaps I can't imagine what it's like to have a screaming, incontinent child. But I do know how it feels to love her and to long to do something to help. I certainly wouldn't switch off my telephone and hope the world would go away and leave me alone."

"I didn't say it was the *right* thing to do," he said softly. "It was what I *had* to do. Are we going to be able to go beyond that? Because I want us to. It wasn't directly personal, Helen. It had to do with years all stacking up until I felt I couldn't take any more."

"I'm not going to add to that," she said, realizing she didn't have any desire to. "In spite of all the rest of it, I like you too much."

"Someone taught you very well," he said with admiring eyes. "Very well."

"You've already met her."

"I fell for your mother at first glance. And then I saw you." He looked down at his hands for a second before meeting her eyes again. "You're very good to be with. No"—he shook his head—"you're too honest for euphemisms. It's just that the timing seems so wrong. I came to find you because of Gena, because Gena needed you and I had to make every effort to provide her with what she needs because I owe her that and much more. But now, being with you, knowing you, I think I came for her sake *and* for mine."

His head came up and he leaned far back in his chair, as if hoping that this small additional distance would heighten his perspective. He came slowly forward, smiling.

"I offered to buy you this evening," he said, the smile flourishing.

"You did what?" It was hard for her to concentrate on what he was saying because she was so involved with the shape of his mouth and the way it moved when he spoke.

"I offered to buy your portrait," he said. "Not knowing, of course, it was you. Your mother was very gracious in her refusal."

"That's very flattering."

"I was damned well victimized by that painting."

"Oh?" It suddenly seemed terribly warm in the restaurant.

"You're a lovely woman," he said, gazing at her. "Beautiful. I love your directness, your honesty, the way you listen. You probably wanted to beat me up when you didn't hear from me, must have thought I was some kind of crude, irresponsible beanbag."

"Beanbag." She laughed. "I planned to murder you. I was going to buy a gun."

"I can't say I blame you. But not yet, please. Let's get to know each other first. Then you may decide to buy a gun. God knows, you've got cause."

"This is new," she said, lining up the salt and pepper shakers.

"What is?"

"The visual seduction. Well, not exactly. Gena does it too."

"It's not something I do every night, Helen. There must be men every day of your life who come at you because you're beautiful. How do you handle it? Tell me about you."

"It usually comes down to whether I want to or I don't. Most of the time I don't. But it's such an awesome weapon. I go home and wonder why, what happened to my mind, what happened to my conviction that it's no good when it's casual."

"I'm not casual. Leaving Gena out of it, do you trust me?"

"Should I?"

"Yes."

"Why?"

"You're a skeptic," he said. "How did that happen?"

"Maybe I am. I was married once upon a time. When Stu died, perhaps I stopped believing. But also, you frighten me a little."

"Why?"

"Oh, I don't know."

"Yes you do. Shall I tell you why?" She nodded, and he took her hand. "It has something to do with mental pictures we both drew and the way we each came armed, prepared to do battle for someone we both love. Gena's no one's concept of a lovable little kid. And you went past all the superficial problems and began caring.

"And you. There are more reasons than the ones you've

given me about Gena. Why don't you feel sorry for yourself? Why? You've been badly treated by the McLarens, but you refuse to be vindictive. Instead, you're compassionate. Why? Tell me. Then I'll say what I've wanted to say for the last three hours."

"You'll find out the prime reason for yourself," she said. "I won't have to tell you. Not about the why's of my caring for Gena. You'll know. As for you . . ." She shrugged her shoulders lightly. "I looked up and I saw you with Mother and I thought, 'There's a beautiful man,' and I couldn't determine why I found you so. It was pure reaction. Then, when you were someone I've been trying to hate for months, I simply couldn't do it. I felt as if I'd had the ladder knocked out from under me. It forced me to start fresh, without preconceptions, because I was drawn to you before I knew who you were. I've spent the last five years entering into once- or twice-weekly tribal mating games with a number of men I didn't especially want or even care for, trying to fill something very empty in my life. Tonight, being with you, I find I no longer care for the ritual. I want to go straight past all of that."

One by one, he kissed the tips of her fingers before folding his hand over hers. "I would like to love you. I think it would make both of us very happy. I also think I have a pretty decent idea who I am, and I'm fairly certain I know who you are. Whatever you want it to be, that's what it'll be. I won't hurt you."

"I know that."

"I want you, and you know that too. But it *is* too fast. It's important that it be right. For both of us. When it's right for you, then . . ." He left the rest unsaid. "I'll take you home now."

He parked in front of the house and peered up at it before turning to her. He leaned forward and kissed her lightly on the mouth, then sat back from her, his hand on her cheek.

"Will you do something else for me?" he asked.

"What?"

"Will you please try not to think too badly of me for everything. I think badly enough of myself. It matters a hell of a lot to me what you think. I don't think I've ever said that to anyone, except perhaps to Gena. It isn't my vanity talking for me now, it's something else. A part of me that very much wants to have what you have—that controlled, reasoning anger and the depth and serenity of the way you care. You're very special. You've given me a look at myself tonight, and it hasn't been pretty. But I'm grateful, and I thank you."

"Don't," she said very quietly. "It's not for me to judge you. And my anger was anything but controlled. Love doesn't follow lines of logic, it just flows in to fill the empty spaces—even the angry ones. *My* vanity was hurt because you didn't respond to my letters. But perhaps I've got a bit more insight now into the problem. It's all a matter of giving and receiving, finding out. There shouldn't be any need for saying please and thank you. Not ever, if it's real."

13

The next afternoon, Wednesday, Norm was restless, unable to work. Grabbing up his hat and coat, he set out to walk it off, and found himself heading in the direction of the high school downtown.

In the front office, he flashed an old press pass under the secretary's nose. She told him what he wanted to know and, as he glanced at his watch, he saw he was in time to catch the end of her class.

He stationed himself at the back door of the room, watching through the inset glass window as Helen leaned against the blackboard with one shoe off and the heel of her shoeless foot resting on the instep of the other. The faces, the eyes of the kids in that room, took her in as they listened to her reading in a beautiful French accent. It was Baudelaire, and he too listened, captivated by her reading.

At the end, there was an audible sigh of appreciation from the class as she closed the book and asked one of the boys to set up a portable record player.

"It's something new," she said, setting a record on the turntable. "Something lovely to end the day with."

With her shoe back on, she moved to the windows, looking out briefly as the sound of Edith Piaf filled the room—"La Goualante de Pauvre Jean," "The Poor People of Paris"—and his head was filled with sudden re-membrances, of moments of intense happiness and some of pain. He stepped back, away from the door, and leaned against the wall, gathering himself together so that when the song ended and the front door opened and the kids streamed out, he was able to quietly enter through the back door—she was talking to one of the students in the doorway—and, unnoticed, take a seat in the middle of the room.

When she saw him, she looked startled, then smiled, and finally laughed as she went back to close the front door.

"*Bonjour, mademoiselle*," he said, removing his hat and setting it down on the desk in front of him. "*Je suis enchanté de vous voir aujourd'hui.*"

"How on earth did you get in?" she asked, sitting on the desk in front of him.

"With this!" he announced, flourishing his outdated pass. "You see before you the Chief Building Inspector of this fair city."

"You're crazy! What exactly did you tell them you planned to inspect in my classroom?"

"Ah now." He smiled broadly. "Any number of items. I wanted to see you. I've spent half the night and most of today thinking about you. Can you come out for dinner?"

"If I don't, you'll probably do something even crazier than this. No, I'd love to, really. I've been thinking about you too." It was true. She'd spent almost two hours walking up and down in her room after he'd left her the evening before.

"In my school days"—he laughed, reaching for her hand—"if there'd been teachers like you around, I'd've become a perpetual student. Do you always read Baudelaire with your shoe off and play Piaf records?"

"Oh, not always. I sometimes read Rostand or Verlaine and play excerpts from *Gaîté Parisienne*. You'll have to meet me outside. I have to pick up some papers from the office. I shouldn't be more than fifteen minutes."

"Give me the directions and I'm on my way."

She sat for a moment longer, looking at him.

"I'm happy to see you," she said finally. "I'm glad you're here."

"I'm glad you're glad. It was a hell of a walk."

"You walked? All the way from Remington Park?"

"All the way. Give you something to think about while you're picking up your papers."

She couldn't ever remember feeling expectant in quite the same way, so lightheaded and weightless. She sailed down the stairs to the front office, totally preoccupied with thoughts of him and anticipation for the hours they'd have to spend together.

"It's too early to eat yet," he said as she got into the car. "How about a drive along the Shore?"

"Would you like to drive?" She handed him the keys. "I like the way you drive."

"Gladly." He got out and walked around the front of the car and slid behind the wheel. "Have to do a little rearranging here," he said, reaching down for the·lever to move the seat back. "That's much better." He beamed over at her. "We're off."

He took shortcuts downtown to the Old Shore Highway, and once they were headed out of town, he unbuttoned his overcoat and relaxed.

"Let's cover the basics," he said, "all right?"

"Like what?"

"Like age, history, likes and dislikes, whatever you want."

"It's brief. I'm twenty-nine. I'm a widow. I love my career. And your daughter. I also love my mother, the zoo, almost all kinds of foods, and I dislike having to list my likes and dislikes. Your turn."

"Forty. Widower. Love my career, my daughter, almost all kinds of foods, and I'm sorry I asked you to do something you dislike. We won't do any more of it. This is one of my favorite spots," he said, pulling into a rest area overlooking the water and switching off the ignition. He swiveled in the seat to look at her, simultaneously reaching into his pocket for a pack of cigarettes and a lighter. He extended the pack to her.

"Thank you, no," she refused. "I rarely smoke. Funny."

She smiled. "I like the smell of cigarettes, but I don't like the taste."

He laughed. "I'll have to keep track of the preferences privately. I enjoy looking at you so much, I keep forgetting what I'm about to say."

"Let's get out. There's a bench over there."

They were silent for several minutes, staring at the late-afternoon sun glinting on the water. She turned slightly to look at him, studying his profile as he smoked. Without examining the impulse, she reached across and took his hand.

"Tell me something," she said, liking the warmth of his large hand, "just so that I understand once and for all. Tell me how you could go off traveling and leave Gena with housekeepers or nurses. Explain it to me, because I don't understand and I want to."

"It was all I had," he said, still not looking at her. "It's a pathetic excuse, I suppose, but I felt as if I was drowning under Gena's weight, as if she was slowly pushing me under. Working kept me on an even keel." He tossed away the cigarette, and his hand tightened on hers. "It's a stinking excuse," he said hoarsely. "The truth is, I don't know why. I've told myself so many damned things and I'm guilty, guilty as hell. I told you that last night. That's why I'm back now, why I'm trying to do everything conceivable to try to fix things. I keep telling myself I've left it too late, and it scares me because it doesn't seem I've done much with her that was right. But Lord God! I'd try to approach her again and she'd cringe and start that screaming, and every bone in my body would start screaming right back at her, the blood pounding in my skull until I thought the only thing left would be to kill her to shut her up. Jesus! What a way to feel!"

He let go of her hand and pulled a handkerchief from his pocket to blow his nose.

"I'm sorry," she said, touching the back of his neck lightly, soothingly. "In differing degrees, I suppose we've all got some form of guilt. I do understand."

He wiped his eyes and looked up at her, attempting to smile, but it didn't work. He put his arms around her and she held him as he cried, "Help me, please. Help us both. I can't do it alone."

"I will. I said I would."

He broke away gently, keeping hold of her hands. "Some hell of a date." He managed to smile. "But I've been needing to do that. Are you cold? You look like you're chilled."

"I am, a little."

"Come on, I'll get you warmed up—buy you a drink and some dinner."

As they reentered the city, she turned to him. "I think you did what you had to do," she said soberly. "I'll leave it alone now. But I had to ask, you understand."

"I know. I'm not sorry you did. It's about time I examined my own behavior and started trying to deal with everything more rationally."

Over dinner he talked books and authors, and she listened, entranced. He was knowledgeable but not smug, and interesting but not pompous. She could easily see how his work had become so successful a refuge.

When he pulled up in front of her house, she said, "If you like, why not take the car and drop it off at the school. It'll be a good deal easier for me to get downtown in the morning than it will for you to get home from here tonight."

"I think I will. It's been a long day. For you too."

"I've enjoyed all of it."

His eyes seemed to glow in the darkness as his arm came around her. He kissed her softly, then let her go. "Sleep well," he said, reaching past her to open the door. "I'll take good care of the car."

"I know you will."

Thursday morning, on her way into the building, she detoured around to the back door to see that the car was in its proper slot. She smiled and continued on her way.

At four fifteen, when she came out, she saw a shadow in the car, and realized he was sitting waiting for her. She opened the door on the passenger side. He moved over and she got in and kissed him.

"I'm going to get used to this," she laughed. "Students with overdeveloped curiosities are going to start talking, and the next thing you know, I'm going to be out looking for a new job."

"Are you serious?" he asked, surprised.

"Partly. It's a long story, but the school board has something against female teachers with affiliations."

"Marvelous," he said, looking disgusted. "I'll have to scout out some more devious means of meeting you."

"As long as you don't stop."

"Come here," he said with a laugh, reaching for her. "I want to kiss you. There's not a kid within a mile."

She felt herself sinking against him and pulled away slowly, her heart thudding heavily. "What's on the agenda?" she asked, touching his lips with her fingertips.

"Dinner? There's a film I thought you might like to see."

"Good. Fine."

He was able to talk more dispassionately about Gena over dinner, and she listened to his recitation of nightmarish incidents, coming to a new understanding of the tremendous pressures he'd been living under.

"She had what appeared to be a total regression six months before she went to California," he said. "I was home the last three months of it, still trying to handle her alone. The very worst of it was . . . When she was about six months old, like every other baby in the world, she did a fingerpainting job on her crib and the walls of her bedroom with a mess she discovered one morning in her diapers. They all do it. Nancy laughed and cleaned it up. She was like that. Treat the worst things lightly and they're minimized. Well, anyway, one morning I went into Gena's room to wake her and she'd done another fingerpainting job. But this time with her menstrual blood. Christ, it was *awful!* I just stood there staring for a couple of minutes, taking it in. Gena was curled up in a fetal ball on the bed in a soiled nightgown, sucking her thumb, smiling at me. Just the way she had as a baby. So I laughed and had the room cleaned up."

"Norm, I don't think I can absorb any more just now," she whispered, feeling ill. "I think I need some fresh air."

Quickly, he paid, helped her into her coat, and hurried her outside to the car.

"Let me sit quietly for a minute or two," she said. "I'll be fine."

"Can I get you something? Is there anything I can do?"

"No, really. It was just the image . . . I'm already better."

"Why don't we pass on the film?" he suggested. "We can always do it another time."

She rolled down the car window and sat with her head back against the seat, breathing in deeply, feeling the sickness passing.

"You have a very visual way of describing things," she said, turning to smile weakly at him. "I'm afraid that last scene was too real. Would you forgive me if I asked you to take me home? I think it would be best if you did."

"Of course."

He pulled the car into the driveway beside the house and came around to open the door for her.

"I'll leave you your car for a change." He smiled, but his eyes looked concerned.

"You're welcome to take it."

"No, it's better this way."

"When are you going up to Hartford?"

"Saturday, in the morning."

"I'll go with you, if you like."

"Good."

"I'm perfectly all right now," she said, nevertheless feeling a slight lingering queasiness. "I'll see you Saturday?"

"Sooner."

He pressed the palm of his hand against her cheek, then hurried away. She waited until he was out of sight, then went inside.

Friday afternoon she experienced a twinge of disappointment as she got into her empty car. She wondered where he was, telling herself she was being foolish to feel so disappointed at his not being there. After all, she'd be seeing him in the morning.

As she drove over the rise of the hill toward the house, she saw the black Buick parked out front and laughed aloud, delighted. She parked the car in the driveway and hurried back to the street in time to see the passenger door of the Buick swing open.

"Hello!" She laughed, sliding in. "Are you always going to turn up in unexpected places?"

"Always. I keep telling myself I'm not going to bother you today, and then out I go to find you and bother you."

"God!" She laughed, moving over to him. "I'm not bothered."

She slipped into the circle of his arms to kiss him eagerly. She felt his hands unbuttoning her coat, then easing around her, and pressed close to him, trembling. When the kiss ended, she bent her forehead to his chest, trying to catch her breath, flushed with desire. When his hands came around to her breasts, she reached for him blindly, opening her mouth to the pleasure rippling all through her. She sat back to look at him, realizing she was sitting on a spreading patch of her own wetness.

"Wait for me," she said. "Give me five minutes."

"I'd wait longer than that." He released her and watched her fly up the stairs and into the house.

She wrote a quick note to Amanda saying she was going to Gena and would return Sunday night. Then she put some things in a small bag and went down to the car.

They didn't speak until he'd opened the apartment door, allowing her to precede him inside. She set her bag down on the floor in the darkened room, then stood as, all in one motion, he swung the door closed and pulled her easily against him.

"I've been wanting you to come here," he whispered into her hair, stroking the nape of her neck. "If you hadn't come today, I'd've probably come tonight and pitched pebbles at your window."

"Don't ever do the 'right' things with me," she said, unbuttoning his coat. "I don't believe in what other people think are all the right things."

He kissed her, then removed her coat, letting it drop on the floor, then kissed her again.

"You're so lovely." he said, his hands on her face. "I never thought it could happen for me again."

"I know," she said, brushing her lips against his hands. "I do know. It's the waiting. It seems so long. Forever."

"Beauty." His mouth was on her throat. "I'm going to take the best care of you."

They couldn't move from that spot. They undressed each other slowly, disregarding where the garments fell.

"You *are* a beautiful man," she said, stroking the smooth expanse of his chest and shoulders.

As their eyes became accustomed to the dark, they stood touching each other, whispering.

"I couldn't have waited any longer," he said. "Not wanting you so badly." She seemed so impossibly beautiful, so warm and real and spontaneous, he couldn't quite believe that she wanted him equally.

"You're better than the painting," he murmured, cupping her breasts, touching her lovingly. "Much better."

"Norm." She let her hands glide down over him, across his hips, down his belly. "I want you now, this minute, this second." Nothing in the world mattered but this man and the boundless love she suddenly had in limitless quantities to give to him. She knelt before him with her hands on his hips, tasting him for the first time, experiencing a fantastic aching heat inside as she felt his quiver, heard him whisper, "God, Helen! Oh . . . Helen!"

His hands fell to her shoulders and he eased her away, down.

"Waiting," he whispered, as she folded under him. "No more waiting. Darling, I can't wait."

She spread herself beneath him, feeling a kind of delirious excitement as she felt him moving slowly forward, entering her so gently, so perfectly. She closed herself around him as he moved all the way inside of her.

"Kiss me." She brought his head down. "I need you. Let me kiss you."

"Nothing's ever been like this." His mouth opened over hers, the tip of his tongue finding hers.

231

"My God," she cried, moving wildly, "I—Norm, I'm—" She went into an instant orgasm, jolted as if she had received an electrical shock, shuddering as he fastened his mouth to hers and seconds later, came shooting into her.

"Darling," he cried, his breath fast against her face. "I couldn't wait. It was too much."

She clung to him, still contracting, too stunned to speak. All she could think was that, from the moment she'd seen him at the gallery, she'd known he'd be the best, the very best.

He broke away after a while and picked her up, saying, "You weigh no more than a child."

"Don't talk," she said, letting her head fall back against his arm. "Just more. Much much more."

"Lights?" he asked, setting her down on the bed.

"Yes, I want to see you."

He turned on the light, then lay down beside her, his eyes traveling over her body. His expression underwent a swift transformation as his hand came down over the scar.

"What was it?" he asked.

"Hysterectomy."

"Oh no," he said softly, his eyes moist with sudden understanding as he drew her close. "Helen." He caressed her. "I'm sorry. God, I'm so sorry."

"Does it matter?"

"No, of course it doesn't matter. Not to me. But it does to you. It has to. When did it happen?"

"When I was fifteen."

"Fifteen. Jesus! Will you let me try to make some of it up to you?"

"I'm in love with you, Norm. I keep thinking I'm making you up in my mind, that it's a fantasy because nothing could be this good."

"No, no. I love you. God, how I love you! I want to give you everything in the world."

"Please," she said very softly, "hold me. Just hold me."

He brought her closer, smoothing the damp hair back from her face. "You're so fine, so rare. Let me look after you, take care of you."

"I want that. I've been waiting for years for you. Years. And now it's like a dream, and I don't want to wake up."

"I feel it too. No one's ever been like you, Helen. Not anyone. I love you so much. This week has been one of the best in my life, because I knew you were alive in the world, because I knew I could see you, hear you laugh, touch you. I won't go traveling on you, I promise you that."

She laughed suddenly, happily. "I know that," she said. "And if the urge happens to take you, I'll pack up and go along."

14

Gena, huddled in her mink, was sitting on a bench in the thin sunshine, staring up into the sky.

"I'll wait in the car for you," Norm said, disengaging his hand. "She didn't even know me last time. There's no point in confusing her."

Helen went down the path and sat on the bench. Gena made no sign that she was aware of her, but simply continued looking up. Helen waited, seeing, with relief, that the fall had left no permanent damage to her face beyond a faint hairline scar on her upper lip. Her left arm was out of sight, inside the coat. She looked thinner, paler, and Helen ached to take the girl into her arms and out of that place.

"This doesn't smell like you any more," Gena said, extending her hand to reveal Helen's handkerchief. "I used it all up."

"Would you like me to put the scent back?"

Gena's head came down and around until she was looking directly into Helen's face. And then she smiled.

"Yes, put it back."

Helen opened her bag, removed an atomizer tube, and sprayed her perfume over the handkerchief. Greedily,

Gena grabbed for it and held it against her mouth and nose, her eyes rolling back ecstatically, then closing.

"They didn't believe me when I told them you'd come for me," she said, her eyes remaining closed. "But I knew you would. I knew."

"I'm sorry I made you wait so long." Helen touched Gena's face. "Will you let me see in?"

Gena shook her head, pressing the handkerchief tighter against her nose.

"If you won't let me see in, will you at least look out?"

Gena opened her eyes. "You mustn't look in," she warned, the handkerchief disappearing into her fist.

"No, I won't. What did you see in the sky, Gena?"

She smiled again and leaned closer to Helen.

"Nothing," She laughed. "Nothing at all. I do it to make them curious. I'm not happy here. It's not a good place to be."

"When you're well again, you'll come home."

"And be with you and Daddy?"

"Yes."

"When will that be?"

"I don't know, darling. Soon, I hope. Would you like me to hold you?"

She nodded, and Helen took her in her arms. "Why do you pretend not to know your father? It hurt him, Gena. Can you tell me why you do that?"

"Because I was waiting for you. He told me you were dead, but I knew you weren't. I was punishing him for lying to me."

"He didn't lie to you. You do know that, don't you?"

"I know," she said, putting her arm around Helen, "but I can't always be sure. I get so mixed up. You call me 'darling.' You always call me that."

"I'm not going to go away and leave you. I'll come back as often as I can. I love you, Gena. You know that I do, don't you?"

"I know that. I can tell."

"So now you can start trying to get better, can't you? You can try."

"I don't want to stay here."

"Then you'll have to try very hard to get better and you'll be able to come home."

"Promise?"

"That is a promise. You have my word."

"And you'll be there to stay with me when I come home?"

"I'll be there."

"Then I'll try. I'll be very good and try very hard. I wouldn't tell them anything," she said, resting her cheek against Helen's. "When I lost the perfume, I thought you were dead, that I'd killed you too."

"Darling, you haven't killed me or anyone. I'll give you the perfume, you can keep it. Would you like that?"

"Oh yes," she said exultantly, "I want it."

"All right then, it's yours. Would you like to walk with me?"

"Yes, let's. I've planted some bulbs," she said, pulling Helen by the hand. "Come on. I'll show them to you." She stopped and stood, faltering. "There is no gardener here," she said. "Do you think they know about me?"

"I think they know how much you enjoy taking care of your own flowers," Helen said quietly. "Where are they?"

Gena stood a moment longer, her hair windblown, her eyes bleak. Helen squeezed her hand gently. "Come along, darling," she said, smiling, "show me the bulbs you've planted."

"Yes," Gena said, shaking off whatever sinister vision had been stalking her mind, looking buoyant again. "Down here," she said, looking devotedly at Helen. "Darling."

Norm came around to open the car door for her.

"How did it go? Did she know you?"

"Yes, she did."

He got in on the driver's side and turned to look at her.

"I don't think I can talk about it for a few minutes," she said. "I'm a little rattled."

"Thank you for coming."

"Don't, Norm. Please, for God's sake, don't thank me!

236

I wanted to run with her, carry her right out of there. I hate the place as much as she does." Unable to go on, she turned instead and looked out the window.

"I'm sorry," he said, handing her some tissues. "That was stupid of me. It's just that there's no way to tell you how I feel about your doing this."

"Then don't try," she said, blotting her eyes. "Let's agree not to state the obvious. All right?"

"I want her out of there myself. I'll never get used to these places. When the hell does it end?"

"Starting now," she said unequivocally. "Let's go somewhere and have a drink. I need one."

"Look, I'd originally intended to spend the night up here. Friends of mine have a place in Avon, just over the mountain. They're away, but I have the use of their guest cottage. It's a quiet place."

"Then we'll go there."

"Fine."

After they'd had a look around and Helen had pronounced the place charming, they poured drinks and sat on the front step.

"I have to say it," Norm said, turning the glass back and forth between his palms. "I'm jealous. I wanted her to light up like a neon sign when I arrived. All I got every time was that face-to-the-sky silent routine. She wouldn't say a word to me."

"I'm jealous of every year of her life you've had her that I haven't. Does that make us even?"

"I think so. I would say it does."

They sipped their drinks, listening to the rustling of the new leaves on the trees.

"We're like people who've known each other for years," he said. "Old, dear friends. As well as everything else. I feel so at peace with you, as if there'd never be any need to call upon all the old tired routines of combat. You know, where I have to impress you with my balls and bravado and your having to demonstrate what a good little domestic you could be if you cared to try. We seem to have cut through all that and come right down to the essentials."

"It seems that way," she agreed, smiling at him.

"Maybe it's knowing what you want when you see it—knowing you're not going to be exploited or manipulated, but simply accepted the way you are."

"I sure as hell know I want you. In every way. What did you and Gena talk about?"

"It wasn't talking in that sense, Norm. She's not that rational. I made her some promises."

"Tell me."

"I promised her that when she was well she could come home. To both of us."

"And you mean to keep that promise?"

"Yes."

"Are you going to marry me?"

"That quiet question just hit me square in the stomach."

"It was more than a question."

"I know that. I know."

"It *is* too fast," he said, taking a long swallow of his drink.

"No, that hasn't anything to do with it. I truthfully hadn't put the thought into words in my own mind. It never occurred to me that I might marry again. I'm not sure if it's what I want."

"Then we'll let the matter drop."

"No, let's talk about it. Are you serious?"

"Very."

"How can you be? Be realistic, Norm. I could be anything at all. You don't know me."

"I *know* you."

"Yes, well, maybe you do. But do *I* know me? Can we walk?"

"Sure."

They set their glasses down inside the door and strolled along the pathway down into the garden.

"This is quite a place," she said. "A pool *and* a tennis court. They've got it all. I've always wanted to learn how to play tennis. It's one of those games that seems so deceivingly effortless from the sidelines."

"I'll teach you. I used to be pretty good."

"And what else were you pretty good at?"

"Oh, the usual college stuff: football, squash, hockey.

238

Junior McLaren, boy athlete. I'll take you to Yale some-time and show you my ugly mug staring out from a gang of group shots."

"Your face is not an ugly mug."

She stopped and looked at him for a long time, knowing what she was going to say and do, but looking nonetheless to see if something mightn't suddenly loom into view to alter her intentions. She knew with certainty that they could very easily spend years together and, married or not, he wouldn't change in the important ways; wouldn't expect or ask her to do or be anything but what she was. And that knowledge contained such warmth, such a vista of anticipated happiness, that there was no way she could withhold it from either of them.

She held out her hand and he took it, bending to kiss her.

"Yes?" he asked.

"Yes," she said, throwing her arms around him. "Yes."

"I'll give you everything, the world."

"Just you. Just give me you. We're crazy. I know it, and I don't care. I love your face too much not to want to see it every day of my life. Make love to me, Norm. Let's go back there and make love."

They ran back through the garden laughing. The sound of it was trapped and held by the encompassing shrubs and trees, picked up in the rustlings of the leaves.

"I forgot to tell you," he said, pulling her to a halt at the threshold.

"What?"

"I work at home. Does that matter?"

"Crazy! No, it doesn't matter. Nothing matters."

PART FOUR

NORM

15

Gena progressed, then slid back, then progressed some more. And every weekend, one or both of them made the trip to Hartford to see her, to touch and encourage her, hopeful when she showed signs of improving, distraught when she seemed worse.

Amanda often went along, taking pencils and sketch-pads. She and Gena sat in the gardens drawing, saying little, simply being together. She could feel that Gena was attempting to gather in facts and information in an effort to reconcile herself to the truth of her life as it had been and was, not to the fantasies she'd elaborately constructed. But it was an inconsistent effort, one that seemed doomed in the sterility of that environment.

She received news of her father's marriage to Helen without so much as a blink, stating, "They've always been married. Otherwise they couldn't have had me." And, for some reason, the remark made such good sense to Amanda that she merely nodded her head, smiling, and proceeded to sharpen her pencils.

Amanda was drawn to Norm by his intense interest in anyone and anything that had to do with creativity, with being productive, and to his impressive fund of knowledge not only about books and writers, but about painting and music. There was little that failed to interest him. And, coupled with this, his gentle strength and impeccable wit seemed like bonuses. There was, too, his powerful love for Helen. Just speaking of her, he seemed to light up, grow. Amanda had, since that evening he'd appeared at the gallery, found him an eminently likable man.

Fraser returned gladly to her position of bearer of the family secret, adroitly fencing off curious members of the Board, fabricating lies to cover Helen's absence while she and Norm spent a two-week honeymoon closeted in his apartment. She was happy for them both, and moved her love for Helen slightly to one side to accommodate the man Helen loved.

Helen settled into the apartment by hanging her clothes beside Norm's.

"You're not going to move the furniture or buy new curtains?" he asked, watching her put her nightgowns in the chest of drawers.

"Nope." She pushed an empty suitcase off the bed. "I like it just the way it is. Housekeeping is not my forte."

"This gets better and better." He laughed, picking up the bag and stowing it at the rear of the closet. "Can you cook at least?"

"*Comme-ci, comme-ça,*" she said, looking around for somewhere to dump the powder that had spilled in one of her bags.

"Here," he said, reaching for a waste basket. "I lived in Paris for ten years, you know. Speak French to me and send me into raptures."

"Take me to Paris and I'll speak French for you."

"Just let me know when you want to go."

"I'll remember that." She laughed.

"You're not even going to rush out and buy new pots and pans? Nothing?"

"Nothing. You've done a perfectly lovely job with this place. I'll enjoy it just the way it is."

"God, you're marvelous!" He grinned, hugging her. "Not going to do a damned thing."

"That's it."

She put her hands on his head. "When did you lose your hair?"

"Who knows? A bit here, a bit there, and one morning, no more. What's hair? So I wear a hat in the winter."

"I love you. I also love the fact that I'll probably never have to buy another book as long as I live. There must be ten thousand of them. I will make one small change, now that I think of it."

"Anything. Name it."

"I'd like to use the shelf in the bathroom. If it's all right with you, I'll move the books elsewhere."

Her first experience seeing him work delighted her. It occurred on the Sunday before she was due to return to work. He'd left a cup of coffee for her on the bedside table and gone into the living room, saying, "I've got to whack out a column. Sleep awhile."

She couldn't. She drank the coffee, then selected a book from the stack on the dresser and, pulling on his terrycloth robe, walked barefoot into the living room. She settled herself on the sofa, anxious not to disturb him. She opened the book but was too curious to read.

Norm, his forehead furrowed, his jaw working furiously, poked out letter after letter on the keyboard with rigid forefingers, maintaining a steady drumroll of sound. He paused, rolling the paper up into the machine to read something he'd written, reaching for a package of licorice lying beside the typewriter. As he scanned the page, he gobbled up a piece of candy, licked his thumb and forefinger, wiped his hand on his shirt, rolled the paper down into the machine, and resumed his frenetic typing. He laughed suddenly, his pace increasing for several moments. Then he continued typing for almost fifteen minutes without further pause. Finally, with a sigh, he extracted the paper from the machine.

He shuffled through three or four pages lying face down, rearranging them, then lit a cigarette and, leaning on his right hand, with the cigarette sending smoke up through his fingers and into his face, penciled his way through the pages. He was left-handed, Helen noted, captivated by this performance. At last, drawing luxuriously on his cigarette, he stretched, his arms reaching for the ceiling as he curved his spine forward, then relaxed.

"Have some licorice," he said, tossing the pack across to her. "Makes your teeth black, but it is, in the vernacular, neat stuff." He laughed and scratched the back of his head, yawning.

"Is this the way you always work?" she asked, setting the candy down on the coffee table.

"Always. Work facing the wall. That way, I'm not distracted by anything. Definitely not by the sight of you sitting there looking like something I imagined in a moment of overwrought exhaustion. Anyway," he went on, smoothing nonexistent hair at the top of his head, "it's how I work best. Words are so powerful. They can be so damned amusing or depressing. It's the closest I can come to omnipotence. I could put any number of combinations of words together and be elated or deflated in the process. Unfortunately, my beauty, others are rarely, if ever, affected by this highly personal view of omnipotence."

"I'm very affected by it, such as it is."

"Well, one takes what one can get, I suppose." He grinned.

"You looked like such a kid, sitting there poking at that machine, eating your candy, laughing, having a grand old time."

"I've always lived with the impression—please don't tell me at this late date it's misguided—that a man's supposed to be happy in his work. I'm happy with all of it."

He got up and walked over, leaning forward with an arm on either side of her, his hands braced against the back of the sofa.

"I can feel myself changing. Being with you is doing something remarkable inside me. For the first time in I don't know how long, I actually feel peaceful, happy." He kissed her, then smiled. "I'm going to try to encourage you to develop an appreciation for the attributes of licorice. Black is good. Cherry is better. The best is all sorts." He kissed her again, then dropped down beside her on the sofa. She watched his hand glide through the overlapping closure of the robe to cover her breast. The contact had the effect of creating an immediate hunger in her, so that when he kissed her she offered her mouth like someone caught up in a dream, someone controlled by a spontaneous interior force over which she hadn't any control.

"I almost couldn't finish that piece," he said, untying the robe, opening it slowly, drinking her in. "The idea that you're staying, that you're here. It's wonderful."

He lowered his mouth to her breast as his arm slid around her, bringing her tight against his lips. She wanted to cry because his love seemed a gift without price—he could bestow it so honestly, it surpassed anything she'd ever imagined. She rested her cheek against the polished warmth of his head, relishing the sweet, plucking sensation of his lips on her nipple.

"God, you're good to me," she sighed, running her hand down his back. "You make me so happy."

He lowered her onto the sofa, saying, "It works both ways. I don't think I could ever see you and not want you. Look how beautiful you are!" he exclaimed, his eyes round and lustrous as he drew his hands down over her breasts, following the curve of her waist to the outflaring of her hips and on down her thighs, then across and up her inner thighs, parting her legs slightly to allow the passing of his hands.

"I love the way you love me," she said, vibrating under his caresses. "No one's ever touched me the way you do, so knowingly."

"No one's ever loved you the way I do," he said, his eyes following his hands. "I love every centimeter of you, inside and out."

She closed her eyes, feeling his fingers on her breast as his mouth opened on her thigh, moving up.

He feasted on the satin softness of her thighs, burying his mouth in the sleek, slippery caverns of her body, devouring her with a devoted deliberation that sent her soaring into pleasure. And when she'd come under his mouth, making senseless word sounds, stroking his head, murmuring endearments, he laid his head on her belly with his eyes closed and his hands on her breasts, feeling as completely contented as she did.

"I'll never be able to tell you or show you how I love you," he said, his long lashes dark and curling against his cheeks, his eyes at peace under their closed lids. "I'd give you anything, do anything for you. Within reason, of course." He laughed softly, opening his eyes, kissing her hand. "Don't expect an unquestioning response to unreasonable demands. I am, after all, merely a reasonable man who loves you. And licorice. We mustn't forget that."

"Come here." She laughed, towing at his arm, bringing him down on her. "Kiss me and tell me all the unquestioning things you'll do for me."

"And what will you do for me?"

"Love you back, of course."

"That's all very well," he said, punctuating his remarks with kisses, "but will you promise never again to come in wearing nothing but a totally concealing, oversized robe while I'm working?"

"What?"

"It's being all covered up that way. Knowing what's underneath. I wouldn't be able to write worth a damn."

"I can't make a promise like that."

"Dear Lord above!" he cried. "Cursed!"

"Like hell," she said softly, nuzzling his ear. "Like hell you are."

Two years and Gena, in the doctors' idiosyncratic idiom, was little, if any, improved. After hearing the review of their findings, Norm drove Helen home. They were both feeling very low.

"She's going to be in that antiseptic nuthouse forever," he said bitterly, his hands tight on the steering wheel. "I don't believe they're doing her a damned bit of good there."

"Then let's send her somewhere else."

"Sure. Where?"

"You've got all kinds of contacts. Ask around. Find out. I agree with you. She's not getting anywhere. Just older."

"I'll look into it."

Aside from the regrettable lack of success with Gena, their life together was very good.

Helen was sitting in bed marking papers one night when he looked up from a brochure he'd been studying.

"My twentieth is coming up," he said.

"Reunion?"

"How would you like to go up for the big do they'll be having on the Saturday night?"

"I've always wanted to see Yale. I'd love it."

"I'll send in the registration," he said, tearing out the form. "I'd kind of enjoy seeing the old place again. I'll even take you to Mory's for a drink before dinner."

They drove to New Haven in June. Helen lit cigarettes for him as he drove.

"How does it feel to be almost forty-three?" she asked.

"Are you by any chance making a crack?"

"No, no. I'm serious. I was just thinking of all the things you've seen and known that I know nothing about. Tell me. How does it feel?"

"Terrific. Better than being eighteen. Why?"

"No reason. I was thinking in abstracts."

He looked over at her, thinking how very young she looked. And beautiful. She was wearing a long white gown of light silk, cut low in the front with long, clinging sleeves. It impressed him that she could completely disregard what was fashionable, selecting unerringly clothes that were so perfectly suited to her that she appeared the essence of good taste.

"You look lovely," he said.

"You make me feel lovely," she said, moving closer to him.

The entire evening was almost diametrically opposed to her expectations. Mory's was alive with the steady hum of conversations, occasional bursts of laughter billowing down the stairs. She looked around at the paneled walls, at the oars suspended from the ceiling, the team pictures on the walls, and tried to decipher the crowded monograms and carvings on their table.

"I gather this is encouraged," she said, tracing her fingers over the table top.

"It's traditional," he said. "It'd be right in keeping if I put our initials down. If there was space, which there isn't. My father's initials are on one of the tables in the other room. We McLarens have always gone to Yale." He laughed. "All two of us—my father and me."

The surviving members of the class of '32 were an attractive group who spoke together in quiet, smiling clusters, commenting on the number of their peers who'd been killed overseas. Helen experienced one moment of wrenching sadness remembering Stu, but tightened her hold on Norm's arm and let it pass.

The dinner was excellent. The speakers were both brief and witty. After dinner, they moved outside to the quadrangle, where large panels had been set up to screen off the area and a band was tuning up. There was a bar manned by undergraduates, and while Norm went to get drinks, she sat on a folding chair and looked at the boys tending bar, thinking they looked wonderfully fresh and full of promise.

It was a warm night with a light breeze, and she listened to the band with a sense of nostalgia. She looked at Norm standing by the bar, tall and distinguished in his dinner jacket, his face creased into a smile as old friends came up to talk to him, their great pleasure in seeing him manifested in hearty handshakes.

"You know," he said, pulling over a chair. "I was standing there, watching the wind blow your hair around, and I thought, Jesus! I'm a lucky man. They're coming at me in droves to congratulate me on the 'little woman.' Would you like to dance?"

The band played pre-war tunes and they danced, listening to the music echo off the surrounding buildings.

"It's just the way it was then," she said quietly, lulled by the comfortable sway of his body against hers.

"It takes you back, doesn't it? I want you."

"I know."

"Let's go for a stroll."

They wandered along the tree-lined streets in contented

silence, followed by the music from the quadrangle and the sounds of other reunions in every building they passed. As they were making their way back to the car, an elderly fellow carrying a drink and wearing a "Class of '99" button came toward them.

"Thought I'd get some air and look things over," he said, companionably extending his hand to Norm. "Fred Russell, 'Ninety-nine," he said, peering at Norm's button. "Norman James McLaren, 'thirty-two. A youngster." He laughed turning to Helen. "And a beauty. Lucky man, Norman James. The old place hasn't changed much, has it? Except for all the rebellious types. Probably thought we were pretty racy back then too. Still, it's a good old place."

Helen was touched to the core by his white-haired fragility and *joie de vivre*. On impulse, she stepped forward and kissed his cheek.

Russell beamed. "That is the nicest thing that's happened to me since our class party in 'Ninety-eight, when pretty Jennifer Hamilton kissed me in the closet. God bless you both," he said, lifting his glass in salute as he ambled on.

"What a sweet, cheeky man," she said, sliding her arm through Norm's.

"Dear old duffer," he said, opening the car door. "Want to go somewhere for a nightcap?"

"I want to go somewhere with a bed."

"You'll never hear me say no to that," he said, leaning across to kiss her. "One of the things I like most about you is your indifference to matters of the physical."

"I've found out about a place I think might be the answer," Norm said. "There's just one small logistical problem."

"What's that?"

"It's in Switzerland."

"Norm, no! That's so far away."

"Helen, you've agreed something has to be done. I think this place is our last hope. It's either this or having her spend the rest of her life in institutions. Neither of us wants that."

"But it's so *far*! I can't imagine how she'll react to not seeing any of us. And for God knows how long."

"Maybe that's what's holding her back, Helen. Maybe the answer is for us to let her go and hope like hell."

"If you think it's right, then it's right. But will we at least be able to go over to see her?"

"In time, of course."

Seeing Gena leave broke her down completely. She cried all the way from the airport and through half the night until Norm said, "Let's talk it out. This is no good."

"There's nothing to talk about."

"There's a lot to talk about. Aren't you really upset because you won't be seeing her on a regular basis? And aren't you a little afraid that if she does recover, she won't depend on you in the same way she has until now?"

She stopped crying and lay looking at him.

"God," she said, "you don't think I've harmed her with it, do you?"

"Of course I don't. But perhaps you've gone as far as you can with her. Now, it's a matter of going back to trusting others to see if they can't take her further. All we can do is wait."

"For how long, though? That's what really worries me. How many more years?"

"It worries me too. But making yourself miserable won't help her, love. It won't help anyone. Please don't do it. It tears me up to see you so unhappy. Especially when you know there's little or nothing either of us can do to change any of it. One way or another, something's bound to give. I've got a hunch this time is it."

"I hope you're right. I'd so love to see her happy and really alive."

"Maybe you will."

It was more than a year before they were able to see her. Gena underwent a serious regression immediately upon her arrival at the sanitarium and was in deep therapy for many months before she was sufficiently aroused even to dress and feed herself.

The psychiatrists' reports were morbidly negative at first, and Helen read them over and over, trying to find

Gena somewhere in all the technical terminology and awkward-English clinical descriptions of her behavior.

When school closed in June of the following year, Norm took a month's leave from the paper to fly with Helen to Zurich. Her enjoyment of the trip was destroyed by her first and only meeting with Gena. Not only did she fail to recognize either of them, but she had declined into silence—which, her therapist explained, was not to be interpreted as a distressing sign.

"We are expecting a break," the austere-looking woman said with surprising kindness. "It would not do to bother yourself because of her demeanor at this stage. She will get better. Of that, I can most certainly assure you."

Helen wanted to believe it, and listened to Norm's sensible opinions with her usual interest, but somehow she couldn't quite muster up enthusiasm for the rest of the trip, the people and places they saw. It all went past her in a colorful but meaningless play. She couldn't get beyond the idea that Gena might spend the rest of her life institutionalized. And she recalled the night when Gena had come groping at her breasts, wanting to be suckled. And she wondered again and again if she shouldn't perhaps have followed her instinct and gone along with it. But she knew she was grasping at implausible if's, and tried not to. Still, her memory was drawn to incident upon incident she might have handled differently, with possibly different results.

"You said yourself—remember?—that you couldn't have prevented any of it from happening," Norm reasoned. "Going back over all the things you might've done is denying the good sense you exercised at the time."

"I'm not sure I can stop. I'm so caught up in it."

"I've got a terrific suggestion."

"What?"

"Just stop! That's all. Stop!"

"Okay, I'll stop. I will stop."

"Good. Now finish marking those things and I'll get on with this piece of drivel I have to review."

Finally a highly encouraging letter arrived. She was unable to believe what she was reading.

"She's getting better!" Helen laughed. "She's asking for us! It's a miracle."

"Two and a half years," he said, staring at the letter. "I'm afraid to believe it."

"We'll go to see her, won't we? Right away."

"Right away," he promised, and booked reservations.

All the way over on the plane, Helen kept hold of his hand, afraid to allow her optimism to get the better of her. What the doctors termed "encouraging" could mean any number of things. It was dangerous to hope for too much.

They scarcely recognized the girl who came running to meet them, her arms outstretched, laughing and calling to them. The three of them stood with their arms around one another, laughing and crying. She seemed so healthy, so alive and vibrant, for the first time ever having a solid application of flesh to her bones.

"You really *are* married!" she laughed. "I've really got you," she told Helen, winding her long arms around her. "It wasn't ever really real to me. It was just that I wanted to have you both. And now I've actually got you. And Daddy," she said, kissing him. "You look so terrific. I'm so happy to see you. Are you going to take me out and buy me a big lunch and a huge bar of chocolate? I'm allowed to go to town by myself as long as I let them know where I'm going."

"Then, by all means, we'll go have a big fat lunch and buy you chocolate," Norm said, leading them to the rented car.

Helen was speechless, lost in wondering what magic key the doctors had found to unlock her. Maybe she *was* the skeptic Stu had once proclaimed her to be. But whatever it was, she was cautious about overtly expressing her relief, for fear that, by giving voice to her thoughts, they might suddenly take wing and fly off. She held Gena's hand and laughed as Gena gave them her considered theories on what had triggered her recovery.

"Mostly," she said, leaning her head on Helen's shoulder, "it was because I was so absolutely furious with both of you. I couldn't believe you'd send me away like that. I screamed and carried on and finally refused to say or hear anything, because I was so *mad* at you. Dr. Lindsner told me that the longer I kept on with not speaking and not hearing, the longer it'd be before I'd be allowed to see you. And that really seemed to click something in my brain. Because I wanted to see you. And I couldn't see you unless I talked and listened to what they said and dressed and fed myself. Suddenly I wanted to do everything in a terrific hurry. I kept thinking, if I do everything quickly, if I hurry as fast as I can, I'll see you.

"And then last year, when you came, I was in the middle of this gigantic fight with Lindsner, because I kept insisting you were my mother and he kept saying things like, 'You muzt agzept ze fact zat zis iz a zurrogate mozzer figure. Zis iz zomeone who luffs you but iz not vot you vish herr to be.' I kept screaming at him that he was a lunatic who didn't know beans about who was and was not my mother. But he wore me down after a while. And now you're finally here and I'm so happy."

"That makes us happy," Norm said, smiling at Helen over the top of Gena's head. "I especially admire your rendition of Lindsner's logic."

"He's as crazy as the rest of us." She laughed. "Why aren't you saying anything?" she asked, stroking Helen's hand, her fingers rhythmically moving up and down. "Are you as happy to see me as I am to see you?"

"Happier," Helen said, believing everything suddenly. "I've missed you so."

"I just can't *believe* you and Daddy are married. It's like one of the little daydreams I used to have when I was leaving those dumb things all over the school for you. You must've really thought I was a fruitcake."

"No, I didn't. And they weren't dumb. They were lovely. You were lovely. I'll never forget that afternoon when you played the piano in the auditorium. Do you remember that?"

"I knew your schedule by heart. I was always planning new ways to trick you into discovering me somewhere. By accident, of course." She laughed, covering Helen's hand with both her own. "How is your mother? Is she fine?"

"She's wonderful, sends you her love. She wants very

much to see you. And told me to tell you she's ready to take you up on your offer to pose."

Gena blushed and looked at her father.

"Does Daddy know about that?"

"I told him years ago," Helen said, glorying in the sight of Gena's blushing beauty. "You're more beautiful than ever," she said. "I can't believe we're here any more than you can."

Lunch came and went in an enthused outflowing of Gena's self-discoveries.

"I can actually paint and draw," she said, eating quickly. "You must be sure to tell Amanda that. I think I'd like to study," she said, glancing over at Norm. "Dr. Lindsner says I'll be ready to come home in another six months. Isn't that something?"

"It certainly is," Norm said, unable to eat. He noticed Helen wasn't eating either. "Would you like to go to an art school?"

"I think I might. I'm not sure. I'll probably know better once I'm home and used to living with people again." She paused, then went on soberly. "I'm still very out of touch with real things and real people. I'm kind of scared to think too far ahead. I don't ever want to go back inside myself the way I was. Not ever."

"I don't believe you will," Helen said. "You've learned the difference between the things that are real and those you made up."

"There is one thing I'll want to do," she said, reaching to take Helen's hand. "I hope you'll understand, because it doesn't mean that I don't love you more than anything, just as much as I love you, Daddy. But I'll want to come back: I'd like to go to Paris sometime, to take it all in, absorb the feeling of the places where everything happened. And see my mother's grave."

"I think your father and I would agree that that's a wonderful idea. Don't you think so, Norm?"

He felt so filled with love and relief and gratitude, it choked his throat. He shook his head, then got up from the table and walked out of the restaurant.

"Did I say something wrong?"

"No, darling. You said something very right. This is a supremely happy day. Come on, I'll pay and we'll go catch up with him and buy some chocolate."

He'd pulled himself together by the time they met up with him in the street. "I've found a chocolate shop," he said, linking arms with both of them. "I think we should buy a lot to take back with us. Pity they don't do licorice, though."

The day was a success beyond their wildest hopes. In bed at their hotel that night, they lay together reviewing the changes in Gena, making speculative plans for her future, her studies, their life as a family.

The second and third days were as good or better than the first, and they returned home alive with hope, feeding and growing off it. Released from their years of fear for Gena, they were able to resume their life together with renewed enthusiasm, convinced now, at last, that she was going to have a life of her own.

True to his prediction, six months later Dr. Lindsner wrote to say he was ready to send Gena off with his blessings. "It is one of my prouder accomplishments," he wrote, "although I would not have conceded at the outset that such a complete and transforming recovery could be accomplished. I wish you all joy in your life together."

Norm sent Gena plane fare and expense money. Then he and Helen set about nervously getting things readied for her return. The night before Gena was due to arrive, they put the finishing touches to the second bedroom, then stood back to admire their work.

"I can't believe it," Helen said, looking at the brightly painted walls and white wicker furniture. "She's going to be here. It doesn't seem possible."

"If not for you," he said soberly, putting his arm around her, "there'd be no one here. There has to be something I can do for you, love. What can I give you? Tell me what you'd like more than anything else."

"I have everything I want, darling. I'm very happy."

"There's nothing?" He turned her so that she was facing him. "Really nothing?"

"Honestly, nothing."

"We could adopt a child," he suggested.

Her eyes opened wide, and she stared at him for several long moments.

"I don't think so," she said at last.

"Are you sure? I like kids."

She put her arms around him and held him, always reassured by the broad strength of his body. "I've gone past it," she said thoughtfully. "I never thought that would happen. But it has. I don't think I could cope with an infant and all its demands. I've been *really* thinking about it for the last few months, since we found out Gena would be coming home. It's enough for me, darling. I have you and Gena. I don't want anything else. I have a suspicion that I might even resent having to give attention in any other directions now. We're fine as we are. Unless"—she lifted her head and looked at him—"it is something you'd like to do."

"Not if you don't, Helen. It has to be both of us or neither. You can't do that to children. You've taught me that. Among other things. You know . . ." He brought her close to him again, resting his chin on top of her head. "I used to think . . . There were times when I thought nothing would ever go right, that Gena and I would both end up institutionalized somewhere. And what was it all for? Why the hell was I running all the time, trying to delude myself that it was serving some kind of worthwhile purpose? It was crazy, absolutely crazy. I had my private cache of guilt and I'd lock myself up with it. But then you came along, and you cut through all my pretensions with your loving, and I realized the pretensions were all I'd had. Until you. Times now, I actually feel I can face that bathroom mirror every morning without wincing, without self-disgust. Sometimes"—his arms tightened around her—"I actually go in there and smile and think there's a point to everything after all. And the point, my love, is you. So, whatever *you* don't want, I *definitely* do not want. But if there's something you *do* want, you're obligated to tell me. Because I don't think there's a damned thing in the world that makes me happier than knowing you're in my life and capable of being pleased by me."

16

Gena came off the plane looking dazed and disoriented. She embraced both of them distractedly, saying, "I had to take Dramamine. Now I can hardly keep my eyes open." She gave them a watery smile and tried to swallow an enormous yawn that shook her whole body.

"We'll take you right home and put you to bed," Helen said. "It's late, and you're tired." Her eyes met Norm's, and he knew she shared his fear that perhaps Gena wasn't ready yet to be with them.

But on the drive back to town, holding Helen's hand, she seemed to wake up.

"Everything's so different," she said, looking first out one side of the car and then out the other. "What's that building? That didn't used to be there."

"University extension," Norm said, easing the car past a slow-moving panel truck.

"Look at that!" Gena exclaimed. "What is *that*? A hotel?"

Norm and Helen both laughed.

"It's the new Power and Light building," Norm explained. "They've got all the power, and lend us a little light from time to time."

Gena laughed, looking questioningly at Helen.

"I feel like I'm still flying," she said, "like dreams I used to have that I could fly around the school and land on the roof, just like that." She outlined a flight pattern with her hand, letting it swoop down and land on top of Helen's. "I wish I wasn't so sleepy. There're so many things I want to tell you."

"You've got all the time in the world to tell us," Helen said softly. "I've taken this week off from school. And then there's only three more weeks left to the term before we go up to the cottage."

"Daddy too?"

"All of us."

"Did you buy a cottage?" she asked her father.

"My mother's summer place," Helen interjected, "up north. I think you'll like it. Fraser will be coming too. Do you remember Fraser? Miss Hilton."

"The tall lady with the gray hair?"

"That's right."

"I remember her," Gena said slowly, her eyes fixing on some indefinite point, "I remember. When I fell. She was there. She touched me here"—she put her hand on her throat—"and then she said, 'Your stars are in ascendance. It isn't time yet.' I thought I was dreaming. What did she mean? That was such a strange thing to say."

"Are you sure that's what she said?" Helen asked.

"I couldn't forget it. It was as if the words were supposed to mean something special, like a clue in a puzzle. I kept thinking of it all the time."

"Fraser is very interested in astrology," Helen said, wondering if Fraser, too, had had a look at that curiously misinforming card in the school file; wondering why, if indeed she had, she'd forecast Gena's horoscope. It seemed an odd thing for her to have done. "I'll ask her about it," she said, puzzled. "I think she was probably trying to distract you in some way."

Gena yawned noisily. "I'm sorry." She smiled lopsidedly. "I'm going off again." She put her head on Helen's shoulder, and within seconds was asleep.

They woke her to get her inside, and the two of them got her undressed. Gena apologized several times more before finally climbing into bed. Norm kissed her good night and discreetly went out, leaving Helen seated on the side of the bed.

"They gave me a shot for the trip," Gena murmured. "Maybe they thought I'd go berserk or something and tear up the airplane. I wish they hadn't. I want to say so many things, and every time I open my mouth to tell you something, a big yawn comes out instead." She smiled dreamily. "I'm so happy to be home."

"We're all happy," Helen said. "Sleep. Tomorrow we'll go shopping or to a movie. Whatever you like." She bent to kiss her, seeing Gena fighting to keep her eyes open. "Sleep now, darling."

Norm was pacing the living room, smoking, leaving a scattering of ash in his wake.

"It's all right," Helen said, stepping out of her shoes and curling up on the sofa. "She said they gave her a shot for the trip."

"Oh!" he said, the fearfulness visibly fading away. "I thought . . ."

"I know." She smiled. "So did I. But she's fine, I can tell. Remind me to ask Fraser about all that business, will you?"

"You know I won't remember," he said, collapsing onto the sofa beside her. "I never remember that sort of thing."

"It feels different knowing she's in there, doesn't it?"

"It feels right."

"Doesn't it," she said softly. "No more waiting and trusting. That's all over and done with."

"Thank God."

"You look so tired." She ran her thumb lightly over his eyelids. "Let's go to sleep."

"Let's not." He laughed. "Let's go to bed."

In the morning, they were awakened by the aroma of perking coffee.

"Gena's making breakfast," Norm said, relishing the sleepy warmth of Helen's body. "Ten dollars says omelettes."

Helen stretched and readjusted herself against him. "She does superb omelettes."

"I love you best in the morning." He sighed, stroking the deep downcurving line of her waist. "All sweet and sleepy. You smell good."

"Mmm," she sighed, gathering him closer. "I am incredibly happy. You know, according to some of those esoteric books you have out there, this part is supposed to taper off sometime soon."

"My parts will never taper off!" He laughed.

She giggled, and he lifted his shoulders so she could slide her arm underneath him. "It's a good thing we have no schedule." She maneuvered her leg under his waist as his hands came down beneath her. She made a soft sighing sound as they joined, the muscles in her thighs hard on his waist.

"Don't think about it." He accurately read her thoughts. "She'll start making noise to let us know breakfast's ready."

"How do you know."

"Another ten says she will. God, I love you in the morning!"

Gena slammed the dishwasher door, startling them awake.

"Told you!" Norm laughed. "Didn't I tell you?"

Gena laughed and came hurrying to kiss them as they entered the kitchen, saying, "I thought you'd *never* get up. We're having omelettes. Everything's ready."

"That's twenty." Norm beamed.

"What's twenty?" Gena asked, heading back to the stove.

"Your father's being silly," Helen said. "Pay it no mind."

"Oh, I know!" Gena turned, spatula in hand. "He bet you I'd make omelettes. Right?"

"Right!" Norm said, pouring the coffee from the percolator into three cups. "Tell her!"

"It's the only food I can cook." Gena laughed. "He knows that."

Norm turned, and for a moment there was complete

silence in the room. He looked at Gena and then at Helen and felt elation filling his eyes and throat.

"Welcome home," he said, holding out his arms to Gena, hugging her hard. "We're so damned happy you're here."

Gena went sketching with Amanda, Norm took the car into town to get the papers, Fraser and Helen sat under the umbrella on the beach, marking papers. Helen became aware of Fraser watching her, and looked up.

"Is something wrong?" she asked. Fraser had an odd, puzzling expression on her face.

"No." Fraser smiled, shaking her head slightly. "I was just thinking."

"That reminds me," Helen said. "Did you do a horoscope for Gena?"

"Well, actually I did. Ages ago. How did you know that?"

"Something Gena said. Why, Fraser?"

"Oh," she said casually, "I do them for almost everybody. Curiosity."

"Hmmm," Helen said, stopping to correct a spelling error on one of the pages. "What were you thinking?" she asked, writing the corrected word inside the margin.

"About you."

"Oh?" Helen picked up the final set of exams and tucked them into her carryall. "What?" she asked, turning to look at Fraser.

"Nothing really. It was . . . nothing."

"It had to be *something*."

"It's just that . . . I was wondering how you'd feel if Gena went away again."

"What does that mean?"

"She seems restless. Have you noticed?"

"I suppose I have. She's only twenty. It's a restless time. If she chooses to go somewhere, she'll go. I'd miss her, but I don't expect her to spend the rest of her life with us, Fraser."

"Good. Well, as long as you feel that way . . ."

"I don't need sheltering from the facts of life," Helen

said gently. "I'm also not in the least unaware of what's going on around me. Gena wants to go to Paris in the fall. Norm and I both agree it would be very good for her to exercise her independence. Sometimes," she said slowly, "I have a feeling you know certain things are going to happen before they happen. Why is that?"

"I don't," Fraser said quickly. "As I said, she seems restless. That's all."

"Oh, here's Norm!" Helen pushed her carryall out of the way.

Fraser stayed on an extra week. She watched Helen with Gena, thinking how closely Helen's relationship with the girl seemed to parallel Amanda's relationship with Helen. She commented on that fact to Amanda one afternoon as Amanda sat on a folding beach chair with a newsprint pad in her lap, sketching Gena and Helen, who were lying nude on beach towels on the sand, sunning. Norm was dozing under the umbrella with a copy of *Time* over his face.

"Perfectly natural," Amanda said, shifting slightly to get a better angle. "Helen has a healthy objectivity about Gena. It enables her to see Gena as someone complete and uniquely individual. As it should be."

"They amaze me," Fraser said softly. "I envy their lack of inhibition. I wish I could be as free about . . . myself . . . as they are." She looked down at her bathing suit. "It doesn't seem to matter to them, to have people see them."

"Does it embarrass you that they're nude?" Amanda asked, keeping her eyes moving between the two figures on the sand and the page in her lap.

"I'm not embarrassed. I just wonder how it . . . feels."

"Comfortable, I expect. I don't think they *think* about it. How do you feel about yourself?" Amanda asked, glancing over at her.

"Ugly. All wrong. I covet their . . . freedom."

"You're not in the least ugly."

"Oh, Lord," she said, looking down at her feet. "I'm totally wrong. I'd give anything to be round and feminine and soft-looking."

"You mean big-breasted?" Amanda guessed.

Fraser flushed and looked flustered.

"The things that bother you," Amanda teased lightly. "Words. Breasts are breasts. Why do the words distress you?"

"I can't . . ."

"I should think a small, neat set of breasts like yours might be very nice," Amanda went on. "It's a question of proportions, like everything else. Helen's breasts aren't Helen, although I somehow feel you believe they are. Be glad of yourself, Fraser. There are those who no doubt envy you your height and your carriage.

"And since you're so evidently tempted, why not forget yourself and take your suit off? I can assure you Norman wouldn't be in the least discomfited, and I'd enjoy the opportunity to make some sketches. I like your lines."

Norm sat under the umbrella watching Amanda dozing beneath her floppy straw sunhat, Helen and Gena on their backs talking quietly, and Fraser's tall, slender silhouette on the raft, her long legs and small breasts giving her a girlish look. He looked around at the women and smiled contentedly, satisfied. His eyes returned once more to Fraser, watching as she sat down on the edge of the raft, her back to the beach. He looked at his wife and daughter —leaning now on their elbows, smiling at each other, talking quickly—and thought, *This is the most beautiful moment*, something he wanted to always remember: the quiet wash of the incoming tide; Amanda asleep in her chair, the sketchpad leaning against the chair leg; Fraser at the edge of the raft, gazing off into the sky; and Helen and Gena, their faces alive with enthusiasm, talking together with that special, semi-secret language they shared in loving. *Beautiful,* he thought, setting aside the magazine he'd been holding.

He got up and walked over to where Gena and Helen were sunning themselves, sitting on the edge of Helen's towel.

"Look," he said quietly, pointing to the raft, "your mother's latest success."

Helen sat up and looked.

"She looks different, doesn't she?" Gena said quietly.

"A lot younger. You wouldn't think a bathing suit would make so much difference, would you?"

"It has nothing to do with the bathing suit," Helen said, still looking. "I sometimes think growing up in a certain sense is really growing younger. She's beautiful and thinks she's ugly. Perhaps Mother's managed to convince her she's anything *but* ugly."

"I'm going to get her to sit for me," Gena said decisively, getting up. "Don't worry," she said to Helen, "I won't make her nervous. Maybe she'll trade off that horoscope for some bad sketches."

She took several steps into the water, then dove under, reappearing a minute or so later by the raft. As Norm and Helen watched, she pulled herself up and sat down beside Fraser and began talking animatedly.

"She's so confident," Norm said. "It speeds up my pulse rate, watching and listening to her."

"Does she remind you of her mother?"

"Not even remotely, except for the combination of eyes and hair. I'll tell you who she does remind me of," he said, planting a kiss between her shoulder blades. "You."

"In what way?"

"She's interested and vital and beautifully constructed. I don't know why, but it does great things for my ego, being surrounded by so many fantastic women."

"I detect a harem fetish developing." She laughed.

"Doubtful. The only woman I see here who does more than stimulate my eye is one small brunette with a sunburned navel. You really should put something on that, Helen."

"Is it really?" She looked down, placing her hands flat on her stomach. "It *is!* Let's go in. I've got some cream."

He watched the muscles working smoothly, strongly, in her legs as she jumped up and turned to offer him her hand, feigning a groan as she helped him up. At the door he stopped her and looked back at the beach.

"Look!" he told her. "Gena's talked her into it. They're swimming back."

"I knew she would." Helen opened the door and went in.

He stood in the doorway watching as she searched the top of the dresser, grabbing a tube of cream. She squeezed an inch of cream onto her forefinger, then replaced the cap.

"I'm sunblind," she complained. "Do it for me."

"A transparent ploy!" He laughed, sitting on the edge of the bed and pulling her over in front of him, transferring the cream from her finger to his. He coated her navel, then wiped the residue off on his trunks.

"I'll remember this," he said, easing her down onto his lap, "as being one of the more memorable days of my life. Does it hurt?"

"No."

"Oh, good." He laughed. "I'd hate to be responsible for irritating any part of you."

"Impossible. You know, you have changed." She kissed the top of his head. "You really have. Not only have you given up traveling, you've given up even thinking about it."

"Which means?"

"I'd like to go somewhere, take a trip. Just think about it, all right?"

"And surprise you, right?"

"That's right."

"Air or sea?"

"Doesn't matter. Do you know you taste delicious?" She moved her mouth from his shoulder to his ear. "Absolutely delicious."

"What was all that tapering-off business?"

"Fiction, obviously. I fully intend to be making love to you when I'm white-haired and saggy and sleep in a beach chair the way Mother does."

"Sounds good," he said. "Sounds very very good."

The last week in August, Gena was ready for her trip to Paris.

"If you run out of money or want to stay longer, just phone," Norm said. "Phone anyway, to keep us posted."

"I will. It's only three weeks. I'll be back before you even notice I've gone."

"You've got the numbers I gave you of people to call?"

'Daddy, please don't fuss. Everything's under control. I've got my ticket, my passport, all those numbers, and everything else. I'll be fine."

"We know that, darling," Helen said. "Have a lovely time and see all the things you want to see. Just try not to do it all in one day."

They saw the plane off. On the way back from the airport, Norm said, "It doesn't seem as if she's been here at all. And now she's gone."

"She *will* be fine, Norm. I think it's time to trust Gena, don't you? Isn't that what it's all been about?"

"I've booked tickets for a holiday in December," he said, "for the three of us."

"Where to?"

"Quebec, Montreal, and Mont Tremblant. Good?"

"Fine."

Two days before she was due to fly back, Gena telephoned from Paris. Norm was at a book-awards presentation dinner, so Helen was alone when the call came.

"You'll think I've gone crazy again." She laughed over the line. "But I've met someone I think I'm going to love, Helen. He's been showing me Paris, taking me everywhere. He's taught me how to eat snails. I'm going to go back to England with him. Here he is! Talk to him!"

Graham sounded intelligent, level-headed, in love, and completely mystified as to how to handle the situation via long-distance.

"I'll take care of her, Mrs. McLaren," he said in a beautifully educated accent. "I'm afraid I've fallen rather hard for your daughter. She's very headstrong, but I'll try to keep her on the track. She's told me *everything*."

"I don't know what to say," Helen said, as much at a loss as he apparently was. "Please, don't go into anything too quickly, will you? She may have an overconfident view of herself right now. Please, take your time, both of you. That's all I ask."

"I understand you perfectly. I'll make certain she's in touch with you as soon as we arrive back. Gena wants the phone again. Please, I know this is an impossible situation, but do try to believe it isn't casual."

"He's twenty-eight and too serious." Gena laughed. "He's a biologist, and he's taking me back with him to Durham University. Are you angry with me?"

"I'm not angry. But will you please call when you're settled and tell all this to your father?"

"Of course I will."

"I can't tell you not to do it, Gena. Just be sure, be very sure, you're doing what *you* want to do."

"I am, honestly. I know this is real. Is everybody well? Your mother and Fraser and Daddy?"

"We're all fine. Take care of yourself, darling. We love you."

"I will, darling. We love you too."

Helen had to laugh as she replaced the telephone. But, as quickly as the laughter came, it evaporated. If she allowed herself, she'd start imagining all the worst possibilities. She wouldn't do it.

Norm, after talking to Gena in England, lifted his shoulders in a gesture of helplessness, saying, "There's nothing we can do. Keep your fingers crossed he's as decent and serious about her as he sounds."

"I'm sure he is."

"There's one other thing," he said, looking pained.

"What is it?"

"She said she wants to do this entirely on her own. Which, translated from her argot, means we're not to make any visits unless invited. She'll let us know when everything's under control."

"I'm not really surprised," she said, nonetheless looking very surprised. "I just hoped she wouldn't ask that."

"She was very specific. Damn it!"

"Norm, I . . ." She got up and walked over to the window and stood looking out at the city lights, in tears.

"Don't, love." His arms slid around her shoulders. "You'll set me off."

"It's going to take a long time." She put her hands over his. "I'm missing her in advance."

"The offer still goes on the adoption."

"I don't think I'd have made much of a mother after all," she said. "If there were three or four children and this happened with each of them, one going after another. It's so hard to let go."

"Makes my traveling a bit easier to understand, doesn't it? That way, you never give it a chance to hit you too hard."

"Don't say that, Norm. I'll cry it out and be fine in a few minutes. You're not bad or remiss, and I hate it when you make yourself out to be something you're not. Whatever you were then, you're not that now."

"Foolish remark," he admitted. "It didn't come out quite right."

"I'm content with you," she said, squeezing his hand. "When you're not quoting Uriah Heep." She laughed and turned to face him. "That's why you said that, isn't it? To sidetrack me."

"It worked, didn't it?" He wiped her face with his fingers. "So who's for the trip? D'you think your mother would be interested?"

"Ask her. She might."

Amanda went with them.

Within days after Norm's conversation with Gena came the first of dozens of letters they were to receive from Graham in the course of the next five years. His letters contained an element of gentle humor and amusement that had failed to reveal itself in either of the telephone calls.

Whenever Gena wrote to them, he felt it vital to write simultaneously in order to render his own interpretation of the events and conditions she outlined, to offset any exaggeration or understatement she might make. It was an effective and ultimately harmonizing touch.

Gena's letters were usually filled with news of her thrice-weekly drawing classes and special Saturday-afternoon private watercolor instruction. She said all too little about her life and relationship with Graham, only that she was happy and getting used to "doing" for somebody else.

The first summer without her was very difficult for both of them.

"I have such damned mixed emotions," Norm said, looking both hopeful and bewildered. "I'm developing a compulsion to drop in on her without warning, or go over and spy on the two of them without letting on that I'm there. I know," he said, seeing Helen about to protest. "I'm not going to do it. But damn it! I miss her."

"We both miss her," Helen corrected smoothly. "But she doesn't want us there, darling. It's something we have to accept. I'm not any happier about it than you are, but I think I understand how she feels."

"Then explain it to me! I'm no goddamned good at this, and I *don't* understand your equanimity."

"Attacking me isn't going to change anything," she said quietly. "Don't, please, take out your disappointments on me!" she said. "I love you, but I won't let you deride my so-called equanimity because you can't supply answers to your own questions. I'm not a damned Pollyanna. Just because there are certain things in life I can accept does not mean I will accept what you just tried to do. Whatever understanding I do have I've worked at for a good long time. Work on your *own!*"

She turned and went into the house. He was on his feet instantly, following. As he came through the door, he saw the bathroom door closing and pushed it open, watching as she threw off her beach robe and reached to turn on the shower.

"Maybe"—he chose his words slowly—"it's a matter of my feeling no longer needed in a number of ways, Helen. Even when Gena was in Switzerland, or Hartford, even California, for all the trips and running away I did, I knew I was needed and had an enormous responsibility to her. Now, after a few months here, she's gone, and God knows when she'll come back—if she ever does—and I'm no longer needed. It's a colossal letdown, but not one I should've directed at you. Oh, Christ!" he said, feeling a kind of delayed shock numbing him. "I didn't *mean* it to end up as an attack on you. I had a moment of sheer childish resentment because . . . because you can sit yourself down and think these things through. It's still new to me. I'm not accustomed to squarely facing up to the ins and outs of things the way you are. I sometimes feel so . . . inarticulate. Whatever it is, I don't know. I'm sorry. I'm . . . sorry."

"I need you," she said, reaching for a hand towel to wipe her face. "It's time for you to let Gena go. Perhaps for good, in the way that you mean it. But *I* need you. I'm the one who's here to share your life for good. I'm the one who sleeps in your bed and makes a career out of loving you and trying to meet your needs. Gena has her own life now, and she has every right to it. I don't think you miss her any more than I do. But we either share it *all* or we have nothing. I didn't marry you for the convenience of legally having certain rights to you. I did it because I need the good qualities you have and because I believe it's mutual. I'd do anything to keep you, Norm. Anything. I love you completely, totally. But I don't want to see what we have together reduced because we can't bridge the problem of Gena. And she shouldn't be a problem. She's a grown woman, living with a fine-sounding young man, trying to make something out of herself and her life. Accept that she's brave and somewhat defiant, and applaud her efforts. You better than anyone know what she's paid. This business about your needing is misdirected. Don't you see that? It's twenty years later, Norm. And I'm here, trying with everything I possess to share your life. There's no room any more for the guilty-father business. I love Gena deeply. But she needs other loves, another kind of life now. I can handle that because I know it does *not* mean she's stopped loving either of us. But I need you. I love you. I sometimes stand at the front of my classroom and go lightheaded wanting you. Can we please put Gena into her proper perspective and the two of us get on with our life? She'll let us know when she wants to see us. It'll do no good pushing at her or wishing she'd somehow include us. We're not meant to be included, any more than she'd expect to come into the bedroom and watch us making love. Do you *see* that?"

"I see it."

She put down the towel, and he took her in his arms.

"Maybe we've cleared the air. I think we have."

"Life wouldn't be worth very much without you, darling. I don't want you to think you have to devote your every waking moment to me—that'd be dreadful. But I need you, and I do depend on you. Please, let's take care of each other and allow Gena the privilege of fending for herself. At least until she indicates she wants us."

"Passing through the eye of the storm," he whispered, holding her closer. "It leaves a lot of wreckage and destruction. I'm glad I have you, love."

"One of the things that makes me happiest about you" —she retrieved the towel and blotted his face—"is that you can cry with me sometimes. I don't suppose it's occurred to you that it makes me love you more?"

"I wouldn't have thought so."

"You see? It's all so silly, really. We're all of us such children at times. We fall down and get hurt and pick ourselves up and cry a little because it helps make the scraped parts feel so much better."

17

The second and third summers of her absence were easier. There were times when, on the beach under the umbrella, Norm sat watching Fraser and Helen sunning or out on the raft and Amanda sitting nearby with a sketchpad, and his mind rearranged time and he saw Gena and Helen side by side on the sand, their heads dropped in laughter, and Fraser's tall form on the raft. That day returned to his mind again and again; that moment when he'd realized that time stood still.

Helen's justified anger that day had knocked something out of him. He felt totally at peace now with himself and with her. And more than ever in love with her. Displacing the final vestiges of what she called his father-guilt had left more room inside him for Helen. And he remembered her saying at their first meeting that love filled the empty spaces, and wondered, astounded by her perception, at her admirable capacity for understanding.

The waiting now was something they did—like everything else—together. And sharing it effectively minimized the impact of Gena's absence.

Initially, Graham again and again apologized for ". . . what must seem an unorthodox lifestyle to you. But I do hope you'll understand that it is not entirely of my own choosing. Gena refuses, on an average of three times daily, to consider marriage just now, and I feel strongly that forcing the issue will do neither of us good."

Gena herself referred only passingly to his wish to marry her and said only, ". . . I'll most likely stay with him for twenty or thirty years and then find someone who doesn't fuss over me quite so much."

Helen said, "She's happy. Can't you feel it?"

"She's awfully good at saying one thing and meaning something else."

"It's not easy for her to declare herself openly, darling. You know that."

"I know."

He did know it, and by the end of the fourth summer of her absence had not only come to terms with Gena's reverse way of emphasizing her feelings, but was able to interpret her letters in simple terms without searching for hidden meanings.

The regularity of their letters, coupled with telephone calls at Christmas and on birthdays, lent a pattern to her absence, and when a period of a month went by without any word at all, they were on the verge of flying over to see for themselves what the problem was, when Graham's letter arrived.

My deepest apologies for not writing sooner, but it couldn't be helped. Gena would not, will not, apparently cannot, bring herself to write to you about it, and I felt that you must be told for any number of reasons. She had a miscarriage at the beginning of March, which I, quite frankly, thought might see her returning to Switzerland. For weeks after, she was in pieces, refusing to get out of bed, but just lay staring at the wall. I was very frightened for her and tried to get her to speak about it, but she rejected my very presence in the flat. It was a gamble—and one I feared was dangerous—but I cleared out, telling her to collect her wits about her or else return home to her family. Within a day, she'd pulled herself out of that morose state and rang me at the University, saying she'd decided it would be wise to get married.

Quite naturally, I wanted to advise you of this, but for reasons she wouldn't reveal, she would not allow it. For this I am, again, sorry. In any event, it's done. We were married in Edinburgh, as Gena was longing to attend the Festival.

Of course, now that we are married, despite the fact that she categorically refused to inform you of it, she is searching the post daily for word from you of your blessings. She is not always logical in her thinking, as well you know, and I hope you'll forgive both the long silence and the haste with which we accomplished the marriage. We both send you our love, and hope we may see one another very soon.

Graham

Norm read the letter first, since he was home working and automatically opened it when it came in the morning mail. He was so pleased, disappointed, and pleased again by Graham's evident good sense and intuitively correct handling of matters that he broke a longstanding rule and telephoned the school, leaving a message for Helen to call immediately.

Since it was something he'd never done, when the note was brought up to her classroom she appointed a monitor and tore downstairs to call him back.

"What's happened?" she asked, afraid to think.

"There's a letter from Graham. Hold on to something!"

"For God's sake, darling! What?"

"They're married. Two weeks ago."

"You scared me to death. I thought they were both dead. Don't ever do that to me again! My heart's about to stop from the fright you've given me."

"I'm sorry." He sounded hurt. "I didn't stop to think. I just knew you'd want to know."

"I do. And you were right to call. If you'd waited until this evening, I'd have probably murdered you. What does he say? Read it to me."

He did and she listened, keeping an eye on Josie, the school secretary, who was doing her best to eavesdrop.

"She must have felt so dreadful, Norm," she said when he'd finished. "If only we'd known."

"I think he handled it all brilliantly. I'm anxious to see them. And I think this is the go-ahead we've been waiting for. What would you think about taking a month before we go up to the cottage?"

"I'd love it. You know I'm longing to see her."

"I know. I am too. Do you want me to go ahead and get to work on tickets?"

"Yes, do. I'm sorry I shrieked at you, darling. I'd better get back before the kids rip the place apart."

"Not your kids." He laughed. "They'll probably wax the floor and dust the desks. The little buggers all drool for you."

The plans grew until they'd extended into a summer-long vacation. Norm accepted an offer to do several foreign pieces, and was mapping out an outline for a new novel.

"I've been deep-thinking it for almost a year," he said. "While you and Gena rush around shopping and having high teas, I'll lock myself in somewhere and start getting it down."

"You haven't said one word about it. Are you at least going to tell me what it's about?"

"We'll see. If you're very, very good, I may let you read the first draft."

"Go to hell!" she retorted. "It'll probably be another of those prurient pieces of inanity that got the people on the committee so worked up they *had* to give you the award."

"That was cruel and rude and only partially true." He laughed, backing her up against the wall. "And to punish you for that cutting critique of my literary abilities, I will now arouse you to a state of such pure, indiluted, and diabolic frenzy that you will not only retract every cynical remark but you will also eat humble pie."

"Like hell!"

"First the zipper," he said, catching her as she tried to

squeeze past him. "Then off with the dress . . . and now for the fancy underwear. Have I ever told you how insanely erotic I find your underwear? All that lace and soft, silky stuff."

"Has anyone ever told you that male undergarments leave a great deal to be desired?" she countered, laughing.

"Another slur." He toppled her over onto the bed. "I think it would be fitting for you to begin reciting the Gettysburg Address at this point. Prior to your public and private retraction of those wounding comments on my old masterpiece, I shall commence with the first part of the program, where the master of ceremonies lathers the culprit into a frenzied state. Nurse!" he called out. "Take the day off!"

She laughed as he came down over her with a menacing expression. "Has it occurred to you, my dearest love"— she smiled—"that I'm going to enjoy this?"

"I know, damn it! When you win, you lose."

They sailed to LeHavre, and from there took the train to Paris. Helen spoke to everyone in her rapid, native-sounding French, and Norm was touched to see how people were charmed by her unassuming manner. She evidenced such interest in everyone and everything she saw that no one seemed able to resist her. They received excellent service everywhere. And wherever they went, the heads of both men and women turned to follow her progress down some street or through a restaurant.

In ten years of marriage, she seemed to have grown younger. When he commented on this fact, she smiled and said, "Just luck, darling. And bone structure, according to Mother. Personally, I think it's all you. And a great deal of highly stimulating physical activity."

"That's all fine and well, but why do I look like a stringy old man with a child bride?"

"Because you *are* a stringy old man with a child bride."

"Just for that, I'm going to urge my wily daughter to turn you into a grandmother."

"Wouldn't that be lovely? I've never even held an infant, do you know that?"

"No."

"I never have. Imagine holding the child of your child! It would be like staring immortality in the face and saying, 'I've done it!' "

"I'll see what I can arrange."

"You can do a great deal, my darling. But that, I believe, is beyond your capacities."

"I can but try."

In Madrid they went to a bullfight. Helen left at once, threatening to be ill. Norm stayed a few minutes longer before experiencing an odd third-person ability to view the action below through Helen's eyes and feeling suddenly sickened. He found her engaged in a laughing conversation with a street vendor and stood watching, marveling at her unlimited affection for people.

They drove through Spain and back into France, on to Germany, then cross-country down to Italy. And three times a day, every day, she ate enormous meals, savoring the new tastes and smells.

"I don't know where you're putting it," he said, pushing away his half-eaten fettucini.

"I never gain weight," she said, sampling his leftovers. "I've never weighed more than ninety pounds. I probably never will. I couldn't begin to explain why, but I'm glad. This is delicious."

In London they stayed at a *pied-à-terre* belonging to a writer friend of his who was away on a fact-finding tour in Nepal.

"You have so many friends with fabulous homes," she commented, examining an exquisite Vermeer on the foyer wall. "I'm beginning to suspect you own all these places and simply fabricate friends to populate them."

They walked for miles, seeing everything from the Tower of London to a kosher delicatessen Helen found in Wardour Street.

They flew to Edinburgh and hired a car there to drive to Durham. And as they drew geographically closer to Gena, Helen's excitement grew. By the time Norm had found his way via Graham's careful directions, she had them both worked up to fever pitch.

Gena was waiting in the road, bundled up in a hand-knitted sweater that had to belong to Graham. It came down almost to her knees and was folded back twice at the wrists. She came running toward them when she spotted the car, her hair sailing out behind her like a billowing black banner.

"God!" Helen declared, laughing. "Isn't she gorgeous?"

"Get out!" Gena insisted. "Get out and let me look at you while Daddy parks the car!"

Norm laughed at the sight of them with their hands on each other's faces, gazing into each other's eyes before embracing.

"You haven't changed one bit," Gena said, taking her hand to lead her into the house. "You look just as fantastic as ever."

"You've changed."

"I should hope so!" Gena laughed. "I'm an old married person with a husband who was supposed to be here half an hour ago. I'll kill him!" She stopped, turning to Helen. "You do understand that I wanted to be sure I could make it on my own without you. I mean, that's why I kept saying not to come."

"I understand. Are you happy, darling? You seem very happy."

"I really am. I don't know why I made poor Gray suffer for so long before I could make up my mind. I want to hear every detail of your trip and all about your mother."

The three of them were sitting in the kitchen having tea when Graham finally arrived. Helen's mental image of him was instantly shattered. Graham was very tall, a powerfully built man with sandy blond hair and a face whose features conveyed both tremendous intelligence and kindness. He looked far more like twenty-one than thirty-three, and gave the impression of being Scandinavian rather than English. His eyes were large and very blue, fringed with white lashes of enviable length.

"Here he is!" Gena cried, her smile filled with love. "The husband! You're a *whole hour* late. Come and meet my parents!"

"Ignore her," he said, coming forward to shake hands

with Norm. He started to reach for Helen's hand, but kissed her instead, saying, "Photographs don't do you justice."

"Which reminds me," she said to Gena. "Speaking of photographs, you've never sent us a single one. Don't you own a camera?"

"She has three," Graham said, straddling a chair, "and a darkroom. She's taken several hundred photographs. But sending them to you is quite another matter. She's definitely kinky, your child."

"They weren't good enough," Gena said, looking embarrassed. "And anyway, I didn't think anyone would want to see them."

"I would have," Norm said, offering Graham a cigarette, which he declined. "You have very primitive ideas about communication, sweetheart."

"Hear, hear!" Graham chimed in. "Has she thought to offer you even a biscuit? She hasn't, I can see. No matter. If you'd care to, there's a very decent pub up the road that does a good lunch. I thought perhaps we might nip round for a pint, Norman, while the women discuss their hormones and whatnot."

"Good idea." Norm chuckled, finding him rather a highly interesting dichotomy.

"I'll give you a hand unloading your gear," Graham said. "We've put you upstairs."

"He's *beautiful!*" Helen said accusingly after they'd gone out. "How could you possibly omit mentioning that salient fact? You really are impossible!"

"Would you like to see your room?" Gena sidetracked.

"Not particularly. I'd prefer to hear all about you and see some of your work, if you'd care to show me."

"It isn't very good, I don't think. Well, that's not true exactly. I'll let you decide for yourself."

Graham had had a small studio built for her in the back garden, and Gena showed it to Helen, saying, "He's always doing things for me. Sometimes it feels like too much."

"You're happy. I can see it. Show me your work, darling. I've promised to report faithfully to Mother."

She was very quiet, introspective, as she showed Helen a dozen or so watercolors that were brilliantly executed.

"They're breathtaking, Gena," Helen said. "You're a very fine artist. I wish Mother could see them. She'd back me up absolutely."

"I'm having a chance to show them in the fall," she said, studying the paintings as if it were her first viewing of them. "I'm starting classes in oils in September. Do you really think these are good?"

"They're very good. I'm tremendously impressed. With everything, especially Graham."

"He has a nice family, a big one. His father's an inventor—was. He made a fortune out of something that goes in car engines and retired at thirty-five. Gray's got four brothers and three sisters. And all the brothers and sisters have at least three kids each. Anyway, Gray's dying to buy a boat and sail down to the Balearic Islands. He's convinced if he can get me off somewhere, I'll start having babies for him."

"Don't you want to have children, Gena?"

"I don't know. Having that miscarriage scared the living hell out of me, Helen. Out of both of us. Gray was positive I'd have to go back to Switzerland, and I was terrified he was right. And anyway, there seem to be a lot of people who are quite contented without having kids. You and Daddy, for instance. You haven't had any."

"We couldn't, Gena. It wasn't a matter of choice."

"I didn't know that," she said softly, returning the watercolors to her portfolio. "I didn't *know*." She walked over to the easel and picked up a piece of charcoal and stood turning it in her fingers. "I should have guessed," she said finally. "I don't know why I didn't. I assumed . . . too much, I guess. Never assume! Gray's forever telling me that. But I had it all worked out in my mind. I thought that because Daddy's eleven years older than you . . . Please give me reasons. I need them for you, and I need them for me too. I have to know."

"Ask me. I'll tell you whatever you like."

"Was it something that happened? Why couldn't you have one? Is that rude of me?"

"I had a hysterectomy when I was fifteen. I'll talk all you like about it. I don't mind."

"*How* old?"

"Fifteen."

Gena reached down the neckline of her sweater and came up with a package of cigarettes. She lit one, then returned the package inside her sweater.

"That's horrible!" she said. "Why? What happened?"

"I had a Fallopian pregnancy and began hemorrhaging. When they started making repairs they discovered I had cancer."

"So they took everything out? Oh, Christ! It's so unfair!" she cried, dropping down to lay her head in Helen's lap. "Is that why you put up with all the awful things I did to you?"

"Part of it. But mostly it was just you, Gena. I've always loved you. And the things you did. Shall I tell you something? You tied a ring from a Cracker Jack box to my car. Do you remember that?"

"I think so."

"My first husband, for a joke, gave me an almost identical ring once. When I found your ring on the car it was as if he'd given you to me. I'm not sure if that sounds too farfetched. But at the time I thought it was an omen."

"Oh, Lord," Gena said, looking up at her, her arms crossed over Helen's knees. "I didn't know *any* of this. Neither of you ever told me you'd been married before."

"Yes, I did tell you. Christmas Eve when you came to the house that first time. I told you then. You've simply forgotten."

"How could I forget something like that? Something so important."

"It wasn't important to you then. It's not particularly important now."

"It is too. I'm reorganizing my entire concept of you. You've been through some pretty bad things."

"So have you. There's something I've wanted to ask for years. How did you get that terrible bruise on your back? Do you remember that?"

"Oh, sure, I remember. I told you I fell off a chair. Right?"

"That's right. What really happened? Do you mind talking about it?"

"No, I don't mind. Not now, anyway. One of Olsen's boyfriends came barging into my bedroom and worked me over. When I tried to get out, he pushed me and I fell over a chair and kind of stunned myself. The next thing I knew, he was on top of me. I just closed my eyes and told myself it wasn't happening."

"Why didn't you tell me? I would have helped you. I knew something very wrong was going on."

"Oh, Helen," she said tiredly, "I couldn't tell you. I mean, that was just one thing. I was so far out of it, I was putting out for every guy in that school just so they'd like me. I didn't know what the hell I was doing. I wanted you to keep on telling me you loved me and having you call me darling. I thought if I told you you'd throw me out."

"God!" Helen said softly. "I had no idea it was so bad. I wish I could have spared you that."

"It doesn't matter. You've given me everything else. And that's the point. You managed to come through everything that happend to you just fine. And I'm still holding my breath, afraid I'll start being crazy for real all over again. Why aren't you crazy too?"

Helen laughed, pinching Gena's cheek. "We're all crazy. Don't you know that? You don't have any special priorities when it comes to being crazy, darling. You just do it a little better than the rest of us. Where you make it rough on yourself is digging for special clues to incidents that don't merit the kind of attention you give them. I've had a very good life. Your father and I are very happy. I couldn't begin to tell you how much I owe *you* for that. And look at you! You're very talented and beautiful, and you've a husband who's responsible and generous and too good-looking to be true. And you love him. It shines all over you. Someone very wise and good once said caring about people is really all there is. And that's true, Gena. Even if it means putting our own egos to one side for a time, it's all so worthwhile in the final analysis. You get such a lot back for your efforts. You're very much loved, darling. You needn't dwell constantly on the bad times of your life in order to properly appreciate the good times by contrast. You've known the bad and come through with flying colors. Now that you know about all that, try relishing the good. I sometimes think being happy is nothing more than a small circuit in the brain that clicks on and says, 'This is a happy time,' and allows us to realize that it is and to value that moment. It's the ability to recognize those moments when they occur and, if you're lucky, as you and I both are, to share them with someone you love."

"You're not so much older than I am, are you?" Gena asked, twisting a strand of hair around her finger.

"No. Fourteen years. I'll be forty-one in January. I'm not that far removed from you in age that I can't appreciate your problems and relate to them. I do understand how you feel, Gena."

"I'm scared to death of having a baby. And I can't give you, or Gray, one good reason why. It just scares me."

"Don't do anything if it frightens you that much. Maybe you shouldn't have children. It's not for me to say. All I will say is, you shouldn't feel driven either way."

"I love you so much," Gena said. "Sometimes I used to think I'd die if I didn't see you. But I had to tell myself that I couldn't keep on depending on you to help me make my decisions and point me in the right direction. I don't know why I didn't want you and Daddy to know about our getting married. I think I thought you'd see it as meaning I didn't need either of you any more and maybe you'd stop thinking about me. I don't know. I had this awful feeling you'd pass me off as some kind of finished business and I'd lose you. Now I'd give anything not to have done it that way. Sometimes I'd start thinking about you and start crying and Gray would say, 'Why don't you phone?' and I'd just cry more and say I couldn't. It hurt, missing you that way. But I couldn't make myself ask you to come."

"You're not going to lose us ever, Gena. Not in the way you mean it. I'm sorry you had to put yourself through such a lot."

"We'd better go meet the men," she said, getting up slowly. "You've always been so truthful. This has been very important to me. I'm sorry if I made you open a lot of old wounds."

"If we benefit from each other's experiences, darling, then everything is worthwhile."

"Just knowing you're there with Daddy benefits me. I love Gray, you know."

"I know."

On the afternoon they were leaving for the last leg of their trip before flying home, Gena enfolded Helen in her arms, whispering, "We're working on a baby. I'll let you know if anything comes of it."

Contented with the success of their visit and the first-hand viewing of Gena's lovable husband, they set off in the rental car to make their way south, eventually to London. In the Midlands they checked into a fine old hotel in Broadway, venturing out from there to tour the Cotswolds. They finished off their next-to-last day in England with tea at The Cobweb in Stratford.

"I've never felt better or happier in my life," Helen said around a mouthful of fresh scone. "It's been like a marvelous fairy tale, this trip."

"I've enjoyed seeing you enjoy it. Maybe we'll do it again soon."

Helen shook her head, still smiling. "It'll never happen. Not like this."

It had begun to rain, and they drove back to Broadway over the narrow, twisting roads in a quiet mood.

"I wish we didn't have to go home," she said. "I'd like to stay here forever. I know we'll never come back."

They parked the car and ran inside to their room. Helen stood by the window watching the downpour while he hung up their wet coats. "I'll never forget one minute of this trip," she said, smiling at a small boy scooting across the road with his jacket pulled over his head.

"If you wouldn't mind being left on your own for a couple of hours, I'd like to go over to the pub for a quiet pint and make a few notes before they escape me."

"I don't mind," she said, stepping out of her dress and draping it over the back of a chair. "I think I'll take a nap before dinner. The rain seems to've made me very sleepy. Run along to the pub, darling, and write down all your brilliant thoughts. Wake me when you get back."

He kissed her and went out, promising to be back in two hours. She got into bed and fell into a deep, dreamless sleep, from which she awakened just over an hour later feeling alert and refreshed. Throwing back the blankets, she swung her legs over the side of the bed, started to stand up, and fell full-length on the floor. She lay for a moment caught beween tears and laughter, trembling, wondering what in hell had happened. Pulling herself to a sitting position, she touched her left leg, which felt dead, as if it belonged to someone else. There was no sensation whatsoever. She leaned back against the bed, thinking she must have fallen asleep in a contorted position and managed to cut off the circulation. It would return in a minute. *I'll just sit here and wait for the feeling to come back*, she thought, forcing herself to be calm. She reached up to the night table for one of Norm's cigarettes and smoked it, watching the ash lengthen with forced concentration. She finished the cigarette, then said aloud, "Now. We'll try again."

She placed her hand on her thigh and was filled with relief. It felt like her own leg again. Carefully, holding on to the bed for support, she got up and took a few experimental steps. She was all right. She went into the bathroom thinking she must have cut off the circulation after all.

By the time Norm returned, looking pleased with himself and saying he was hungry, she was dressed and waiting for him. But, catlike, he sensed something and crossed the room, studying her eyes.

"Did something happen?" he asked, holding her face between his hands.

"Why do you ask that?"

"Just a feeling I got the minute I came through the door. What happened?"

287

"I'm not sure it's even worth mentioning," she said, trying to laugh it away.

"Let me be the judge of that, okay?"

"It's really very silly."

"Just tell me."

"It's so stupid. I tried to get out of bed and couldn't stand up. Fell right on my face."

"Darling Helen, that is *not* stupid. What happened?"

"I think it must have been the way I slept. You know how it is when you fall asleep on your arm and when you turn over your arm wants to stay where it is because you've cut off the blood flow. That kind of feeling."

"Maybe you should give Leon a call when we get back."

"Oh, really, it's not worth it. Listening to myself now, it sounds so minimal. He'd laugh me right out of the office."

"Well," he said, unconvinced, "if you're sure you're not bothered."

"Honestly. Let's just forget it."

At the end of September, Gena wrote saying she was pregnant:

> . . . the baby's due in early April, and you should see Gray! He's rushing here and there, starting things and forgetting to finish them; flying home at all hours to make sure the embryo and I are still alive. We're going to do a natural-childbirth course, and I'm very excited about it. It's fantastic, but I'm not scared. Now that it's actually happening, I feel very healthy and sane, and keep wondering what I was so frightened of all that time. We're going through name books trying to find something terrific, but so far nothing sounds right. Anyway, you can both start cleaning out your wallets to make room for the dozens of baby pictures you'll have to carry around. We all love you both and send love to Fraser and Great Grandmama.
>
> Gena

Helen wanted to go out at once and start buying gifts for the baby, but contented herself with writing a long congratulatory letter and hurrying out to mail it at one in the morning.

"You'd think no one ever conceived before," Norm said, cuddling her affectionately after she'd returned from her trip to the mailbox.

"I'm thrilled, period. In fact, I'm so worked up about it, I probably won't be able to sleep a wink tonight."

"Let me think . . ." He screwed up his face.

"You know something else?" she said, gliding over top of him. "I also think all that mental exercise is slowing down your reactions, dearest heart. Just a little slowed down."

"You really think so?" He grinned, lifting the hem of her nightgown.

"On reconsideration," she said softly, "no. God! Can you imagine anyone not enjoying this?"

Just after the New Year, she fell again. Norm was in the bathroom shaving, with the door half closed, and didn't see. She sat on the floor holding a conversation with him, hoping the whole time he wouldn't come out. She couldn't bear the thought of having him see her helpless. The idea of it sealed off any impulse she might have had to call him. She told herself she was being childish and oversensitive, but she simply couldn't bring herself to tell him.

Her dreams took a bizarre turn. Night after night she fell asleep to find herself collapsing in front of her students, having them step unnoticing over her as they went on to their next classes. Or she dreamed the apartment was in flames and Norm was shouting to her to get up and run but she couldn't and just lay disabled, slowly suffocating in acrid clouds of smoke.

They were in the living room one evening near the end of March when she suddenly swiveled around in her chair and said, "I simply can't mark another paper. I'm exhausted. I don't think I've ever felt so done in in all my life. I'm going to go to bed."

"All right, darling," he said, not looking up from his paper, which unaccountably enraged her.

"Can't you at least *look* at me? I'm *talking* to you."

He put the paper down and stared at her.

She stared back at him for a moment, then stood up.

"You're angry!" he said, his eyebrows lifted. "What did I do or not do that I should or should not have done?"

"Nothing," she said. "Just nothing. I'm going mad."

Then, stupefied, he watched as she crossed her arms over her face and sobbed, her whole body shaking with the force of her crying. He was up and holding her instantly, asking, "What is it? What's wrong?"

She shook her head fiercely, unable to stop, giving in to the fear that had been building inside her for months. It wasn't just the falling down or the constant tiredness that alarmed her. It was the paper cut on her finger that refused to heal; the sudden loss of her appetite; the spells of dizziness; the nausea. It was everything—all the things she'd convinced herself were insignificant symptoms of growing older. Intimidated by her sudden belief that these things were anything but insignificant, she sought refuge in the circle of his arms, crying convulsively.

"Please, Helen. Tell me what's wrong. You're scaring the hell out of me."

"Nothing," she sobbed, "nothing. I don't know what I'm doing. I'll stop in a minute. Just hold me."

"Come lie down. I'll get you a drink."

He settled her on the bed, then went to pour some brandy, noticing, as he held the bottle over the glasses, that his hands were trembling. He'd never seen her go to pieces before. It unnerved him completely. Something was critically wrong. He could feel it in his bones, had been feeling it since they'd returned from their trip.

"Drink up," he said, sitting on the bed with her, watching her gulp down the brandy like water. "What can I do? Is there anything I can do?"

"I'm frightened," she admitted. "Something's wrong. I know it. I feel so . . . jittery. This falling down worries me. I keep trying to tell myself it's nothing, but I know it's *something*."

"Maybe you're overworked."

"Maybe."

"We could go somewhere for a few days. Take the sun.

Then, if you're not feeling any better, I think you should go see Leon. What do you think?"

"I like the idea."

"Okay. How about Easter? Bermuda? We could play tennis or just loaf around. Whatever you like. There's a very good place I know. How does that sound?"

"It sounds terrific, as Gena would say. Would you mind if I go to sleep now? I think I've cried myself into a stupor."

"Are you sure you're all right?"

"Just sleepy now. I'm sorry, darling. You're probably right, and I've been pushing myself too hard. I do feel terribly worn down."

"All right," he said uneasily, not completely persuaded. "I'll come say good night. Give me a shout when you've finished your ablutions."

For the first two days, everything was perfect. As always, she turned golden brown after only a few hours in the sun, and her appetite returned. They were both lulled into a disarmed state by her apparent good health. They were expecting word any minute on the arrival of the baby, and left messages where they could be reached at all times.

They were in the middle of the second set of a good doubles match with a young honeymooning couple when Helen became aware of a pain fanning out from her hip. She flubbed several easy shots, and Norm looked at her quizzically. "Sorry," she said, stopping to mop her face. The sun was burning right through the top of her head, distorting her vision, sapping her strength. They lost the game, and Helen moved back to serve. Her heart was pounding erratically, double- and triple-beating. The racket seemed impossibly heavy. She threw the ball up in the air and lifted her racket, thinking, *I can't breathe.* The ball fell in front of her, and she stood panting, trying to catch her breath, sweat pouring into her eyes, down her neck, saturating her.

"Helen?" Norm turned from the net, the color bleaching from his face. He threw down his racket and ran toward her.

Her entire body was in a spasm, fighting for air. The sun had magnified itself a thousand times, burning up the air before she could breathe it in. She opened and closed her mouth as her heartbeat echoed deafeningly inside her skull. She collapsed into his arms, thinking, *I'm dying. Dear God, I'm dying.*

She regained consciousness half an hour later, trying to figure out what was covering her mouth.

"It's oxygen," Norm said, beside her.

She turned her head and looked at him. His eyes were round, terror-stricken, and she tried to smile but realized he couldn't see her mouth. She lifted her hand and he clasped it, saying, "It's all right, love. We're going home."

18

Norm had telephoned Leon immediately after her collapse, and he was waiting for them. They went from the airport by limousine directly to his office.

"Okay," Leon said brusquely. "Let's have a look."

"Nothing superficial," he said, beginning a series of taps and touches, working his way up her leg from the knee, asking, "Does that hurt?", to which she replied, "No." He continued on until he reached her left hip. She held out her hand. "If you pound me there, Leon, I'll probably pass out."

"I see." He placed his hands lightly on her hip, bending close to examine the surface. "Now," he said, straightening up, "tell me about this falling down. How many times has it happened?"

"A few. Three, no, four times."

"I see. And what else? Any other problems?"

She told him about the nausea and dizziness, how she'd been unable to breathe on the tennis court.

"And this cut." She held out her hand. "It won't heal."

"Let's see that," he said, studying her finger. "That's a mean infection. How long?"

"Three months at least."

"I see," he said, putting her hand down gently. "You

rest here. I want to talk to Norm for a minute and make a phone call. I'll be back shortly."

She lay on the examining table soaked with perspiration, consumed by cold fear. She couldn't stop shivering. Leon returned with Norm.

"I'm putting you in the hospital for tests," Leon said as Norm came around to help her up. "I'll take you over now and get you admitted. Take it nice and slow, Norm. My car's right outside. You can go out the back way. I'll get my coat and meet you at the car."

"What did he tell you, darling?"

"Exactly what he told you, that he's putting you in for tests."

"If you lie to me now, Norm, I'll never forgive you."

"I've never lied to you. I don't think this is the time to start."

"Promise me," she said, "promise me you won't lie about any of this. You might, thinking you were sparing me. I'd rather face everything."

"You don't know that you'll have to *face* anything."

"Darling, please, don't let's try to duck around this. We both know something's gone haywire. I'm scared. Be scared with me. What I don't need is for you to be brave and heroic. Be a coward right along with me."

"I'm scared," he admitted. "I'm scared silly."

At the hospital, a nurse took over while Norm went with Leon to complete the admitting forms. Within minutes, she had Helen out of her clothes, into a hospital gown, and into bed.

"My name is Cora," she said, giving Helen's hand a friendly pat. "I'm the head nurse on this floor. If you need anything, just pick up the buzzer. You relax now. The doctor'll be along in a minute."

Leon came in, accompanied by two other doctors.

"Helen, this is Lou Ramirez. He's an osteologist—a bone specialist. This other fellow is Mac MacAllister, a hematologist. These two will be running your tests. The three of us will look after you while you're here. I've got to get back to my office now. I'll look in on you later when

I do my rounds. Norm's gone to your place to pick up some things, and he told me to tell you he'd call Amanda."

"Good, Leon. Thank you."

The pain of the tests surpassed the pain of whatever was wrong. Blood was taken from her several times. Then the X-rays. Racked almost beyond endurance, she was turned this way and that until she was praying she would faint. Finally they were finished and took her back to her room. Cora came at once with a painkiller.

When Leon returned later, he said, "Take it easy, dear. I know none of this is pleasant. There'll be more tests tomorrow, and then you'll be able to relax a bit while the findings are analyzed."

"What other tests?"

"A spinal tap and a bone-marrow sampling are the two most important. Try to get some sleep. I'll be back in the morning."

"I won't sleep."

"You sure will." He smiled encouragingly. "I've left a whopping medication order. See you tomorrow."

When the door opened just minutes later and she saw Norm standing there with her suitcase, she sat up, holding out her arms.

"I hate seeing you here," he said, sitting on the bed, holding her. "I know how you must be feeling."

"I hate every bit of this," she said, her tears spilling over onto his jacket.

He grabbed a handful of tissues from the box on the bedside table. "Here, let me." He dried her eyes. "What have they done so far?"

She told him, for the moment omitting her suspicions.

"I feel a thousand times better now that you're here," she said. "It's idiotic, but just the smell of this place gives me the willies."

"I know. I know."

"Is Mother all right?"

"Fine. I told her you'd prefer her not to come all the way down here. Right?"

"Right. I love you, Norm. Thank you for handling everything."

"Don't, love. You and I don't do those thank-you things. I'm just trying to be practical and keep my wits about me. It isn't easy."

He left when the night nurse came in to give her her medication.

"You'll have a good sleep," she said, fluffing the pillows. "Those little yellow babies are dynamite. Is there anything I can do for you before I go?"

"No, nothing. Thank you."

"Sleep tight," she said, switching off all the lights but the one over the bed.

She lay waiting for the pills to take hold, crying softly; gripped by fear; hounded by the dreaded word that kept lighting up against the backdrop of her consciousness, standing in neon italics, shouting out for her attention. *Cancer.* She knew it. She knew it absolutely. The very word rang of death, making her grow cold. She thought of Norm, of his having to go through another cancerous death, and wept harder.

The pills began to take effect, and she abandoned herself to weightlessness, lifting out of herself, opening her mind to the respite of drugged sleep.

The day began at six A.M., when a new nurse came breezing in, shaking down a thermometer.

"Sleep well?" she asked, waiting for Helen's response before inserting the thermometer under her tongue. "That's good," she said, smiling. "Now your pulse."

Pushing off the residual effects of the pills, Helen watched the girl count off the seconds on her wristwatch. The kindness and consideration of these nurses comforted her. Feeling as defenseless, as susceptible to injury, as she did, any kindness was greatly magnified. Love from strangers—it was synthetic but appeasing, distracting.

"Breakfast in an hour," the nurse said, retrieving the thermometer.

"What's my temperature?"

"Ninety-seven point five. You're cold."

"Freezing."

"I'll get you an extra blanket. Anything else you'd like?"

"Am I allowed up?"

"Sure. If you can manage it."

Her left leg dragged, hanging uselessly like a dead branch, and the effort of getting from the bed to the bathroom depleted her. But she felt it was imperative not to be bested by her physical weakness.

Through sheer force of will and fierce determination, she used the toilet and then the shower. Finally, pulling on one of the nightgowns Norm had brought, she made her way back to bed. She rested for several minutes, then reached for the tray table and, using the mirror in the lid of her overnight bag, applied some make-up to conceal her pallor. Last, in defiance of her circumstances and surroundings, she sprayed her throat and wrists with perfume. There was something terribly important in continuing, to the best of her ability, the routines of bathing, grooming, being herself. The effort involved helped greatly to alleviate her sense of frozen isolation.

After an inedible breakfast—her appetite gone again—Ramirez, Mac, and a technician came in with Cora, who was carrying a covered instrument tray. The doctors began their tapping and touching, making authoritative medical remarks to each other that only helped confirm her fear. All that careful camouflage of her earlier efforts blew away like so much inconsequential fluff.

Despite the local anesthetic, the tests were painful, the marrowing in particular. She lay on her stomach feeling dehumanized as the sample was taken and her legs jerked out like those of an insect in the throes of death as the needle penetrated her spinal column. She concealed her face in the pillow, trying to suppress her tears. When Cora reached out and held her hand, smiling with genuine sympathy, Helen looked at her in speechless gratitude and clung to her hand like someone drowning.

Norm came at midday with flowers and champagne, cheerfully giving the flowers to Cora to put in water, then sitting gingerly on the side of the bed to open the champagne.

"You look better," he lied, pouring the wine into two water glasses.

"I look like hell," she said. "We agreed not to do this, Norm."

"When do we get some answers?" he asked, abandoning the pretense. "This is rough."

"Supposedly later this afternoon. You look tired."

"I am. It was a long night. Did you sleep?"

"Fairly well, all things considered."

"I have this impulse to take you the hell out of here," he said dismally. "It's all so ominous."

"Worse than that. Good champagne," she said, finding it easier now to smile and kiss him.

"How were the tests?"

"Demoralizing, humiliating."

"Jesus!"

"Do you know something, darling?"

"What's that?"

"This whole business bothers me more for your sake than it does mine. I'm upset, understand that. But I can't help feeling once we both know what's happening here, we'll be able to get past this 'wedge' that's come between us."

"Are you imagining the very worst?"

"I'm positive of it."

"God! Don't say it! It's bad enough we're both thinking of it. But saying it . . ." He closed his eyes and bore down hard on her hand. "Okay!" he said, gathering her close to him, "okay! God damn it! I'll be back later and we'll shout the whole fucking thing out loud together. Let's drink up."

Watching him go wasn't difficult. Trying to talk, holding him, seeing his anxiety was crippling. She drank the rest of her champagne, then set the tumbler down, staring out the window at the building across the way. Nothing served as a diversion. Every few seconds her mind shouted, *Cancer!* and she stood to mental attention, amazed that one word could be so terrorizing, so terminal in its implications.

The three doctors came in shortly after three, wearing grave faces. She knew. Norm reached for her hand, and she turned to see that he, too, knew.

Leon pulled up a chair and straddled it, resting his chin

on the back. The other two stood at a respectful distance, looking disconcerted.

"Okay," he said, "here goes! No fooling around, no euphemisms. You have cancer. It's in the bone marrow. The particular brand you've got is called dysproteinemia. There's not a hell of a lot we know about it at this stage of the game, so I can't go into an explanation of what rules it runs by. There is also a possible sarcoma on your left hip cutting off the flow of blood to the leg, which is why you have no sensation or mobility in the limb itself. We can't be sure how extensive the growth is or even if it's another malignancy until we do an exploratory. I will say, if the X-rays back me up, as they seem to, there's a good chance we can remove the growth and return to you the use of the leg. Providing it's nonmalignant. I suspect it is. I'm hoping it is."

"How long do I have?" she asked, dry-mouthed.

"Hard to say. Until we've had a look at your hip, I don't know. If we're dealing only with the dysproteinemia, you could have as much as two years. I won't be able to give you any kind of realistic answer until after surgery."

He looked at Norm, then back at Helen.

"Any questions? Anything you want to ask?"

"No," she said, not sure if it was her hand or Norm's that had gone very hot and damp. "We'll wait along with you."

"You're a hell of a pair," he said, climbing off the chair. "I'm not going to say a lot of useless things about how I personally feel. It wouldn't do anyone any good. I admire the way you're handling it. Talk it all out! Don't hide it away and pretend it isn't happening! That's all the advice I'll offer. I'm going to get out of here now and let these two get some more information, more blood. Don't let their attitude put you off," he said, casting a disapproving glance at the two younger men. "They think I'm a gruff, heartless old son of a bitch. But I think I know you two well enough. There's not a damned thing to be gained from avoiding words like 'cancer' and 'death.' They're real and they're happening. Death isn't always the worst thing that can happen to you. It doesn't have to be ugly or shameful. It's a function, something in most ways as natural as living. It's possible to treat it as such if you accept from the outset that it *is* happening and can be accomplished with dignity.

"I'll let these two get on with the samples, then everyone will leave you two alone to try to come to grips with it. Would you like me to call Amanda?" he asked, his hand on Helen's shoulder.

"I'll do that," Norm volunteered, his respect and admiration for Leon overcoming the horrific initial impact of the truth.

"All right. I'll be around again later."

Norm bent to kiss her, then went out to wait in the corridor.

More touching, probing, and tapping, the painful drawing of arterial blood samples.

"Have you ever taken any of the following drugs?" Ramirez asked, reading off a list of medicines she'd never heard of.

"No," she said, tired, her hip throbbing.

"Have you ever sustained an injury to that hip? A severe fall? Anything like that?"

"No," she said automatically, then, "Wait. A long time ago, years ago, I had a car accident. I was thrown against the door handle."

Ramirez noted that down.

"You should've had it checked at the time," Mac said, checking her other hip.

"It was bruised, but that went away. I didn't think about it." They'd been holding a mock burial for Stu.

"We'd like to do the surgery as soon as possible," Mac said, drawing down her gown and pulling up the blankets. "There's an availability in the O.R. tonight," he told Ramirez. "I'd like to book it."

It sounded as if she were a roll of cold cuts about to be sliced up in a delicatessen. The idea of neat, even slabs of her flesh lying on a plate was so grotesque that it actually made her smile. And then, realizing how macabre she was being, she carefully drew composure around herself.

When Norm came back in, she faltered, fear words

poised on her tongue like some vile pill she had the option of spitting out. She looked at his face, at the depth of fear and loving in his eyes, and let her own fear dissolve on her tongue.

"They're going to do the surgery tonight," she said, falling against his consoling body. "Then we'll know it all."

He touched her hair, wanting to say something, groping for some palliating phrase he knew was nonexistent.

"I'm going to die," she said, voicing the reality for both of them. "God, Norm! Last night and all day today, it's been all I could think of. It kept going around and around in my head, until there wasn't room left for anything else. Now that we know—I guess it sounds irrational—but I'm relieved. Somehow, only having suspicion is so much worse than having the truth to contend with."

"It's not fair," he said, his mouth in her hair. "Jesus! It's not fair! I'm not sure I can handle this, Helen. I've got to go somewhere and think, get it into some kind of comprehensible shape."

"It's even more unfair to you," she said, fingering the buttons on his jacket. "This makes twice." She gave up attempting to express herself, and wept.

His tears dropped into her hair, and he held her, thinking it didn't seem possible, it couldn't be happening, because she was still there—still soft and warm, taking air in and out of her lungs. And now there was something else inside of her, something that was slowly going to eat away all the softness and warmth until nothing—nothing at all—remained.

They broke apart and looked at each other, their hands entwined.

"Well." She sniffed. "That helped, don't you think?"

"It did," he said, reaching for his handkerchief. "What the hell do we do now?"

"Take some time to ourselves to think about it, try to come to terms with it, as Leon said. I have to think, and so do you."

"Right," he said, letting her take the handkerchief from his hand and wipe his eyes. "That makes sense."

"I'll tell you one thing," she said, looking determined.

"I'm not going to quietly give up and crawl into a closet and die. If I'm going to have another two years, by Christ, I'll live them. We'll live every damned minute. Agreed?"

"You're quite a lady," he said, a smile forming on his mouth. "I'm going to go do some thinking before I see your mother. Do we tell anyone?"

"No! No one. No, wait! I've got to think. Fraser should know. Dear God!" Her eyes opened wide. "Gena. Oh, Norm, this could devastate her."

"I'll handle it. I'll be here when you come out of surgery. You do understand I need some time?"

"We both do."

Before he left the hospital, he called Fraser. He saw nothing to be gained by playing it down, and got directly to the point.

"Helen's dying," he told her, marveling at how easy it was to say the words. "She wants you to know. No one else will be told but the family."

There was a long silence on the line.

"Is there anything I can do for either of you?" she asked at last.

"Not that I can think of at the moment. Thank you for offering. I'm sorry, Fraser."

"No, no, Norman. It's I who am sorry. You're a dear man. Thank you for calling."

He went on out to the parking lot and got into the car. He drove along, listening intently to the music from the radio, captured by each song he heard, finding every set of lyrics suddenly very personal and meaningful. He chain-smoked, driving mechanically, not thinking or caring where he was going. It was crucially important to hear every word of every song, to notice the way the sunlight slanted through the still-naked branches and glinted on the windshield. He drove, reviewing his life with Helen, his mind darting here and there to pick random incidents: the night they'd met, the class reunion, Fred Russell. Helen chattering in Spanish to a grinning, toothless street vendor. Helen standing at the front of her classroom, the focus of all those adoring young eyes.

Helen and Gena in the road, their hands on each other's faces, their eyes alive with wonder. Helen. Helen.

He pulled off the road and sat for a long time, letting the incredulity wash over him as something gnawed inside, saying, *Think of this! Think!* and he suddenly knew that Gena had to be told.

He was caught again by the sunlight as he wiped his face, mesmerized by the brightness and beauty of the day. No. He blinked away the temptation of being blinded to the things that needed doing. It was time to go back, time to tell Amanda.

She listened closely, her eyes in no way reflecting that what she was hearing was out of the ordinary. When he had finished, she exhaled slowly, and continued to sit still, studying his face. He could see Helen in her mother as Amanda closed her eyes for an instant, her hands folded in her lap. He waited almost eagerly for her words, sensing that what she'd say would contain some wisdom valuable to his own understanding and handling of events.

"I think, perhaps, you might help her die, Norman," she said. "I have to believe it is something that might be done almost . . . beautifully. Yes, I think it could be. You needn't necessarily share my philosophy—it would be understandable if you don't. But I hope," she went on, ignoring the tears that had filled her eyes, "I will pray, in my irreligious fashion, that you can do that for her. It is as much a gift of love as any I can imagine. Helen will want to die well. You love her, Norman. Help her! I'm too old to attempt to do more than face the inevitable and try to attain some degree of acceptance. This is a time when we will all have to examine our souls very scrupulously. If we're to be completely realistic, we'll have to air our very worst fears—the ones we have for ourselves because we're losing her. It's that loss, that terrible hole she'll leave in our lives, that makes the knowledge so hard to bear."

She stopped and looked down at her hands.

"My instinct is to rail against fate and make a lot of preposterous promises such as offering my life for hers.

But that's time-wasting and tasteless. Enough of that," she said, impatiently brushing the tears from her face. "There is something you should have, something I should have given you long ago. I'll have it sent to the apartment tomorrow. It will explain itself. I think I'll go for my siesta now. You'll call me later, after the operation?"

"Of course."

"I love you both. My heart goes to you, Norman. This is the ultimate test of love. I think you can pass it. Forgive me if I leave you now. There's such a lot to think about."

The operation didn't take very long. He waited in the room, walking up and down, picking up this and that of Helen's, standing for a long while in front of the window holding her nightgown, breathing in the scent of her in the silk fibers.

Ramirez came in to say, "She's in the recovery room. I'm going down to Pathology. We should have some answers soon."

"Was it a success?"

"We got out the growth. She should be ambulatory within a matter of days. I'll have more for you later. They'll be bringing her up in about twenty minutes."

That's how she'll look dead, he thought when she was returned to the room. *Like a sculpted image of herself, pale and still and beautiful.* He lit a cigarette and sat waiting, never taking his eyes from her face.

Her eyelids twitched, and he thought she'd awaken then, but she didn't. Her hand moved slightly, causing a chill of panic to run down his spine. *God,* he thought, *what am I scared about? We know about all there is to know.*

He glanced out the window, reviewing Amanda's words and the truth they contained, knowing that what he was engaging in at that very moment was a consideration of the yawning hole there'd be in his life. When he turned to look at her again, her eyes were open.

"Hello." He touched her hand.

"Hello," she whispered. "Will you get me some water?"

He rang for the nurse, who came, listened, then went off to get juice for Helen and some coffee for him.

"How do you feel?" he asked after the nurse had gone.

"Not too bad." She smiled groggily. "Better than I thought I would. It's lovely to see you, darling."

"It's even better to see you."

"Did you tell Mother?"

"Everything's taken care of."

"Good. It's hard for me to talk."

"Lie quietly then," he said, holding her hand.

The nurse returned with the drinks, saying, "They just called up. About half an hour more."

Norm's hands went wet; his heartbeat accelerated. Half an hour and they'd get the verdict. He imagined he knew now how criminals felt when they stood in front of a silent courtroom awaiting sentence.

He held the glass while she sipped some of the juice through a bent straw.

"That's better." She rested against the pillows. "Why do operations make you so damned dry?"

"Can't say. I've never had one."

"Don't look that way, darling." She smiled. "It can't get too much worse."

"Do you *really* believe that?"

"Yes, I really do. And so should you."

Mac and Ramirez came in, looking tired and anxious to go home.

"The growth was nonmalignant," Ramirez said. "You should have no further problem with the leg. As far as the dysproteinemia is concerned, Leon's already explained how little we know about it. The treatment so far is totally hit-and-miss. We've been able, for the most part, with medication, to achieve remissions lasting anywhere from ten months to two years. But nothing appreciably longer. I don't want to give you any false hopes. I'm not as blunt as Leon, but I don't disagree with his feelings for telling the truth."

"How long?" Helen asked.

"I'd say eighteen months."

"But it could be less?"

"It could be as little as five or six months. Then again, you could stymie us all and go on for two or three years. It's just not that predictable. At the moment, the peripheral blood indicates low hemoglobin. Ditto on the white cells. The marrow findings aren't good either. We'll want to transfuse you—probably first thing tomorrow—see if we can't stabilize the counts at a safe level. If we can do that and maintain the safe level, you should be able to go on for a while. The danger lies in sudden unexplained drops, like the one that occurred in Bermuda. When the hemoglobin drops below a safe level, the heart has to work harder. The pumping is a lot more difficult because the blood is not oxygenated sufficiently, since the hemoglobin is so low. It's kind of an overcharged chain reaction. If your counts should drop to a low point where transfusion and medication fail to raise them, then that's that. The heart can't take the strain. It just keeps working away until it finally gives out. Think of it as a pump that burns itself out from being overworked. I'm painting a grim picture, I know. But so far this has been the pattern. We'll try transfusing and hope the pattern holds.

"Symptomatically, the initial stages of the disease resemble leukemia: fatigue, nausea, loss of appetite. Sometimes, rarely, impaired vision. Superficial lesions refusing to heal because the white-cell level is low. It's a difficult disease, because the research boys aren't sure they've pinned down the marrow function totally.

"Once a month—possibly more often, depending on your counts—you'll come back for a sternal narrow puncture and blood samples. And a course of X-ray therapy over a period of a few weeks. That's about it. We'll go now and let you rest, unless you have questions."

"No," she said, "no questions."

MacAllister slipped quietly out of the room. Ramirez stood a moment longer, toying with his clipboard.

"You're good people," he said finally. "I'm sorry there isn't more I can say or do."

"We appreciate that," Norm said. "Thank you for giving us a realistic picture."

"You never know, man," Ramirez said. "*Vaya con Dios*."

"Eighteen months is quite a lot of time, if you think about it," she said after Ramirez had left.

"It's nothing," he said, forgetting everything. "It's a minute, a split second, nothing."

"It's quite a *lot* of time," she insisted, squeezing his hand. "It could be worse."

"Yes," he said quietly. "It could be."

After leaving the hospital, he put a call in to Gena. When he told her, she drew in her breath in a sharp gasp.

"How long will she be in the hospital before she can go home?" she asked in a steady voice.

"About ten more days, probably."

"Okay. I'll be there. I can't talk any more now, Daddy. Don't tell her I'm coming, okay? There's something I want to do."

"All right, sweetheart. I'll be waiting for you."

It could *be worse,* she thought after Norm left. Now at least she'd be mobile again. And eighteen months. She'd be able to teach through to the end of her contract, a year from June. What seemed most important was not spending the remainder of her life crying over the fact that she was losing it, squandering precious time on useless rejection of the truth.

She stopped, asking herself if she was being honest, if she wasn't attempting to philosophize the facts right out of existence. *I'm dying,* she thought. *I am dying.* Somehow the concept no longer held any fear. What she feared now was not that she knew approximately when and how she was going to die. Better than stepping out of the apartment building some morning and being struck down by a truck. No, what she feared was the impact on Norm's life, on his state of mind.

Granted, she went on, there was no longer margin for wishful thinking or distant, future plans. This knowledge they possessed eliminated the compulsion to speculate on the future. She knew the future. And there was someone else who'd always known. She was suddenly very awake, very alert. So many seemingly eccentric acts that hadn't—in retrospect—been quite so eccentric as she'd mistaken them to be. All at once, she had answers for almost every question she'd ever asked herself about Fraser.

When she came, first thing in the morning on her way to school, Helen was waiting. She had known she'd come.

"How is it?" Fraser asked, her calm manner serving to verify Helen's previous night's assessment.

"You've always known, haven't you, Fraser? How long do I have?"

"What do you mean?" she asked, her startled eyes betraying her exterior calm.

"Fraser, your stars don't lie! You know that. It's what you've always told me. And all these years I believed it was about Stu, about his not coming back. How long, Fraser?"

"But you're wrong—I—"

"No more lying! Just tell me! I've got to know."

Tears welled up in Fraser's eyes, and she glanced around nervously, as if looking for an exit.

"Pull yourself together," Helen said softly. "This is no time for hysterics. Please tell me. I know you know."

"A year and a half," she said, downcast. "That's all."

"That's what they said. I just wanted to be sure."

"Why believe now, when you never would before?"

"Why not?" she said simply, grasping Fraser's hand. "Aside from miracle cures, I'm willing to believe in all kinds of things."

Fraser sat down tiredly, covering Helen's hand with her own long, aristocratic hands.

"You were so young, so beautiful," she said. "I love you. I couldn't have told you what I thought I'd seen. I wouldn't have been your friend if I'd told you. It would have spoiled all these years for you, Helen. And I couldn't be certain I hadn't made a miscalculation. There was that too. You're the only real friend I've ever had, the only one who didn't judge me or run away from me. The only thing I had to offer you was not telling you what I'd learned. I can't stand to think of how . . . empty my life will be without you."

"Your life won't be empty, Fraser. You'll still have my mother and Norm. They're not going to disappear because I don't happen to be around. And you've got your lectures and charts to prepare. You'll be fine."

"How can you be so calm? I think I'd go mad if it were me."

"I'm anything but calm. The amazing part of knowing is how it's changed my concept of time. I've been thinking a lot about that. I used to think time was merely a commodity, something I could use without regard for the possibility of its ever being in short supply. Death was something far off down the road, out of sight. It's not dying I'm afraid of, Fraser. I can't honestly say I'm afraid now that it's happening. I have a feeling that when it comes, I'll be more than ready to meet it. I'm just a little scared time will play more tricks on me, that there won't be time enough to do all the things I still want to do."

"What about Norman?" Fraser asked quietly. "How . . . how is he taking it? He must be . . . ."

"He's shocked and angry and scared, like me. But he's being honest. There's something so unreal about all of it, Fraser. I mean, to lie here and say a lot of words I think I mean. I wonder, from minute to minute, if it's just a brave face—if I'm attempting to delude everyone, even myself. But I don't think so. I love him. I keep imagining how I'd feel if he were dying, and I know I'd want to kill him for dying on me." She laughed. "You see what I mean, I think. He can't help being angry, any more than I could if our positions were reversed. And suddenly all our plans are just meaningless illusion, because most of the things we'd thought we'd do we'll never get to. There is a very real horror that I feel—it's the finality of it all. I'm going to be dead, and he's going to have to reshape his life and his concepts and go on. I know that. When Stu died, I blamed him for every miserable condition of my life. Everything. I wanted him alive so I could tell him just how totally he'd screwed me up by dying. I wanted to tell him how furious I was, how much I wanted to strike back at him for leaving me alone with photographs I couldn't look at and letters I couldn't read. And, worst of all, the way he'd tainted me for other men. I couldn't give myself, couldn't make love without—at some instant—remembering him, thinking of the way we'd been together. Until Norm. And when Norm came along, the anger and misery had dissipated themselves. Time had been a catharsis, too. I'd changed, grown up. And I was ready for Norm, ready to relegate Stu to the past. Not forget him. Even now I think of him, find certain moments tremendously real, vivid. But Stu and I only had seven months together, Fraser. Norm and I have already had almost eleven years. Much more to go back over.

"I've never asked you for anything, Fraser. Now there's something I want you to do for me." Her hand tightened on Fraser's, and she studied her eyes hopefully.

"Please ask me! I'd do anything."

"This might be something you mightn't wish to do, my dear. But someone's going to have to, and I'd like it to be you."

"Whatever it is, I'll do it. You have my promise."

"When the word came, finally, that Stu was dead, I felt as if I'd died too. I needed someone to hold on to, someone alive—someone to show me that the life process would go on, even without Stu. There was a man. He'd been through it all and understood the numbing terror of those first hours when you're alone, completely alone. He stayed with me that night, until the worst of the shock had passed."

"I think I know," Fraser said, color rising in her cheeks.

"Just those first hours, Fraser. So he won't be alone. Knowing he won't be alone . . . it'll make such a difference. Please, I know you're appalled at what I'm asking you, but understand that I'm asking you because I love you both, Fraser. He's going to need someone to hold on to for a while. Do it for both of us. Or just for me, if it's easier to think of that way. Those first half dozen or dozen hours are bad, Fraser. You could make it all better. I love you enough to ask. Love me enough to say you'll do it."

"I'll do it," she said, looking away.

"Look at me, Fraser! You've always tried to deny yourself to me. You can't do it any longer. Your kindness and generosity have always betrayed you. Just as your yearning for my life has. Now here we all are, and the yearning comes to nothing, doesn't it? Because if you had my life, you'd have my death too. I want you near me, Fraser. Perhaps, if you're with me, you'll see you'd rather keep the life you have."

"Don't!" she said. "Don't ask me to watch you die and learn, in the process, how to live. That's expecting too much of me. Too much."

"Can't you understand that I need you? No matter how honestly Norman and I face this, I still need someone I can say *everything* to, Fraser. All the truth, everything, would leave him nothing to go on with. I *need* you. Mother's too old to hold my hand now. I'm asking you to help me, not to learn lessons. Let me hold your hand from time to time when the going gets rough. It'll happen, I know. And there's no one else I'd want with me, Fraser. Because I trust you."

"Yes, all right," she said, meeting Helen's eyes. "But . . ." She stopped, her gray eyes at once aged and mournful. "All right," she said abruptly. "I'll do whatever you ask."

She fell asleep after Fraser left. Cora awakened her just before lunchtime to give her additional medication. The food was nondescript, and she ate only because she knew she had to. Then it seemed she'd only that moment set down the cup when once again she was wooed and won by sleep. She became aware, as she settled into it, that her sleep now possessed new qualities. Physically she surrendered herself to it completely, falling easily into a depth of rest that left her mind clear and sharp and acutely aware of everything around her. She looked forward to sleep in the same way she'd once anticipated growing old. It was a reflective, restorative time that enabled her to return to life with heightened perception and clarified vision.

She was sleeping when Norm arrived. He opened the

door, saw she was asleep, and backed out into the corridor in time to see Gena coming out of the elevator.

"You got here so quickly," he said, embracing her, then easing her away to look at her. "Are you all right?"

"I'm fine, Daddy. How is she? How's she taking it?"

"Better than I am. She's asleep right now. Come on, there's a private waiting room down here where we can talk."

"I called Gray's father and begged him to help, and he got me a ride with a friend of his in his private plane. Close the door, okay?"

She looked around, then opened her cape to reveal the baby strapped to her front by a canvas sling with loops fitting over her arms.

"Those officious fools downstairs wouldn't let me in with her. So I changed clothes and smuggled her in. This is Claire. Meet your Granddaddy, Claire," she said, handing the baby to Norm.

He sat down with the infant, unable to stop grinning.

"Isn't she terrific?" Gena laughed.

"She's wonderful," he said, leaning forward to kiss her. "Why didn't you let us know?"

"I was going to cable you in Bermuda. Then I decided to call trans-Atlantic instead, and when they told me Helen had been taken ill and the two of you had flown home, I went up in smoke. Gray spent two days trying to quiet me, trying to get me to call again, but I couldn't because I was terrified you'd tell me she was dead or something." She paused, her face falling. "And then you called. Daddy, isn't there *anything* they can do for her?"

"No." He couldn't take his eyes off the small, sleeping face. "Isn't it risky bringing a small infant on a trip like this?"

"The doctor said as long as I feed, change, and bathe her at regular intervals, he didn't see any reason why I shouldn't. I *had* to bring her, Daddy. For Helen. It was the right thing to do. It isn't going to be the same, is it? You know. The way it was with my mother?"

"No," he said, returning the baby to her. "Different disease, thank God."

He watched as Gena strapped the baby back into the sling and readjusted her cape.

"I'm reconciled to this, Daddy," she said, her hand on his cheek. "It's not going to destroy me. I couldn't do that to Gray or to Claire. I have responsibilities to other people now. To you, too. And Helen. I *hate* it. I don't want to believe a bit of it, but I do believe it, and I'm going to handle it. You don't have to worry about me. Just take care of yourself and her. I want to go surprise her. Will you stand guard so no one comes charging in and catches us?"

"Go on. I'll be along in a minute. I'll stand watch in the corridor. Sweetheart, I'm very glad to see you."

"I'm glad to see you too. But I wish none of this was happening."

"I know. Go on."

She stood beside the bed watching Helen sleep, the baby stirring slightly under the cape. "This isn't real," she whispered to herself, feeling as if she'd just stepped over the edge of reality and into the middle of nightmarish impossibilities. She studied Helen's sleeping face, the angle of her jaw, the way her hair curled behind her ear, the steadily regular pulsing in her throat. Her eyes followed the line of Helen's neck down, noting the delicate edging of lace on the neckline of her nightgown, the tiny gatherings of fabric beneath the lace. Steadying the baby with her hand, she sat down carefully on the side of the bed and bent to kiss the sleeping face, surprised at the coolness of Helen's cheek.

"Wake up, darling," she whispered, feeling she might suddenly detonate, feeling sharp pangs of grief exploding inside her. "Wake up."

Helen's eyes opened and looked straight into hers, sending an infusion of hope through her.

"I'm dreaming," Helen said, her arms coming up, her hands cool on Gena's face. "It's the best dream ever."

"Am I dreaming too?" Gena asked softly, her hands reaching up to cover Helen's. "Is this for real?"

Helen looked into the darkened depths of Gena's eyes,

for the first time wanting to say, *No. It isn't real. None of
this is happening.*

"It's real," she said instead.

"Do you know," Gena whispered, "I never call you
Helen in my thoughts. When I'm thinking of you, even
when I talk about you to other people, it's never Helen."

"Gena. . ."

"I just want you to know. But I thought you'd hate it or
want me not to, because I know you're not old enough.
But I call you Mother. I've brought someone to see you,"
she said quickly, leaving no room for Helen to respond.
She threw off the cape, and, unhooking the sling, she
said, "If you can, sit up a bit, and I'll introduce you."
She placed the baby in Helen's arms. "This is Claire H.
Richardson. The H, of course, stands for Herman."

"Of course." Helen smiled, awed. "Oh, Gena! This is
too much! She's so lovely. So little. I can't believe it."

"She's two and a half weeks old and weighs almost ten
pounds already. She seems fantastic to me, too."

"Why didn't you let us know?" Helen asked, looking
at the tiny fist curled on her breast.

"I told Daddy. I telephoned Bermuda and they said
you'd . . . had to fly home. It panicked me. I was afraid
to call and find out. I'm sorry . . ."

"Never mind. It doesn't matter. Claire." She laughed
softly, gazing at the baby's face. "She looks like Graham."

"Yes, I think so."

Gena watched Helen's fingertips touching the baby's
face, fascinated by the length of her polished fingernails,
the ease of her movements.

"Darling, don't dwell on it," Helen said. "Don't make
yourself unhappy. Not when you have so much to be
happy about."

"I can't help it. It's so —*unfair.* Are you in pain? Do
you feel . . . ?"

"I am *not* in pain. I feel just fine. Seeing you and the
baby is exactly what I've been needing. I'm very happy
you're here. I love you and I love your child. Was it
frightening?"

"No." Gena brightened. "It hurt more than I expected.

But that didn't matter, because it was secondary, somehow. Gray was with me the whole time. We . . . It was very exciting."

"This," Helen said, gesturing at the room, "is *very* secondary."

The baby emitted a small squeal, and Gena said, "She's hungry. Do you mind if I feed her?"

"Not at all," she said, returning Claire, thinking Gena was reaching for a bottle as her hand burrowed in the depths of her bag. But the hand came up with a cloth diaper, which Gena set on the bed as she unbuttoned her shirt. A surge of elation took Helen's breath away as she watched Gena hold the baby to her breast. There was something so perfect in the sight of Gena's fingers curved tenderly under the baby's head as she fitted the searching mouth against her nipple that Helen's eyes spilled over with tears. As the baby nursed, Gena held Helen's hand, smiling.

"She's your baby too," she said, before lapsing into a long, shared silence.

Norm came in quietly just as Gena had shifted the baby to her other breast. He came round and sat down on the far side of the bed as Helen, with a sob, pressed her face against his chest. Gena looked up questioningly, and he said, "We're very happy, sweetheart. Don't disturb the baby."

19

After Gena had left to settle into the spare bedroom at the apartment, Helen lay back, looking at him.

"How long will she stay?"

"Until you're well enough to go back to school," he said, lighting a cigarette. "She wants to see for herself that you're actually going to get out of here. Then she'll go home."

"I want to hold you," she said, taking the cigarette from him and setting it in the ashtray. "We've done everything else in this room today. I don't see why you can't lie down with me for a few minutes."

"It's rotten sleeping without you," he said, lying down and taking her in his arms. "I can't sleep worth a damn. I keep rolling over and there's nothing there."

"I know. Are you repelled by me now, Norm?"

"Repelled? What the hell is that?"

"I don't know. For a moment, holding the baby, it struck me so hard. That it's real. You know—that for all the talking and moral philosophizing, I'm slowly but surely turning into dust. Hold me."

"God, Helen! I love you. Even more now. Everything seems so magnified—all the feelings, all the caring. I want you more than ever. Don't say things like that, love. For both our sakes. I need you the same way I've always needed you—more. Knowing all this makes it seem so important that you know exactly how much I do love you, how much I want you. Dust!" He kissed her slowly, finding her mouth soft and responsive, but desperate.

"I think," she said, their faces very close together, "once I can come home, once I can make love again and I can hold you inside me, then I won't feel quite so close to the finality of it as I do just now. I'm sleepy again. I'm always sleepy lately. Will you stay until I fall asleep, hold me until I do?"

"Close your eyes, love. Tuesday you'll be home and this part will be over."

She nestled against him, and he watched her drift into sleep.

Tuesday, as they were coming into the apartment, they met Gena with the baby on her way out.

"I thought this might be a good time to visit Great-grandmama," she said. "We'll be back later this afternoon." With a kiss for each of them, she smiled and went on her way.

"Very subtle, that girl," Norm said, steering Helen into the bedroom.

"It's marvelous the way she runs about with that baby slung to her front. You'd think she'd never done anything else. Mother will go into raptures over Claire."

"Into bed," he ordered, pulling off the spread. "Leon gave me specific instructions. You've got four more days of bed rest before you're allowed to return to the stage."

She laughed. "And how do you think you'll enjoy spending four days in bed?" She smiled meaningfully, starting to undress.

"Is it all right?" he asked, concerned.

"I have the assurances of my three medical men. It is perfectly safe. And wanted and needed."

His kiss was long and deep, his hold on her so gentle, so infinitely tender, she felt she'd break apart with loving him.

"I'm afraid of hurting you," he said, looking at her mouth.

"Even if it hurt, which I know it won't, it'd be worth any amount of pain to be with you, touch you. I *do not* care."

"I care," he said, running his hand down the fragile curve of her neck and over her soft, heavy breasts. "I'd hurt myself first."

"I crave what you've suddenly decided to call hurting, darling, having you inside me. It's real and alive. It makes me feel alive. Right now you're the only one in the world who matters. I don't care about anything else. Only you. I want you so much. Don't think about hurting. Love takes all that away."

Her arm encircled his neck, drawing his mouth down to hers, shifting, opening as his hand moved down. She sighed into his mouth as if she'd been holding her breath for a very long time, then returned to the kiss, sinking under his hand.

"I want to make love to you," she said, turning with him, kissing his chest, his belly, lowering her head over him, delighting in his familiar smooth sweetness as he pressed her hand to his mouth. She closed her eyes, blotting out everything but him—his mouth, his hands, his body, his knowledge of her most private ways and most personal secrets. She felt utterly removed from time and thought, lost in feeling, in motion.

She gave herself to him, took him to herself with finely honed emotional awareness, valuing beyond anything else the depth and consideration of his love. When she lifted her head to look at him, she saw love in his eyes, pure love, and felt the truth of her own words piercing her pleasurably because it was true: Nothing and no one else mattered.

He rose up to enfold her in his arms, looking deep into her eyes.

"I love you," he whispered.

They joined together in a state of perfect peace. She received him, holding him fast inside, closing around him, coupled so completely, so deeply that his body was her own, his thrusting tumescence her own. His broad strong chest pressing against her breasts was an extension of her own self. Their two mouths together were one with mutual caring, common destination. His arms and legs twined about hers, their bodies matched like interlocking puzzle parts fitted with perfect symmetry, body into body. They were entirely one.

He kissed her eyes as they closed, her head straining back as she rose around him, rolling like ocean swells, rising in waves, surrounding him, sucking both of them forward toward oblivion.

She rose tautly, her body tight, rigid, as she approached the perimeters of a spiraling, liquid pleasure.

"Oh, *God!*" she cried, her eyes flying open to fix on him, "how I love you! Kiss me. It's—now."

He couldn't sleep afterward. She lay on her right side, her face on her arm, curled against him, her breathing light and even, her hair lying damply over her cheek. He lit a cigarette and sat up, leaning against the headboard, watching her readjust herself against him in her sleep. He drew the blankets over her. *How can you die?* he asked her silently. *How can that be possible?* She was alive, sleeping against his chest, her breath like blown feathers grazing his skin. Her taste and scent were all over his body, on his hands, in his mouth. She looked so young. Her clear, peachy skin flushed with sleep was like a child's; her tiny nose, the nostrils moving slightly as she breathed, her pointed chin just touching his ribs—young. And so beautiful. The very sight of her moved something deep, something enormous, inside him. And by next summer's end, she'd be dead. *Good God above,* he thought, *how can that be?*

He butted the cigarette and lit another, still watching. Her sleep began to change, her breathing becoming jagged, her jaw working, eyelashes fluttering. He could see her eyes moving under the lids. Her hands jerked suddenly, her body tensing. She began folding in on herself, until her knees were bent almost to her breasts and her small fists were jammed protectively against her throat as her mouth moved. A film of perspiration covered her face.

"Helen, wake up!" he whispered, gathering her into his arms. "Wake up, love!" She emerged from it, opening her eyes wide, taking in his face, sobbing uncontrollably, crying out, "The dream! Norm, a terrible dream!"

"I know," he said, rocking her as her tears dropped on his arm. "I know, love."

"I infected Claire," she cried. "I put a white mask over the baby's face and her body started crumbling in my hands. *God!*"

"It was just a dream," he said comfortingly, "just a dream."

"It's real." She shivered. "All the words in the world can't change any of it."

"You can't infect anyone, Helen. You can't harm the people you love."

"I know that. I do know. I love you so. It's so hard trying to go on as if nothing matters. Why is it happening to us? Why?"

"I wish I knew."

"I don't want it to end. I've been so happy with you. Have you been happy?"

"You know I have. And we'll keep right on being happy. Try to go back to sleep. I'll stay here. Everything will be fine."

"Darling, are we playing games? Don't let's fool each other, please."

"We won't, I promise you. Sleep now, love. It was just a bad dream."

"I wish that's all it was."

He said nothing about Amanda's gift, but allowed Helen to discover it as she wandered into the living room to find something to read while he prepared dinner. She stood looking up at the portrait, knowing that by making a gift of it to Norm, her mother had, in her particular way, made peace with the truth.

"She never fails to surprise me," she said, sitting down in the kitchen to watch as he cooked. "Her acceptance of things, of life patterns, of death. She faces it all so squarely, as if these were subjects she might paint. She comes to terms with the definition, the shape, the essence of what it is she sees."

"She made me feel as if what's happening is simply a logical progression," he said. "an adjunct to our relationships. Not just yours and mine, but mine and hers, yours and hers, yours, mine, and Gena's. She lifted a good portion of my fear with the neatness and dexterity of a pickpocket. I was scarcely even aware of it until I'd left the house and was standing in the street, where it occurred to me I wasn't as afraid as I'd been when I'd first gone inside to tell her."

"We have to make plans, Norm."

"I know it."

"Shallots?" she said, fascinated.

"You'll love this. Chicken breasts sautéed in a wine sauce with mushrooms and shallots."

She laughed. "You're so talented."

"Plans," he reminded her. "Yours first."

"I haven't any beyond being positive I want to finish out my contract. Through to the end of June next year."

"That's cutting it close, don't you think?"

"Possibly. I want to try. Heavy cream too?"

"I told you you'll love it. My plan is for us to take a cruise this summer, as soon as Leon says your counts are stabilized. I brought home some brochures for you to look at. What would you think of that?"

"I think it's fabulous. But what about your book? And the summer school? And the paper?"

"They'll still be here when we get back. And anyway, I had an idea."

"Oh?"

"A combination of a little helpful therapy and also a useful means of getting another viewpoint."

"On what?"

"You and Gena. The beginnings of the relationship.

How she was. How you felt. I thought it might interest you, and at the same time give me an insight into how the attachment was formed. I've hit a mental block on it."

"You didn't tell me you were writing about Gena."

"I'm telling you now. Do you think you'd like to try?"

"What would I have to do?"

"Just keep paper and pens handy and jot down whatever you remember."

"I'm interested. Leave it with me, we'll see what happens."

They stared at each other for a long moment.

"Something's boiling over," she said.

"Don't get up. It's just the rice. I forgot to turn it down. Do you want to take a look at the brochures?"

"It smells heavenly in here."

"Do you want to look?"

"Surprise me! Make the bookings and take me to all the places I've never seen."

"Okay. Here." He deposited a colander full of greens and a salad bowl in front of her. "Tear gently and arrange artistically in bowl."

"One would think I'd never made a salad."

"Anyone who chops lettuce with a knife the way you do has never made a salad."

"Tear *gent*-ly." She laughed. "Does it cry out or something?"

"They say the flowers cry when they're cut from their stems."

She thought of popping a baby mum into her mouth while Stu stood gaping at her and the band was playing.

"What is it?" Norm asked, handing her some vegetables to slice into the salad.

"Just remembering something that happened years ago. It was what you said about the flowers that reminded me of it."

"Tell me."

"It's idiotic." She laughed, remembering Stu's face. "I ate a chrysanthemum at a wedding party."

"Oh swell!" he said, quickly slicing the vegetables and

tossing them into the bowl. "I wouldn't trust you within a mile of any garden of mine now that I know that." He laughed, stopping to kiss her, overcome by the success of their return to the rapport of their everyday life. "I love you. It's so damned good to have you home."

"I think I would like to do that," she said, planting a kiss on the inside of his arm.

"Not before dinner."

"That too." She smiled. "The writing thing, I meant. It appeals to me."

Gena left on the evening before Helen was to return to school.

"I've arranged for a limo," she said, standing holding Claire as she surveyed her bags. "I hate airport scenes and good-byes. I'll be back. You know." She shrugged, her eyes beseeching.

"I know," Helen said, loving her more than ever for keeping such a tight grip on her emotions. "Give our love to Graham. You'd better go now, or you'll miss your flight."

Gena kissed them both and escaped.

"She'll be fine," Helen said after Norm returned from seeing her down to the limousine. "She's got it all under control."

"It's the baby, I think."

"Some. But mostly it's Gena. She meant what she said about never going back 'in.' She's sticking to it."

"The other part is you," he said, his arm around her shoulders. "You've always shown her there are ways to keep on going, to get beyond the past."

"You're making me out to be something I'm not, Norm. All I've done is muddle through the best way I know how."

"That's just it, my love. The best way you know how is a damned sight better than most. Time for bed. You look a little tired."

"You did the absolutely right thing telling her, you know. I don't know that I would have. In fact, I know I wouldn't have. Don't credit me with too much, darling. It's having you around that makes me look good by reflection."

"We'll massage each other's egos in bed," he said, leading her down the hall. "Or whatever else we decide on."

Returning to school seemed to reinforce the illusion that nothing had changed. Now that she could move with relative freedom, it became increasingly difficult to keep it in mind that her life had become temporary. It was Fraser who held her on the right track. Her willingness to talk, to listen, to discuss anything and everything, intercepted Helen's thoughts when they began to stray. The very fact that Fraser was there, carrying her entrusted fund of knowledge, just steps away, five days of every week, was a constant reminder that what was happening really was happening and not just the remnant of some waking nightmare.

Not that Fraser was overattentive or mollycoddling in her concern. On the contrary, she exercised a discretion and compassionate objectivity that proved very consoling when Helen experienced infrequent moments of terror. The discrepancy between her healthy-looking exterior and her slowly disintegrating skeletal structure was so petrifying that at times Helen found it almost impossible to maintain a realistic outlook. Reality now seemed something so totally relative that she was compelled to concentrate on externals—the classes, the children, the examinations, and reports to be written—in order to escape the convoluted whorls of thought that tempted her to reject the truth.

They talked over lunch, after school over drinks, in the evenings over dinner, either at Fraser's place or the apartment. And Norm left them to their conversations, sensing Helen's need to confide to Fraser certain thoughts and feelings that she couldn't reveal to him.

When the school year ended, with Leon's approval, they packed their bags and flew to New York. Settled aboard ship in their stateroom, Norm handed her half a dozen ruled pads and a box of ballpoint pens, saying, "No more stalling. I need your viewpoints. Start writing down whatever occurs to you, and when you've got a few free minutes, pass it all on to me. Okay?"

"I'm not sure what you expect me to write about."

"You and Gena. Or about yourself, how you feel, what you think. Anything, everything. Just try."

Initially, sitting on a deck chair, distracted by the pungent, salty sea air, she found it hard to get started. But she kept recalling moments with Gena, and decided to go back to the beginning and make a chronological stab at relating the growth of the relationship.

As he'd hoped might happen, once started she found she couldn't stop. At random moments throughout the day and night, she reached for her pen and sat writing line after line in her bold, unfussy handwriting. When she presented him with the first sheaf of closely written pages, he went off to the bar for a drink to read them while she napped.

And what she'd written and the way in which she'd done it so surprised and impressed him, he hurried back to the stateroom to tell her.

"This is so good, love," he said, waving the pages excitedly. "You can write. I mean really write. It's so straightforward, so wonderfully evocative. I can literally see the two of you marching right off the paper. More," he said. "Keep it coming. I'm getting an idea."

"You wouldn't con me, would you?" she asked, smiling at his enthusiasm. "I'm not a writer, darling."

"The hell you're not! Just don't stop, all right? I'm getting a fantastic idea."

So she kept on. And when she'd gone through the supply of ruled pads, he got more. He kept the completed pages carefully stored in his briefcase, and from time to time she awoke to find him making notes on the backs of pages she'd written, or comparing her words to his own steadily increasing stack of completed manuscript.

It was a quietly good time. They toured Nassau and Bermuda, sending postcards home, buying souvenirs to take back for Gena and Amanda and Fraser, returning home after two weeks feeling relaxed and heartened, only to learn the brief remission had ended and her counts had begun to slip. The X-ray treatments were resumed.

Her reactions to the X-rays were very severe, and for the first three or four days after treatment her skin had a positively gray tinge, her face puffing out doughily. Norm helped her when she was repeatedly and violently sick. The second week, she'd be regaining her strength and appetite, and by the third be back to a reasonable facsimile of herself.

Aside from the side-effects of the treatment, the disease hadn't yet begun to overtly manifest itself. The external symptoms, they learned, would be minimal. But, waiting, watching, they both wondered if, somewhere along the line, a mistake mightn't have been made.

"It hasn't," he said, bathing her face with a cold cloth after one of the treatments. "No one could be so inhuman as to make you suffer this way if the X-rays weren't doing an important job."

"My hair's starting to fall out," she said, looking distraught. "Handfuls of it."

"Perhaps they could change to something else, something that doesn't make you so sick."

"Something that makes me sicker," she said wretchedly. "Something that leaves me completely bald and permanently incapable of keeping food down. God!"

"I know how you feel, love. I know."

"Christ! You *don't* know! You're not the one who's doubled up in the damned bathroom vomiting half the day and night. It's not *your* goddamned hair that's falling out."

"No," he said quietly, enveloping her in his arms. "Mine's already gone."

She laughed tearfully, looking at him with tortured eyes. "I'm sorry. I'm taking it out on you. It's not fair."

"Sure it's fair. That's what I'm here for. You've got every right to be angry. Be angry! Maybe I'll buy you some boxing gloves and we can get into a ring and really fight it out."

"You're an ass," she said, her face against the warmth

of his chest. "Boxing gloves. It's going to get worse, and I'm scared."

"So am I. We'll be scared together."

"I want to hit you for being so reasonable. I can't fight you."

"I *won't* fight that way, Helen. If you want to yell and carry on, go ahead. By all means. It'll make you feel better. But I'm not going to rise to it as if I don't know what's prompting all this. Keep writing everything down. When you feel like striking out, write instead."

"You're taking this good-natured understanding too far. You frustrate me. I *need* to fight. I have a right to my anger. You said so yourself. I'm not some damned martyr, so stop trying to turn me into one. Leave me alone, Norm."

"I can't, Helen! Understand that! We're different. We have different ways of handling what we feel. I *do* know how you feel, but I can't fight you. It solves nothing. I love you too much."

"*You* understand something! You understand that as much as I love you, I hate dying in front of you. I hate having you hold me while I'm being sick, hate having you patiently clean up my messes. I can't ignore the humiliation of having you witness all of it. It *shames* me."

"It's because I do love you that I want to help. You mustn't separate yourself from me that way. Please, love, don't do it to yourself or to me. Can't you believe that my view of you, my love for you, isn't in any way diminished by any of this? Your body's sick, but you're not. Not you, the person I care about. I can't do anything to change any part of this. All I can do is try to make it better in whatever way I can. Every day we get through brings us another day closer to the time limit. I believe absolutely that if it was me and not you, we'd be doing every bit of it exactly the same way and I'd be the one screaming at you for all your loving reasonableness. And you'd be just as adamant in your refusal to fight me. For all the same reasons. I want you to express what you're feeling. It's vital that both of us do. But if we go backward, the way we almost did about Gena, if we attack the relationship itself and start chipping away at the foundations of our loving, then we'll end up with nothing but empty hands and bitter, regretting memories. It doesn't have to be that way. I deplore this disease, and the X-rays and the medication and what they do to you. But I will not allow anything to interfere with our feelings for each other. I'm facing the truth. I've faced it. I can't die with you. It wouldn't make you feel any better if I could. I want you while I've still got you. As long as you're here, every second that you're here, I want you and need you and love you. I won't waste love on bitterness. Or time, either. I care too much for you to reduce the last months of our life together to an arena where we grapple and claw at each other over what's happening."

"It'll pass," she said, meeting his eyes. "All of this will pass. I can't be brave about this any more than you can pretend all your dreams aren't going up in smoke. I'm tired, darling."

She looked hollow with fatigue, her cheeks streaked with tears, her eyes red-rimmed and slightly sunken.

"I have no illusions, love," he said, drying her face. "I may not actually feel the pain, but it isn't always necessary. I feel all the rest, and I'm as angry, as frightened, as apprehensive, as everything as you are. But, as you say, it'll pass."

"Everything is passing," she said resolutely, letting him tuck her under the bedclothes. "Even anger."

20

By the end of that summer, it seemed the anger had passed. It left no apparent empty space crying out to be filled. It was as if the love they had for each other simply expanded to take over the space previously occupied by the outrage.

Helen had several long talks with her mother, soaking up Amanda's words in the portion of her consciousness she drew on at times alone, regardless of whoever else might be around, when she felt an immense need to reflect on her decreasing life span.

"It has occurred to me—somewhat capriciously, I'll admit," Amanda said, as Helen kneaded her aching hands, "that you're fortunate in having a deadline of sorts. It's possible that it could lend a positive definition to the importance of various things you might want to do. Do you see, darling? By knowing your time has unquestionable limits, you can exercise a special selectivity. Perhaps this comes across as banal babble, but I find myself thinking in those terms. In my case, it's age. In yours, it's illness. But there's time for consideration. And time, too, for accomplishment. But time, in any case, that can be used wisely if one is to 'retire' with a sense of fulfillment.

"I go to far greater pains now, for example, to try to express what I see than I did twenty-five years ago. There's no longer a need for the extra frills I added then only because they seemed to embellish and even overstate what I saw. Now I can see that what is real speaks for itself, and adding nonessential flourishes only detracts from the truth of what I'm attempting to depict. I don't think it's an unreasonable analogy, darling. Art, after all, is life seen through the eyes of different talents. I think life—death too—might be considered arts effected by different viewpoints."

Her notebooks were everywhere. In the apartment Norm came across them on the stove, tucked between the cushions of the sofa, in the bathroom, under her pillow. He was aware of her awakening frequently at four or five in the morning to reach for a notebook, the sound of her pen a heartening disruption of his rarely deep sleep. And while she wrote, unaware she was being observed, he could see the pain she went to such lengths to hide from everyone. It rippled along her arms as she tried to write; loitered menacingly in the corners of her eyes; hovered close to the surface of her skin like a swarm of nettlesome gnats, causing her body to go rigid as her eyes closed and her teeth sank down hard into her lower lip. Then she'd take a deep breath and keep on writing.

He found, as they silently counted down the months, that he clung to the top layer of sleep, always alert for sounds or activity that might mean trouble. The only times he was able to relax completely were times when, after making love, they slept entwined, so totally attuned to each other that he felt no need to set his mental alarm. At those times, with her body safely wrapped in and around his own, he felt at peace, secure in the knowledge that, for however short a time, she was so close that fear failed to exist for either of them.

They were drawn to lovemaking with an urgency and passion that were acutely intensified by the knowledge that, within weeks, the patterns of their lovemaking would begin undergoing alterations.

The pain crept up on her insidiously, starting out as

minor, discomforting stresses she accepted without inordinate attention. Her visits for marrowing, blood tests, and X-ray treatment were switched to a twice-monthly and then a weekly basis. And she went along, studying the faces of her fellow victims in the waiting room, listening to the recitals of her various white-cell and hemoglobin counts with a detachment vitally necessary to the maintenance of her emotional balance. The medications were changed. After much discussion, she and the three doctors agreed to discontinue the chemicals and X-rays that were merely making her feel sicker and, to all intents and purposes, were not, in any way, arresting the progress of the disease.

The distressing part of these visits to the hospital was having to see the faces of the children with leukemia, who sat quietly, without any of the fidgety restlessness of other children, waiting for their tests and medication. Their faces haunted her. Without discussing the decision with anyone, she went to see her lawyer to rewrite her will, adding a codicil donating the bulk of her estate to leukemia research. It was a small gesture, she thought, but one that eased her when she reviewed those closed, resigned little faces every week.

By early spring the pain had become a permanent partner to her waking and sleeping hours. It was always present, although rarely spoken of. It spread itself throughout her body with malevolent obstinacy, gaining proportionately in power as it slowly sapped her energy.

There were more drugs: painkillers, peace-givers whose qualities she became more and more dependent upon until time was measured by the various pills and injections to be taken at different hours in order for her to get past the day and into the night.

When her contract finally came to its end and she collected her things for the last time before leaving the school, she wasn't sorry, as she'd once thought she'd be.

"I'm actually glad it's over," she said as Fraser drove her home. "I'm looking forward to staying home, scribbling in my notebooks, sitting in the park if it's what I feel like doing."

"It won't be the same without you there," Fraser said. "But it's too much for you. All those raucous children demanding attention, the papers to mark, meetings."

"I'll miss the children," she said, gazing down at her hands. "I've always loved that first day, seeing each fresh crop of lovely new faces."

"Are you going up to the cottage?"

"We're not sure. Possibly for a few days. Norm's doing the galley proofs. If he gets them in on schedule, we might go up for a longer stay."

They didn't go at all. During late June and all of July, Fraser came at least once a week, more often twice or three times, bringing armloads of flowers from her garden, library books she thought might be of interest, gifts of all kinds. She couldn't arrive empty-handed; the offerings, she thought, would let Helen know how very much she cared.

"Try not to think about it so much," Helen told her. "Concentrate on all the things you have to do."

"Yes," Fraser said, nodding her head. "Yes. That's what I must do. I forget sometimes."

"It's all right," Helen said. "I love seeing you. I look forward to your visits. Norm's very busy now. It's a nice break in the day to have you come."

"It's probably in bad taste to say this, but you look better as time goes by. More beautiful. Every time I come, I see it just a little more."

"I don't feel it," Helen confided in an undertone. "I feel as if I'm being gradually eaten alive. I'm living on narcotics." She laughed. "I expect to be raided at any moment and have all my magical capsules and tablets and vials confiscated by the drug squad. But, God! Fraser, the euphoria of an entire pain-free hour!" She looked at Fraser solemnly. "I'm getting ready," she said softly. "I'm looking ahead, seeing visions of painless eternities. I have daydreams about floating on cotton clouds that hold me in a perfectly serene state where nothing hurts, nothing matters. Don't be sorry, Fraser. I always suspected I'd arrive at a point where death lost its sinister overtones and assumed peaceful attributes."

Norm sent in the edited proofs at the beginning of August.

"You'll read the first author's copy," he promised.

"After all my contributions, you're rotten not to at least have let me read the proofs."

"It's going to be a surprise I hope you'll like."

They had slightly over three months left together, according to their estimated schedule, when that end they'd both been dreading came to their lovemaking.

He cradled her in his arms while she cried.

"I hoped somehow—idiotically—it wouldn't ever happen. I kept insisting to myself it wouldn't be the way Leon said. I had it all worked out that it would be beautifully romantic, like *La Dame aux Camellias*, where I expired in your arms, lost in ecstasy. With Armand in attendance." She laughed, then cried harder.

"We still have all the rest," he said. "It doesn't matter."

"I know, darling. It's just that it was something we've always had that was so good, so unifying. And now that's gone too."

"Oh, love, it doesn't matter. You know it doesn't."

"I keep telling myself that. But sometimes words are nothing. Every time you hold me now I think of how I want you, and wanting you, just physically responding to you, brings me pain. I'm not even allowed to *want* you, never mind that I can't have you. And there's nothing you and I together can do about it. All you can do is give me my drugs and hold my hand while the grains stun my cells senseless for an hour or two. This isn't living any more, Norm. I'm just existing, not even functioning. Please, darling, start letting me go in your mind. I've already started."

"No!" he cried, startling them both. "Not yet. Just a little longer, for both of us. I don't want you to suffer. I can't stand the agony you're going through. But don't give up on life yet!"

"It's not a choice that's mine to make, darling. Now it's a matter of conceding graciously and welcoming the unavoidable. I don't want to go on and on. The pain's taking me over, Norm, dominating my brain, my consciousness, my every thought, every breath. I'm falling in love with death, darling. It's taking all my attention. A year ago I wouldn't have believed it possible to make a statement like that. But there has to be an end. This business of sustaining myself on pills, narcotics. It's a fiction. A few hours of fiction out of every twenty-four of fact."

"Can you mean that? Is it really that bad so suddenly?"

"Not suddenly," she said, putting her hand on his cheek, overcome with sympathy for him. "It's been gaining ground, sneaking up on me. And now it's here." She laughed softly. "I feel like one of those poor degenerates you see downtown early Sunday morning, crouched in doorways, living from handout to handout so they can go into some liquor store and buy another bottle in another brown paper bag. That's how I feel with all of this, with the pills, the drugs; being marrowed like some frog in a zoology lab. I can't fight something that has such unrelenting weapons. There's no point in even *trying* to fight. I don't *want* to."

Just under two weeks later, they were sitting in the living room after dinner when she started gasping for air. Her heart was thudding wildly, spasmodically, and she opened and closed her mouth, unable to speak or breathe. *It's too soon,* she thought, feeling herself going under. *It's not time yet. I shouldn't have said what I did.*

she pitched forward. Not wanting to waste time waiting
Norm happened to turn and see, catching her just as
for an ambulance, he picked her up and carried her down to the car, laid her on the back seat, covered her with a blanket, then drove like a maniac to the hospital.

He left her in the car while he ran into the emergency room, shouting at the nurse on duty to send for Ramirez or Mac or Leon. Then he bolted back to the car, got Helen, and deposited her on the stretcher the nurse had waiting, backing away as an oxygen mask was slapped over Helen's face. People came running from all directions. Ramirez and a nurse came down one corridor; Mac, a technician, and an aide came from another. The duty

334

nurse shoved the stretcher into Mac's hands. With the aide holding the oxygen tank and the technician pushing from behind, they sped off down the corridor and through the swing doors. The duty nurse then ran to call the blood bank while the crowd of people flew down the corridor after the stretcher, shouting instructions and calling for special equipment. Norm stood watching all this in breathless gratitude.

Ramirez emerged after a short while.

"Come on," he said to Norm. "I'll buy you a coffee. She'll be all right. They're transfusing her. It'll take several hours. We'll talk in the doctors' lounge."

Norm followed him into the empty room and dropped heavily into an armchair as Ramirez poured a large quantity of Scotch into a cup of black coffee and handed it to him.

"Go on, man, drink it! It'll scare away the shock."

He drank half the cup and felt better.

"What now?" he asked Ramirez, lighting a cigarette.

"Could you spare one of those?" he asked, patting the pockets of his white jacket. "I'm all out."

Ramirez lit up, then sat back. "She's going into the final stages," he said, drawing deeply on the cigarette. "It's time to number the days."

"How long?"

"At the most, three, maybe four, weeks. If we can sufficiently raise the counts, it'll give her heart a chance to relax, maybe add another week or two. But face it," he said, not unkindly. "It's about over."

"I know. But even knowing, I still wasn't ready for tonight."

"Man, you *saved* her tonight! Ten more minutes and she'd have been gone. You made all the right moves."

"Will I be able to take her home? She wants to be at home."

"In a couple of days. Hire a private nurse. It's going to be heavy going from here on in, and if you feel about each other the way I think you do, she's not going to want you to see her incapacitated. And you're not going to *want* to see it. She'll have to be helped with everything. Get a nurse, take my advice. It'll allow her to maintain her dignity, and that's very important to her, we all know that. She's a beautiful human being," he said, getting up. "We've never had anyone like her here. I've learned a few things from your wife, man. We all have. You don't have to worry about her being alone tonight. The floor nurses have agreed to take turns keeping her company. They *asked* to do it. So you go see her in a while, then take yourself home and unwind. Stay with it, man," he said, opening the door. "You're all right."

Helen watched the blood dripping into her arm—the last of the bottles—too enervated to speak.

Norm sat without stirring, his eyes, too, fixed on the slow, steady dripping of blood into the tube. Finally, knowing he was fulfilling no purpose being there, knowing she was too drained to really be aware of him, he got up and leaned over her.

"I'm going home now, love." He touched her hand. "I'll be back in the morning. Don't try to say anything. Just close your eyes and sleep. Get that good blood going."

After interviewing half a dozen women, Norm found Lorna Barrington. She was a young West Indian with a wonderful aura of serenity and quiet competence. Her qualifications were the best, having received her training in England. But what clinched it for him was when, after studying Helen's portrait for several minutes, she said, "I think I would like to know her."

He hired her and took her along to point out the spare bedroom and explain Helen's prognosis.

"I'll spend the nights with her," he said. "I'll also be here during the day. But it'll be up to you to attend to all her personal needs."

"I understand," she said in her musical accent. "I see in her eyes, she would not wish to show anyone her pain."

"You're wonderful," he said. "Helen will love you."

"How long will she have, sir?"

"Not long. A month at the most."

"She is so young," she said sadly.

"Forty-two."

"I will be here at eight o'clock on Saturday morning. Will you wish me to wear my uniform?"

"I think not," he said, anticipating what Helen might feel. "I'm glad you'll be with us, Lorna."

After she'd gone, he sat down to start making the necessary calls. Gena said she'd come right away.

"I'm bringing Claire," she said, in a voice that left no room for argument. "We'll stay with Amanda. I've already written asking if we could. I won't get in the way, Daddy."

"You couldn't ever be in the way, sweetheart."

"I've got another surprise for Helen."

"What's that?"

"I'm going to have another little Richardson."

"That's great!" He laughed. "I can't wait to see you and Claire. I don't suppose Gray can get away?"

"He's in Majorca collecting some kind of marine samples. I don't think he'll come, Daddy. He gets long-distance upset, you know. He wants to remember her the way she was."

"I understand."

"And don't meet the plane! I'll call you when I get in, and we'll work it from there. Okay?"

"Okay."

"Is she still beautiful, Daddy?" she asked in a hesitant voice.

"More so. Nothing shows, Gena. She looks glorious, just a shade thinner. Call me when you get here, okay?"

"Okay, Daddy. I love you."

After hanging up, he lifted the phone again and called Amanda to tell her that Gena and Claire were on their way.

"I'll have Mary make up the rooms. How long will they be staying, Norman?"

"Not more than three weeks. Four at the absolute outside."

"I see." Her voice contained the barest hint of a quaver. "I will come by the apartment midweek, if it's convenient."

"Any time at all."

"Yes," she said indistinctly, and replaced the receiver.

There were several more calls to make, including one to Fraser, and finally he stood up, rubbing his ear, and went to stand in front of the windows, looking out.

Time to start counting days, he thought, finding the concept morbid. He thought of the pain—which was so staggering in its totality he was unable even to imagine it—and knew he wanted an end to it for her now, perhaps even as devoutly as Helen did herself. The idea of his selfishness in begging her to hang on to a life no longer bearable to her repulsed him. How could he have been so egocentric? It was her privilege to seek an end to suffering. And, for purely selfish reasons, he'd tried to induce her to suffer just a little longer on his behalf. *It's immoral,* he thought, leaning with his forehead against the cool glass. Let her go, leave her to her hard-won rest. God! How ruthless, how vain to deny her that! It was well past due time to begin letting go. And everyone knew it.

He drove to the hospital Saturday morning to collect her, finding her packed and waiting, impatient to be away from there. In the car, she looked out the window, breathing in the late-summer air. "Let's go for a ride," she suggested. "I'd like to look at the world."

"Right," he said, swinging the car into the traffic. "I drove out this way the day we found out," he said, turning on the radio.

"What did you do, darling?"

"Drove around for hours listening to the radio, got mad, cried awhile."

"Norm." Her fingers brushed the back of his neck. "This has been hell for you."

"No, no." He turned to smile.

They drove along listening to the music. She looked at the cloudless perfect blue of the sky, the green of the trees, a group of children on bicycles pedaling furiously up an incline in the road, their small legs pumping, their wholesome laughing faces forming an image suggestive of promise, of health, of the future.

"Aren't they beautiful?" she murmured, turning stiffly for a last look as they drove past. "I think it's time to go

338

home and meet this marvelous nurse you've been telling me about."

"She's very special, Helen. Hey!" he said, spotting an open confectionery store. "How about an ice cream?"

"Lovely!" She laughed. "Chocolate."

"Okay." He pulled over to the curb. "I'll be right back." He left the key in the ignition, and she let her head fall back against the seat, listening to the music as she watched him stride into the store. He looked so dapper, so trim and handsome. As he returned, carrying the ice cream, his magnetism and energy seemed to radiate out of him.

He drove with one hand, glancing over at her from moment to moment, grinning. "Pity they've never taken up on my idea for licorice ice cream." He laughed. "Probably sell millions of gallons."

"Only to you." She laughed back. "The idea of it strikes me as totally revolting." She made a face, then laughed again.

"All these years and you wait till now to admit you're totally revolted by my weakness for licorice."

"Not your weakness, just your taste buds."

He deposited her on the sofa while he went back down to the car to get her bag and cane. Lorna introduced herself and sat down opposite, smiling.

"I've heard such a lot about you," Helen said. "If it's all true, I'm going to wonder how I ever managed without you."

"Yes, mistress," she said.

"Helen."

"Mistress Helen." Lorna laughed softly.

Norm came in and took her things to the bedroom, then returned to help her into bed.

"Gena's coming at one," he said, "with surprises."

"Always with surprises." She smiled.

Lorna set about unpacking the bag. Helen watched her for a moment, appreciating her strong, comfortable-looking body.

"I think I'll try to take a nap before Gena comes, darling. Lorna will stay with me."

"Good idea. I've got to run out for about an hour. I'll be back sooner if I can, depending on the traffic."

Lorna got her into bed with hands that seemed incapable of any but the gentlest touch. Then she crossed the room to close the curtains.

"Stay awhile," Helen said. "I'd like your company."

"I am happy to stay," she said. "I get my book and come back. Close your eyes and be resting. I stay close by if you need me."

Lorna sat in the chair by the dressing table, quietly turning the pages of her paperback novel.

"What are you reading?" Helen asked.

"An old book by Agatha Christie."

"I can't stand Agatha Christie."

"No." Lorna laughed. "She's not so wonderful."

At twelve thirty Lorna lightly touched her on the shoulder, whispering, "It is time now for you to be awakening, my dear. The girl will be coming, and I wish to give you medication."

Helen's eyelids moved and she came to the surface, calmed by the sight of the smooth brown face, the slightly slanted large black eyes gazing down at her.

"Thank you," she said, touching the soft face with her hand. "I like you, Lorna."

"And I you, my dear. You must be readying yourself now."

Norm had returned from his errand, and let Gena in almost before her finger came off the buzzer. With Claire clinging to her skirt, she flew into her father's arms, hugging him, then standing back, trying to smile.

Lifting the child into the air, she said, "Give Grand-daddy a big kiss and a lovely hug, Claire. And say what Mummy taught you."

Without an instant of uncertainty, the little girl held out her arms and wound them around Norm's neck, pressing her mouth against his cheek.

"Go on," Gena prompted. "You remember what Mummy taught you."

With her huge blue eyes shining, Claire peered up

into Norm's nostrils, probing his nose with a tiny fore-finger.

"Claire!" Gena laughed. "You're not to do that! Tell Granddaddy what you're supposed to."

The blonde head turned, and Claire looked at her mother for a moment, then laughed and tightened her hold on Norm, saying, "I lulloo!"

"Good girl!" Gena applauded, beaming.

"I love you too," he said, squeezing her. "I love your face! You are beau-ti-ful. Beau-ti-ful!"

Claire lowered her eyes, having done her duty, and proceeded to stick her fingers into Norm's mouth.

"Can we see her? Is she awake?" Gena asked.

"Awake and itching to see you and this delicious kid."

Gena took Claire from him. "We'll talk later, okay?" she said, starting down the hallway. "Okay, Daddy?"

"Okay, sweetheart. Go on in."

Lorna looked up from her book as the door opened, and she had to smile at the sight of the tall, black-haired, violet-eyed woman holding a golden child. She glanced over to see Helen's face transformed radiantly, her arms held out.

"Gena! Come let me see you! And Claire! God, isn't she lovely!"

Lorna continued to watch, entranced, as the woman set the child down and sat on the side of the bed, enveloping Helen carefully in her arms, burying her face in the curve of Helen's neck. They remained that way for a long time, until Claire managed to clamber up on the bed, putting her hand on Helen's arm to steady herself. Lorna saw a swift darting of pain travel across her eyes, but Helen said nothing, smiling as the mother lifted the little girl over to be held and kissed.

"She looks more like Graham every day," Gena said. "I thought I'd say it first."

"Not altogether. She has your eyes, darling. Great, gorgeous saucers."

"I lulloo," Claire volunteered. "I lulloo."

"Oh, that's lovely," Helen whispered, holding the child

against her. "I like what you're teaching her," she said, her eyes large and loving.

"All the important things first."

"Gena, this is Lorna," Helen said, as Lorna set down her book and rose, her smile revealing large, white teeth.

"Lorna," Gena smiled, extending her hand. "Would you be kind enough to take Claire for a bit so we can talk?"

"Come, darling," Lorna said, swinging Claire into her arms with a jubilant laugh. "Come to Lorna, my darling."

With Claire's laughter bubbling around them, Lorna left the room. Norm looked up from his newspaper at the sound of them coming into the room.

"Look at you!" she was saying, pointing her finger at the tip of Claire's nose. "Look at you! Lorna take you to make coffee, darlin'. Ooo, you be rude! Look at this rude child! Put your fingers any place at all, rude girl!" She laughed, tousling the blond curls with loving fingers. "Lorna give the rude child some nice milk, eh? Come, darlin'."

They went on through to the kitchen, and Norm sat listening to the continuing stream of Lorna's amused monologue as the sounds of her making coffee filtered out to him. He realized that Lorna's manner of speaking had undergone a complete change. She'd abandoned her precise English and lapsed into a dialect he'd heard before in the Islands. Claire's arrival had brought Lorna into the family.

When they returned from the kitchen and Lorna sat with Claire on her knee, wiping the child's fingers, Norm could scarcely contain his fascinated curiosity.

"She is wonderful to see, your daughter," Lorna said. "A fine-seeming woman. She loves her mummy. The mistress shine when she see her."

"Gena is my daughter," he explained. "Not Helen's."

For an instant something shadowed her eyes. Then she set Claire down on the floor and shook her head slowly.

"No, sir," she said quietly. "They be mother and child. I see that. Make no difference Mistress Helen not bear she. She be her true mother. I have a daughter. I know how it be."

"Where is your daughter?" he asked, compelled by her intuitive understanding.

"At home, in Antigua with my mother."

"But she should be with you."

"No, sir," she said, firmly but politely. "She be where she belong. I go home to her soon."

"You must miss her. How old is she?"

"Twelve. I miss her, but it's not so good to think about."

Gena sighed and took hold of Helen's hand. "Daddy told me you looked well, but you look better than ever. And your hair's so long. I've never seen you with long hair. It all seems so hard to believe . . ."

"Gena, believe it," Helen said gently. "It's happening, and I want you to understand something. I *want* it to happen. Don't be shocked, darling. It's the truth."

"Oh, Christ!" Gena's face changed slowly with understanding. "I . . . I'm going to cry. I'm sorry, I can't help it. I swore I wouldn't. What should I do?"

"Talk to me. I hear you have your usual store of surprises."

"I'm pregnant again." She wiped her eyes on her sleeve.

"That's marvelous! When?"

"Six more months."

"I'm happy for you. How's Graham? He must be so pleased."

"He's . . . we . . . He's fine. I'm painting full time. Your mother and I have talked ourselves stupid for the last twelve hours. She's been showing me her early work and some one-minute sketches she did when you were a little girl. They're so beautiful. They have such economy, so much insight. You *can't* want to hear all this!"

"I do. It's heaven just to look at you, to hear your voice. I'd love to see some of your work."

"I brought a portfolio with me. I'll bring it tomorrow when I come." She stopped, trapped again by her own misgivings. "You'll tell me when not to come, won't you?"

"Yes, darling. I'll tell you."

"If it's what you *want*," she said, "Then I want it for you. But I can't stay right through. I can't. It's so important to keep you in my mind this way, the way you look this minute, the way you've always been. I love you too much to try to lie to you. It's like telling myself I'll come in here and make you laugh when I know damned well *I* can't laugh about losing you. I need something to take back with me, Helen. To keep all the love alive, intact. Because it'll always be there, you know. Always. I can't imagine how it's going to feel not being able to pick up the telephone and call you. Not to see you or to come running when I need you to set me straight. I think about it and I tell myself: That's the way it's going to be. I know it. I accept it. But I'll still be here, loving you, holding you in my mind, the way I always have."

Their eyes held for a long time before Helen said, "I've never thought of you as anything but mine." She applied a light pressure to Gena's hand. "Now tell me about what you and Gray have been doing, your work, all of it."

"Okay," Gena took a deep breath. "Stop me when it's time for me to go."

21

After Gena left, Helen held her hand over her mouth, trembling with fatigue, rapidly dissolving into the pain she'd kept in abeyance during Gena's visit. It hadn't been an attempt to hide anything from Gena, but rather an effort to concentrate on more important things for that half-hour. And, with that time gone, there remained nothing to stand between her and the savagery of the pain. When Lorna opened the door minutes later, Helen lifted her hand mutely, unable to speak.

"I will hurry, my dear," Lorna said, seeing the tears pouring down the sides of Helen's face, the tendons standing out prominently in her neck and shoulders as she strained away from the dampened pillow.

By the time Norm came in, she was already experiencing the familiar tranquility induced by the drugs.

"I'm so happy," she said dreamily. "Gena gets better and better. And Claire!" She closed her eyes for a moment, then opened them and smiled at him, finding it impossible to focus.

"I've got a surprise today, too." He placed a package on the blankets. "When you wake up," he said, kissing her. "There's no rush."

"Thank you," she whispered, plummeting into sleep.

He and Lorna prepared dinner and set out the meal in the living room so that Helen, on the sofa, could take her dinner with them.

"I can't eat," she said. "I'd love some brandy."

Norm looked at Lorna, who smiled and said, "Dr. Ramirez say she may have whatever she please. I will fetch it."

Helen drank her brandy and lay waiting for them to finish.

"I like sharing my surprises," she said, after the table was cleared and Lorna moved to leave. "Stay, Lorna! We'll see what Norm has given me."

She removed the wrappings, lifted the lid of the box, and parted the tissues inside. Her eyes were round with disbelief as she picked up the book and held it, staring at the dust jacket.

"God, Norm! What have you done?" she said almost inaudibly, instantly in tears. "What *have* you done?"

"You wrote it, love," he said, reaching for her hand. "It's your book, not mine. I wanted everyone to know that. I simply edited it and added bits and pieces here and there."

"*Words of Love*," she read. " 'By Helen McLaren, edited by Norman McLaren, with paintings and drawings by Amanda Kimbrough and Gena Richardson.' It's a plot you three cooked up. Is this real?"

"You'd better believe it's real. We're already into our third printing."

"You tricked me," she accused. "You all tricked me. All that so-called therapeutic writing. God, I'm scared to death to read it!"

"I'm ashamed to admit it, but some of the imagery you used was so good, what you said so honest and inspired, I was eaten up with jealousy. I'm very proud of you, love. I wanted everyone to know you as I have. This is the only way I could do it."

"I'm flabbergasted! Look at this, Lorna!" she said, holding out the book. "The damned man's turned me into an author."

Lorna looked at the book, then turned it over, studying the photograph of the pair of them on the back.

"Lord, Lord!" She laughed. "This be wonderful! You famous, Mistress! I shall tell all my friends."

"I've got a copy for you too," he said. "And Amanda has hers, as does Gena. And I didn't forget Fraser!"

"You're mad!" she said. "I want to read it this very minute."

He couldn't sleep. He lay smoking quietly, listening to Helen turning the pages, feeling like a kid who's just handed in his first essay, afraid to look over at her. He didn't dare predict her reactions to what he'd put into the book, and sat listening and waiting, chain-smoking, trying not to distract her.

The alarm went off at two, rousing him. He got up and went into the bathroom for her medication. She swallowed the pills and drank the water without taking her eyes from the book, then held out her arm for the injection, clutching the book as her body contorted for a moment. Then, blinking away the involuntary tears, she picked up where she'd left off reading.

He disposed of the syringe, turned off the bathroom light, and, fully awake again, lit a fresh cigarette and resumed his waiting, determined not to fall off to sleep again before she'd finished.

Just before six, he turned and looked at her, finding on her face an expressive mix of nostalgia, melancholy, and complete love. She closed the book soundlessly—like a bible, he thought—and clasped his extended hand to her breast with a long sigh.

"Darling, thank you," she whispered, kissing him soft and long. "Thank you, Norm. I don't know what to say. I can't even begin to imagine how you managed to find that little drawing Gena did of me on the broomstick, or how you induced Mother to resurrect all those drawings she made of me as a child. I should have guessed when Gena mentioned Mother had been showing them to her. You've given meaning to everything, even to dying. How could you know so well all I've been thinking and feeling and trying not to let you see? How?"

"I just *knew,* love. There wasn't any other way for me to show you."

"You're the best thing that ever happened to me," she said, gazing into the depths of his eyes. "You've given me everything. And now this. It's too much."

"You've got it backwards," he said huskily. "You've given me more than I ever believed it possible to experience. Helen, don't you know? Once, for a couple of years with Nancy, I thought I had something. And it was fine, something sweet. But it ended almost before it began. Then, all those years with nothing to do but feel sorry and guilty, trying to cope with a problem I thought had no possible answer. Nothing in sight but more of the same. Then you came along with so many answers, such hope in a hopeless situation. You're everything, love. Coming home to you, knowing that no matter what happened I had you to come home to, gave me a direction to go in. This book is almost a trifling way to attempt to demonstrate just what you've meant to me from the first. We've had almost thirteen years of a happiness so real, so tangible. I wish I had more to give, much more. The only other thing I have left to share with you now is my understanding that I know you can't go on and don't want to. I'm letting you go. But just for this moment, just for these few seconds, I . . ." He stopped, choked up.

"I want to hold you against me the way I used to. Help me out of this thing, darling." She pushed the nightgown over her shoulders, lifting herself with an effort as he eased it down over her hips. "Hold me," she whispered.

He kissed her throat and breasts, stroking her tenderly, wishing he could draw the pain out of her body through his fingertips, wishing futilely that love could make her live forever.

"Kiss me," she murmured. "Then I'll sleep."

For the duration of the kiss, he forgot time and days to be counted and medications to be given—even that he couldn't hold her properly in his arms because it would cause her pain. But with her body warm and still under

348

his hands, death seemed far removed, something so distant it mightn't ever claim her.

Amanda came Wednesday of the following week, and they exchanged good-byes tearlessly, like people so close they knew without any doubt whatsoever they'd be seeing each other again very soon.

Thursday, Fraser came, her eyes gleaming as she said, "The most beautiful book, Helen. To think so many people will know you now, that I . . ."

"Sssh," she said. "None of that. Quickly, before it slips my mind—I'm getting terribly absent-minded—you won't forget your promise, will you?"

"I won't."

"Good. Now tell me all the news. How's school? What've you been doing? I want to hear it all."

Friday Gena came, alone.

Helen had just had her medication and felt very lazy and dopey.

"It's time for you to go home to Graham," she said after they'd talked for several minutes. "Take Claire and go home to your husband, darling. There's nothing more for you here. You'll see your father again soon. He's promised me that."

"I've been gearing myself up for this, but now that you're telling me it's time to go, I don't want to. I'll never see you again."

"Things happen that way sometimes, darling. Seeing you and Claire has been so good. You'll never know how happy it makes me to know you have a fine life. I love you with all my heart, Gena. You're a warm, beautiful woman."

"I wouldn't have a life at all if I hadn't had you," Gena said, bending to kiss the face that had first appeared to her like a beacon in the depths and darkness of her terror and confusion. "I love you."

She stayed a moment longer, seeing Helen struggling to keep her eyes open, then turned away and, with a faint smile, pressed Lorna's shoulder and went out.

* * *

By Sunday morning it was obvious she was failing. She asked to speak to Lorna, and Norm went out to smoke a cigarette and steady his nerves.

"I want to be alone with him, Lorna. But I wanted to thank you for being here. I've left something for you. Norm's put it on the desk in the living room. He'll explain it later. Would you please bring me my medication now. I know it's too soon, but I need it. Norm will give me the injection."

"Of course, my dear," she said, going into the bathroom.

"I'd like to kiss you, Lorna," she said, trying to lift her hand.

Lorna rested her cheek against Helen's. "The Lord take you sweetly, darlin'," she crooned, smoothing Helen's hair. "He hold you in His arms and love you. I will be near if you wish me."

Outside, Lorna said, "She wants you to give her the injection. It is not wise, sir. Please, you will hold to her hand and I do it quickly. She has bad bone pain now. I can do it fast, so the pain not so terrible."

"All right," he said, going back into the room with her.

Helen was scarcely aware of Lorna preparing the syringe. Her eyes were shrouded in pain, the muscles of her face and neck twisted with it. When he took her hand, the strength of her grip alarmed him. He watched Lorna lift Helen's arm, dab the inside of her forearm with alcohol, then, with lightning speed, bring the needle down into the vein. Helen's entire body arched off the bed, and he felt the incredible agony travel through the length of his own body, leaving a quivering tension in his stomach. Lorna vanished, and he sat down on the side of the bed, feeling Helen's grip on his hand easing as the drug rapidly went to work.

"I'm cold," she said, opening her eyes to look at him. He pulled the blankets close around her.

She laughed drowsily. "I'd love to have you hold me, but I think I'd break. God, it works fast," she said, the dreams and memories starting to weave themselves in amid the reality. "I feel lovely and light. It's like floating.

Don't let yourself be lonely, darling," she said, opening her eyes again. "You've got such a lot to do. Don't mourn me! I hate the thought of it. Norm?"

"I'm here, love."

"Have me cremated. Don't put me on display, will you, darling? Have the damned lid nailed shut. You could sprinkle my ashes on the beach at the cottage. I like to think of that."

"Whatever you want."

"My eyes keep opening and closing all by themselves. It's fantastic. My tongue's even starting to do its own talking without me. Oh, darling," she said, forcing her eyes open. "I'm so glad it's ending. I'm ready, so sleepy."

She was quiet for several minutes, then looked at him again. "You gave me talent," she said. "I never had any."

"You always had talent," he said, feeling her slipping away from him by inches. "The best kind."

"We've been so happy, haven't we?"

"Very happy," he said. Her fingers were relaxing in his hand.

"Thank you for all the love and the living we've had, and for Gena." She lay utterly still for a few seconds, then opened her eyes very wide and smiled at him. "Don't look so glum, my darling," she said, thickly. "It's beautiful. Nothing hurts."

She didn't open her eyes or speak again. He sat holding her hand for a long time before letting it go and lighting a cigarette. He continued to sit, smoking and looking at her for another hour before reaching to touch her throat. There was no pulse. With an enormous sense of relief, both for Helen and for himself, he got up and went out.

Lorna covered her eyes with her hand.

"I told her about your daughter," he said. "She wanted you to have the money to go home to her."

She shook her head, unable to talk. The buzzer sounded, and Lorna's hand came away from her eyes. They looked at each other until Lorna said, "The mistress. She asked me to call her friend."

Confused, he went to the door to find Fraser standing outside, waiting.

"I thought you might like to come out for a bit while Lorna does what has to be done," she offered quietly.

"Yes," he said, "I'll get my coat and come with you."

Bestselling Books
from Berkley

___ $4.50	09291-7	**THE ACCIDENTAL TOURIST** Anne Tyler
___ $4.50	09103-1	**ELVIS AND ME**
		Priscilla Beaulieu Presley with Sandra Harmon
___ $5.95	07704-7	**"...AND LADIES OF THE CLUB"**
		Helen Hooven Santmyer
___ $4.50	08520-1	**THE AUERBACH WILL** Stephen Birmingham
___ $4.50	09077-9	**EVERYTHING AND MORE** Jacqueline Briskin
___ $4.50	10004-9	**SAVANNAH** Eugenia Price
___ $4.50	09868-0	**DINNER AT THE HOMESICK RESTAURANT**
		Anne Tyler
___ $4.50	08472-8	**LOVE, HONOR AND BETRAY** Elizabeth Kary
___ $4.50	08529-5	**ILLUSIONS OF LOVE** Cynthia Freeman
___ $3.95	08659-3	**MATTERS OF THE HEART** Charlotte Vale Allen
___ $4.50	08783-2	**TOO MUCH TOO SOON** Jacqueline Briskin
___ $4.50	09203-8	**TO SEE YOUR FACE AGAIN** Eugenia Price
___ $4.50	09557-6	**SEASONS OF THE HEART** Cynthia Freeman
___ $4.50	09633-5	**THE LeBARON SECRET** Stephen Birmingham
___ $4.50	09807-9	**TIMESTEPS** Charlotte Vale Allen
___ $4.50	09472-3	**LET NO MAN DIVIDE** Elizabeth Kary
___ $3.95	09702-1	**ONE OF MY VERY BEST FRIENDS** Shirley Lord
		(on sale August 1987)

New York Times bestsellers— Berkley Books at their best!